The
Beach
House

Books by Helen McKenna

The Beach House Series
The Beach House
The Perfect Proposal (short story)
Third Offence

Other Novels
Room 46

Short Stories
Flashback

Combined Editions
The Perfect Proposal and Other Stories
Room 46 & Short Story Collection

All titles also available as e-books.

The Beach House

Helen McKenna

The Beach House

By Helen McKenna

Originally published by Joshua Books, Australia (2011)
Revised edition published by Lightning Source (2017)

ISBN 13: 9780994479471

Website: www.helenmckenna.com.au
Email: info@helenmckenna.com.au

Contents

Prologue

*T*he Sunset Point School of Arts Hall was not used to such commotion. Built in the 1950s, the modest timber structure had hosted Saturday night dances, debutante balls, ballet classes and the local Eisteddfod each year since 1974. Over the years, it had also seen many town meetings, but never one quite like this. All two hundred seats were filled and dozens more people lined the sides and crowded at the back of the hall. A loud buzz of conversation permeated the room. Four people seated at a long table at the front struggled to maintain order and correct meeting procedure.

'Order please,' Moira Bell said into the microphone. 'Everybody needs their chance to speak.'

When the crowd ignored Moira's request, in fact the noise seemed to increase, Jim Stewart gave a shrill whistle. 'All right!' he shouted. 'Calm down! Mr Walton here has something to say.'

Max Walton stood, but was drowned out before he said his first word.

'Boo! Boo! Boo!' chorused a gang from the back section.

'Greedy land grabber!' bellowed a man in the second row. Heavily built, bearded and dressed in King Gee work clothes, to Max's eye he looked the type who enjoyed this kind of civil protest.

A young woman standing at the side started a chant. 'Go away! Go away! Go away!' It was soon accompanied by rhythmic claps and foot stamping.

Max shook his head, amazed at the ignorance of these people. He wasn't suggesting a Vegas style casino or a brothel, just a luxurious resort.

Reclaiming the microphone, Jim held it near the amplifier, causing an ear-splitting electronic shriek. The hall gradually fell silent. Jim spoke again, now with no need for the microphone. 'We all feel very strongly about this, but in the tradition of a democratic society let Mr Walton speak.'

Max took the microphone again. 'Please just hear what I have to say,' he began, ignoring the few diehards who continued to boo.

Jim held up his hand and the noise trickled to a murmur.

'I know you feel very attached to the beach house and you're right, it is a beautiful building. I want to assure you that it won't be demolished, just moved to another site right here in Sunset Point.'

'Yeah, to a scrubby block near the highway with no view,' said an elderly woman in the front row. Max stared at her in surprise. She looked like such a frail old thing. He was glad her words couldn't be heard over the increasing volume of conversation returning to the room.

Gamely he continued. 'You have to understand; the way it is now it is only accessible to a small group of people each year. With the resort I'm proposing, this wonderful site will be available to hundreds at a time. And don't forget the people staying there don't just spend money on accommodation; they spend it in your shops, your cafe and your cinema. It means your town can expand and grow.'

'We don't want it to grow!' yelled a middle-aged man from the fifth row. 'We like it just as it is! We don't need city problems up here.'

Max shook his head. 'There doesn't have to be city problems. We're talking about modest growth. This is motivated by a genuine desire to help your community.'

The audience erupted again. 'Come off it,' yelled the same man, 'it's motivated by money and greed. We're not just small-town hicks without a clue.'

This time the microphone on the amplifier had no effect and Max was booed off the stage.

• • • • •

Two weeks later in the Brisbane office of news magazine *The Queensland Reviewer*, Jessica Stanton sat at her desk admiring the beautiful bouquet of flowers just delivered to her colleague Vanessa. 'You're so lucky Ness,' she said, trying to keep the envy out of her voice. None of her boyfriends had ever done something so romantic for her.

'I told you he was perfect,' Vanessa said as she inhaled the scent of the pink and white roses. Picking up the florist's card, she read aloud, 'Budding Blooms. Hmm, I'd heard they do fabulous arrangements. Weren't they mentioned in a story we did recently?'

Jessica nodded. 'Yeah, it was one of mine. They did the flowers for that society wedding, you know Amanda McMillan-Byrne and William Ashton?'

'Oh yeah. It was at Mt Tamborine, right?'

'Uh huh. The bouquets and centrepieces from Budding Blooms were so exquisite that I interviewed the florist as well and did an extra piece about her.'

'I don't remember reading it.'

'Grant hasn't run it yet,' Jessica said.

'Well, I think I'll keep their card. I might need their services in the not-too-distant future.' Vanessa smiled dreamily as she reached for the vase on top of the filing cabinet.

Rolling her eyes, Jessica turned her attention to the memo the editor-in-chief Grant Morris had deposited in her in-tray ten minutes earlier. It was her new story assignment: *Landmark legal case in the works for small coastal village of Sunset Point*.

Jessica sighed inwardly as she eyed off the attached pile of printed pages. Grant loved extensive background information and he always questioned his staff to make sure they'd actually read it.

With nothing else pressing to finish for the day, Jessica decided to make a start on it before heading over to Indooroopilly. It was late-night shopping and she'd arranged to meet her sister so they could buy their mother's birthday present.

Turning off her computer to avoid distractions, Jessica leaned back in her chair and began to read the background synopsis.

Sunset Point is a small town on an undeveloped section of the central Queensland coastline. Featuring a popular swimming and surfing beach, the town, with a permanent population of around three thousand, is flooded with holiday makers during the summer months and school holiday periods. A beachfront caravan park/campground and several small beach shacks cater for holiday visitors.

The other landmark of Sunset Point is a heritage-listed Queenslander known locally as "The Beach House". Set on what is considered to be the finest piece of land in the town, it was built almost 100 years ago by Clem McMaster, a local sawmill worker, after winning the lottery.

Jessica paused in her reading and studied the exterior photos of the house. It was indeed a beautiful old building. She could imagine holidaymakers relaxing on the veranda enjoying the cool beach vibe while their beach towels hung drying on the wooden railings.

I haven't been to the beach in ages, she thought. I might head down to the Gold Coast this weekend. It's still too cold to swim but I'll go early and have a nice walk and … Realising she was daydreaming, she shook her head and turned her attention back to the pages in her hand.

Clem's eldest son Richard inherited the house and initially it was a private holiday retreat but was later converted into an exclusive health resort. On Richard's death, ownership of the house passed on to his only son James, a man of vision who was cynical about the class structure that still existed in twentieth century society. Although born into wealth – thanks to his grandfather's careful investments – James felt restricted by wealth and the associated expectations of society. Determined that the beach house would not be an exclusive domain of the wealthy, James opened it up as a regular holiday rental.

Glancing at her watch, Jessica noticed it was almost five o'clock. Her workmates were starting to pack up, including Vanessa with her huge bunch of flowers. She should get going too. But now she was this far into her reading, she may as well finish before she left. Waving goodbye to her colleagues, she slid off the uncomfortable shoes she'd been trying to wear in for the past week and continued reading.

Critical of the trappings of the modern world, the only conveniences James allowed in the house were a radio and a telephone, ruling that no television was ever to be installed. Further clauses were added by the Beach House committee (see note below) as technology developed to also prohibit the internet and any electronic devices.

James never married nor had any children, so he willed the house to the town of Sunset Point. However, in order to maintain ownership, the house could never be sold or removed from the site, nor the land subdivided. The aforementioned conditions instigated by James also needed to remain intact. The rental income from the property was to be divided among approved local charities. A management committee, with strictly regulated membership, was formed to oversee the house and to ensure that James's wishes were upheld.

Jessica turned the page but the back of the paper was blank. Annoyed, she shuffled through the pages in her In tray, but the rest of the information wasn't there either. Knowing Grant would still be in his office, she made her way down the hall.

Looking up when Jessica appeared at his door, Grant checked his watch and shot her a quizzical glance.

'Yes, I know - it's after five and I'm still here. That deserves some brownie points, doesn't it?' Jessica smiled hopefully.

Grant shrugged. 'I guess so. You came down just to tell me that?'

'Of course not. That background info you gave me about the beach house story, there's some pages missing.'

'I'm still reading it myself,' Grant said, holding up a few sheets of paper. 'I figured I had at least until tomorrow before you got around to reading the first part.'

Jessica came in and sat down. 'I had a few spare minutes so I thought I'd get started on it today and I hate leaving things half-read. I'm just up to the part about the committee.'

'Intriguing story, isn't it? Not your average small-town-versus-developer scenario.' Grant raised an eyebrow and leaned back in his chair.

'No, it's way more than that. But you left me hanging. What happened with the committee?'

'Well, the committee, a group of upstanding local citizens, has done its job excellently for the past twenty-five years without any problem. The community is happy, the people who stay in the house are happy.'

'What's the angle, then? How can the developer even mount a court case?'

'Ah, this is where it gets a bit murky. Their local council was amalgamated two years ago. So now their former mayor, who is very conservative, is just one of fourteen councillors on a much larger regional council. And the new mayor is very pro-development.'

'What about the heritage listing?'

'Well, because he's promising to move the building fully intact to another site in the same area, it's not an issue.'

'How did this Max guy even find out about the house?'

'His car broke down and he spent two days in Sunset Point waiting for a new head gasket. Apparently, he did some exploring and cast his developer's eye over the house site and adjoining blocks. His expensive legal team then found him a loophole in the regulations – the local council, which is now the regional council, has the discretion to modify the ownership clause in extraordinary circumstances.'

'How is this extraordinary?'

'Two of the amalgamated shires had major debt and one of the former mayors was deposed for embezzlement just before the election. The sale of this land would make a fair hole in their budget deficit.'

'What about the adjoining blocks? Can't he buy them instead?'

'Yes, possibly, but they aren't worth much without the beach house site. It's got the access and the beach frontage. This resort he's planning is huge and he needs all the land.'

'So now it's going to court and you want me to follow the case?' Jessica asked, her eyes lighting up at the prospect of her by-line appearing on something that was sure to capture a lot of public attention. *This* was the kind of story that could get her noticed. After almost a year working here, Grant was finally giving her something exciting to write about.

Grant held his hand up in a calming gesture. 'Hang on there, Jess. Yes, you can do the court case, but I want to set the scene first. We ran a brief filler piece last fortnight that also ran in the New South Wales and Victorian editions. I've had a stack of emails, letters and phone calls from people who've stayed there and they've all got a story to tell. So, I want you to interview five of them and see what comes up. They're all surprisingly passionate about saving the house.'

Jessica reached over and took the pile of printed pages from Grant. She stood up but paused before leaving. 'I get how they can block the internet by not having any kind of modem or wireless set up in the house, but how can you stop people taking their gadgets with them?'

'Ah, young Gen-Y Jessica, we can survive without technology you know,' Grant said with a smile. 'Apparently, they use the old-fashioned honour system. Obviously they can't search people's belongings but each tenant is asked not to bring those items and, on arrival, the real estate agent reminds them again of the house rules. Maybe it's like the old adage, if you do cheat then you're only cheating yourself.'

Jessica, who was very attached to her own gadgets, raised her eyebrows. 'How so?'

'Read the emails and my phone call summaries and you'll start to understand.'

Jessica took the pages back to her desk but set them aside. She would humour Grant and do the human-interest stories, but her first priority was getting some background information on Max Walton. Then, when she wrote about the court case, the thoroughness of her research skills would be evident. That was the kind of thing major daily newspaper editors looked for in their staff.

Turning her computer back on, Jessica logged onto the internet and googled "Malton Construction and Development". Scrolling through the numerous pages returned by the search, she felt a frisson of excitement. This thing was going to be *big*. Max Walton was a heavyweight in coastal development and he wasn't afraid of controversy. He'd already won two lawsuits against local governments that had tried to block his construction projects in their areas.

Clicking on a link Jessica looked at a photograph of Malton's newest resort in Western Australia. It was magnificent but, according to the caption, not entirely welcome. Apparently the town of Moon Bay had also been divided about whether it should go ahead. Jessica scribbled the name in her notebook. She'd have to find out what their local paper was called and look up some story clips. Hopefully it would give her some ideas.

Grant stopped at Jessica's cubicle at six thirty, carrying his briefcase. Totally engrossed in an article about Max's last court case, she jumped in fright when he spoke.

'Jess, you know I love a dedicated worker but I don't want you walking to your car in the dark by yourself.'

Jessica bookmarked the web page and hit the hibernate key. 'Yes, I know, safety first. In any case, I'm supposed to be at Indro now, selecting my mother's birthday gift. My sister will kill me for being late.'

Grant held the back door open and Jessica walked past him into the almost empty car park. Waiting while she unlocked her car, Grant checked his phone. 'My wife just texted me to say that if I wasn't home in twenty minutes, the dog is getting my dinner,' he said, sliding his Blackberry into his back pocket.

'I hope the traffic's not too bad then.' Jessica grinned as she threw her bag on the passenger seat.

'Me too. If that mutt gets lasagne and I'm stuck with beans on toast I won't be very happy.'

Jessica paused for a moment, standing between the open car door and the driver's seat. 'Thanks for walking me out. You get here about seven most mornings, don't you?'

'I do indeed, sometimes a bit earlier when we're on deadline. Should I expect to see you here early too tomorrow?'

Jessica nodded. 'I can't wait to get started.'

• • • • •

Almost a week later, Jessica finalised her list of interviewees. It had taken longer than planned to sift through the emails and call summaries to determine which ones to use. Frankly she thought Grant was putting too much emphasis on this angle, rather than backgrounding Max Walton and his development empire, but she had to keep him sweet or he might put someone more experienced on the court case.

Just play by the rules Jessica, she kept reminding herself.

Sitting in Grant's office later, she tapped her foot on the carpeted floor, as he examined the list. Grant had the ability to read through information without showing any change in facial expression, so Jessica had no idea what he was thinking. Eventually he looked up and nodded.

'Good work, Jess. I like the mix of backgrounds and it's a nice even timeline.'

'Well, that just kind of fell into place. I wasn't really aiming for any particular era. But I think it would be good if we ran them in sequence.'

'Yes, I agree,' said Grant. 'But what about the interstate ones? Phone interviews? Or are you going to Skype them?' Grant had no problems with using technology, but he did think that sometimes the younger staff relied on it too much, rather than developing more intuitive journalistic skills.

'No, it's all old school, face to face, and it's not costing you much at all. I managed to work them into my Melbourne trip.'

'Trip?'

Jessica swallowed her impatience. 'I'm going to Melbourne for a wedding. Remember, I asked you for next Friday off? I'll need the Monday and Tuesday too, now, so I can come back via Sydney.'

'Right, right, sure, I remember and yes, you can take the extra days. That's good if you can do it that way.' Grant eyed his newest reporter. 'This is a pretty big task, Jess. Are you sure you're up to it? We can divide the interviews up, if you want.'

Jessica shook her head. There was no way she was letting anyone muscle in on this assignment and potentially steal the story of the year. 'No, it's totally fine. I don't mind doing some extra hours.'

'All right, then. I must say, I'm glad that you seem to have lost your aversion to human interest stories. Like I've told you numerous times already, journalism is not always about the big headlines.'

Jessica smiled benignly, desperately hoping she looked sincere. 'What can I say? You're right again, boss.'

Kate

1991

*K*ate Green added another fancy swirl to the elaborate doodle she was creating in her notebook. It was one of her best yet, taking up almost half a page. Turning the book on its side she was eyeing her work of art critically when she heard her name called. Flinching, she cast her eyes to the front of the classroom, mortified to have been caught daydreaming.

The blackboard was covered in writing and diagrams, but gave no real clue of the question she had just been asked.

Kate opened her mouth to respond, but then noticed other students returning to their seats holding papers and realised the lecturer was handing back their last assignment. Breathing a sigh of relief, she slunk down to the front desk, keeping her eyes downcast as she grabbed her assignment from the pile so as to avoid the stern gaze of Associate Professor Harold Frezwar.

A tall, rotund, balding man who habitually wore a starched white shirt and a tie, Harold Frezwar lived and breathed economics and expected the same enthusiasm from his students. Considering she had *zero* passion for the subject, theirs was not a very warm affiliation.

Kate's heart began to pound as she made her way back to her seat. I'm sure I've failed, she thought grimly. I threw this together at the very last moment with only the vaguest understanding of the subject matter. Harold is such a hard marker, there's no way he would have passed it.

Sitting back down, Kate put her assignment on the desk but couldn't bring herself to flip it over and read her grade on the back. She had hoped for another few days of grace before this particular nightmare came back to haunt her.

Harold's voice broke into her thoughts. 'All in all, the standard of the essays was reasonable,' he intoned. 'Although, of course, there were several that I simply could not pass.' Pausing dramatically, he cast his unyielding gaze around the room, settling, it seemed, right on Kate.

Heat suffused her neck and face. Just get it over with, she thought. Open the stupid thing and see how badly you actually did. Taking a deep breath, she turned the stack of pages over to reveal the grading sheet with her mark written boldly in red.

53%.

Kate stared at the numbers for a moment, certain she must be seeing things. She had passed! Just barely, but it was enough. Exhaling sharply, she smiled in relief. Somehow, she had scraped through again, but, at the same time, she knew her luck couldn't hold out forever. At some point she was going to have to shake off this apathy.

Noticing the time, Kate packed up her belongings and as soon as Harold dismissed the class, she bolted out the door.

It was a hot October day. Kate fanned herself with a notebook as she sat near the main entrance to Queensland University of Technology, sweltering in the midday sun. Checking her watch, she sighed impatiently. Her friend Fiona was always late. Even when she gave a fake meeting time quarter of an hour earlier than the actual time, Fiona never showed up first.

Ten minutes later Fiona finally emerged. She jostled her way through the crowds of students milling around the campus entrance and jogged towards Kate. Why does she bother rushing now? wondered Kate, as she stood and slung her backpack over her shoulder. She's already this late, what's another minute?

'Sorry, sorry,' Fiona said, as she bustled over. 'The queue for the photocopier was huge and then I couldn't find my library card. I had to unpack my whole purse, then I realised it was in my pocket all along.'

Kate nodded. At least her excuses were original. She rarely used the same one twice.

'How come we're meeting this early, anyway?' Fiona asked, as she unscrewed the lid off her water bottle. 'Didn't you have that tute for accounting?'

'Nah, decided to ditch it.'

'Well, shopping is definitely more exciting,' Fiona said before taking a swig of water. 'And you've gotta love the fact that the Queen Street Mall is right on our doorstep.'

'Absolutely,' Kate agreed.

It was late afternoon when they disembarked from the bus, each holding a shopping bag. 'Are you sure your mum doesn't mind me coming over for dinner again?' Kate asked.

'Nah, she sees it as her civic duty to ensure you get a home cooked meal as often as possible.'

They both laughed.

A carpet of jacaranda blooms littered the nature strip in Fiona's street. 'They're so pretty,' Kate said, as they sloughed through them. 'And they make you realise summer is not far away.'

'Yeah, but watch your head,' Fiona advised.

'What?'

'Haven't you heard the University of Queensland legend that if a bloom falls on your head during exam time then you're destined to fail?'

Kate leapt back onto the bitumen and cast a fearful eye up at the tree, lest a whole branch come crashing down on her. Then she laughed. 'We don't even go to UQ and exams are still ages away.'

• • • • •

Even with the end of the semester looming, The Victory pub was packed on Saturday night two weeks later. Happy hour was in full swing and Kate was relieved to see that she and her friends weren't the only ones who had ditched studying for the night.

'Mel and her friends are working on some group assignment,' she yelled in Fiona's ear. 'So it's not like I'd be able to study anyway with them all there.'

Hiking up her precarious strapless top Fiona gave a wry smile. 'Yeah, how inconsiderate,' she yelled back. 'Forcing you to go out and party instead.'

Kate poked out her tongue. Fiona grinned in reply as she adjusted her top again.

Fixing a carefree expression on her face Kate sipped her West Coast Cooler and bopped along to Hunters and Collectors. Fiona was *so* lucky she could get away with such a revealing outfit. Her own top was much more sedate. No matter what they said about black being slimming, it was difficult to disguise the eight extra kilos she had gained this year. She wasn't overweight exactly, but not slender anymore either. It was something she had always taken for granted before.

Fiona leaned over to shout in Kate's ear again. 'Are you going to stay sharing with Mel next year?'

Rolling her eyes dramatically, Kate shrugged. 'Who knows? Anyway, I might not even be here next year.'

Placing her empty glass on a table, Fiona grabbed Kate's wrist.

'You're not really thinking about leaving, are you?'

Sighing, Kate shrugged again. 'I don't know! I just can't stand the thought of studying business for another two whole years.'

'Then change courses. You're getting good at that,' Fiona smirked.

'I know, I know, all the chopping and changing has been a bit ridiculous – but I really wanted to do criminal psychology. I can't believe they rejected me.'

'Well they're a bit of a snobby bunch at SEQU,' Fiona said, pronouncing it *SeeKwoo* rather than by its initials. 'Would you really want to go there?'

'Yes, I would, I really had my heart set on it. Two more years is such a long time to endure economics and accounting.'

Fiona adjusted her top again. 'Yeah, maybe, but think of the partying you'll miss if you leave. Come on, Kate, nobody enjoys studying, it's the lifestyle we're here for. We've got two more years to have fun, enjoy long holidays and make the most of being young and carefree. Then when we're finished we can bum around Europe for a year or something.'

Kate took her last mouthful of West Coast and set the bottle on the table. 'Fine, I'll think about it.'

'I know you, Kate – the minute you have to start writing job applications, you'll cut your losses and decide to stay.'

Early the next afternoon Kate stared glassy eyed at the cars hurtling around the racetrack. I'm really scraping the bottom of the barrel, she decided as she lay listlessly on the couch. Motor racing is the watching paint dry of weekend TV and I'm using it as a distraction.

Hauling herself to her feet a few minutes later, she flicked the TV off before gathering the various sections of *The Sunday Mail* into a semi-neat pile. Salvaging the sealed hand wipe and extra napkin from the KFC box, Kate dumped them in the junk basket on the kitchen bench before heading to her room.

Finally seated at her desk, Kate ploughed through her economics questions. Frustrated to know so few of the answers, she started doodling. WHO CARES??? she scrawled under question five. Well, it was lucky that some people *did* care, or else the world economy would be in lots of trouble. It wasn't that she didn't see the point of economics, she had just realised early on that it wasn't something she wanted to spend time thinking about.

Eventually tossing the worksheet aside, she moved on to accounting. No more appealing than economics, Kate struggled to stay focused once again. Having missed tutorials for the past three weeks, she cursed her own laziness. She would definitely attend tomorrow and round up notes from someone.

At eight thirty Kate shuffled out to the kitchen in search of something to eat. While Mel's shelves held a reasonable stockpile of food, hers were depressingly empty. Even if she had the energy to go out in search of take-away, her options at this time on a Sunday night were limited. And she wasn't quite desperate enough to risk eating a hot dog from the servo down the road.

Making a face, Kate grabbed her last can of baked beans and stole a slice of Mel's bread to make toast. Upending the beans into a bowl, she stuck it in the microwave and set the timer.

Nothing happened.

'No, don't do this now,' she cried, giving the console a well-practised thump.

Still nothing.

I've had it with this stupid thing, Kate fumed, banging her hand down on top of it. This time she was rewarded with a welcome hum.

As the beans spun around slowly, she clicked the TV on. I'll just watch while I eat, she reasoned. Then I'll get back to it.

Beans and toast in hand Kate plonked onto the couch and channel surfed for a few moments, eager for any diversion from uni work. She found it in *Back To The Future*. 'Cool!' she exclaimed, happy to have stumbled across one of her favourite movies.

Having seen the movie countless times on video, Kate decided she would only watch until nine thirty. But inevitably that deadline came and went. At ten o'clock she conceded it was too late to start studying again and instead kept watching until the credits rolled. As she collapsed into bed at ten forty-five, Kate promised herself that this coming week she would *really* get motivated.

• • • • •

Five days later, Kate took in the familiar surrounds of her guidance counsellor's office, before glancing again at the commemorative World Expo '88 clock on the wall. The secretary had shown her in and assured her that Patricia was coming, but it was now nine thirty and her appointment had been for twenty past. Like Fiona, Patricia always seemed to be running late.

When she finally bustled in, Kate was sure she caught a hint of impatience in her greeting. 'Kate, hello... again,' she murmured, dumping a pile of folders on an already overloaded desk.

A short, plump woman with steel grey hair, Patricia always looked a little harassed. Or maybe it's just in my presence, Kate thought. I must be one of the ficklest students she has ever come across.

'So, what can I do for you today?' Patricia asked, lowering herself carefully onto her bright pink swivel chair.

'I'm just letting you know I'll soon be out of your hair,' Kate said. 'I'm going to withdraw.'

Patricia's face softened. 'Well, we did talk about that. I think taking a year out would be a really good thing for you. It will give you a chance to work out what you really want to do. And you'll have this year's credit to use as a building block for something else. Just let them know at admin.'

'No, I mean I'm withdrawing now. As of today.'

Patricia's jaw dropped. 'What on earth for? There's only one week until study break.'

'I've had enough. All week I've been sitting in lectures and tutes gradually coming to the realisation there's no way I can catch up. What's the point in sitting exams I'm going to fail?'

'But you'll get four fails on your transcript anyway if you withdraw now. If you at least try, you might make a conceded pass or even a pass. It will give you lots more options.'

'No, my mind is made up,' Kate assured her. 'Not getting into criminal psychology was obviously a sign. I'm just not meant to be at university. Thanks for all your help anyway.' Kate smiled as she stood to leave, revelling in the sense of relief her decision had brought about.

Patricia stood too. 'Oh Kate, I wish you wouldn't. Please think about this more! At the very least don't officially drop out yet. I'd hate you to change your mind.'

Kate shook her head as she walked to the door. 'Trust me, I won't.'

• • • • •

Kate sat up straight and peered out the window at the green road sign in the distance. Could it actually be…? Yes, it was! Sunset Point 10km. She sighed in relief. Long bus journeys were such a bore and thanks to road works on the two-lane highway, this one had turned into a marathon.

She couldn't believe she was doing this. Reaching into her backpack Kate pulled out the letter and read it again.

Dear Miss Green,

We are pleased to advise that your application to enrol in the Bachelor of Criminal Psychology course has been tentatively approved. Once we have been officially advised of your successful completion of this semester's units with a GPA of at least 4.5, you will be sent the next part of the application pack. Please note that any fail grades on your academic transcript will disqualify you from entry to this program. Furthermore, should you not accept this position you will not be eligible to reapply for three years.

Yours truly,
Sarah Lowes
Assistant Dean, Department of Psychology
South-East QLD University

It had taken a lot of convincing, on both Patricia and her mother's behalf, before Kate decided to give her exams one more shot. As Patricia had pointed out, she had managed to bluff her way through the year without much effort and she had a favourable exam timetable, with her first exam five days in. If she really put her mind to it, maybe she could pull it off.

Twenty minutes later, Kate watched idly as the driver unloaded the luggage, not minding that hers was the last to come off. Anything that delayed the reality of serious study was welcome at this point.

Dragging her bag behind her, Kate hailed the lone taxi waiting nearby. The house wasn't far away but her bag was full of textbooks and way too heavy to carry any distance.

'Whew,' the taxi driver said, putting it in the boot. 'Are you building a house with those bricks?'

Kate smiled politely but didn't encourage any conversation. She was lost in thought as the car made its short journey towards Blue Pacific Boulevard, summing up in her mind the pros of coming to a beach house to study. Firstly, getting away from people and things that could distract her made sense. Secondly, there wasn't even a TV in the house. Thirdly, she'd always found the beach to be very relaxing. Maybe being close to the ocean would help her really focus.

The driver carried her bag up onto the veranda. Kate handed him a ten-dollar note and told him to keep the change.

'No, love, I couldn't,' he said, handing her back some dollar coins.

He gave a friendly wave as he drove away and Kate hoped that such a positive start to her time here was a good omen.

The note was taped to the front door.

Kate,
I'm at the library. Key in previously disclosed location. Wriggle it a bit if it sticks. Lock up if you go out. Jane

Kate rolled her eyes. The brief note seemed to sum up Jane's personality perfectly. Formal. Stern. Uptight. Well, maybe the note wasn't uptight, but her cousin certainly was.

Only a year older than her, Jane hadn't always been so serious and straight. They'd actually been good pals when they were younger. Kate thought that leaving her small hometown in country New South Wales to attend uni in Sydney might have loosened Jane up a bit. Obviously it hadn't.

After locating the key (fourth pot plant, second row, slightly raised), Kate let herself in. Taking in the simple, old-fashioned décor, she smiled. Although her preference for a beach holiday would generally be a luxurious resort with an on-site day spa, there was something very welcoming about this old house.

Heading upstairs, Kate surveyed the spare rooms and chose the end one. Big and breezy, with two huge four-poster beds, an antique dressing table, and a desk it also featured a window seat directly overlooking the beach. *And* the two spare bedrooms between it and the master bedroom would create a decent buffer zone between her and Jane.

Once her unpacking was finished she flopped down on the bed taking time out to appreciate her surroundings and recover from the long bus ride. She could start studying tomorrow.

Kate's scrawled note to Jane was even briefer. *Gone to town. K.*

She locked the door then carefully hid the key. Heaven forbid if she put it in the wrong place. Kate was glad the house was within easy walking distance of the town. She wouldn't have coped without some kind of civilization nearby.

Taking her time, she strolled through the town centre of Sunset Point. There wasn't anything too exciting – a little Four Square Supermarket, greengrocer, chemist, post office, second hand bookshop, jeweller and clothing boutique lined one side of the main street. A café, newsagent, surf shop, ice cream parlour, haberdashery store, butcher and bakery lined the other.

Although Kate felt like she was in a bit of a time warp, she was impressed with how nicely it was set out. There were car parks in the centre of the wide street, interspersed with beautiful gardens. The footpaths were wide and the shopfronts well maintained with plenty of seats where people could sit and chat.

A little further down the main street was a pub, library, cinema and a Chinese restaurant. An elegant looking seafood restaurant, Leo's, was set a little bit back from the road and a sign saying 'Professional Offices' pointed to a street on the left. Used to living in a student area with a Night Owl convenience store nearby, Kate was surprised to see Four Square was about to close for the day. Dashing inside, she grabbed a few things as the sole checkout operator tapped her foot impatiently.

Taking the long way back, Kate passed the caravan park and the RSL. She also noticed a corner store/fish and chip shop just across the road from the beach. A sign proudly proclaimed that the newly refurbished Sunset Point Surf Club would be re-opening in two weeks. It was such a shame she wasn't here for fun, because it looked like the kind of place for an old-fashioned, idyllic beach holiday.

The front door was unlocked when Kate got back. She's home, Kate thought, so be nice. It's not that hard to give a pleasant greeting.

But all was quiet as she traipsed through the lounge room into the kitchen. After stowing her cold things in the fridge, Kate walked out onto the veranda. Jane wasn't there either.

Heading upstairs, she paused in the hallway outside Jane's closed bedroom door. The fact it was closed was a statement - or was it? Jane had always been very studious, maybe she just kept it closed to make sure she had the quietest possible environment. Maybe she was having a nap. Or maybe she was putting off coming face to face with her cousin for as long as possible.

Kate raised her hand to knock, but then lowered it again. They'd run into each other eventually.

As well as some basic food supplies, Kate had bought herself a pile of magazines. She was flicking through *Cleo* and eating a bowl of ice-cream on the couch when Jane appeared downstairs. Having inherited her Italian father's black hair, brown eyes and olive skin she had never fit the "plain Jane" stereotype.

Kate had always been envious of her cousin's natural beauty. Her own light brown hair was always carefully styled, she took time to do her make-up and people told her that her blue eyes were her best feature. So she didn't believe herself to be unattractive. But seeing Jane standing there in an old pair of shorts and a t-shirt, with her hair in a ponytail and still looking gorgeous didn't seem fair.

Has she always been that skinny? Kate thought, knowing how frumpy she must look sprawled on the couch. Of course she's tall too, so she can carry an extra kilo or two without it showing up instantly, unlike me.

'Hello Kate. Long-time no see.'

'Yeah, it's been a while,' Kate replied politely, as Jane walked past her into the kitchen. 'I've stocked up on ice-cream if you want some,' she called, in an effort to break the ice. 'Choc chip and caramel swirl, they didn't have any rocky road unfortunately.'

Jane dropped a chamomile tea bag into a china mug while she waited for the kettle to boil. 'I try and stay away from sugar while I'm studying, but thanks all the same,' she called back. 'Would you like some tea?'

'No thanks, I'm more of a latte girl,' Kate said, determined to keep things civil even though she could already feel her hackles rising. Trust Jane to fortify herself with just tea. No wonder she was so slim; she didn't even allow herself the luxury of a sugar binge during swot vac. 'When did you get here?' she asked.

'Yesterday arvo.'

'That must have been a long bus ride?'

'Yep.'

'You're on study break too, then?'

'Uh huh.'

I've made some effort, Kate thought, do I really need to keep trying? Jane answered the question for her by taking her tea and heading back upstairs without another word.

Kate made a face at her cousin's retreating back. Throwing the magazine aside, she lay down on the couch and stared up at the high ceiling. As much as Jane annoyed her by being such a goody-goody, she felt some sympathy towards her. Having her father walk out when she was twelve and watching her mother suffer from chronic health problems couldn't have been easy. Still, she didn't have to be so prickly.

'Great idea, Mum,' she mumbled sarcastically. 'Yeah, Jane and I can really take the time to re-connect.'

After reading both the *Cleo* and *Woman's Day* cover to cover, Kate wandered out on to the veranda and listened to the pounding ocean. Although there was only a sliver of moon, there was an abundance of stars. They're like little diamonds in a black velvet box, thought Kate. And they're much more visible here, away from the city lights of Brisbane.

Her father had always been a keen amateur astronomer and she could remember many nights spent out in the backyard with him pointing out constellations to her and her brothers. Once she hit her mid-teens, though, she was much more interested in staying inside watching TV and hadn't star gazed for years.

It took Kate a while to find the Southern Cross, down low on the horizon as it was in November. Dad would be shocked at how much I've forgotten, she thought sadly. I can't even remember what other constellations are visible in spring.

When she went up to bed at ten, Jane's light was already off.

Kate couldn't believe it when she slept in until nine thirty the next morning. So much for getting off to an early start.

'Kate, phone,' called Jane, and she realised that the ringing had probably woken her. There was an extension in Jane's bedroom, but Kate opted to take the call downstairs. She didn't need to advertise the fact she had just crawled out of bed. No doubt Miss Smarty Pants had been up since five, steadily reviewing work that she had already studied.

'Hi Katie,' her mother said cheerily when she picked up the receiver. 'I just wanted to make sure you had settled in all right and that the studying was coming along okay.'

Kate didn't have the heart to admit things were off to a shaky start. 'Yeah, it's fine. It's a very peaceful little town and the house is great,' she said, neglecting to mention she hadn't yet opened a book.

'And you and Jane are getting along?'

'Yes, we are,' Kate replied. Well she wasn't lying – they hadn't spent enough time together for there to be any problems.

'Good, that's very good. See, I knew if you could just get away somewhere and focus you would be fine. You're such a smart girl and Dad and I know you will do well.'

'Thanks for the vote of confidence,' Kate said. Her mother thought she'd been exaggerating when she had told her how behind she was. Obviously she still did.

'Oh, I saw Mrs Wheeler today and she said to pass on her regards. She's looking forward to catching up with her favourite past student when you come home for the holidays.'

'Yeah, that'll be great,' Kate murmured, wondering how she could avoid that meeting.

'All right, I'll let you get back to the books. Study hard now.'

'Yes Mum, I will,' Kate said, trying to swallow the lump in her throat.

Six hours later Kate lay her head back against the pillow and closed her eyes for a moment. She had moved from the desk to the spare bed so that she wouldn't be distracted by the view out the window and it did seem to have made her more productive. But now she had a pain in her wrist from writing at an unnatural angle and her knees were aching from being bent so she could lean her papers against them.

Kate had finally plunged into tackling one of the most tedious sections in Introduction to Taxation, but right now she was thinking more about what her mother had said than the latest revisions to the tax laws.

It wasn't that she didn't want to go home for the holidays, in many ways she looked forward to it. She loved the scenic beauty and the community feel of Elderfield, in the Brisbane Valley. The problem was that she had left her school and hometown as a star with seemingly unlimited potential. To go back having failed to live up to what others believed she was capable of, was going to be humiliating.

She was snapped out of her reverie by the ring of the telephone. Kate had grown so used to the softer buzz of modern phones that she'd forgotten how shrill the older ones sounded.

'Kate, it's for you,' Jane called. Going by the tone of her voice Miss Perfect didn't approve of frivolous phone conversations when you were supposed to be studying Kate decided as she trekked downstairs to take the call.

'How's it going, Kate?' Fiona asked, sounding like she didn't have a care in the world. 'Tell me about that gorgeous beach. I bet you're tanned already.'

Kate looked out the window down to the soft white sand that she hadn't even set foot on yet. 'Uh, it's going okay and the beach is beautiful, not too crowded or anything. No time for sunbaking though, I've spent most of today doing those stupid tax revisions and I think some of it has actually sunk in.'

Fiona laughed. 'Oh dear, you might not want to hear this then.'

'Hear what?'

'Well I had to return some library books today and found a notice on Gordy's door. Because he cancelled the last lecture yesterday, he decided it wasn't fair to include that question in the exam. So you can scratch the tax revisions.'

Kate slumped down on the couch. 'You have *got* to be kidding me,' she wailed.

'No, I'm not.' Fiona chuckled.

'It's not funny,' Kate snapped. 'Do you realise how many hours I've wasted on that?'

'Hey, chill out Kate, don't shoot the messenger. I thought you'd be happy.'

'Sorry, I'm just a bit stressed out and now I've wasted a whole day on something useless.'

'Come on, Kate, we've still got heaps of time left. Chalk it up to experience and go for a swim. I'm just heading out to the pool myself, it's really hot here today.'

After making small talk for another couple of minutes, Kate hung up. Fiona could be so annoying sometimes. She seemed to put as little effort into her work as Kate yet she still did well in her exams. Either she was super bright, or she studied far more than she let on.

So disheartened about her wasted day, Kate took the rest of the afternoon off. She lay on her bed and read the *Cosmopolitan* and then headed to town in search of something edible to dampen her sorrows. Chips or chocolate, she debated as she walked along the quiet street. I'd love some KFC chips, but I'm not desperate enough to take a bus ride to another town to get some. Maybe some sour cream and chives Thins? No, she decided as she saw a child eating an ice-block, a Magnum is what I want. Oh yeah, today won't seem quite so bad once I have a Magnum.

Five minutes later she stared in dismay at the ice-block cabinet in Four Square. 'You don't have any Magnums?' she asked the checkout operator.

The teenaged girl, whose name badge read Janine, shook her head. 'No, I'm so sorry we don't,' she replied politely.

'You're sure?'

Janine nodded. 'The supplier comes on Monday's. Some weeks we run out of the popular ones.'

'No Drumstick's either?'

Janine shook her head again. 'What you see is what you get. How about a Splice or a Paddlepop?'

'No thanks,' Kate sighed.

'A chocolate Billabong might hit the spot.'

'Nah, I'll have chips instead,' Kate said, selecting a large bag off the display next to the cash register.

Kate sat on the veranda to eat her chips. It was wider than an average veranda with an assortment of loungers and chairs, as well as a few small tables and a timber outdoor setting, down one end. She watched the waves rolling in on the beach and thought how restful it was to just sit there and take in the awesome view.

Caught up in her ocean gazing, Kate got a fright when the screen door banged against the wall and Jane came out holding steamed vegetables in one hand and a bowl of fruit salad in the other.

Great, now she knows exactly why I've chumped it up, Kate cringed, hastily scrunching up the foil packet and brushing the crumbs off her shirt. She hadn't intended to eat the whole bag in one sitting, but having made no other dinner plans they ended up being an easy option.

Jane didn't look very happy to see her. 'Oh, Kate, I didn't realise you were out here.'

'I'm pretty much finished,' Kate replied, thinking to herself that her cousin must be one of the few nineteen-year-old uni students in the world who voluntarily ate fruit and vegetables.

Jane nodded and smiled in a polite but vague way.

She's just as uncomfortable to be around me as I am around her, Kate realised. I can't think why. She's the skinny, pretty one who is sailing through her studies, while I'm the one who has crashed and burned. Still, she did let me stay here with her, I should make some effort.

'So,' she said, 'how are you enjoying nursing?'

Jane speared a piece of broccoli before answering. 'I really love it. It's harder this year now we are doing prac hours as well and I'm also doing shifts at the volunteer campus clinic for extra experience.'

'That sounds like a tough workload.'

'It can be but it's all I've ever wanted to do. Anything that helps me get there is worth it.'

'Right,' was all Kate could think to say at that point, wondering why anybody would voluntarily undertake extra work. But Jane had always been one of those people who went above and beyond what was expected of the average human. She had held down two part-time jobs from the age of fourteen as well as running a neighbourhood mowing service when she was at school. It seemed that she couldn't bear to waste a minute that could be used productively.

Deciding to cut her losses and not force any further conversation Kate was just about to excuse herself when Jane spoke.

'So, what happened with law?'

Kate cringed, as she always did, when people asked her that question. 'Oh, I just decided it wasn't for me after all.'

'Oh, right. And you knew that right from the start? You didn't think it was worth sticking it out a bit longer?'

'No,' Kate said, 'it was one of those instinctive things, you know?' not adding that it hadn't even taken her six days let alone the six-week grace period to know that law was a big mistake.

'And you're doing business now, right?'

Kate nodded.

'Oh, Mum must have got the story wrong somewhere. She told me you had changed from law to computer programming,' Jane said with a little laugh. 'I'm not sure how she got that so muddled.'

Kate considered lying for a moment, but knew she would get found out. 'I did go into IT for the rest of first semester, but it wasn't for me either.'

Jane just nodded (smugly Kate thought) and she took that as an opportunity to escape back inside so she wouldn't have to answer any more embarrassing questions. Stopping in the kitchen she made some vegemite toast and a cup of strong coffee. After carrying them back up to her room she sat at her desk and started reading through her accounting textbook, determined not to go to bed until she covered at least five chapters. It didn't feel like she was taking much in, but at least she was doing *something*.

She woke at two o'clock with her head resting on her open textbook and her hand still clutching her pen. Gazing blearily at the page she contemplated making herself stay awake and finish that chapter at least. But when she realised she couldn't even focus on the text, she cut her losses and crawled into bed.

Despite her late night, Kate still managed to drag herself out of bed by eight thirty the next morning. After having a quick shower and bolting down a bowl of Fruit Loops, she made it to her desk by nine o'clock. But before she had a chance to start work the phone rang.

'It's for you!' Jane snapped rudely.

Well excuse me for maintaining communication with the outside world, Kate thought, as she ran down the steps.

'Hi Kate, it's me Mel,' her flatmate said when she picked up the receiver.

'Oh, hi, how's it going?' Kate and Mel got along well enough, but they weren't good friends. She hadn't expected to hear from her.

'Oh, it's going all right. I'm trying really hard to stick to my study timetable. It's the best way to make sure I spend time on everything I need to, including the horrible stuff I'd rather forget.'

'Yeah, well that's true. It can be easier to ignore the unpleasant things in life,' Kate said, still not sure why Mel had rung.

Finally, she got to the point. 'I noticed you left your Business Practices book of readings behind and I thought you might need it. You want me to post it up?'

'Oh, yeah, could you?' Kate hadn't even started on BP yet, which was why she hadn't noticed the readings were missing. I really am the worst student ever, she thought as she made her way back upstairs. I haven't even thought about a study timetable.

Two hours later she put the finishing touches on a colour-coded, precisely detailed work of art. Right, now the timetable is done I can really start work, she decided with a smile.

By eight fifteen that night, Kate was weary. Accounting took so much *effort*. As mind numbing as the tax revisions had been yesterday they were just straight rote learning, she didn't need to understand them like she did journals and ledgers. She couldn't skip ahead either, as each new section built on knowledge introduced in the previous ones.

Trudging downstairs in search of food, she found Jane in the kitchen preparing her meal. Kate poured herself a big bowl of Coco-Pops and a tall glass of Coke while Jane put the finishing touches on a huge salad just brimming with healthiness. It was a roomy kitchen so they weren't in each other's way, however Kate still felt crowded in by her cousin's presence.

'Did you have a good day?' Jane asked.

Kate took a mouthful of cereal and nodded slowly. 'Yeah, I guess. I was at my desk pretty much for seven hours straight so that must mean something hey?'

'Whatever works for you.'

'What's *that* supposed to mean?'

'It means what it sounds like,' Jane replied calmly. 'Different people study in different ways, so if that way works for you then that's great.'

'What do you mean *that way*? You make it sound like I'm learning impaired.'

Jane held up her hands in surrender. 'You're totally over analysing everything I say. It was just a simple remark enquiring how your day was. I'm not trying to criticise or suggest you don't know what you're doing.'

'No, you're not saying it, but you're thinking it.'

'Don't presume to know what I think, Kate - just don't.' Jane still looked calm but her tone was cold and measured.

'Well I don't have to presume too much. You're making it pretty obvious that you don't want me here, disturbing your precious study haven.'

Jane didn't respond verbally to Kate's barb, instead she crossed her arms, raised her eyebrows and shrugged

'I'm *sooo* sorry for not being perfect like you.' Kate slugged another mouthful of Coke.

'I never said I was perfect,' Jane retaliated as she opened the cutlery drawer and selected a knife and fork.

'No, *you* don't have to say it - everyone else says it for you. All I ever hear is how great Jane is. Why did you even agree to me coming here anyway?'

'Because your mother asked me,' Jane replied bluntly.

'You could have said no.'

'Yes, I could, but I felt like I should give you a chance like she said. You know what? If she hadn't—' Jane trailed off mid-sentence.

Kate glared at her. 'If she hadn't what?'

Jane just shook her head. 'Forget it. I foolishly agreed and here we are. I'll make up a time-table for meals tomorrow so we won't have to interact any more than is necessary.' She picked up her salad and went out to the veranda, banging the door in her wake.

'I knew this wouldn't work,' Kate yelled after her.

There was no reply from the veranda.

Kate tipped the remainder of her cereal down the sink, turning the tap on full force to wash it away. After gulping down the rest of her Coke, she stomped upstairs and threw herself on her bed, still fuming. Lying there for half an hour didn't help her sort anything out in her mind, rather it made her more stressed about study and more annoyed with her cousin for being so *good*.

Her family, and especially Kate's own mother, always made such a fuss of Jane. Even the most mundane accomplishments were praised and talked about endlessly. On her acceptance into her nursing degree there was as much fanfare as if she had been accepted as a Rhodes Scholar.

And, to top it all off, Jane had chosen a noble and unselfish kind of career, while all Kate's choices were motivated by their potential income level.

Scrunching up a stray piece of paper Kate threw it viciously in the direction of Jane's room. Maybe if people made as big a fuss of me and what I was doing, I might have had a more successful year, she fumed.

Hearing footsteps on the stairs, Kate got up and opened the wardrobe to find something to wear. She was going down to the pub. It wasn't something she normally did by herself, but tonight she was desperate to get out of the house. Earlier she had seen a banner advertising the rugby union world cup to be shown on the big screen at the King George Hotel. That sounded like it might just be fun.

Forty-five minutes later Kate strode purposefully into the pub and straight up to the bar. If she was going to carry this off, she had to look like she was meeting someone, not like a lonesome loser who went out alone.

The place was packed. All the tables were occupied and dozens of other people stood in groups around the room. Green and gold streamers hung from the ceiling fans, swirling lazily. Matching balloons were strung along each wall. A small but vocal contingent of English supporters dressed in red and white occupied one corner. 'Always look on the bright side of life,' they sang.

'Give it a rest!' yelled a young man good naturedly. Decked out in a Wallabies jersey and beanie, he must have been roasting, given the warm temperature.

The big screen TV was on, but the sound still muted waiting for the kick-off. Permission had been granted for the pub to stay open past midnight to cater for the northern hemisphere match time.

The two bar staff looked like they were in a speeded up old fashioned movie as they worked feverishly, trying to satisfy all their customers. Finally, the harassed looking middle-aged woman made it to Kate.

Before she opened her mouth, a voice beside her said, 'Champagne for the lady and a VB for me thanks.'

Shocked, Kate turned towards the owner of the voice. It was the jersey/beanie guy. Up close he had reddish-brown hair and light brown eyes. A sheen of sweat glistened on his forehead. 'Aren't you hot?' she blurted, then felt immediately foolish for saying something so stupid.

Grinning, he mopped his brow. 'Yeah, I am a bit. But you've got to get in the spirit of these things, right?'

Kate nodded and smiled. 'Thanks for the drink,' she said. 'My name's Kate.'

'My pleasure Kate. I'm Travis. Would you care to join my friends and I? We saw you walking down here by yourself and thought you might be lonely.'

Kate was about to deliver a vague story about maybe meeting up with somebody later, but then realised it didn't matter. 'I'd love to,' she agreed.

The atmosphere was electric as the match neared its end. Kate couldn't believe she might have missed such a fun night. She was having such a great time with Travis and his two female companions, Libby and Robyn. They were on holidays from Canberra and had met Travis that afternoon in the laundry at the caravan park.

'I love David Campese!' Libby declared with a woozy smile.

'He can play all right,' Travis agreed, jumping to his feet as an English player made a spectacular dash with the ball. 'Noooo!' he yelled in unison with half the crowd. The sense of relief in the room was palpable when he was finally tackled.

'Whew, that was close,' Travis said, taking another swig of beer.

The frenzied crowd stayed on the edge of their seats for the final five minutes, before the countdown to the twelve to six victory. A rousing rendition of Waltzing Matilda broke out, amid cheers and general revelry.

Linking arms with Travis and Robyn, Kate allowed herself to be swept along in the crowd. This is so much better than studying, she decided with a grin.

Someone was repeating her name. At first it was just an irritating background kind of buzz, but now it was building up to an annoying, nagging tone.

'Wha—,' Kate mumbled, determined to get just a little bit more sleep.

Stomping footsteps were followed by the sound of curtains being opened and an explosion of light that she could sense, even with her eyes closed.

'KATE!' Jane yelled.

Forcing one eye open, Kate was hit with a laser beam of bright sunlight. Using her hand to block it she focused on the stern figure standing at the end of her bed. 'What's going on?' she asked.

'There's some guy downstairs to see you.'

'Guy?'

'*Travis*'

'Oh, yeah, right,' Kate murmured. 'Tell him I'll be right there.'

After Jane flounced off, Kate dragged herself out of bed and threw on yesterday's discarded clothes. Her watch read eight o'clock. It was almost three by the time they got home. She couldn't believe he was up and about so early.

Grabbing a glass of water on her way past the kitchen, Kate ventured out to the veranda to find Travis leaning on the railing, taking in the view.

'Hi,' she said.

Travis smiled as he turned to face her. Although his eyes were red and his face pale, he looked ready to face the day. 'Great house!' he exclaimed.

'Yeah, it's pretty cool.'

'I don't think your cousin likes me.'

Kate waved her hand dismissively. 'Don't worry about it, she's a bit stand-offish.'

Travis parked himself on one of the loungers. 'So, what are we going to do today? Libby and Robyn are just having their showers and getting organised.'

'I can't do anything, I've got to study,' Kate said, sitting down on the other lounger.

Travis stared at her in astonishment. 'I honestly thought you were joking. Come on, Kate,' he wheedled, 'you can't study on a day like today.' He extended his arms to take in the panorama of the beautiful summer's day.

'No, really, I'm so behind…'

'You know you want to Kate.'

'Well…, maybe, just something this morning. But I need to be home by two at the latest.'

'Sure, no problem.'

Kate took another handful of Twisties and checked her watch. Four thirty. She should have been back two hours ago. But then she would have missed all the fun. The girls had hired a Mini Moke and they'd had an amazing drive along the sparkling coastline, before heading inland.

She smiled as she took in her surroundings. She, Libby and Robyn were relaxing on a picnic blanket while Travis was sprawled on the lush green grass nearby, snoring gently. She'd never even heard of the Hidden Gorge Rock Pools before today. Located downstream on the Archibald River, the pristine pools were an amazing place to swim and the adjacent grassed area a perfect place to relax. Dappled sunlight filtered onto the blanket, creating the ultimate lazy summer afternoon.

'What's Travis' story anyway?' Kate wondered out loud.

Libby shrugged. 'I'm really not sure. He just turned up at the caravan park yesterday, by himself. Said he was having a break away from his stressful job, but won't say what it is.'

'Yeah, I noticed he doesn't talk much about himself.'

Robyn popped open a can of Diet Coke. 'He did let it slip that he's from Adelaide, but that's about all.'

'It is a bit weird that he doesn't drive,' said Libby. 'I mean, a guy of that age not having his licence is pretty unusual.'

'Maybe he lost it for speeding or something,' Robyn said.

Kate and Libby nodded in agreement.

'He must be a reformed smoker too,' Kate said softly. 'Did you hear the way he wheezed when we walked up here, despite it being pretty flat ground?'

Robyn took another sip of her drink. 'I get the impression he lives pretty fast. Obviously having afternoon naps is his way of keeping up the pace.'

'Are you coming to the pub again tonight?' Libby asked.

Shaking her head Kate said, 'I really need to do some work.'

Travis stirred just as she spoke. 'Aw, come on, Kate, you're not still on that boring track, are you?' he said, blinking in the sunlight. 'All you've done is moan how much you hate it, why are you even bothering?'

'Because it means I might get to do something else I really want to.'

'Yeah, but what if you hate that too?'

Good point, thought Kate. She had been so sure she'd love law but instead she'd detested it. Maybe she was just stabbing wildly in the dark. She had come to the beach house thinking everything would magically fall into place and it hadn't.

'I left school in year ten,' put in Robyn. 'I couldn't get out of there fast enough. I don't get why people study for so many more years than they have to.'

'Hear, hear,' agreed Travis. 'Life's way too short to spend time doing something you hate. You've got to get out there and enjoy every single minute.'

'All right!' Kate smiled. 'I'll just pop down for a while.'

It was the sound of voices that woke her the next morning. Loud voices. Somebody downstairs was having an argument. Kate groaned and rolled out of bed. She knew who she'd find down there.

She could hear Jane's angry tone as she came down the stairs. 'You're distracting her!'

'Maybe she needs to be distracted. Maybe you do too. You're way too young to be so hung up on everything.'

'Please! I don't need your advice about anything. This is about Kate.'

Kate jogged down the last few stairs. 'Yeah, it *is* about me,' she agreed, glaring at Jane. 'So I'll thank you to keep your opinions to yourself.'

'You know what, fine, if you want to throw away your own future but I need to study and I can't do that if you're dragging people home at all hours, talking and laughing and *drinking*,' Jane said viciously.

Kate took in the state of the lounge room. Two empty pizza boxes lay discarded on the coffee table. Travis had given a cab driver a fifty-dollar tip to go and pick them up from the next town. Three beer cans and a wine bottle sat on the floor. A deck of cards was strewn in front of the radio. Although she'd tried to keep the others quiet last night, they had been a bit loud.

'All right, I'm sorry,' Kate said. 'I'll clean this up and we won't come back here again. But don't think you can tell me what to do.'

Jane shook her head and stormed back upstairs.

Travis looked at Kate and grinned. 'Don't mind her, I've got something really cool planned for today.'

They set off in the Mini Moke again, this time heading south. Travis gave directions but wouldn't say what they were doing. 'You'll love it,' he assured Kate, as they sat in the back. 'It's just what you need to rediscover the adventurous spirit your cousin is trying to kill.'

Kate felt a stab of disloyalty, even though she and Jane weren't really speaking. 'She's not that bad,' she said. 'She's just very conscientious.'

Travis rolled his eyes. 'Sounds pretty unadventurous to me.' Focusing back on the road he pointed ahead. 'Here's the turn off Lib,' he said excitedly.

Looking over at the smaller sign attached to the pole of the road sign Kate did a double take. 'We're not seriously doing this, are we?'

Travis's eyes gleamed. 'You bet we are!'

A battered Pajero took them most of the way up the steep track, but they had to walk the last part. Libby and Robyn had decided not to come, saying they were happy to watch, so it was just Kate and Travis making their way to the platform. Kate was swinging between extreme nerves and excitement. Travis was playing it cool but by the way he was sweating, he must have been pretty nervous too. Then again, maybe he was just very unfit, Kate thought as she listened to his laboured breathing.

'Are you okay?' she asked, eyeing his pale face.

He nodded. 'Just a touch of asthma.'

'Asthma!' exclaimed the guide who was walking just in front of them. Stopping abruptly, he made Travis and Kate do the same. 'Didn't you read the disclaimer?' he barked. 'You can't do this with asthma!'

Travis held up his hands in surrender. 'All right, my mistake. I'll go back down. But Kate here still wants to go ahead.'

'No, no, it's fine, I'll come back too,' Kate said.

Travis turned her around and gave her a gentle push. 'No, you have to do it. For me as well as you.'

The guide raised his eyebrows impatiently. 'Well?'

Taking a deep breath, Kate nodded. 'All right, I'll go!'

A wave of nausea hit. Kate was sure she was going to be sick. Closing her eyes, she took a deep breath and tried to calm herself.

Boom-boom. Boom-boom. Boom-boom.

She had no idea her own heart could sound so loud or beat so fast.

Opening her eyes again Kate looked down at her feet. Strapped together they barely fit on the tiny platform. She couldn't believe she was about to do this.

The nausea hit again and she thought about trying to wriggle her way back. But she couldn't. Once you were out here you had to go.

She didn't want the countdown to start, but inevitably it did. 'Three, two, one...BUNGY!' yelled the man in the black t-shirt.

Kate squeezed her eyes shut and jumped over the edge.

They were still talking about it that night as they cooked a barbeque in the picnic area adjacent to the beach.

'Seriously, I don't know how you stood out there, knowing you had to leap off,' Robyn said, as she fried the onions.

'Yeah, I'll admit that was terrifying,' said Kate. 'And to be honest I'm not sure I'd do it again – but the feeling of flying through the air was pretty amazing. It was like, for those ten seconds or whatever it was, nothing else mattered.'

'Yeah, it's almost as cool as sky diving,' Travis agreed. 'You need to try that next Kate.'

Kate smiled as she stuck the sausages onto the hotplate. 'One thing at a time.'

'You've got to admit it was better than wasting the day stuck up at Stalag Beach House,' he said.

A stab of guilt assaulted Kate as she glanced up at the house. She hadn't even checked in with Jane. It wasn't like they were supposed to be keeping tabs on each other, but it was almost eight thirty and she might be wondering where Kate was.

'Uh, I'm just going up to get my long-sleeved shirt,' she said casually. 'It's a bit breezy down here.'

The others nodded and kept talking as she made her way back to the house. I don't have to actually speak to her, Kate thought as she headed up the path towards the back steps. I'll just go in and out and make enough noise for her to hear me. She's probably sitting at her desk not even thinking about me.

Jane was, in fact, sitting on the veranda with the light off. Kate wasn't sure if she was waiting for her or not. But having not seen her in the dark, she got the fright of her life when Jane spoke.

'I'm not doing this anymore, Kate,' she said. 'One of us is going to have to leave. I'd prefer it to be you, but I'm not going to fight about it. If you're not prepared to go, I will.'

Kate exhaled loudly. 'What does it matter? I told you I won't bring them up to the house anymore. I was out all day today, so how is that affecting you?'

'It's too unsettling. I'm not going to stand by and watch you self-destruct.'

'Since when does having a good time mean that you're self-destructing?'

'I don't understand you Kate. All you have to do is focus for a couple of weeks and then you can have all the fun you want.'

'Spare me the lecture. You don't know the first thing about me.'

'You're right, I don't. You're not the girl I once knew.'

'Nor are you! You used to be adventurous as well and have a sense of humour. Now you're like a fifty-year-old.'

'Yeah well I'm a fifty-year-old with a future.'

Kate was incensed. 'How dare you say that?' she yelled.

The sound of footsteps on the stairs made them both look up. Travis stood there with his hands held out in a calming gesture. 'Ladies, please there's no need to fight.'

Jane rolled her eyes. 'Perfect. More pearls of wisdom.'

Travis took another step up and then dropped to his knees with his hands crossed over his chest. 'Kate…,' he began.

'There's a time and a place Travis and I can fight my own battles thanks,' Kate said, annoyed that he had followed her up. She wasn't in the mood for his carefree witticisms right now.

He didn't move. 'No, Kate I…I,'

'I mean it Travis!'

Without a word, he pulled himself up the last two steps. Then he collapsed.

· · · · ·

The tiny private hospital was right on the outskirts of town. As soon as the taxi pulled up in front of the building, Kate leapt out and ran inside, leaving Jane to pay the driver. Ignoring the young nurse who was manning the front desk, she ran along the short hallway, peering into each room.

She found him in the third on the left. Her heart almost stopped at the sight that greeted her. Travis's eyes were closed and an oxygen mask covered his face. An IV bag hung next to his bed, connected to his arm by the cannula she had seen the ambulance officer insert earlier. A series of wires snaked over the top of his hospital gown and attached to a monitor that was beeping softly every few seconds.

A short, red-haired young man with a stethoscope around his neck was writing in a chart. Glancing up, he looked at Kate expectantly. 'Are you a relative?'

'No, I'm a friend. He's just on holidays here.'

'Well good work calling the ambulance so fast, it meant we could get him straight onto oxygen and up his medication.'

Kate gasped. This was worse than she thought. 'Is he okay?'

The man shook his head. 'Not really.'

Kate's hand flew to her mouth. 'What's wrong with him?'

Realising he had frightened her, the man hung up the chart and motioned for Kate to follow him into a small lounge across the hall. 'My name is Joe Nichols and I'm a registrar at Rosethorn Hospital, which is the next major town around here. Sometimes I get called over here after hours if their doctor is unavailable.'

Kate nodded impatiently, not really caring about any of this information.

'It's lucky he was wearing that medic alert bracelet, it meant I knew what I was dealing with straight away and who to contact.'

Kate nodded again, numbly this time. She hadn't even noticed anything special about the bracelet. 'Will he have to stay here long?'

Joe shook his head. 'No, he can't.'

Kate gave him a puzzled glance.

'We can't treat him here; he needs much more specialised care.'

Kate's hand flew to her mouth again. 'Why?' she whispered.

'He's got a serious heart condition.'

Without either of its occupants having to voice it, a white flag had been raised at the beach house. The angry words that had been exchanged mere hours earlier were forgotten as Kate and Jane sat on the veranda, each nursing a cup of tea.

'I still don't understand,' Kate murmured. 'I mean how can someone who's that sick act so normal?'

'Well, apparently he's held pretty level for a while, but it was only a matter of time before the heart really started to weaken. Also, the medication masks it, but he was probably overcompensating as well. By keeping up the hyper façade, you don't really notice when he's short of breath or a bit lethargic.'

'He did wheeze a lot, but he said it was asthma.'

'Well that sounds plausible to anyone without medical training.'

'But why do it?' Kate asked. 'I mean why take off from his family and friends and go on some crazy holiday?'

'He's facing huge surgery in a few weeks. It will either vastly improve his quality of life or eventually he'll need to go on the transplant list. I guess it was his last hurrah while he felt he still had some control over his destiny.'

'Do you think he'll be all right? I mean you know a lot about medical stuff.'

'I honestly don't know,' Jane said quietly.

For the first time since she had arrived, Kate awoke early the next morning. Even without looking at her clock she could tell that the sun hadn't long been up. Flinging off the sheet, she wandered over to the window seat and opened the curtains.

Another beautiful day greeted her. Only a few wispy clouds dotted an otherwise perfect azure sky. The ocean gleamed in the early sunlight. Kate could see a few surfers in the water, gliding along the waves with apparent ease.

Early morning was so perfect, so full of potential. Yet she felt so trapped and weighed down. Glancing over at the desk and the pile of textbooks, a tear slid down her cheek. This time last year as she prepared to leave high school the world seemed so full of possibilities. She had been presented with opportunities that many seventeen year olds could only dream of. And somehow, she had managed to throw them all away.

Thinking about Travis, Kate started to sob. His future was so uncertain, but he'd got out there and done something, no matter how ill advised. He, at least had an idea of what he wanted to get out of life, while she was totally lost.

Stumbling back over to her bed, she threw herself face down and cried like her heart might break.

Kate was still lying on her bed an hour later. Having cried the worst of it out of her system, she was now caught in inertia. She knew she should move and do something, but couldn't seem to get her brain to connect with her limbs.

She was shocked when Jane appeared at her door holding a cup of something. She thought last night was probably a blip on the radar of their troubled relationship.

'Come in,' she said listlessly.

Walking over, Jane handed her the cup. 'It's coffee,' she said. 'You said you're a latte girl. This isn't a latte, exactly, but I thought it might help.'

Kate was touched. 'Thanks.'

'I rang the hospital. Travis has been airlifted to Brisbane to be monitored for a while before they send him home to Adelaide.'

'Thanks,' Kate said again. 'You didn't have to.'

'Hey, I yelled at him yesterday, I feel pretty bad about that.'

'How do you think I feel? He almost bungy jumped with me!'

Jane shook her head in wonder. 'I can't believe you did that.'

'Me either. It was one of those crazy, split second decisions,' Kate admitted, bracing for the lecture.

It didn't come. Instead Jane asked, 'Was it fun?'

Kate eyed her in surprise. 'Yeah, it was, kinda,' she said. 'I had my eyes closed most of the tim,e though.'

'That's understandable.' Jane smiled.

Kate took a few sips of coffee before speaking again. 'So, what you said yesterday about me leaving....'

'Look, Kate, I don't want to be the heavy here, but I think you're at the crossroads. So, stop dithering. Decide what you're going to do and do it.'

'I wish I could! I keep thinking about what Travis said about not wasting a moment on things that aren't important.'

Jane sat on the edge of the bed. 'Sometimes you've got to look at things in context. Yeah, it's a good philosophy not to waste a second of life, but it's not always entirely practical.'

'Why not?' Kate challenged. 'Maybe we'd all be happier if we lived like that.'

Jane sighed. 'Travis is staring down the barrel of risky surgery with a forty percent success rate or a potentially long and desperate wait for a donor heart. For him the concept of not wasting a second is pretty much a necessity.'

'Yeah, but you know what they say, anyone can get hit by a bus.'

'True, but it's not really very likely. You have the luxury of time on your hands and in the greater scheme of things a few weeks of effort towards something you're not very interested in isn't that big a sacrifice to make.'

'I think I've left it too late.'

Jane's exasperated sigh reminded Kate of Patricia. 'When's your first exam?'

'Next Friday.'

'Right, that's eleven days,' said Jane briskly. '*Come on*, Kate, this is not unsalvageable. You just have to focus on one thing at a time and sometimes you need to make yourself sit down and do it by sheer force of will.' Reaching over she took the cup out of Kate's hand. Then she grabbed her wrist and hauled her to her feet.

'Hey!' Kate protested, taken aback.

'Get dressed, go for a nice long walk to clear your head and then come back up here and get to work.'

They eyeballed each other for a second. Kate didn't appreciate the bossy tone and her hackles rose at being told what to do. But then she took a breath and finally made a decision. 'All right,' she said.

Having woken up so early, it was only seven thirty when Kate stepped onto the cool, soft sand. The still gentle heat from the sun was like a soft embrace on her skin as the waves rolled in lazily with a gentle rhythm.

A young family walked past her. Three small children decked out in a bright array of new-looking swimwear ran eagerly ahead, while their parents staggered behind, weighed down with towels, hats and beach toys. Kate smiled, remembering how much easier it was to go to the beach when you didn't have to be responsible for your own stuff.

Looking further along she noticed the red and yellow patrol flags flapping gently in the breeze. Two men wearing lifeguard shirts stood talking on the sand, while keeping a close eye on the ocean in front of them. Just beyond the flags a crew of four men and two women were hauling a wooden boat emblazoned with *Sunset Point S.L.S.C.* into the waves.

Smiling wistfully Kate cast her mind back to her last two years of high school as a member of the rowing team. They had trained twice a week at six a.m. and she had always enjoyed the beauty of early morning when everything seemed so fresh and quiet. She had planned to join the QUT rowing team, but with so much upheaval in her life at the start of the year she'd never gotten around to it. Now she wished she'd made the effort.

The sight of a seagull soaring peacefully through the air brought her back to the present. Don't start the day off in a negative frame of mind, she reminded herself, focus on being productive. Pulling on her cap she pushed the unpleasant thoughts away and started walking.

When she strode back up the walkway to the house forty-five minutes later, Kate couldn't believe how alive she felt. Sunset Point beach was beautiful, there were no high-rise buildings in sight and very few people to crowd the shoreline. She'd forgotten just how magic a walk on the beach could be. Bouncing up the back steps, Kate hoped she could hold on to that energetic feeling throughout the day.

A pang of déjà vu hit when Kate flung open the pantry cupboard at one o'clock. This time it was Jane's, rather than Mel's, shelves that were well stocked, while hers boasted only two boxes of cereal and a jar of vegemite. I guess I could have ice-cream, she thought, but then shook her head. That's the epitome of laziness she scolded herself. It'll take ten minutes to walk down to the shops and get some bread.

This really is a quiet little place, Kate thought, as she strolled down the main street. Even though it's lunchtime, there's still not that much activity. Walking past the bustling Sunset Café seconds later, she smiled. So that's where everybody was. Pausing for a second, she half turned and looked through the front window. Maybe I could just have lunch here, Kate thought, save myself the trouble.

She dithered for a second, then turned away. Bungy jumping had carved a huge hole in her finances. There was no way she could afford café lunches. Sighing, she kept walking towards the bakery.

Kate was shocked when she took her sandwich and apple out to the veranda and saw Jane flipping through her *Woman's Day*. Catching the look Jane glanced back uncertainly. 'Uh, you don't mind do you? I mean it was just lying on the table.'

Kate shook her head. 'No, of course not, I'm finished with it.'

'What's that look for, then?'

'Well, I'm just shocked to see you doing something so unproductive. I mean *Woman's Day*, that's pretty frivolous.'

'As compared to the *Cosmo* I read yesterday?'

Kate chuckled, remembering the times they had giggled together as primary schoolers. She hasn't totally lost her sense of humour after all, she realised.

'I'm not that much of a drudge,' Jane said.

'You've just looked so intense since I've been here. I didn't realise you came up for air sometimes.'

'I just build in some relaxation breaks, you know half an hour here, an hour later. It's too full on otherwise.'

Kate sat down. 'I like the sound of that but I still think it's different for you because you're so naturally studious. You've got a real advantage,' she said glumly, taking a bite of her sandwich.

'Honestly, Kate that's not true. I've always been a plodder. I *need* to spend a lot of hours at my desk going over stuff until it sinks in. My HSC year was a long, hard slog and I still only just scraped into uni.'

'Really?' Kate was dubious. The way she had heard it from Jane's mother the nursing faculty were humbled beyond belief that such a brilliant student had deigned to study with them.

Jane nodded. 'It was literally by a few points.'

Kate raised an eyebrow, still not sure if that was the truth. 'I'm so glad that Queensland ditched external exams.'

'I'm with you on that, I'd never want to go through that year again, or this one to be honest.'

'Has it been hard?'

'Brutal. I was downplaying it the other night. I have definitely struggled to keep all the balls in the air at times.'

'You honestly have to work hard all the time to keep up?'

'Definitely. Between study, prac, volunteering and my part-time jobs I'm lucky to see daylight some weeks.'

'Oh, do you still have more than one job? Don't you get Austudy?'

'Yeah, but that only covers my rent. There's food and transport and I have to, oh, you know, there's always extra stuff.'

'You're very independent. I just ask my parents for money for the extra stuff.'

'Lucky you.'

By four thirty Kate's fingers were aching. Wriggling them she examined the middle one and realised she was getting a blister. Throwing her pen down, she gazed out the window and was so caught up in the inviting scene that she didn't hear Jane come into her room. When she spoke, Kate clutched her chest in fright. 'You'll put *me* in hospital if you scare me like that again,' she gasped.

'Sorry,' Jane said. 'I just came in to see how you're going.'

Kate motioned to the pile of written pages she had amassed since that morning. 'Well I've written a lot. Not sure how much of it has sunk in yet though.'

'You've got to start somewhere and remember what Nanna always says?'

'You need a light hand to make a sponge cake?'

'No,' Jane chuckled. 'Remember, how do you eat an elephant?'

'One bite at a time.'

'That's it! I also came to ask if you want to go for a swim.'

Kate raised her eyebrows.

'It's my afternoon break,' Jane said defensively.

'I'm getting a copy of your timetable.'

'Sure, if you want to,' Jane agreed. 'Are you going to come? I discovered a storage cupboard downstairs yesterday, it's full of beach equipment, you know boogie boards and stuff.'

Kate hesitated. She loved swimming but hated the idea of standing next to Jane's slender form. Still, boogie boarding did sound like a very welcome respite from study and her togs were black (and thus theoretically slimming) after all.

'I'd love to,' she agreed.

As the girls prepared dinner they listened to the local radio station — first the news and then a trivia contest.

'Come on, you have to know this one,' cried Kate when the contestant couldn't remember the name of the middle Brady Bunch boy. 'It's Peter!'

Two questions later Jane was shouting at the radio. 'We breathe out carbon dioxide you silly man, not hydrogen.'

'We should have a go one night,' Kate said. 'There's a hundred-dollar prize.'

Jane nodded and handed her some carrots to peel for the stir-fry.

Apparently sensing how the last few days must have strained Kate's finances, Jane had suggested sharing the food expenses. Kate had readily agreed, even though it did mean she had to also pitch in with meal preparation. I'm not opposed to healthy eating, she thought, as she chopped the carrots, I'm just lazy.

Moving onto the zucchinis, she bopped her head and started singing along to the radio as she sliced. 'Don't go now…' she crooned.

Jane raised her eyebrows.

'My flatmate Mel is a huge RATCAT fan,' Kate said. 'I know all their songs by osmosis.'

'Sure. If you say so.'

Kate stuck out her tongue and kept singing.

While they ate, they talked about their achievements for the day.

'Well, I still feel like I'm never going to get through what I have to, but I did make some progress,' Kate said as she finished the last of her rice. 'I could answer more than half of the review questions for the first chapter of economics.'

'They say a journey of a thousand miles begins with the first step.'

'I think my journey is more like ten thousand miles, but you're right. I'm further along than I was yesterday. How about you?'

'I got through a lot of chemistry, which I was a bit behind in. But it feels like I'm starting to make a dent.'

Kate didn't really believe that Jane would be behind in anything, but she didn't comment. It was nice to be on friendly terms again instead of walking on eggshells.

Having carefully copied down Jane's daily schedule, Kate knew that between eight and nine was relaxation and wind down hour. She's really onto something here, Kate decided, as she made two mugs of hot chocolate. Studying is much more bearable if you have something fun to look forward to as well.

Jane searched through the shelves of board games. 'It's nice to have someone to play a game with,' she said, as Kate emerged from the kitchen holding the drinks. 'We've got Scrabble, Uno, Skipbo, Rummykub, chess, draughts or ordinary playing cards.'

'Um, how about Scrabble? I haven't played for years and I'm totally over numbers today.'

'Scrabble it is,' Jane replied, bringing the dog-eared box over and setting it up on the long dining room table.

Half an hour later the friendly game had become quite spirited. Beneath Jane's reserved, ultra-responsible persona lurked a serious competitor.

'Kakapo?' she asked suspiciously, as Kate arranged her tiles on the board.

Kate nodded. 'Yes, kakapo. It's a native New Zealand bird. Look it up,' she said, motioning towards the huge dictionary sitting on the bookshelf.

'Okay,' Jane conceded after finding the word, 'you are correct.' Then with a glint in her eye, she asked, 'what else can you tell me about it?'

'It's nocturnal and it rarely flies.'

'You got me. Obviously my education has been lacking thus far not to have ever heard of it.' Jane was gracious in defeat.

Kate laughed. 'I did a project about them in grade five and it was such a weird name I never forgot. It's not the first time I've used it in Scrabble.'

Despite Kate using her old standby, Jane still won, although not by much.

'You're on notice, Miss Moretti,' Kate said as she gathered up the tiles and dropped them back in the box. 'Now I know how you play I'm coming after you next time.'

'Oooh, I'm scared.'

They looked at each other and laughed, an action that conveyed how nice it was to be pals again.

'So,' Kate said as she put the game back on the shelf. 'Do you really get up at five thirty every morning?'

'Yep, I do. I like to go for a jog before I start work.'

Kate blanched. 'I won't be jogging, but I can walk.'

'You don't have to follow the timetable to the letter,' Jane said, as she locked the back door.

'No, I said I would and I'm going to. But I guess I'll actually have to use my alarm clock now.'

• • • • •

Beep-beep. Pause. Beep-beep. Pause. Beep-beep...

Eventually the tinny sound permeated Kate's consciousness. Keeping her eyes closed, she felt along the side of her travel clock and depressed the small, round button. Whoever had invented the snooze button was a genius, she decided as she buried her head under the pillow for another ten minutes of sleep.

She felt slightly guilty the second time she did it, but not so much that it kept her eyes open.

When the third series of beeps started, she finally flung back the sheet and dragged herself out of bed.

The next morning, she only hit snooze once. You've just got to ease yourself into these things, she conceded as she rolled out of bed after the alarm sprang back to life the second time.

Kate didn't even need the alarm the following morning. It had finally occurred to her to leave the curtains open and so her eyes fluttered open five minutes before it was due to go off.

She was still bleary eyed when she headed down the walking path five minutes later, but like always, it didn't take long to blink away the last vestiges of sleep once she set foot on the cool, soft sand. The early morning beach scene was becoming familiar now, an integral part of her daily routine.

Gazing towards the southern end of the beach she could see the jutting cliff that marked the border of town. Right, today I'm going that way, Kate decided, instead of taking the shorter path north to the lighthouse. I have to tackle that last section of economics and I'm going to need a clear head to do it.

The walk took longer than she anticipated. The cliff was like a mirage in the desert, seeming closer than it actually was. Not that Kate minded. I don't think you could ever really get tired of this, she thought, as she watched the sun's ray's dance across the turquoise water. Even with my appalling lack of fitness, it's an easy enough walk.

Eventually she made it, smiling to herself as she strode right up to the huge formation and symbolically touched one of the boulders at its base. Pausing for a moment, she stared out to sea and thought about how lucky she was to have somehow ended up here, finally taking some positive steps after a year of false starts and dead ends.

A rogue wave crashed to shore, ricocheting off the rocks and drenching her shorts. But Kate was in such a good frame of mind she didn't care. They would dry on the walk back and the water temperature was so pleasant, anyway. She didn't even flinch when an even larger wave splashed her a second time. Laughing, she squeezed the bottom of her shorts. That water is so nice I think I'm going to have a swim when I get back, she decided.

The water was perfect. I really don't think it gets much better than this, Kate thought, as she bobbed up and down in the waves, with some of the other early risers of Sunset Point. I could honestly stay here all day.

She'd been in the water about ten minutes when the lifeguards began setting up. A tall man who looked to be in his mid-forties directed operations. When the flags were up and the beach conditions recorded on the information board, he removed his shirt and waded into the water. Diving expertly under the small waves he moved through the water with surprising speed and swam out much further than Kate dared to go.

She was surprised when the man approached her as she dried off. Up close he had bright green eyes and the weather-beaten complexion of someone who worked outdoors. 'I see you changed directions on your walk today,' he said.

'Uh, yeah, I did,' Kate replied, puzzled that he seemed to know who she was.

'Enjoy your swim?'

Kate nodded. 'Yeah! It was sublime.'

'Too true. But you know I never like to see people in the water before we set up. I know this is generally a calm little beach, but we still get rips and sweeps and I'd hate to see a nice young lady like you get into any kind of trouble in the water.'

Embarrassed that she had ignored one of the basic rules of surf safety Kate was also touched that a stranger was concerned for her safety. 'I'm sorry,' she said, 'it was a careless oversight and I won't do it again.'

'That's what I like to hear.' Pausing a moment, he said, 'You looked like you enjoyed the game the other night.'

'Game?'

'The Wallabies.'

'Oh, *that* game,' Kate replied. 'Yeah, it was fun, such an amazing atmosphere.'

'And a great result too.'

'Yeah, definitely.'

Moving away, the lifeguard nodded politely. 'Enjoy your stay up at the house now.'

Kate smiled in reply, as she wrapped her towel around her waist. I wonder how he knows so much about me, she thought, as she scuffed through the sand back to the house.

Jane shrugged it off when she mentioned it over breakfast. 'It's a small town, Kate, just like the one I grew up in. People love to talk about new faces in town. Also, I think the locals are pretty possessive about this house, they like to know there's no riff raff staying.'

'You think we've passed the riff raff test, then?' grinned Kate.

Jane smiled back. 'Apparently we have.'

The girls sat out on the veranda that evening so they could enjoy the thousands of stars that decorated the inky night sky.

'Look, there's the saucepan,' Kate said, excited to have remembered one of the constellations her dad had shown her.

Jane nodded. 'Yeah, it's part of Orion.'

'Which part?' Kate asked, turning her head various ways to try and get the most accurate view.

'It's his belt and the handle is his sword,' Jane explained, doing a quick diagram on the margin of her biology notes.

'Oh, right.'

Over the last few days they had started a combined evening study session. It involved each of them explaining a particular topic to the other. Because neither had any clue of the other's field of study, it was an interesting way to test if they could impart knowledge.

Kate laboured through the theory of economic cycles, aware of how dry and dull it sounded and unsure if she made any sense. But Jane was interested – or at least she acted interested - and supportive. 'Kate I'm so focused on what I'm learning I don't have a clue about how the economy works, well at least I didn't until you told me all of this,' she admitted. 'Now I'll be able to watch the finance report on the news and at least have some inkling of what they're talking about.'

Kate tried to be equally enthusiastic when Jane walked her through cell metabolism. 'I actually do remember learning about mitosis and meiosis, although I can see that what you learn in high school biology is a very scaled down version of the process. I know I could never be a nurse because I'm too squeamish, but it is kind of interesting to know how the body functions.'

Both girls came away from the session a little more confident about what they considered their greatest academic hurdles of the day. Kate knew she was still on the back foot, but at least she wasn't crushingly overwhelmed anymore. Dumping her books on the dining table, she made a beeline for the games shelf.

'All right, tonight we're playing Uno and I've got to warn you I'm the family champion. I hate to be the bearer of bad news Jane, but tonight you're going down.'

Buoyed after another amazing early morning swim, Kate bounced up the back stairs in good spirits the next morning.

Jane eyed her with obvious amusement as she sat on the veranda, eating her toast.

'All right I know, I know, you've converted me into an early riser,' Kate admitted.

'No, I just suggested it, you made the leap all by yourself.'

'Yeah, I did, didn't I?' Sitting down onto the other lounger Kate sighed wistfully.

'What's wrong?'

'Well I love this part of the day, but hate the next. I don't know if I can face accounting today.'

'Yeah, you can. Remember sometimes it just has to be sheer force of will.'

'That sounds *so* appealing.'

Jane gathered up her breakfast things and stood up. 'I'm heading down to the library soon. It'll be a treat to get out of the house for a while.'

'What's at the library?'

'I've got a short essay due that I've been putting off. I just need to do some research.'

Since being at the beach house Kate had grown used to the constant background noise of the crashing surf. It was a peaceful, reassuring sound that she had grown to love. But today it seemed to be taunting her, reminding her what she was missing out on, while she was stuck inside most of the day.

I've never actually waded through molasses, she thought as she made notes, but I'm sure it must be pretty similar to trying to come to grips with doubtful debts. This must be the most boring topic in the known universe.

Kate was examining the callous on her middle finger when Jane appeared at her door. 'Wow, you're an efficient researcher,' she said, happy for any kind of distraction.

Shaking her head, Jane sat down on the bed. 'Well, I can be when I have the right resources available to me. But I couldn't even find out what it means. It didn't come up on the computer.'

'What is the topic anyway?' asked Kate.

'Women's suffrage in Australia. Who's heard of that?'

Trying not to smile Kate said, 'It was when women gained the right to vote.'

'Oh, right.'

'I take it you didn't do history at school?'

'Nope, I was too busy battling chemistry and biol.'

'What are you doing an assignment about that for?' Kate asked, with a puzzled glance. 'How is that related to nursing?'

'It's for a scholarship prize. Five grand. I'll try anything for that kind of money.'

Doodling on her notes, Kate wondered why her cousin was so big on being financially independent. It wasn't something she worried much about.

Jane was back to business. 'Well, knowing what it means is something, but where can I research it? Like I said, it doesn't even come up on the library computer.'

'Yeah, well, a town library is pretty general, it won't necessarily have anything on that subject, specifically.'

Flopping down on the bed, Jane groaned. 'So how can I possibly write an essay about it?'

Kate came over and sat next to her. 'There will be info about it, you'll just have to be a bit sneaky about how you get it. Come on, I'll give you a hand.'

A woman in her forties with the nameplate "Moira Bell, Librarian" on her desk eyed the girls suspiciously as they walked through the front door of the small brick building.

'Where's the reference section please?' Kate asked politely.

Moira paused before answering, as if she was weighing up whether her reference section would be safe in the hands of anybody under the age of fifty. 'In the back, left corner,' she replied. 'None of that collection is for borrowing,' she added.

'Thanks,' Kate said. Ignoring Moira's pointed glance, she made a beeline for the back of the building, motioning for Jane to follow her.

Standing back, Jane watched as Kate scanned the shelves before handing her a large, heavy book.

'The Australian Student Encyclopaedia?' Jane read doubtfully as she studied the cover. 'Uh, I don't think you're allowed to use encyclopaedias for uni essays, even unofficial ones like this.'

'Think outside the square,' said Kate. 'Use it to get all your facts about the topic so you know what you're talking about. Then we'll just have to find some books on Australian history, gather some quotes from a few different historians and there you go. How many references do you need?'

'A minimum of six.'

'Easily done. The main trick in bibliography padding is to credit general facts that everyone says to the unhelpful books and use the more helpful ones for your main argument.'

'I've been at uni two years and I've never heard of bibliography padding.'

'Well that's more of a sad reflection on me than on you,' Kate admitted, 'but we won't worry about it now. Come on let's get to work before Moira throws us out for talking.'

Even though she had pushed through the tedium of accounting

revision and accomplished a fair day's work, Kate was still eager to escape right on the dot of four thirty, which was afternoon break time. Jane looked up in surprise when she stuck her head in on the way past.

'Oh, is it that time already?'

'You bet!' Kate replied, wondering if Jane ever slacked off with anything. She was just so driven.

They walked companionably down the path to the beach, each carrying a boogie board and flippers. 'I can't thank you enough for your help this morning,' Jane said, as they hit the sand.

'It was nothing. You just picked the right person to ask about fudging the rules of assignment writing. Like I said it's not necessarily something to be proud of.'

'But it's a helpful skill to have, nonetheless.'

'Come on now, admit it, you're just amazed that the last-minute crammer has some underlying academic ability.'

Jane shook her head. 'No, that's not true, I've never doubted your academic ability. The only reason you got into such a jam this year was because you have no interest in what you're studying. If you liked these subjects, then the exams would be no stress at all.'

'You really think so?' Kate asked, as she dumped her towel on the sand.

'Yeah.' Jane dropped hers on top.

In their combined study session that evening, Jane spoke about the basics of counselling. 'Sometimes people don't tell you that something is worrying them,' she said. 'You have to try and pick it up by what they're not saying or sometimes by their actions.'

'I didn't know they taught you that in nursing. I thought it was all medical stuff.'

'I'm doing a social work elective. I thought counselling would be a helpful skill for a nurse to have.'

'That's true. But isn't it hard to interpret someone's actions?'

'Not always. The more time you spend with someone, the easier they are to read.'

'Really?'

'Yes, really.'

'So, what are you reading about me?'

'I think the law thing was your first major life challenge and it really knocked your confidence. You were used to having everything go your way and you realised that life doesn't always work out exactly how you want it to.'

Kate's eyes widened. 'You've hit the nail on the head,' she said. 'I felt so lost when I realised that what I thought was my life ambition was way off base. It felt like nothing made sense.'

'But you hung in there, you changed courses.'

'Twice.'

'Yeah, but that's not unheard of. And now you've found a new vocation, right?'

'Sure.' Kate glanced around the room before meeting Jane's gaze again. 'What?' she asked.

'You tell me.'

Kate sighed heavily. 'Criminal Psychology was a much more appealing goal when it was unattainable. Now it's a possibility I'm not even sure if I want it.' She stared at Jane again. 'I can't believe you just got me to tell you that. How did you know?'

'Like I said, by what you weren't telling me.'

'Then what's the point of me even doing this, then?'

'It's finishing off something you started, giving yourself as many options as possible. It might be something you want, after all.'

'Yeah, that's true. I've put in this many hours, I may as well see it through and try to salvage the semester after all.'

'Absolutely. You deserve it.'

Kate was glad when the rest of the session moved away from her problems. But even then, she couldn't get Jane's comment out of her mind. "You deserve it." She wasn't so sure that she did.

• • • • •

Kate dressed quietly, leaving her shoes off so she wouldn't make any noise. Tiptoeing out into the hallway she stayed still for several moments, listening for any sounds from Jane's room. The light was off, but she might still be awake.

An animal of some kind scurried across the tin roof startling her. Clutching her hand to her chest, she paused for another moment, before continuing her silent journey along the hallway and then down the stairs.

It was ridiculous sneaking out of the house like this. After all she was an adult now and Jane wasn't her mother. But she would disapprove and Kate didn't want to face that. For the moment, she just needed to escape without answering any questions.

Clasping the handle on the front door she turned it slowly and eased it open. Pushing the button in to lock it, she slipped through and closed it silently. Making her way along the veranda, she sat on the top step and put her shoes on. Then she tiptoed down the stairs, along the driveway and out onto the street.

The pub was much quieter that night. All the green and gold decorations had been removed and the big TV wasn't on. A much smaller crowd were scattered around the room in small clusters. Most were at the tables, but a few men were leaning against the bar.

Scanning the room, Kate noticed Libby and Robyn in the corner and made her way over. They were surprised but pleased to see her.

'Kate!' Libby exclaimed, her face rosy from the red wine in her glass as well as light sunburn.

Robyn was drinking chardonnay. 'We thought we'd lost you to the study slave driver,' she said. 'How'd you manage to escape?'

'Ah, Jane's not so bad, after all. She was so good with Travis the other night. I mean I just totally freaked out and she knew exactly what to do.'

Libby sighed heavily. 'Poor guy. I can't believe he's sick. He was so much fun.'

Kate nodded. 'Yeah, he was. Hang on, why are we saying was? He's still alive and might make a really good recovery after the surgery.'

'I hope so,' Robyn said softly.

Libby drank her last mouthful of wine. 'So, are you up for a big night? We're leaving tomorrow and want to go out in style, but none of these other people look like the partying type.'

Kate pulled a chair over from a neighbouring table and plonked herself down. 'I'm totally up for a big night.'

The girls were incensed when the barman stopped serving them at eleven thirty. 'I am not drunk!' Kate said.

Libby was standing next to her. 'You are a bit,' she stage whispered. 'So am I,' she added with a giggle.

Robyn, who was the soberest of the three, nodded. 'We all are.'

A couple of men at the bar looked over at them. 'Stop staring!' Kate said, much louder than she intended to.

One of the men stood up. Tall with brown hair, his face was familiar. Kate was sure she'd seen him around somewhere but just couldn't put her finger on it.

'Why don't I walk you girls home?' he said.

The barman breathed a sigh of relief. 'Would you, Jim?'

'You're just trying to get rid of us,' Kate said.

'No, it's nearly closing time anyway. If you stay much longer Johnny will make you help him wash the glasses,' Jim said.

'Johnnie?' Libby giggled. 'You mean Johnnie Walker?'

Jim smiled benignly and escorted them out the door.

• • • • •

Somebody was pounding on her skull. It was the only explanation Kate could come up with for the jackhammer like sensation. 'Stop it,' she mumbled, wrapping the pillow tightly around her head and encasing it with her arms.

It didn't help.

I think my brain is going to explode, she decided. If I could just get some ice it would soothe the pain. There were ice cubes in the freezer, she knew, but the freezer was downstairs. Too far to contemplate right now.

Just go back to sleep, she willed herself. You haven't slept enough, that's why your head hurts.

She was just drifting back off when she heard footsteps come down the hall and stop at the doorway to her room. 'Hey Kate you lazybones, I'm just cooking scrambled eggs for breakfast. You want some?' Jane opened the door and peered in.

Suddenly her pounding head became secondary to her heaving stomach. Leaping out of bed, Kate bolted across the room, down the hall and into the bathroom, leaving an astonished Jane in her wake.

Jane did all the right things any good nurse would. She hung a blanket over the window to darken the room, gave Kate Panadol and made her drink a tall glass of water. She soaked a face washer in cold water and draped it over her forehead. She even found a bucket and put it next to the bed. Then finally she told her to go back to sleep in a soothing voice.

Kate couldn't fault any of Jane's actions. She couldn't have been more supportive or helpful. But she could also feel her disapproval. It wasn't voiced, but it was there, as heavy and dark as the blanket on the window.

When Kate woke again at eleven thirty she felt a lot better. The headache had gone and her stomach had settled somewhat. She probably couldn't face lunch yet, but she wasn't on the verge of throwing up either.

She lay there for a while, feeling strangely out of sync in the darkness when she knew it was daylight outside. Eventually she climbed out of bed and pulled the blanket down from the window. Sunlight flooded the room, causing her to squint. Standing there she became aware of how bad she smelt. Cigarette smoke and sweat, what a delightful combination, she thought as she headed down to the bathroom.

Kate didn't bother turning the shower on to warm up while she undressed. I think a cold start to my shower will be nice today, she decided as she stepped into the bathtub. Although it was an old-fashioned bathroom, the showerhead was modern and delivered great water pressure.

Reaching over, she turned both taps on hard, eagerly anticipating the welcome blast of cool water to wake her up. It didn't come. Instead there was a short spurt of tepid water which rapidly dwindled to a few pathetic drops. 'Argh!' she grumbled, turning the taps to maximum in a fruitless attempt to get wet.

Flinging the shower curtain back, she stepped back out of the bath, threw her smelly pyjamas back on and stomped downstairs.

By the amount of banging coming from the kitchen, Kate expected to see a plumber. So she was genuinely shocked at the sight of her cousin crouched under the sink, wrestling with the pipe. 'Stupid thing!' she yelled, banging it with a tool of some sort before attempting to loosen the coupling.

Kate couldn't hide her annoyance. 'What's going on?' she demanded. 'I really need a shower.'

'Then go down to the beach,' Jane snapped, all vestiges of her earlier sympathetic manner gone.

No, I wasn't imagining it, Kate acknowledged, the disapproval was real. 'Why are you doing that? What's wrong with the sink?'

'It's blocked. I first noticed it yesterday, but it was worse this morning.'

Kate winced as another series of ear-splitting bangs rang out. 'Aren't you supposed to call the real estate office?'

'I'm quite capable of fixing a blocked pipe. When you can't afford a plumber, you get pretty good at D.I.Y.'

Kate selected a glass from the cupboard, then realised her dilemma. 'So, I can't even get a drink of water?' she moaned.

Jane stopped banging for a moment and sat cross legged on the floor. 'No, I suppose you can't. Still feeling a bit dehydrated, are we?'

Banging her glass down on the bench, Kate folded her arms and glared at Jane. 'Why are you so sure I'm hung over? How do you know it's not some stomach bug?'

Chuckling mirthlessly Jane shook her head. 'I may not be as naturally smart as you Kate, but I can put two and two together. Your going out clothes flung on the floor, the fact the front door was unlocked this morning when I was certain I locked it last night and a seemingly weird comment one of the lifeguards made when I went for my jog. I didn't give it that much thought until I saw the state you were in, then it all made sense.'

Kate's stomach plummeted. Oh, that's where I knew him from, she cringed. How embarrassing! I'll never be able to swim at the beach again. 'All right, I went out and wrote myself off,' she said. 'Not a smart thing to do, but why is it such a big deal for you?'

'Because I hate seeing people kill their brain cells one by one.'

'Then why were you so nice this morning when you clearly disagree so strongly with alcohol in any form?'

'Why was I so nice?'

'Yeah, why?'

Jane stared at her for a moment, apparently having some kind of internal debate. But finally she answered. 'Years of practice,' she said quietly, leaning back against the cupboard door and gazing unseeingly at the hardwood floor.

'Huh? You don't even drink.'

Jane exhaled sharply. 'My father is an alcoholic, Kate. I grew up with the morning after routine.'

'What?' Kate reeled in shock. She honestly couldn't think of anything to say. From her memories Jane's father had seemed so friendly and fun, which was why it was such a shock when he deserted his family.

Jane picked up the wrench and focused her attention on it. 'He hid it well, both my parents did,' she said flatly. 'It's not the kind of thing you want to share with your extended family.'

'That must have been really hard to live with,' Kate said, 'especially for a young child.'

Jane nodded but didn't meet Kate's eye. 'It was awful,' she murmured.

As she tried to blink back the tears welling in her eyes, Kate felt helpless that she couldn't say anything to make the situation better. 'Jane I'm so sorry, this is just horrible and I had no idea...'

Jane's eyes were still downcast. 'He didn't hurt me or Mum, he wasn't violent or verbally abusive. He was just so... helpless I guess is the word. He couldn't hold down a job for very long and he drank any money we did get. He couldn't cope when Mum was sick. He used to tell me and Mum that we couldn't understand why he drank and he was right we couldn't, but he wouldn't get help either – he wouldn't admit he had a problem.'

'And then he left?' Kate asked, feeling that she should say something.

Jane got up and walked out to the veranda railing, fussing with the beach towels that were hanging there.

Kate hesitated a second, then followed her. 'Jane?'

'He didn't walk out on us Kate, I asked him to leave, begged him to actually.'

'Oh,' was all Kate could think to say.

'I was twelve years old and I couldn't do it any more. I couldn't look after both of them. It's so hard when you're an only child. You don't know how lucky you are to have siblings.'

Kate's two younger brothers drove her crazy sometimes, but she couldn't imagine life without them. I *am* lucky, she realised.

Jane kept talking. 'At first he cried and pleaded but then he agreed it would be the best thing for all of us.'

'And your mother?' Kate worked hard to keep her voice impassive.

'She had no idea what I did, but she could see how much easier life was when he went. After I took that step I knew I had to be the strong one. I worked myself ragged at school, at my jobs, at everything I did because I was determined that I would never, ever end up like that. When I got older and understood that alcoholism was a disease and that I could have inherited the tendency for it I decided that I would never drink and I haven't.'

'So how did you cope financially?'

'Mum got the single parent pension until I was eligible for Austudy and now she gets a sickness benefit.'

'But even with that it must have been hard - all those times she was in hospital, the medication and all that.'

'Well most of it's free with the public health system, but yeah, there were some gaps to fill.'

'That's why you've had so many jobs, why you still do. You had to provide income just to survive and you still send money home now, don't you?'

Jane nodded slowly. 'I don't mind, I really don't, but it can be hard sometimes knowing that somebody relies a lot on you, just for survival.'

Kate was lost for words again. 'Jane, I…'

They were interrupted by the shrill ringing of the phone. 'You'd better get that,' Jane said. 'I'm going to go and finish fixing this stupid pipe.' With that she headed back into the kitchen.

Kate jogged in to answer the phone, only to find that it was a wrong number.

The relief after diving under the first wave was immediate on many levels. It was a hot day, so it was nice to get cool. It removed the grungy, unwashed feeling. It helped restore some equilibrium, like being in the surf always did. And, finally, it kept Kate out of sight of the lifeguards momentarily. She'd managed to avoid Jim as she slunk down onto the sand, dumping her towel on the fly before heading into the water.

Jane had ignored her when she tried to talk more, pretending not to hear over the banging in the kitchen. Obviously she wanted to be left alone and Kate was happy enough to comply. Jane's revelation had floored her and she really wasn't sure where they would go from here in their troubled relationship.

As she surfaced after diving under an uncharacteristically big wave, Kate had a sudden realisation. Her mother and other family members must know about the alcoholism and the struggles Jane had endured. What Kate had selfishly viewed as undeserved praise, had been her mother's way of trying to support and encourage her niece to succeed in life.

Preoccupied with that thought, she didn't notice another big wave rolling in and it knocked her off her feet. Kate let it pummel her a little as it washed over, before pushing herself back upright and wading out of the surf. She felt bad that she had simply let her friendship with Jane slide, never wondering what may have caused her cousin to become an adult well before her time.

Kate scanned the beach carefully before making the break for her towel. Jim was right up the other end of the patrolled area, so it was safe to have a shower. Letting the cool water cascade over her and wash off the salt, she pondered just what lay ahead up at the beach house.

When she noticed the clock hands approach six o'clock Kate dropped her pen and leaned her chin on her hands as she gazed out the window. She couldn't believe she'd worked steadily all afternoon, stopping only once to slip over to the shop for a lemonade Popsicle, a can of Coke and a packet of salt and vinegar chips. I never realised you could use study as a distraction, she thought. I've been doing the opposite all year.

It was almost dinner time and she was starving, after eating so little all day. Jane usually organised the meals, with her as offsider. But there had been no sound from her room all afternoon, she hadn't even emerged for a drink or snack.

Venturing down the hallway, Kate paused outside Jane's closed bedroom door, feeling like she did the day she arrived. Any of the same reasons she had pondered that first day could apply again today and once again she raised her hand to knock, then lowered it again, too unsure to take the chance.

The kitchen had been restored to order. The cupboard under the sink was closed and the toolbox put away. Kate had a quick peek, noting that all the pipes seemed to be intact. Tentatively she turned the tap on, just to make sure it was all working. The water flowed easily down the sink, with no evidence of a blockage and there was no leak in the pipe below. Jane obviously knew her stuff.

Flinging open the fridge, Kate leaned on the door and gazed at its contents. Sure, there was a reasonable selection of food there, but she had no idea what to do with it. Pushing the door closed, she leant back against it for a minute, working out how much money she had left. Maybe it could extend to a Chinese takeaway. Then she shook her head. No Kate, she scolded herself, that's your problem. You give in way too easily.

Taking another look around the kitchen she spied a selection of recipe books on one of the shelves. Scanning the titles, she pulled down *Simple, Everyday Cookery*. Surely she could manage something from that.

It was quarter to eight by the time she knocked on Jane's door. There was a pause before the listless reply came.

'Come in.'

Juggling the two plates, Kate nudged the door open. Jane was sitting at the desk, surrounded by neat piles of paper. She eyed Kate warily, an unreadable expression on her face.

'I just brought you something to eat,' Kate said.

'Thanks,' Jane replied flatly.

'It's macaroni cheese.'

Jane's face softened. 'Like Nanna makes?'

'Well not as good as hers, but the intention is there.'

'Let's sit on the bed to eat it.'

They settled themselves on the Queen-sized bed and ate in silence for a while. Finally, Jane spoke. 'It's good,' she said.

'Thanks.'

'Sorry Kate, but it's just a bit weird, knowing that you know.'

'It must be.'

More silence as they finished eating. Then Kate spoke. 'Can I ask you something?'

Jane shrugged.

'I understand why you were so mad about last night. But you've had this disapproving attitude for a few years now, long before I went to uni and started drinking.'

'It's not disapproval, it's envy. Everything came so easily to you. You had a normal family, you were really popular and school work was a breeze. Your life was so carefree. I had to struggle so hard to get half the things you had.' Jane paused a moment, rolling her fork between her hands. 'That's why I was so standoffish when you first arrived. I thought you were just going to have a relaxing break, sleeping in every day and chatting to your friends on the phone and maybe occasionally opening a book.'

'Well given the start I got off to I can see how you might have thought that.'

'You seemed so flippant and just didn't get how important doing well is for me. I literally can't afford to fail and this whole year has been so tough. It wasn't your fault because I'd never told you how things really were, but it still made me mad.'

Kate shrugged helplessly, not sure what to say.

'You know when I heard you'd dropped out of law I was glad, as horrible as that sounds,' Jane said. 'I thought, *finally*, something in Kate's life isn't perfect. I could sense you didn't want to talk about it but I asked you anyway, just to rub it in a bit.' She looked at Kate uncertainly, unsure how she might react. To her surprise, her cousin was smiling. 'Didn't you hear what I just said?'

'Yeah, I did. It's just kind of nice to know that it wasn't only me having mean thoughts.'

'Trust me, Kate, I have plenty of mean thoughts.'

'If you don't mind me asking, how did you afford to come here for these two weeks? With the bus fare, rent and food that must have set you back a bit.'

'It was a gift from someone that I'm really glad I accepted,' Jane said. 'I'm going to have an early night. You don't mind if we miss the study session, do you?'

Kate shook her head. 'No, I think I need an early night too.'

Striding back up the beach the next morning, Kate did a quick once over of the patrolled area. She was dying for a swim, but prepared to forgo it if Jim was around. She was trying to ignore the vague, unsettling flashbacks of belting out a Madonna medley while using a pool cue as a microphone. Seeing Jim face to face would be too much to bear.

Greatly relieved to see a younger, shorter man at the helm near the lifeguard tower, Kate dropped her towel, pulled off her shirt and shorts and splashed into the waves.

When she got home, Jane was already in the kitchen preparing her breakfast. Not sure what to say, Kate was glad when Jane spoke first.

'Morning - isn't it a gorgeous day?'

'Yeah, the water was perfect as usual,' Kate said, pulling her towel tighter around her waist. 'Are you okay?'

'I'm fine. Let's just refocus and get on with it.'

'That works for me.'

'Are you going to eat out on the veranda?'

'Yep, I'll be there in a sec.'

Settling themselves at the outdoor table, they ate in companionable silence for a while. Then Kate spoke. 'Do you ever think about your dad?' she asked gently.

'Yeah, all the time, I see him once a week or so.'

Kate stared at her cousin in surprise.

'I said I asked him to leave, I never said we lost touch. He moved to Sydney to live with his brother. He and his wife look after him as best they can. They run a restaurant and Dad does a bit of work for them when he's up to it.'

'And do you give him money too?'

The pause said it all. 'Occasionally,' Jane admitted, which Kate knew, meant often.

Kate shook her head in wonder, amazed that such a young person had so many burdens to carry. Gathering her plates together she said,

'I really envy you too, you know.'

'What?' Jane stammered, almost choking on her juice.

'Well, apart from the fact that you're beautiful and skinny, you know exactly what you want and you've got the drive and determination to go after it. Trust me that's a real gift.'

Jane looked at her for a moment and then nodded slowly. 'I guess it is,' she agreed.

Although there were no formal rules in place regarding their combined study session, the idea was that a new topic would be discussed by both of them each night. Kate trudged through the ins and outs of proprietary limited companies and was surprised when Jane started speaking about counselling again. 'You already did that subject.'

'Yeah, I know but I want to try something different,' Jane said. 'I've come across a bit of a case study and I just wanted to run it by you.'

'All right. I'm not sure I'll be much help but fire away.'

'Okay, basic information is you have a young woman not long out of high school. She's a real go-getter - school captain, chairperson of the student council, on various senior committees. She's also a bright student who doesn't have to kill herself to get good grades. Are you with me so far?'

Kate glanced over sharply. 'Yes.'

'So, as well as these things she's also quite athletic, she jogs, rows and plays water polo. In fact, her team are the state champions and she has the option to train with the development squad when she goes to uni in Brisbane.'

This time Kate delivered a hard stare but didn't speak.

Jane pressed on. 'So for all intents and purposes uni should be great, but somehow it isn't. Things don't work out and the young woman feels like she has lost direction. Her grades slip, she doesn't bother with water polo or get interested in student government like she thought she might.'

'You forgot to mention how fat I've got.'

'You're not fat.'

'Okay how about plump, chubby, hefty….'

'Kate, there's nothing wrong with your size.'

'That's easy for a *slim* person to say.'

Jane exhaled. 'Look, I really don't want to get into a debate about your weight. We're getting right off the topic here.'

'All right, fine. Why don't you keep outlining how spectacularly I've failed this year?'

'You haven't failed, Kate, like I said, you've just lost direction. You've always known how to study; you just chose not to even when you knew the consequences. Now I know we talked about the law thing the other night and I understand that was your first big life challenge and it really shook you up. But there's something else going on here and it only just occurred to me today that your big night out was a reaction to our first chat.'

'Really?' Kate replied sarcastically.

'Yes. You're punishing yourself for something by self-sabotage. You've done it all year and it was only that letter from SEQU that stopped you dropping out. Then you regrouped and came here and after a dubious start you made some great progress for a few days. Then you regressed back again by doing something that could ruin all your hard work.'

'Okay, but then I regrouped *again* and kept going.'

Jane sighed. 'Yes, you did, but can't you see the pattern? Unless you resolve whatever it is, you'll just keep doing the same thing. Ultimately there will come a time when you won't have the energy to regroup again.'

Kate didn't answer.

'My guess is that something happened fairly early on this year, something you're still grappling with.'

'Why do you think that?'

'Because self-sabotage is a pretty normal reaction to an experience that was out of your control.'

'No offence, Jane, but I think you need to study up on your counselling a bit more.'

'All right,' Jane said.

Kate stood. 'I'm not really in the mood for games tonight, I think I'll just sit outside a while.'

'No worries.' Jane headed into the kitchen to make herself some tea.

It was beautiful out on the veranda. The moon was full and the reflection on the water was breathtaking. It's just like nature's own spotlight, Kate thought, transfixed by the way the waves kept rolling, never once breaking their steady rhythm.

The chirp of the crickets seemed so much louder in such a quiet place. She knew she heard them in Brisbane too, but not to the same volume. A tabby cat padded up the back steps then came to a dramatic halt when it noticed Kate sitting there. It froze for a moment, its bright green eyes seemingly glowing in the dark, then squeezed through the treads in the steps and disappeared under the house.

She'd been out there almost an hour when the door opened. 'You're not going to the pub again, are you?' Jane asked.

'No. I couldn't even if I wanted to. I'm down to my last twenty bucks.'

Jane walked out and sat down. 'You can tell me Kate. You'll feel much better when you do.'

'You're wrong, you know,' Kate said quietly. 'It wasn't an experience that was out of my control.'

'Okay.'

'There was this girl called Angie in my class at school. We'd known each other since pre-school, but were never really friends per se. I mean she was nice enough but we just never moved in the same circles. She was very quiet and timid and kept very much in the background.'

'All right, I get the picture.'

'She got into QUT as well and before we started she seemed so tense about it while I was so excited. She was so anxious about not knowing anybody and I told her that we'd know each other, so it wasn't all that bad. I didn't mean it as an invitation to be best friends, I was just trying to reassure her.'

'Uh huh.'

She's good at this, Kate realised. Encouraging me to reveal the details without being pushy about it.

'So, fast forward to O Week. Angie spots me there the first day and clings to me like a limpet. I know it sounds horrible, but I didn't want to hang around with her all day every day. I was happy enough to say hello but I wanted to focus on meeting new people, fun people and with Angie there acting like a wallflower I felt they would put me in the same category.'

'Right.'

'So, on the third day I gave her the brush off. I tried to be nice about it, but in the end, I had to be a bit forceful because she just didn't take the hint. From then on, I went out of my way to avoid her. I felt kind of bad, but I figured she'd make her own friends eventually.'

The squeals of a cat fight shattered the still night, startling them both. Kate wondered if it was the same cat she'd seen earlier. It looked the type that might like the occasional rumble.

'So, back to Angie,' Jane prodded gently.

Kate sighed heavily. 'I saw her around once or twice, tried to be nice but she wasn't having any of it. Then, a couple of weeks later Mum tells me she's had some kind of breakdown and was in hospital. It was a shock and I felt sorry for her, but I didn't dwell on it too much. At that point I was too depressed about how much I hated law. But then I got the letter. I honestly don't know if the hospital she was in sanctioned it or if she smuggled it out somehow, but it was pretty vicious.'

'Really?'

Kate gave a mirthless chuckle. 'Oh yeah, really. She told me how I had ruined her life by refusing to be friends. How I'd abandoned her when she needed my help and destroyed her dreams of going to uni. It literally made me sick. I couldn't eat for days.'

'Kate…,' Jane began.

'I realised how desperate she must have been and how selfish I had been in doing what I did. Mixed in with the whole law thing I didn't know which way was up for a while there.'

'Kate, you don't honestly think this was your fault?'

'I really don't know. Some days I hardly think about it, other times it really preys on my mind.'

'All right, you did something that was mean but it wasn't horrendously cruel or evil. Angie was obviously already on the brink and this was just one of the things that tipped her over. You can't take on responsibility for all her problems.'

'But maybe I could have helped her.'

'Yeah, maybe short term, but inevitably it would have still happened. Breakdowns are generally the end result of a thousand small issues, building over time.'

'I should have gone and seen her or done *something*.'

'If she was in hospital she was getting the best possible care from people trained to deal with it. Have you seen her since?'

'No.'

'Well, maybe that's the next step, when you're both ready. You'll probably find she's moved way past the idea that it's all your fault.'

'You really think that?'

'If she had treatment, then yeah, probably. Look, you can take this as a lesson in how to treat people. A hard lesson, definitely, but a valuable one. Forgive yourself for being a seventeen-year-old grappling with her own problems.'

Kate sniffled. 'I just want to be me again.'

'Don't worry, you can be.'

For the first time since arriving, Kate's comfortable bed and relaxing room were not enough to bring about a good night's sleep. She tossed and turned, first feeling too cold without a blanket and then waking an hour later bathed in sweat because it was too hot. A series of intense dreams also plagued her, the kind that she couldn't remember when she woke, but at the same time on a sub-conscious level knew were unsettling.

Although her morning walk and swim restored some of Kate's energy, Jane soon noticed the dark circles under her eyes as they sat down to breakfast on the veranda.

'Rough night?' she enquired kindly, as she poured milk over her Sultana Bran.

'Yeah.' Kate buttered a piece of raisin toast and reached for the honey.

'You know there's a saying, "strong and bitter words indicate a weak cause".'

'I've never heard that.'

'Highly emotive terms like *ruined* and *destroyed* have a lot of impact and make things sound worse than they really are. Sure, Angie may have had to put her study plans on hold for a year, maybe even two but they aren't ruined, QUT is always going to be there.'

'I guess so.'

'You can't destroy anybody else's dream Kate, only they themselves can stop believing in it.'

'She must have really thought I did, though.'

'People who are in a lot of pain often lash out at the nearest target. In this case that was you. Writing that letter was an opportunity for Angie to assign blame to *somebody* amidst the chaos of what she was going through.'

'You really think so?'

Jane nodded.

They ate in silence for a few minutes, each lost in their own thoughts. Then Jane spoke again. 'Kate, you know you really can't change anything right now. Losing your concentration after all the hard work you've put in won't have an immediate positive impact on Angie's life. Like I said it's probably a good idea to see her at some point but another week or two after all this time is neither here nor there.'

'Yeah, I know. That's actually not what is bothering me the most right now.'

Jane looked at her expectantly.

'Well, I just realised that maybe the whole law thing went bad because I was so stressed about the Angie situation. Maybe everybody hates the first weeks and I needed to just stick it out for longer. If I've been sub-consciously sabotaging myself like you said, then maybe I really should have stayed in law after all, instead of chasing my tail around all year.'

Jane pushed her empty cereal bowl away and reached for a slice of rockmelon. 'Okay, so what you're saying is that you actually enjoyed the law lectures you went to and were excited about the course of study that was outlined? You found it interesting and exciting?'

'No, I found it boring, the most boring thing I'd ever encountered. It seemed so rigid and exact and there were so many rules to follow. But maybe I only thought that because I was so upset.'

'Look Kate if you find something boring, then you find it boring whether you're upset or stressed or not. The fact that you knew so soon and so certainly that law wasn't what you wanted is a good example that your intuition is very strong. There is absolutely nothing wrong with a law degree if that's what *you* want, the same goes for IT or business. They obviously just aren't your thing and you shouldn't feel bad about that.'

'Yeah, but I just don't feel like I'll ever find my *thing*,' Kate said, holding up her fingers to indicate inverted commas. 'You would think out of all the careers out there I would be interested in something.'

'Don't get so worried. Sometimes the harder you try to look for something the more elusive it becomes. I think you're a creative type but you've been pursuing areas of study that are logical and rule-based. No wonder you've struggled.'

'So, there's a chance that criminal psychology might be what I'm looking for after all?'

'Yeah, for sure. But for now, just get through these exams first and then worry about the rest later.'

Kate leaned back in her chair and closed her eyes. 'Okay, I'll try.'

Both girls worked industriously all day, each of them aware that their time at the house was drawing to a close, which also meant that exams were rapidly approaching. When a thunderstorm rolled in mid-afternoon and cancelled out their afternoon swim, neither was too perturbed, thinking instead about how they could use the extra hour to get more work done.

Kate was amazed when Jane bounded into her room at five thirty, her eyes dancing. 'I just rang in for the trivia contest and got through! Quick, come in while I answer the questions, we're on in three minutes!'

Dropping her pen, Kate ran into Jane's room, still amused at her excited state. She listened as Jane chatted with someone on the other end before the official questions began. Due to the seven second delay, Kate felt out of step as she heard Jane answer each question, but not if it was right or wrong until it came through on the radio.

After Jane sailed through the first six questions Kevin the radio DJ built up the suspense. 'Okay Jane, you are up to question seven the best result we've had for weeks. If you get this right you win the one-hundred-dollar cash prize. Are you ready?'

'Yes, let's do it!'

'All right what does the abbreviation GDP stand for?'

Jane's face lit up. 'Gross domestic product!'

Once the seven seconds passed Kate cheered heartily, as did Kevin, who had been trying desperately to give the prize money away for the past month.

After Jane gave her details to Kevin and made arrangements to pick up her prize, she hung up the phone and gave Kate a big grin. 'Well Miss Green, I have you to thank for winning. Until five days ago, I didn't have a clue what GDP was.'

'Don't mention it and you did manage the other six on your own.'

'True enough, but without the last one, the prize would have only been a kilo of sausages from Barry's Butchery.'

'Nothing against Barry but I think you just might enjoy the hundred bucks more.'

Once they were over the initial excitement, Jane surprised Kate for the second time that afternoon. 'Where will we go?' she asked.

'Go?'

'To spend our money, Kate. You've seen more of Sunset Point than I have, there must be somewhere we could have a night out.'

Kate tried to hide her shock. 'But you can't get the prize until tomorrow.'

'I'll just use my money tonight and replace it later.'

'Oh, okay.' Kate had been sure Jane would want to keep the money for own expenses and she would have been perfectly happy for her to do so. If there was anyone that deserved a windfall it was Jane. She was also amazed she was suggesting a night away from study.

Jane's eyes were still dancing. 'Come on Kate, you're the socialite, where will we go?'

First, they dined at the seafood restaurant, Leo's. After a week of simple home cooked meals, it was bliss to indulge in such scrumptious food. They were impressed to find such upmarket dining in a small town like Sunset Point. From the elegantly decorated interior to the cutlery, crockery and glassware, everything was of the highest quality.

The staff were also top shelf. Their young waiter, decked out in black trousers and a starched white shirt couldn't have been more attentive. 'Everything all right ladies?' he asked, hovering at Jane's elbow yet again.

She's got no idea how pretty she is, Kate thought, as she held up her water glass for a refill.

'They were the nicest crab cakes I've ever tasted,' said Jane, patting her mouth with her monogrammed, starched linen napkin.

'Mmmm, the salmon was exquisite. I wonder if Leo is the chef?'

'Whoever it is they know their stuff. Hey look there's the lady from the library.'

Kate swivelled around and met the gaze of Moira, who did a double take when she saw the two girls sitting there. They giggled at her reaction. 'Obviously she doesn't think we're classy enough to dine here,' Kate said.

It was only a short walk over to the little cinema to see *City Slickers*. Neither of them had seen it when it had screened in their respective cities a few months before. They were chuckling when they came outside.

'I liked that,' said Kate. 'Billy Crystal is such a laugh.'

'Yeah, he is. I never would have picked that movie on my own but it was great. It kind of makes you want to go and take riding lessons.'

To round off the night they opted for a hot chocolate in the Sunset Cafe. As they waited for their drinks, the girls took in the old-fashioned décor.

'I can't believe they still make those vinyl fly strips,' Kate said softly. 'I feel like I'm eight again, our corner store used to have them too.'

'Look at the milkshake maker and those jars of mixed lollies. Remember that time Nanna gave us thirty cents and we got those two bulging bags? You wouldn't get that many now.'

Kate nodded. 'She's got milkos! I didn't know you could still get them.'

'Or Golden Roughs.'

'I didn't think this place opened at night,' Kate whispered. Although she wasn't sure why, she was a bit wary of the woman who appeared to be the proprietor. Her name badge said Marge and to Kate this suggested a strict, no-nonsense kind of person who might be offended by a comment about her café being old fashioned.

Jane pointed to a sign on the door, "Now open Tuesday/Saturday nights after the movie."

Marge came over with their drinks. Setting them down she looked at the girls thoughtfully and said, 'You're not some of those schoolies, are you?'

Kate stifled a smile. As much as she loved Sunset Point, Surfers Paradise it was not! Fortunately, Jane was composed enough to give a sensible answer.

'Oh no, we're both university students well past the crazy school leaver mindset.'

'Are you on holidays already when it's barely November?'

'No, it's our study break before exams.'

'No wonder it takes so long to finish a degree. What's wrong with studying on the weekends?'

Both girls shrugged, knowing it would be futile to argue the point.

'We don't get many girls holidaying here by themselves,' Marge said. 'A few people said they saw some young lasses drinking at the hotel, that's why we thought you might be schoolies. We don't want that kind of nonsense around here.'

'Yes,' agreed Jane, 'It would ruin the feel of the place.'

Marge peered at them closely again, but could find no fault with that comment. 'Well, work hard then,' she said before moving to the next table to take an order.

The girls managed to stay composed while they finished their drinks, but burst out laughing as they walked home, sharing the bag of mixed lollies they couldn't resist buying.

'Somehow, I don't think Sunset Point is in any danger of becoming the next Schoolies mecca,' Kate said as she chewed on a milko. 'And you managed to nicely sidestep admitting that I was one of the bold lasses down at the pub.'

Jane shrugged. 'If you act sensible and agree without really agreeing you can usually bluff your way out of any situation.'

'I'll have to remember that.'

Still buoyed after their fun night out, Kate forgot to be vigilant as she waded out of the ocean the next morning and almost walked right into Jim as he stood on the sand, watching the water. 'Oh! Sorry,' she mumbled, moving over towards her towel.

'Haven't seen you in a while,' Jim said.

'Uh, yeah, I've been studying hard, you know.'

He nodded, his expression somewhere between a smile and concern.

Picking up her towel Kate wrapped it around herself, ready to make a fast escape. Then she sighed and turned back around to face Jim. 'I'm sorry for my behaviour the other night. I don't usually do that; I was just a bit stressed about something.'

'That was quite a repertoire you had there.'

'Well, like I said, I don't usually…,'

'And we still can't work out what a kara-okay machine is.'

Kate's face burned with humiliation as another hazy flashback assaulted her mind, this one involving her yelling at the barman that the pub needed karaoke to be taken seriously as an entertainment venue.

She decided to cut her losses. 'Thank you for looking out for me.'

'That's all right. I'd like to think that somebody would do the same for my daughters.' He nodded politely as he moved away. At least he hadn't delivered a lecture, Kate thought. That would have made any further time on the beach very awkward.

Engrossed in her last chapter of economics, Kate got a shock later that morning when Jane burst into her room, without knocking.

'Can I help you with something?' she asked, taking in the unusual sight of her cousin in, what looked like, a hyperactive state.

'Oh, I'm sorry I didn't knock, but I'm just so excited and I needed to tell somebody!'

'Tell somebody what?' Kate asked.

Jane waved a piece of paper around. 'This was waiting for me at the post office. I applied for a scholarship and I got it! I get six thousand dollars in February. It's going to make such a difference for me.'

'The Women's Suffrage thing already?'

'No, no this is another one. I'm always applying for them, I've just never got one before.'

Kate jumped up and gave her an impulsive hug. 'That's so great! Nobody deserves it more than you. Well done!'

Jane's pretty face was beaming. 'Thanks. Oh, I just feel so *great* – no more kitchen hand shifts at The Steakhouse.'

'Sounds like a good thing to be giving up.'

'Trust me, it is!'

The feel-good vibe was still evident when they relaxed on the veranda after lunch. Stretching contentedly Kate smiled. 'You do realise that we have broken all the traditional rules of swot vac by what we have accomplished here don't you? I'm convinced this is actually an alternate reality.'

Jane laughed. 'You think so?'

'Totally. We're supposed to be highly stressed, living on caffeine and sugar and severely sleep deprived. Instead we're relaxed, barefoot, we're getting heaps of sleep and despite some hiccups we're studying like machines. We are enjoying leisure time. And, I'm actually starting to *kind of* get economics. It's not even that hard, I've just never bothered reading the textbook before.'

'It is a magic place and the house is great. But you have to take some of the credit yourself. You could have let your rocky start put you off, but you got stuck into it. You should be really proud of yourself.'

The words "yeah, right!" were on the tip of her tongue but then Kate thought about what Jane had said. Sure, the circumstances had been put in her lap and she had procrastinated at first, but in the end, she'd come through. Kate was certain she would never study anything business related ever again, but in the greater scheme of things it didn't matter at all.

'You know, for the first time in a long time I don't want to swap places with you,' Jane said.

'Gee thanks!'

'Oh, no offence,' Jane added hastily, 'I just mean I'm satisfied with what I have. I agree I'm so lucky to know exactly what I want to do with my life.'

Kate laughed. 'I know what you mean and I'm really happy for you. Even if I did fail I've got a safety net to catch me. You've made me realise just how lucky I am too.'

• • • • •

It was their last night there together. An air of sadness hung over the Beach House. Their visit was almost over. Kate was leaving late the next afternoon and Jane would be gone the morning after. They had splurged on fish and chips and there was a Viennetta in the freezer for dessert.

As they sat down to eat Jane said, 'You could have got some wine if you wanted. I know most people like to have it for a celebration.'

'I'm fine without it,' Kate said. 'I'm not that much of a drinker, you know. When I was out with Travis and the girls those first couple of nights I only had a few. I wasn't drunk or anything. The pub was just a fun place to hang out.'

Jane contemplated this. 'You know I never go anywhere there might be drinking - whether to see a band playing, or into a pub or bar or to a party. I won't meet people for drinks and I've never been into a nightclub.' She glanced over at Kate. 'Yes, I know that officially qualifies me for freak status'.

'Two weeks ago, my answer would have been yes, but now I would just say that you are unusual among your peers,' Kate said.

Jane smiled. 'Thanks! That's *much* better! Seriously though, I've always had a chip on my shoulder about alcohol. I thought it was just about Dad but I've realised it's also because to me it represents students having the luxury of having fun and wasting money on something frivolous, something that wasn't an option for me.'

'I'm sorry…' Kate said.

'No, don't be sorry. You don't need to apologise for having had a normal life.'

'But things will be easier for you now with the extra money.'

'Yeah, much easier and I won't have the excuse of no money for being a social recluse. Since spending time here I've been thinking about how driven and controlling I have been in certain areas of my life. I'm fairly sure that I will never drink but that doesn't mean I should cut myself off from a whole range of socialising just to keep proving a point to myself. I've never been a party animal and don't aspire to be one, but that doesn't mean I can't let my hair down a bit more.'

Kate nodded. 'That's so true. In any case, it's all about doing what you think is fun — whether it's square dancing or quiz night at the pub, just don't count yourself out because other people might be drinking there.'

'That's a sound plan. I guess alcohol is always going to be one of my issues, I'll just have to learn to be more accepting about it.'

'Let's face it, we've all got issues. I've let alcohol cloud my judgement on occasion. Staying away from it isn't such a bad choice.'

Jane sighed. 'You know I always took the moral high ground that I was above all that kind of thing. It's been niggling at me for a year or two now that I was being too restrictive with myself but I was too scared to admit that I was allowed to change my mind. I took this big, bold stance and couldn't back down.'

Kate took a sip of water, then burst out laughing, spraying it everywhere.

'Would you look at the pair of us?' she said. 'Both riddled with insecurities while thinking the other one has got it together. Yet somehow, we've managed to find some common ground and help each other. Is that weird or what?'

'Some people say that there are no accidents in life. Supposedly we're put in situations to learn something and move on. Maybe this was just our moment of truth and we've both managed to embrace it.'

'Considering how distant we'd become I never would have come here if I wasn't desperate. Maybe fate did throw us together.'

Jane smiled. 'Fate *and* your mother.'

'Well, yeah, it was so lucky she knew you were coming, when I told her I was dropping out.'

'Uh, yeah,' Jane hedged.

Kate looked at her. 'Wait a minute, how *did* she know so much about it – the exact address, how much the rent was, the house rules and all that? I'm sure you didn't bore her with every detail when you mentioned it.'

'She arranged it all Kate. She was concerned about how much pressure I was putting on myself and was worried that you weren't taking your study quite seriously enough. I think she thought some time together might help us both find some middle ground. I'll admit I wasn't that thrilled about the idea, but she's always been really good to me and the prospect of an all-expenses paid beach break was too good to pass up.'

'So this was all in place before I almost dropped out?'

'Yep, she arranged it back in September. She just put off telling you until the last minute to try and ambush you, so you wouldn't think up an excuse not to come.'

'She didn't realise quite what she was setting up did she?'

'No, but she couldn't have asked for a better result, though.'

Kate shook her head. 'No, she couldn't.'

· · · · ·

Kate was torn on her last day at the Beach House. As much as she couldn't wait to be finished with her exams and studying, she was genuinely sad that her time at Sunset Point was ending. She decided then and there that she would come back another time without the stress of study and enjoy being there just for fun.

As Kate worked through the final set of review questions for economics, she couldn't help but feel proud of what she had accomplished in just two weeks. While she would never recommend the "cram at the last minute" approach, she had proven to herself that with discipline and determination you could turn a very bad situation around. For the first time in her life she could see the value and reward of hard work, rather than just taking the easy road.

Kate knew she wouldn't come away with a high distinction for economics, but a pass was fairly certain and a credit was not outside the bounds of possibility – depending of course on just what kind of exam Harold had set.

Jane sat on the spare bed while Kate packed the last of her things. 'Just think, this time tomorrow your economics exam will be almost over.'

'Well, hopefully I'll still be frantically writing. As much as I still dislike it I do want to show Harold that I have learnt something.' Kate shoved her last textbook down the side of the bag. Glancing around the room she said, 'I think that's everything.'

Jane nodded. 'Looks like you're all set. I'll miss our study session tonight.'

'Me too and I'll miss Scrabble.'

Their conversation was interrupted by the toot of a horn. Looking out the window, Kate saw it was her taxi. 'I can't believe it's all over, didn't I just get here?'

'Feels like it.'

Kate gave her cousin a goodbye hug. 'I'm so glad you and Aunty Judy are coming up for Christmas. It will be great to hang out and have some fun instead of hitting the books.'

'Yeah, I can't wait,' Jane said, returning the hug. 'Good luck with your exams. Give me a call after each one and tell me how it went.'

'I will. You're the only one who will truly understand what an accomplishment even sitting them will be.'

After another toot of the horn Jane ran down to tell the driver to wait while Kate took one last look at her room. Staying here had changed her and after her exams were over and done with she was going to take some time to think about what direction her life was going to move in next.

With a last wistful glance, she picked up her bag and went downstairs.

Simone

1994

S imone Ryan closed the lid on the washing machine, set the dial to the correct cycle and turned her attention to the pile of ironing stacked on the laundry bench. The girls' school uniforms and her linen shirts took time and effort, but she took pride in the way they were all wrinkle free when they left the house each day.

She also took pride in the way her home looked. It was a large house that required a lot of upkeep, so it was lucky she had so much time to devote to it. Light coloured carpets needed so much maintenance and the polished floors showed up every speck of dust.

Pasta, Simone thought, as she slid the iron over an Egyptian cotton sheet. We need more pasta. As soon as the ironing was done she would finish off the meal plan for the week. She couldn't believe she never used to do one. The thought of facing a week now without a plan made her chest constrict.

Simone lifted the ironed sheet carefully onto the laundry bench and folded it precisely. People who said it was a waste of time to iron sheets had obviously never slept between a set that had been pressed. It was worth that bit of extra effort.

So many people had told her she needed to keep busy and they were right. It was the only way she had found to deal with the pain.

Simone's daughters were lounging in front of the TV, putting off the kitchen clean up as long as they could.

'I can't believe Shane and Angel are getting married,' fourteen-year-old Jill said, as the closing credits of *Home and Away* came on.

Sixteen-year-old Elizabeth picked up the remote and began flicking channels. 'It's a soapie, they have to have a wedding every now and then.'

'Yeah, that's true,' Jill agreed. She moaned as a thought struck her. 'Please tell me we didn't leave that Bolognese sauce to harden on those pasta bowls.'

'Mum would have rinsed hers. I say we just put them in the dishwasher as is and see what happens.'

'But Mum likes us to rinse them first,' Jill said. 'Besides, if you leave the food on, it clogs up the filter and you have to scrub it with a toothbrush.'

Elizabeth made a face. 'Okay, fine, we'll do it your way.'

The girls knew if they kept watching TV for another half hour their mother would clean the kitchen. But she already did too much of that. Mum had always liked to keep things neat and organised, but now she was so focused on housework and everything looking perfect that she didn't seem to have time or energy for anything else. It worried them but they just didn't know what to do about it.

The girls were singing a Kylie Minogue medley as they cleaned up, so they didn't hear their brother Matt come in the front door. Although his uni contact hours were minimal and their home in St Lucia only streets away from the University of Queensland campus, the nineteen-year-old student's movements were difficult to pinpoint. He often appeared as late as nine or ten o'clock at night, or sometimes as early as two in the afternoon. Whatever the hour though, he always made a beeline for the kitchen.

Dropping his backpack behind the couch Matt wandered into the kitchen and smirked at the scene before him. Jill put down the detergent bottle she had been using as a microphone and poked her tongue out at her brother.

'Oh, and you've never played air guitar or sung in the shower before?'

'I didn't say a word.' Matt's amused expression said it all.

Elizabeth poured the powder into the dishwasher and turned it on. 'Your dinner is in the fridge before you start ransacking the cupboards. I can't believe you ate my last packet of popcorn on Monday! It's my special study treat.'

'Sorry. You should write your name on it or something.' Matt reached into the fridge and pulled out his meal as well as the last slice of mud cake.

Elizabeth took the bowl of pasta from him and put it in the microwave. 'Let Mum know you're here, you know how much she worries.'

Matt took a bite of cake and ambled off in the direction of the laundry.

The bedside clock glowed in the inky darkness. 2:05 again. Why did her eyes always spring open at that moment? Sighing, Simone sat up and switched on the reading lamp. Of all the things she missed most about her old life, getting a full night's sleep was the most prominent.

Simone hated taking sleeping pills and tried other ways to fight the frustration of insomnia. She subscribed to just about every magazine in print, had become an expert at crosswords and logic puzzles and watched a lot of mindless TV. She'd even taken up knitting again and had made everybody in the house two pairs of bed socks and a scarf each. They'd come in handy during the colder than normal winter Brisbane had experienced that year.

No matter what everybody said about time healing all wounds, it wasn't getting any easier. The ache in her heart hadn't even begun to subside. In fact, some days she felt it was getting worse.

Simone picked up the photo she still kept by the bed and traced her finger over her husband's boyish, smiling face. She'd always loved this photo because it captured the essence of him so well, his charm and laid back nature. Opening the top drawer of her bedside table, she picked up his stethoscope and hugged it close to her chest. Andrew's black medical bag still sat on the edge of the dressing table, where he always left it, and one pair of his surgical scrubs still hung in the cupboard. Her sisters had helped her sort his other belongings, giving some away and storing most of it for when she was ready to face it. But Simone wasn't sure when that might be.

Just over a year had passed since Andrew's death and Simone was no closer to coming to terms with it than she was that horrible day. She hated Wednesdays now. Hated what one day of the week had taken from her and the kids. Andrew was coming back from lunch when a woman had a heart attack at the wheel of her car and ploughed through a pedestrian crossing just outside the hospital where he worked. Three others were knocked down as well, but he was the only one who died.

Her wonderful, loving husband was gone in the blink of an eye. A forty-three-year-old highly skilled surgeon with so much more to offer the world, snatched right from their grasp.

Simone picked up the TV remote and pressed the on button, hastily pressing mute when the small set came to life. Everything seemed so much louder in a dark, silent house and she didn't want to wake the girls. After switching between a B grade horror movie featuring a scantily clad young woman attempting to lure a vampire back into his coffin, highlights of a golf tournament in Scotland (which in itself should have been enough to induce sleep), and an infomercial featuring an electronic duster, she flicked the set off again. As usual, early morning TV was not riveting viewing.

Plumping her pillows into a comfortable position, Simone picked up a magazine from the pile she kept near her bed. *How would you cope in a life-changing crisis?* asked one of the cover headlines. As Simone well knew it was the kind of question you could only answer when you had been through such a crisis. In truth, she didn't know how she *had* gotten her through those awful, dark first days – the funeral and dealing with all the associated paperwork and trying to comfort the children and Andrew's family. They'd come through it somehow, but she had no real memory of it, nor did she want one.

Picking up another magazine, Simone took a deep breath and fought back the tears that were never far away. She had heard all the platitudes and the genuine advice, but none of it seemed to help. She had refused her doctor's offers to refer her to a counsellor or psychologist, believing that if other people could cope with loss then so could she. Leaning down, Simone opened the bottom drawer of her bedside table and removed the box of sleeping pills. Tonight, she *was* desperate enough to take them.

• • • • •

Her eyelids felt heavy. Eventually Simone forced them open. The clock read 11:53. The room was bathed in bright sunlight. It took her a moment to get her bearings. She jolted upright. Immediately panic over the morning she had lost began to overtake the groggy, disorientating after-effects of the Temazepam. She'd slept for nine hours. She hadn't made lunch for the girls. She hadn't been to the shops for groceries. She hadn't even had a shower. The kids must have been so worried when she wasn't in the kitchen when they got up.

Simone splashed some water on her face in the en suite bathroom and sighed in dismay on catching a glimpse of herself in the mirror. Still six months away from her fortieth birthday, today she looked years older. Her hazel eyes were muddy and tired and without the camouflage of makeup the dark circles beneath were much more pronounced. Her short, wavy blonde hair resembled a bird's nest and she could see her collarbone clearly through her nightie. Of slim build anyway, she was still three kilograms under her usual weight and hated how gaunt she looked.

Pulling on her bathrobe Simone headed to the kitchen to make some tea. She was pleasantly surprised to see Matt sitting at the table eating a sandwich. She didn't often get to spend time with him in the middle of the day.

'And just what time do you call this?' he asked, pointing at the kitchen clock.

Simone ran her hands through her tousled hair and picked up the kettle. 'I know, it's dreadful. I can't believe I slept so long. I wasn't up to get the girls off.'

'Mum, I was joking; it's okay to sleep in whenever you want. The girls can feed and dress themselves and I took them to school.'

Matt had actually enjoyed the school run in Simone's car. He had never before considered the kudos of a nineteen-year-old guy pulling up in a silver, late model BMW at an all girls' school.

'Thank you darling, you're so good to me.'

Simone came and stood alongside her son and put her arm around his shoulder. Matt had been supportive and caring, despite losing his father at a critical time in his young life. She knew she wouldn't have coped without him or the girls and tried hard not to burden them with her grief.

Pouring her tea a few minutes later, she decided that sleeping tablets were not the answer and that she would go and see the doctor again as soon as she could.

Even though she was busy studying for her end of year exams, Elizabeth called an impromptu sibling meeting the following week. They gathered in Matt's room, a large self-contained area above the garage. He still had one exam left, but was apparently not too stressed about it, as he was reclined on his unmade bed, channel surfing, when the girls came in.

Jill threw a pile of dirty clothes on the floor and sat on the lumpy couch. 'You didn't need to clean up just for us, Matty,' she teased.

'Hey, nothing's too good for my little sisters,' he said, his eyes still on the TV.

Elizabeth plonked down on top of the pile of papers on the desk chair. 'Mum was wondering where the rest of her mugs got to,' she said, surveying the collection of dirty coffee cups lined up on the desk.

Matt was engrossed in *The Simpsons*. 'Yeah, yeah, I'll take 'em back later.'

Elizabeth peered out the window to check that their mother hadn't returned from the supermarket. Then she leaned over and turned off the TV.

'Hey!' protested Matt.

'Come on, we need to have a proper discussion for a few minutes. It's about Mum.'

'All right, talk away.' Matt laced his fingers behind his head and closed his eyes.

'I'm serious, Matt,' Elizabeth said. 'You need to pay attention.'

'I am paying attention. What's this all about?'

Elizabeth sighed. 'We really need to do something to get Mum to slow down a bit.'

'She always looks so tired,' Jill said.

'Apparently she went to the doctor the other day and she told her that she has to have a holiday and totally relax – like no housework or anything,' Elizabeth said. 'So, I'm not sure what she's organising, but whatever it is, we have to all agree to go along eagerly.'

Sensing his sister's gaze upon him, Matt opened his eyes and glared back. 'I never said I wouldn't go on a holiday or anywhere else for that matter.'

'All right keep your shirt on, I'm just saying please be enthusiastic and don't act like you're giving up a week on the French Riviera to slum it with us,' Elizabeth said.

'And just when have I ever done that?'

'Uh, how about when you got back from your trip last year? You name-dropped for months afterward.'

Matt had taken a year out between school and university when he was chosen as a speech writer for the national youth debating team. The highlight of their program was a three-month tour of Europe.

Plumping his pillow, Matt gave Elizabeth a hateful smile. 'Well, forgive me for trying to educate you of places and cultures beyond our familial experiences.'

Ever the peacemaker, Jill laughed. 'Come on Matty, you were totally showing off, but we did love hearing about it.'

'Let's not get off topic here,' Elizabeth said, glancing out the window again. 'All you have to do is be your wonderful, golden-haired boy self and it will all be great.' Before Matt had the chance to refute the golden-haired comment she continued on. 'We all have to agree to do all the work wherever we end up going. So that means the shopping, cooking, cleaning – everything, okay? Are we all agreed about this?'

'Yes,' Jill and Matt chorused.

'I'm really serious, guys. We can't back down on this at all, okay? We have to stick together, right?'

Jill and Matt nodded and Elizabeth knew they meant it.

• • • • •

Almost three weeks later, Simone and her children climbed out of the car, weary after an early morning wakeup, the stress of packing and a long drive. Matt stretched his tall frame and yawned. As much as he loved driving the BMW, he was glad to finally be out from behind the wheel.

It always amused the girls how Matt modified his driving style when their mother was in the car. He had stuck religiously to the speed limit and hadn't complained once about the choice of CD or adjusted the volume up to where he usually had it. As they approached the outskirts of Sunset Point he had slowed down, allowing everybody to appreciate the scenery and relaxed atmosphere of the small town. As much as they chided him about being the golden-haired boy, he was very good to their mother.

Jill stood in front of the house and smiled. 'It looks just the same,' she said. 'You know how sometimes you have a great memory about something and when you revisit, it's changed somehow?'

Simone nodded. 'I know exactly what you mean. And you're right, it hasn't changed one bit.'

They were finally back at the Beach House; the location of their best ever holiday five years earlier. Simone's doctor had been blunt. She needed a complete change of scenery and as much relaxation as possible. She had to break out of the almost manic state of activity with which she filled her days.

Although Simone knew it would be painful to come back without Andrew, she also knew without doubt that this *was* the right place to come.

Forbidden from helping to unpack the car, Simone sat on the couch and watched the kids haul the luggage inside. After a failed attempt at assisting, she had decided it was easier to give in and let them do it.

Looking out the open back door onto the uncrowded beach, Simone was glad they were here before the official school holidays began. It meant they could enjoy the sleepy little town before it swelled with summer holidaymakers. Matt had finished his exams almost a fortnight ago and the girls had finished theirs only days before, two weeks earlier than the public schools.

'Okay Mum, I've got your stuff,' Matt said, leading the way up the stairs and depositing her luggage in the first room. Simone trailed behind, not sure how she would feel.

It was difficult to walk into the master bedroom. As she stepped over the threshold Simone tried not to dwell on the fact that she would be sleeping in here alone this time. She could have swapped rooms with Matt, who would have eagerly taken the big room, but decided to see how she coped first.

Exhaling sharply, she looked around the room. It's been rearranged, she thought, and there's a new bed. The old one didn't have a wooden headboard. It had been moved to the opposite wall and the wardrobe was in the right corner, instead of midway along the wall. Maybe someone in the real estate office was into feng shui?

Simone scanned the room for other changes. A chest of drawers that hadn't been there last time sat near the window seat. New curtains fluttered from the windows. This wasn't so bad. She *could* stay in here.

The kids had brought their own things up and she could hear the girls reminiscing as they unpacked. They were laughing about how they had scared themselves so much by telling ghost stories when their cousins visited, that seven of them had ended up sleeping in one room.

Simone looked down into the yard below and saw Andrew's surfboard on the car roof racks. It was old and battered, but Matt had refused Simone's offer to buy him a new one for their holiday and she could understand why. The board had been Andrew's most prized possession when she met him and his attachment had never waned. He'd always loved the ocean. Although he worked long hours and didn't have much free time Andrew always managed to squeeze in a few hours or surfing here and there. As Matt got older he went with him.

Elizabeth and Jill had been downstairs to get the last of their things and stopped in Simone's room on their way back. She smiled at them wistfully, thinking how fast they were growing up and how alike they were. Both had hazel eyes and curly light brown hair, although Jill had cut hers much shorter this year because they were tired of being called twins. They had both inherited Simone's petite build, although Elizabeth was now slightly taller than her mother.

Jill sat on the bed next to Simone and sighed contentedly. 'This really is the coolest house ever. You don't mind that there is always sand on the floor or salt spray on the windows, it's all part of the fun.'

'I totally forgot there was no TV,' Elizabeth said, plonking down next to Jill. 'We were so busy last time I don't even remember thinking about it.'

'Yes, we were, we didn't have time for TV,' Simone replied. 'In fact, we were so impressed with how well you coped without it we considered getting rid of ours at home.'

The girls exchanged an alarmed glance.

'Seriously?' asked Jill. 'I'm glad you didn't. I mean holidays are one thing, but at home it wouldn't have been the same.'

'Don't worry I'm not reconsidering.' Simone smiled fondly and leaned over to hug them both.

The girls went back to their own rooms to finish unpacking and Simone sat on the window seat for a moment as a montage of happy memories from that idyllic first holiday danced through her mind. They'd all fallen in love with the Beach House and had vowed to come back. Yet, somehow the return had been shelved. One year they had gone skiing and the next to Disneyland. Two years ago it had been booked, but both girls had come down with severe chickenpox, much to everybody's disappointment. As for last year – well it had been hard enough to function at all, let alone plan a holiday.

Feeling her chest constrict, Simone took a deep breath to calm herself. 'Just going for a walk,' she called and fled down the stairs and out the door before the kids could answer. Although the wind had picked up and it looked like it was going to rain, Simone stumbled through the soft sand to the water's edge. Pausing for a moment, she scanned the beach, noticing that the south end towards the cliff was practically deserted. Putting her head down against the bracing wind, she headed off in that direction.

When she got back ninety minutes later, Simone sat on the almost empty beach and watched the stormy sea for a few minutes. The brisk walk had cleared her head and she did feel calmer. Maybe she just needed to do lots of walking to force the grief out of her system.

A raindrop plopped onto her head, startling her. Standing up, she dusted off her shorts and headed up the path to the house.

Simone was surprised when she got inside and saw that the kids had been to the small Four Square supermarket and bought some groceries. She had planned to get Chinese takeaway or fish and chips from the shop across the road. Instead, the girls were busy making a salad and Matt was manning the barbeque. Trying not to be obvious about it, Simone peered into the cupboard to see what they had bought. Before she got a good look, Jill stepped in and closed the door.

'Uh uh, you're not allowed to worry about that. We'll do the shopping and the cooking.'

'But we're all on holidays darling, I can help out too.'

Elizabeth shook her head. 'No, you can't. You need a proper break Mum, you're so thin and worn out and we can do this, we're not helpless you know.'

'Of course you're not; you're very capable. But what will I do with myself?' Simone asked.

Jill washed some cherry tomatoes under the tap and dried them on paper towel. 'Whatever you like. You can read or see a movie at the cinema and there's some of those huge jigsaws that you love doing on the shelf. Remember last time, you finished that mountain one in a day when it rained.'

Smiling at the memory, Simone nodded. 'Yes, I did and I nearly went blind in the attempt. You're right, I do enjoy doing them.'

'We just want you to relax and have fun, Mum,' Elizabeth said. 'Promise us you'll try and do that.'

'All right, I promise I'll try. Now, am I allowed to pour the drinks?'

The room was light when Simone opened her eyes the next morning. She stared at the clock in amazement. 5:33! Maybe it was the long walk, or the sound of the ocean that had helped to bypass the 2:05 barrier for the first time in weeks. Simone stretched and looked out the window, where the sun was already shining on the beautiful blue ocean. Maybe getting a full night's sleep was a sign that she could and would regain control of her life.

Already, there was plenty of activity on the beach when Simone made her way down fifteen minutes later. Dozens of people dotted the shoreline, some in twos or threes and others, like her, walked alone. There was something almost primal about walking along the beach, she decided, as she headed south towards the cliff. People are just drawn to the shoreline and it's different to other walking. You can go for miles without getting tired.

Meandering along the damp, cool water's edge and watching the sun dance on the ocean, Simone felt the same calmness she had the day before. Nothing seemed as bad when you could feel sand between your toes and see waves breaking.

By the time she got back to the patrolled area the sun was higher in the sky and there was a fair crowd in the water. It didn't take long to spot Matt on his surfboard. Simone hadn't seen him surf for a long time and was surprised how good he was. She could also see the girls bodysurfing and swimming. Elizabeth was the more fearless but Jill did her best to keep up, even if it meant getting knocked off her feet occasionally.

Jill saw her mother and waved. Attempting to catch a wave in, she collided with a child on a surf mat, which sent her sprawling under the water. Clambering to her feet, she waded out of the water and walked over to her belongings. Picking up her towel, Jill shook the sand off and wrapped it around herself before coming over to Simone. 'Did you have a nice walk?' she asked.

Simone knew they all wanted her to start feeling better, she wanted it too. 'Yeah, it was great, an amazing way to start the day.' She smiled, squinting a little in the sun.

'Well we're cooking breakfast today; it's going to be a big feast. Early morning swimming gives you the hugest appetite.'

Forcing herself to keep smiling, Simone nodded. Andrew's fried holiday breakfasts had been legendary. They used to joke about a doctor serving up so much cholesterol. She hadn't eaten a cooked breakfast since he died, but she was going to do it today. Maybe it was just another hurdle on the path back to normality.

Simone waited while Jill signalled the other two to come to shore and they walked back up to the house together.

They had a lazy morning and Simone and the girls were relaxing on the veranda that afternoon when Matt bounded up the back steps, a rolled-up newspaper in his hand.

'So, how does it feel to have a genius for a brother?' he asked the girls, donging them playfully on the head with the paper.

Jill swatted the paper away. 'I wouldn't know.'

Matt donged her again. 'Come on Jillsy, don't be like that,' he said.

'Will you stop that!' Jill growled, making a grab for the paper.

Lifting it out of her reach, Matt grabbed Elizabeth's glass of sarsaparilla cordial with his other hand. He took a swig and handed it back to her.

Elizabeth made a face. 'Yuck! You can keep it.'

Matt gulped down the rest of the drink. 'I'm a bit parched from running back from town.'

Annoyed she would have to go and fix herself another drink, Elizabeth scowled at her brother. 'What's with you anyway? Why all the hyper behaviour?'

Matt waved the paper like a relay baton. 'My results were in the paper today,' he grinned.

'And judging by your behaviour you failed miserably?' asked Jill.

Matt ignored her comment. 'Two sevens and two sixes,' he

announced, 'which means a GPA of six point five.'

Elizabeth's eyes widened. 'Seven is the highest, right?'

Matt nodded.

'Quite frankly, I'm bewildered that somebody who spends so little time studying could get those kind of results,' Elizabeth said sourly.

'Says the girl who watched the federal election results coverage on TV instead of doing her English assignment.'

Elizabeth poked out her tongue. 'That was an act of desperation, not laziness.'

'And who stayed up with you after the winner was declared and helped you finish said assignment?'

'All right!' Elizabeth conceded. 'You're a legend! I'm just jealous I have to actually spend time at my desk to get good marks.'

Jill smiled. 'That's great Matty!'

Standing up, Simone gathered her son in a hug. 'I'm so proud of you Matthew,' she said, hoping the surprise didn't show in her face. Elizabeth's comments hadn't been too far off the mark and she was also surprised he'd done so well.

'I do study you know,' Matt reassured his mother. 'It's just that most of the time it's when you guys are in bed asleep.'

Later, when the girls had gone down to the beach, Matt came back out onto the veranda. Although taller and broader than his father had been, Matt had inherited Andrew's blue eyes, black hair and facial structure, as well as many of his mannerisms. When he stood quietly and rubbed his chin, Simone knew that he wanted to say something and, eventually, he did.

'Do you think Dad would mind that I'm doing Arts? I know in his heart he wanted me to do Medicine.'

Shaking her head, Simone sighed sadly. 'Matty come on, we've been through this. Dad knew you loved to write and he was proud of you for that. Medicine was his calling, not yours and he understood that.'

Matt rubbed his chin again. 'Just, sometimes, I remember when I was little, I always told him I'd be a doctor too. I never got to tell him my final decision and sometimes I feel like I'm betraying him.'

'You didn't get the OP score for medicine even if you did want to do it,' Simone said.

'Yeah, for the undergrad degree, but now it's going post-grad I could apply in a couple of years. I'd have to transfer to science though and get a bit more serious with my study.'

Simone reached over and squeezed Matt's hand. 'You're not betraying him Matthew, you need to do what you want to do - what you love to do - and follow your own path.'

'Yeah, I know, he told me the same thing. He said Grandad wanted him to be a mechanic like him and if he hadn't won a scholarship for uni, he probably wouldn't have been able to go.'

'Yes, that's true. Grandad gave him a hard time about it for a while, but he got over it. You know how proud he was of him.'

Dropping his mother's hand, Matt extended his arms straight and examined his own hands. 'Well, remember, Grandad tried to convince me to become a mechanic too. He said I had the right hands for it.'

'I think we can safely say that the world of mechanics is better off without you or your dad being in it,' Simone said with a smile.

• • • • •

By the third day of the holiday Simone had experienced a tangle of emotions. She knew the change of scenery was good for her. She was sleeping better and the twice-daily walks were helping her to stay calm. Spending time with the kids was wonderful. They were fussing around her and trying so hard to make her happy. Playing Monopoly and Scrabble, going shopping with the girls and getting involved with putting together one of the thousand-piece jigsaws had given her periods of normalcy that she hadn't known in all the past year. But the pockets of emptiness and despair still lurked in the shadows, waiting to pounce.

After lunch Simone sat down to write her Christmas cards. As always, she'd chosen tasteful, expensive cards rather than cheap supermarket ones and had already made out her mailing list. Simone always wrote a newsy account of the past year and after not sending out cards last year, she wanted to make the effort again this Christmas.

Simone spread the cards out on the beautiful silky oak dining table and chose one to send her friend Anna, in Perth. She only got as far as the basic greeting before the tears welled up. After writing "with love from", she had almost written Andrew. Taking a deep breath, she wrote "Simone and family". Fortifying herself with a glass of wine, Simone wrote a basic message that covered the positive events of the past year and copied it into each card.

Jill wandered downstairs when Simone was three quarters of the way through her list. Spying the empty wine glass, she sat down and offered to address and stamp the envelopes. They chatted as they worked, which allowed Simone to finish the task without any further deep contemplation. When Jill and Elizabeth left for the post office to mail the cards, Simone started working on the jigsaw again to keep the pain at bay.

· · · · ·

The sound came out of nowhere, shattering the peacefulness of a warm, November night.

Bang! Bang!

Simone jolted upright, her heart pounding. Having to deal with unexplained noises at night was one of the many downsides of widowhood. She sat perfectly still, as if that alone might somehow solve the problem.

Silence.

She strained her eyes against the inky darkness of the room. Gradually they adjusted. A sliver of moonlight peeked in through the curtain. She sat for another few minutes. Maybe she'd dreamt it.

No sooner had she laid down, when it started up again.

Bang! Bang! Bang Bang!

Somebody was rocking the roof. Why here of all places? Sunset Point was supposed to be a quiet little village. She'd have to wake Matthew or maybe call the police. She couldn't go outside alone and confront whoever it was.

Simone was just about to get out of bed when a violent gust of wind slammed the window shut. Then came an avalanche of bangs on the roof and heavy raindrops pounding against the window. The penny dropped. It was hail. She'd forgotten it sounded so loud on a tin roof.

Content to listen to the universally soothing sound of rain on a tin roof, Simone lay back down and drew her sheet around her. Just on the cusp of sleep, she was once again startled by mother nature.

The first rumble of thunder was like a bomb exploding. It was closely followed by a flash of lightening that lit up the room for several seconds. Then the wind started. Simone had never been in a cyclone, but she imagined the eerie moaning outside was very similar. It howled furiously, shaking the timber house to its foundations. She was fairly sure she'd closed all the windows downstairs, but didn't want to leave her bed to go and check.

When her bedroom door swung open, Simone jumped in fright.

'Mum, are you awake?' asked Jill. 'We're scared.'

Simone switched on the lamp, revealing her daughters standing near the foot of her bed. Elizabeth had plaited her hair but Jill's was a tangle of wild curls. She smiled and patted her bed. 'Come and keep me company.'

The girls jumped in and huddled under the sheet. 'Will we be okay here Mum?' asked Elizabeth. 'It feels like the roof is going to come off.'

One of Andrew's favourite sayings came to mind. If you don't know the answer bluff your way through.

'Of course, Darling. We're just feeling the brunt of it because the house is so close to the ocean.'

They all jumped as an especially fierce gust of wind seemed to lift the house right off its stumps.

'It was designed to withstand cyclones,' Simone ad-libbed, hoping they didn't detect the uncertainty in her voice.

'This is kind of like the storm scene in *The Sound of Music*,' Elizabeth said, huddling closer to her mother.

Simone laughed. 'Well, I'm sorry girls, but I don't have the energy to dance around the room and sing about my favourite things.'

Matt appeared in the doorway then. One side of his hair stood up like a cockatoo's crest and he had a sheet print on his face. 'What are you guys doing?' he asked, blinking against the lamp light.

'We're scared,' Jill said.

'It's just a storm,' Matt scoffed.

'Oh yeah, then what are *you* doing?' Elizabeth retorted.

'I need to take a leak.'

'Matthew! That's a very vulgar expression.'

'Sorry, Mum, I meant to say I need to go potty.'

Elizabeth gave him a withering glance. 'And again, you prove that age doesn't equal maturity.'

Matt smirked back.

'Do you want to come and sit with us?' Jill asked.

'No, I'm fine thanks, ladies. It's just a storm,' Matt repeated and headed to the bathroom.

'Do boys ever admit they're scared?' Elizabeth asked, as another rumble of thunder boomed.

'Rarely.' Simone cuddled her close.

Simone and the girls didn't wake until eight the next morning.

'Wow Mum, you're usually up at the crack of dawn,' Jill said, surprised to see her mother still in bed.

'Don't I know it? It's lovely to have a sleep in now and then,' Simone replied.

They looked outside for signs of damage, but apart from a few fallen tree branches, the house didn't bear any scars from the night before.

After breakfast, Simone sat on the veranda, reading the paper. It's so peaceful here, she thought, so far away from sitting in traffic doing the school run or wandering aimlessly around Indooroopilly Shopping Centre. She smiled at the sound of the girls bickering as they cleaned the kitchen. Well, it was mostly peaceful.

The cheerful sound of birdsong drew her attention to the yard. Several rainbow lorikeets had congregated to feast on the nectar of a large bottlebrush tree near the back steps. They're such beautiful birds, Simone thought, studying their brilliant blue, red and green feathers. It had been a long time since she'd slowed down enough to appreciate the simple beauty of nature.

The shrill ring of the phone interrupted her musings.

'I'll get it,' Matt yelled.

Judging by the easy-going conversation and laughter, the call was obviously for him. Simone didn't mean to eavesdrop but her ears pricked up when she heard him say, 'Sure, that'll be great. Bring your board, there are some great waves up here.' After pausing a moment he added, 'yeah, it's fine to stay here, there's heaps of room.'

Simone looked down at the paper but couldn't concentrate. It was reasonable that Matt should invite a friend, but the idea made her feel uneasy. She wanted to work through the emotions she needed to, but not in front of a stranger.

Matt's friend Liam arrived late that afternoon. He looks like a lost waif, Simone thought as Liam struggled through the door with a surfboard and a bulging backpack. Liam's dark blond hair was tousled, he was unshaven and his clothes were wrinkled and well worn. He wore Reefs on his feet. A whole head shorter than Matt and with a much leaner build, he looked a lot younger.

Liam put his bag on the floor. 'Man, that was a rough trip.'

'You didn't hitch, did you?' Matt asked.

'Of course not. I caught the bus like other law-abiding citizens. We don't all have a Beamer at our disposal.'

Matt took Liam's surfboard and put it out on the veranda with his own board. 'Well, aren't buses a pretty civilised form of transport?' he asked as he came back inside.

'Yeah, normally, but not this time. First, we got a flat tyre and had to stand outside in the midday sun while it got changed. Then the air-conditioning broke down. A few of the guys managed to get those little top windows open but it was like a sauna in there.'

'I can imagine it must have been,' Simone said.

Liam nodded. 'Tell me about it! I was glad I could get off when we got here, the other passengers had to wait for a replacement bus.'

After showing Liam around, Matt set off with the girls to buy some barbeque supplies while his friend headed for the shower. Simone decided to work on the jigsaw to keep her mind occupied.

She was surprised when Liam emerged and seemed happy to sit and chat. Most of Matt's friends were shy around her if he wasn't there to act as a buffer. Showered, shaved and dressed in clean clothes Liam scrubbed up very nicely. Simone made them both a cup of tea and they sat on the veranda, enjoying the balmy late spring afternoon.

'So, you're a surfer too?' Simone asked, casting her eyes to Liam's board.

Liam nodded. 'Almost since I could stand. I'm from Kingscliff, so I pretty much grew up on the beach. How about you? Do you surf?'

Simone chuckled. 'No, definitely not. Matthew gets his talent from his dad. I've never been on a surfboard, although I did long to try it in my teens. We used to go up to Mooloolaba for holidays and I thought that it looked like a really fun thing to do.'

'So why didn't you have a go?'

'Girls didn't surf back then. We were supposed to admire the boys and look pretty on the sand.'

'That's a real shame,' Liam said.

Simone shrugged. 'Let's face it we all have whimsical dreams as teenagers. More tea?'

'No thanks.'

'Did your parents grow up in Kingscliff too?' Simone asked as she topped up her own tea.

'My grandparents won a block of land there in the 1950s and Grandpa and Dad ran a fishing business until Grandpa retired. It's hard work but it's a pretty steady living most of the time. My brother works with Dad now.'

'And you didn't want to go into the family business?' Simone probed gently, hoping she wasn't being too nosy.

'No, it's not in my blood like it's in Dad's. I like going fishing to relax, but that's about it.'

'So, are you a budding writer like Matthew?'

'No, definitely not. I'm doing science. Matt and I met through the UQ tennis club.'

'Oh, I see. Any particular kind of science?'

'Well, I'm going to be a meteorologist, but that's post-graduate. So for my undergrad degree I'm doing lots of physics and chemistry, as well as some astronomy.'

'Wow, that's an interesting career. My father is a bit of an amateur weatherman, but he's never done any formal study.'

'I've always been fascinated with the weather. Even as a kid I loved thunderstorms,' Liam said. 'I just want to know how it all works, really.'

'You should have been here last night, we had a huge storm. Very scary, actually.'

'Yeah, I heard about it on the news. Any damage?'

Simone shook her head. 'Amazingly, no.'

'Crazy things, thunderstorms.'

Simone looked at Liam and noticed what an unusual pale blue his eyes were. 'Do you mind me asking why you came here for a surfing holiday when your own family live at the beach anyway?'

'No, it's a fair question. When I go home I have to work pretty flat out, firstly because Christmas is such a busy time for seafood and then to give both Dad and my brother a chance to have a break. Mum suggested I go away for a couple of weeks after exams to relax, before heading home to work.'

They continued to talk until the others arrived back and then Liam insisted on helping with dinner preparation too. Simone poured herself a glass of wine and relaxed, feeling more content than she had for a long time.

• • • • •

Liam proved himself to be an easy guest. He and Matt got up just after sunrise to surf and then collapsed for another half hour of sleep. But they always made sure they were up when Simone came back from her walk to help get breakfast ready. Liam fitted easily into their daily routine and insisted on sharing the chores with them. Still, Simone felt guilty at the sight of him doing the breakfast dishes one morning while she sat reading on the veranda. Setting the *New Idea* down she came into the kitchen.

'Liam it's so nice of you to help out, but I can't possibly sit out there and have you wash my breakfast dishes when you're a guest. It's not right.'

'It's no problem Mrs Ryan. I'm gate crashing your holiday so the least I can do is help out.'

Simone took the tea towel that was hanging on the oven door. 'Well, at least one of my children should be in here helping.'

'Jill will be down in a minute and she'll get mad if I let you do that.'

Simone hung up the tea towel. 'Make sure you put your dirty clothes out and I'll wash them.'

'Liz is already onto it.'

Now that she was inside Simone could hear the washing machine going in the laundry. She decided not to worry if the whites were separated from the colours. Pouring a glass of water, she watched as Liam scrubbed the frying pan. He was familiar with household chores, probably more so than her own kids. They always helped out, but generally did as little as they could get away with. Simone was touched that they had arranged things between themselves so well to make sure everything was covered.

'Where's Matthew, by the way?' she asked. He was very adept at making himself scarce when there was work to be done.

'He's vacuuming upstairs.'

Simone almost choked on her water. 'This is Matthew Ryan, my son, we're talking about?'

Liam laughed. 'I know it's not something you see every day but he does appear to know how to operate the vacuum cleaner.'

As if to illustrate the point, Matt appeared downstairs with a large dust patch on his navy blue shorts. Jill followed, ready to do the wiping up. Looking at her brother she laughed. 'You don't have to sit in the dust before you vacuum it up you know.'

Matt gave her an insincere smile. 'Thanks, I'll remember that.'

Elizabeth and Jill had never played chess before. They had grown up watching their father and brother spending hours huddled over the chessboard and thought it must be the most boring game in the world. So, Matt couldn't believe it when they sat down with Liam and learned the rules. In fact he was annoyed, because it meant they had to have a round robin system so everybody got a go each evening, after dinner.

The other three played cards. Liam had suggested Skat that night and although Simone and Jill had never played before, they proved to be surprisingly competitive.

'I'm beginning to see where Matt gets his talent for cards from,' he said, as he shuffled the deck in readiness for the next round.

'I'm not sure you'd call it a talent exactly,' Jill replied, remembering the seventy-five dollars Matt still owed her and Elizabeth after his last poker game.

'I didn't know he played that much,' Simone said, looking over at the chess game.

Feeling his mother's gaze, Matt glanced up from where he was engaged with Elizabeth on the chessboard. He had a guilty expression on his face. 'Sorry, I didn't mean to swear, but she couldn't even play a week ago, and now she's got me in a stalemate.'

Liam laughed. 'I was only telling your mum about your card playing skills.'

A look of alarm crossed Matt's face. He shot Liam a warning glance. 'Come on, we've only been to Jupiter's twice and it's not like we really *officially* gamble or anything at poker nights.'

'Too much information there, buddy. I was just talking about our friendly, social games.'

Simone tried to look stern. 'What's this about gambling?'

'It's little things, you know a bottle of beer, small change, that kind of stuff,' Matt said casually.

The girls looked on with interest as their brother tried to redeem himself. They often threatened to tell their mother about some of his activities, but in the age-old tradition of sibling solidarity they were never very serious about it. It was funny to watch him get himself into trouble though.

Simone decided to let him off the hook. 'Andrew was a good player too,' she said quietly. 'My husband,' she added.

Liam nodded and watched the change in her face.

'Yeah, he was a good player,' said Matt. 'We had some great games at family get togethers.'

Don't get teary, Simone willed herself, you'll upset everybody else. Needing to keep busy she said, 'How about some hot chocolate?'

'Yeah,' the kids chorused.

'I'll help,' Jill offered, putting an arm around her mother as they walked into the kitchen.

· · · · ·

The tide was right out the next morning when Simone went for her walk. She strode briskly right along the water's edge, enjoying the feel of the water splashing over her toes. There were some kite surfers in the water and she watched with interest as they skipped along the top of the waves, aided by the ocean breeze.

A lone seagull floated lazily on the breeze, circling around her.

She'd noticed him earlier on too as he had a black oil stain on his feathers. Her mind drifted back to a conversation she'd had years ago with the elderly woman next door. After her husband died the woman was convinced he came to visit her in the form of a kookaburra that sat on the outdoor table each morning, as she had a cup of tea. Simone had told Andrew the story and they'd laughed heartily at the idea of it. He'd joked that it would be pretty cool to come back as a bird.

She sat down on the sand for a moment and studied the bird again. He seemed to be watching her just as intently. Simone was startled when it flew down and stood beside her.

'Hello Mr Seagull,' she said, feeling foolish as she uttered the words.

Up close its beady bird eyes looked nothing like Andrew's startling blue ones and it soon became clear the seagull was much more interested in scratching in the sand than looking at her. Simone laughed and shook her head, glad that there wasn't anybody nearby to witness her odd behaviour.

You are losing it Simone, she chided herself as she stood up. Just keep walking and stop looking for things that aren't there.

'Did you meet anybody interesting on your walk?' Elizabeth asked, as they sat around the breakfast table later.

Simone thought about the seagull and stifled a smile. 'Not really, just a few regulars I've struck up a nodding acquaintance with.'

Jill poured herself some orange juice. 'Liz and I thought we could go over to the new shopping centre in Rosethorn this morning,' she suggested. 'As cute as Sunset Point is, we wouldn't mind checking out some real shops.'

'Sure, I'd like that,' Simone said. 'You boys want to come?'

Matt and Liam shook their heads. 'We've got plenty of guy stuff to do,' Matt assured her.

Simone and the girls had a lovely morning. They each had a manicure and a facial and explored the shops to their heart's content. The girls talked Simone into buying some new togs and a pair of board shorts. She was holidaying at the beach after all. They ate lunch at the Sunset Café in town and when they got home all three of them retired to their rooms to read the pile of magazines they'd picked up that morning.

Simone left for her long afternoon walk at four o'clock. The tide was much higher now, each wave encroaching a bit further on the soft, white sand. A little girl of about two scampered along the sand with her parents, squealing in delight each time a wave splashed over her feet.

The south end of the beach was almost deserted. Not many people walked that far, although there were a few surfers in the water. Simone was almost up to the cliff when she noticed Liam sitting at the edge of the dunes with a huge surfboard next to him, gazing out to sea.

Scuffing through the soft sand she walked over and smiled at him. 'Hello stranger. What are you doing all the way down here?'

Liam smiled back. 'Waiting for you.'

Simone did not give in easily. She and Liam argued good-naturedly for almost half an hour before she even considered what he was suggesting. He didn't accept her argument that wanting to learn to surf had been a fanciful teenage idea and that watching Andrew and now Matt was enough to keep her satisfied.

'Mrs Ryan, the fact you even mentioned it to me shows you haven't forgotten it. I could tell by the expression on your face it meant something to you.'

Realising she couldn't win that particular argument, Simone switched to safety. 'Liam I'm not a confident swimmer. I'm not too bad in the safety of our pool but I'm nervous in the ocean.'

Liam's pale blue eyes held her gaze. 'I understand that but let's look at what we're working with. The whole shoreline of Sunset Point is pretty protected and I've picked a great spot. We're using a long board, which is much easier to learn on *and* I've worked as a surfing instructor, so I know what I'm doing.'

'But what about those people you hear about who get serious injuries from being dumped?'

'Mrs Ryan, I promise you if there are dumping waves we won't go in the water.'

Simone gave an exasperated smile. 'For someone so laid back you are very persistent. All right! I'll give it a try.'

'That's the spirit!' Liam smiled victoriously.

Simone stood up. 'Well it's a shame we can't start right now but it would take me too long to go back and get my swimming gear. Tomorrow will do just fine.'

Liam smiled again as he laid the board down flat and brushed the sand off the surface. 'For the first lesson, you don't even go near the water.'

Simone knew her children must have been in on Liam's idea when they didn't question why she was an hour late returning from her walk. Apparently they could also sense she wasn't ready to talk about it, as they had dinner and assumed their normal night-time routine without any mention of surfing.

When she and Liam took their turn on the chess board, Simone attempted to dissuade him from continuing with the lessons. 'I really am scared in the surf Liam,' she said, as she dithered over moving her Queen or her rook. 'I almost drowned once.'

'Really?' Liam gave her a quick glance across the dining table.

'Yes, really. Remember how I told you we used to go on holidays at Mooloolaba?'

Liam nodded that he was listening, while he considered his next move. For someone who hadn't played chess much, Mrs Ryan was pretty good at it.

'Well one time I got caught in a rip and got carried way out. It was such an awful feeling; I still shudder when I remember it.'

Liam moved his bishop. 'What happened?'

'Andrew rescued me. It's how we met'

'Seriously?'

Simone nodded. 'Yes, can you believe it? He was working as a labourer on his uni holidays and was down cooling off in his lunch hour. We agreed it must have been fate because our paths probably wouldn't have crossed otherwise.'

'That's actually a pretty cool way to meet someone, the danger factor aside.'

Simone smiled sadly. 'Yes, I suppose it is.' She studied her chess pieces for a moment. 'You don't think it might hold me back with the lessons?'

'No, not at all,' Liam assured her.

Simone went to bed early enough but didn't sleep well. In fact she spent much of the night thinking up a tactful way to get out of the lessons. The whole idea was crazy; she just wasn't the sort of woman who learned to surf. She was sorry she'd ever mentioned it to Liam.

She would be polite but firm. Short of dragging her down to the water, Liam couldn't *make* her keep doing the lessons. She was an adult after all.

Deliberately skipping her walk and coming downstairs in her bathrobe at eight thirty instead of Liam's suggested time of eight, Simone breathed a sigh relief at sight of the empty lounge room. He must have got the message, thank goodness! She smiled as she filled the kettle. There was a lot to be said for passive resistance.

Making her way out to the veranda with tea in hand, Simone's heart sank when she saw Liam sitting there quietly, reading the paper. He was wearing board shorts and a rash vest and the long board and his towel were sitting by his feet.

He looked up and smiled. 'Ready?'

Simone's carefully prepared excuses deserted her. He'd gone to so much trouble. It seemed very mean spirited to pike out.

'Just let me drink this and I'm all set.'

After Liam and Simone had left, Matt and the girls congregated on the veranda. Matt was waxing his surfboard and the girls had brought some postcards out with them to write.

Elizabeth got comfortable on one of the loungers and looked at Matt expectantly. 'Well, what did Liam say about how the lesson went?'

Matt shrugged. 'Not much. Liam's the kind of guy who only tells you things in his own time. He just said that it went well.'

'What is it with boys and getting no details?' Jill sighed in exasperation.

'Hey, feel free to ask him yourself, see how much better you do.'

'I just can't believe she agreed to it,' Elizabeth said. 'I know we've all said we wanted Mum to start having fun again, I just never thought it would be surfing. It's weird though, how come we never knew that about her? It made me feel a bit bad.'

Matt paused his waxing for a moment. 'I think sometimes an outsider can see things that people close to the situation can't see. I think she'd kind of forgotten about it herself. I know Dad would have taught her if she asked him.'

The girls nodded in agreement and the three of them were lost in their own thoughts for a while. It was Jill who spoke first.

'I don't often say it to Mum, because I know it upsets her, but I still miss him so much.'

'I miss the way he always came and said goodnight, even if it was late and we were asleep,' Elizabeth said.

Matt looked out at the ocean. 'I miss our early morning swims. He used to have to drag me out sometimes but I always felt good afterwards. Every day I wish he was here to motivate me.'

Jill tried to blink back the tears, but they spilled down her cheeks. 'It's not fair,' she whispered.

Elizabeth started to cry too. She tried to speak but couldn't.

Matt came over and put an arm around each of his sisters. 'You're right Jill, it's not fair,' he said hugging them both. 'But we owe it to him to keep going, to be everything he wanted us to. He's still around us, you know - I feel his presence sometimes.'

The girls clung to Matt for a moment. As much as he gave them a hard time sometimes, he had always been their fiercest protector and never more so than the past year. They knew he would always look out for them.

They sat in silence for a while before Jill spoke again. 'I think he would like to see Mum learning though. He loved teaching me and Liz.'

'Oh yeah, he would definitely like it,' agreed Matt.

• • • • •

The pain was awful.

It woke her out of an exhausted sleep that night. Every time Simone moved, it seemed to squeeze her chest and abdomen. My heart, she thought. I must be having a heart attack. There was heart disease in her father's family. Her great uncle had dropped dead at forty-four. But she'd always been careful with her health; she didn't smoke and ate well. She had regular check-ups and there had never been any indication of cardiac disease.

Simone curled into the foetal position and moaned softly as

another stab of pain hit. Why did it have to happen here of all places, she thought. The nearest major hospital was half an hour away, much too far if she needed some kind of urgent treatment.

She grabbed at her neck until her index and middle finger found her pulse. That's weird, she thought as she felt the steady throb in her carotid artery. I thought your heart either sped up dramatically or slowed right down when you had a coronary. Hers felt normal. She reached down to her wrist and got the same regular beat.

Her mind raced with the other symptoms of a heart attack. Feeling feverish or cold and clammy was one. She slapped her hand across her forehead, relieved but puzzled to find it felt normal too. She wasn't sweating nor was she nauseous. Simone rolled onto her back and took some deep breaths. Maybe she was having a panic attack. The pain subsided for a moment.

It was only when she rolled over to sit up and have a drink that she realised the pain was muscular. Her abdominal muscles burned with the exertion of the movement. Leaning back against the pillows she remembered how Liam made her practise extending her arms to lift her chest off the board. She must have done it fifty times.

Gingerly lowering herself down onto her back she sighed in relief. As long as her heart was okay, she could live with some muscle pain.

Simone rolled awkwardly out of bed the next morning, amazed at just how many movements were influenced by her abdominal muscles. It hurt to pull her bathrobe on and brush her hair. She'd have to send the kids out to buy her a heat pack and spend the next week recovering on the couch.

Four sets of eyes focused on her as she hobbled down the stairs at nine o'clock.

'I'm as stiff as a board,' she announced grimly.

'Ah, the old abdominal agony,' Matt said.

'It kills hey, Mum?' Jill sympathised.

'I'll say! I can't believe you didn't warn me about it. I thought I was dying last night.'

Liam shrugged. 'No point in putting you off before you even got started. The upside is that it only hurts the first time, your muscles soon adjust.'

'Oh, great. Considering I'll be unable to climb onto a surfboard in the foreseeable future, there's not much comfort in that.'

Elizabeth guided her to the couch and helped her sit down. 'Oh, no, you have to work through it. Go back out today and try again.'

Simone shook her head. 'Oh no, there's no way I'm going anywhere near that board again.'

An hour later, she was paddling slowly across the unusually flat ocean. At least the lack of waves was one thing in her favour. After being unmercifully ganged up on, she had given in and agreed to attempt her morning lesson. Annoyingly enough the kids seemed to be right. Moving her muscles was helping the stiffness.

'That's it Mrs Ryan,' Liam said. 'Really dig your arms into the water.'

I can't believe I'm doing this, she thought. When Doctor Randall suggested a relaxing seaside holiday, she hadn't said anything about undertaking a physically demanding activity like surfing. But, somehow, Simone didn't think she would object to the idea either. She'd been urging her to exercise for the past six months.

Two seagulls swooped down close to the water. She studied them intently, looking for the tell-tale black mark. It wasn't there.

So much for *that* theory.

The birds screeched at each other and flew away again.

Could Andrew see her? she wondered. Was he trying to make a connection by steering her towards something that he had loved so much?

Simone paused in her paddling for a moment and rested her head on the board. Because it was so big, she could lie easily on top of it. Although there was almost no swell, the gentle rippling motion of the water was enough to cause the board to sway delicately. How peaceful, she thought. A moment of perfect calm and stillness.

She was sure Dr Randall would approve of that.

Even though she had started to stiffen up again, Simone didn't even try and get out of the afternoon lesson. There wasn't much point when she knew the cheer squad would keep at her until she went.

She could hear the kids laughing on the veranda as she walked downstairs.

'Remember how Dad lost the house keys last time?' Jill said.

'Yeah, and he blamed it on me!' Elizabeth said. 'The woman in the real estate office gave me a lecture about not touching things that weren't mine.'

Matt laughed. 'He found them a month later under the car seat but said not to tell Mum.'

'Well he knew he'd get in trouble if you did.' Jill giggled.

They were laughing about something else by the time Simone got out onto the veranda. Liam picked up the board and they made their way down the stairs, with Matt and the girls waving them off cheerfully.

Simone did her best to smile as they started walking along the water's edge, but she couldn't stop the tears welling up. Annoyed with herself for not wearing her sunglasses, she attempted to discretely dab her eyes with her towel and keep her composure.

'I hope it's not the company that's upsetting you,' Liam said, in his usual calm manner as he glanced at Simone.

'Oh Liam, you're very kind, but it's sort of hard to explain.'

'Lots of things are, but it usually helps to tell someone.'

Simone dried her eyes and sighed, a deep sigh that seemed to reach down to her toes. 'I heard the conversation you were having about the lost keys.'

'Oh, okay,' Liam said. 'Are you upset about what Jill said about Mr Ryan getting in trouble off you?'

'No, no, that was true. I would have told him off. He was always losing things – buttons, cufflinks, keys, sunglasses…he was hopeless.'

'And do you feel bad now for getting mad at him about things that didn't matter?'

'No, that's not it either. Sure, I chided him about it, but it was light hearted.' Simone shook her head wearily. 'No, what's wrong is that I envy the way the kids can talk and laugh about Andrew so easily. For me it's like a physical pain to remember him fondly like that.'

'That must be tough.'

'Yeah, it is. I feel so torn sometimes. I want the kids to be happy and get on with their lives, but at the same time I don't understand how they've managed to move on and I haven't.'

Liam hefted the huge surfboard to his other arm. Although lean, he was wiry and, despite the board's bulk, he carried it easily 'Well,' he said, 'you're comparing two different experiences.'

Simone stopped walking and stared at him. 'What do you mean? They adored their dad too, you know.'

Liam shook his head. 'No, I didn't mean that. You're grieving for the same person but from two different perspectives. You lost your husband, your life partner – the kids lost their father. They've never been married so they don't know how you feel. Your father is still alive, right?'

Simone nodded.

'So, you don't know how it feels to be without a father.'

Simone stared at him again. 'You know Liam, nobody has ever put it to me like that before. The thought hadn't even crossed my mind.'

Liam shrugged. 'It's easier to see things like that from outside the square.'

Simone started walking again. 'I'm sorry Liam, you offered to teach me to surf, not to be a sounding board for my problems.'

'It's all right. We all need a sounding board sometimes.'

They walked the rest of the way in companionable silence.

It was almost six forty-five when Simone's eye's fluttered open the next morning. She lay there for a moment under the crisp, white sheet enjoying the gentle transition between sleep and wakefulness. It was so long since she'd experienced it. She'd grown used to jolting awake with a racing mind and, more often than not, a headache from lack of rest.

She stretched gingerly. Her muscles were still sore, but not nearly as bad as the day before. Simone cast her eyes over to the window. She'd left the curtains partially open and they were rippling gently in rhythm with the soft ocean breeze. Through the window she could see a patch of blue water bathed in sunlight. It was another beautiful Sunset Point day and although she wasn't exactly thrilled at the prospect of doing another two surfing lessons, at least they would give the day some shape.

The swell had returned that morning and Simone panicked when Liam told her she'd be paddling out in the face of the waves.

'I really don't think I can do that yet,' she said.

'Sure you can,' Liam replied easily.

Simone waded into the waves slowly. The water that had seemed so calm and inviting yesterday felt menacing today. Lowering herself down onto the board, she attempted to paddle out to where Liam was waiting. Before she'd moved very far a wave crashed over the board and drenched her face. She sputtered as the salt water stung her nostrils and burned her throat.

Stay calm, Simone, she told herself, as her arms thrashed through the water. The paddling skills she'd build up yesterday seemed to have deserted her now. Liam was saying something to her, but she couldn't hear it.

The next wave knocked her off the board all together. Panic set in as she plunged into the water. The leg rope felt like an anchor and she twisted and flailed in the water, trying to fight her way to the surface again. It wasn't that deep, but she was so off balance she just couldn't get her footing.

Finally she felt a hand grasp her elbow and help her to her feet. 'Are you okay?' Liam asked.

Simone shook her head. 'I can't do this!'

Keeping a firm hand on her elbow, Liam steered her back to shore. Picking up the board, he held it patiently while Simone bent down and undid the leg rope.

Simone wrapped herself in her towel as they sat on the sand, but Liam just let the warm air dry him.

'I know it must seem silly to someone like you who is so at home in the water, but those waves really scare me,' she admitted. 'They're so unpredictable and knock you down when you're trying to climb back up.'

'Kind of a metaphor for life hey?'

Simone nodded wearily. 'Yes. Exactly.'

'Well you're right, waves are unpredictable and you can't change the way they come at you, but you can prepare yourself for most eventualities. And, if you get knocked off your feet, you can find your way to the surface again, once you get your bearings.'

'That sounds like you're going to make me go back out there.'

'You got it. But I'll jump on the back of the board and paddle with you. Then when you're ready you can have another go.'

Matt was napping on the couch that afternoon when the girls started nagging him to take them surfing.

'Come on Matty,' wheedled Jill, 'you promised.'

Matt's eyes stayed closed. 'Yeah, all right, we'll go a bit later,' he murmured drowsily.

Elizabeth took the baton. 'No, Mum needs the board later. We want to use the long board; you know we're not good at the short one yet.'

'That's all right, I can miss a lesson,' Simone said, looking up from the jigsaw puzzle she was working on.

Liam reached his leg over from the recliner he was sitting on and nudged Matt's foot. 'Come on Ryan, you lazy oaf. Take your sisters surfing. We can't have your mum missing a lesson.'

Matt levered himself to a sitting position and scowled at the girls. 'Fine, let's go.'

Although they hadn't surfed in a while, both girls were surprised at the skills they'd retained. Matt soon got over his bad mood and shared their enthusiasm as they practised.

'Hey, great ride Lizzie,' he said an hour later, as Elizabeth proudly stood almost all the way to shore.

She grinned and splashed through the shallows to where Matt and Jill were standing. 'Yeah, well I can't have Mum showing me up. It sounds like she's getting pretty good, from the limited information that's flowing back.'

'I told you, Liam only tells you things in his own time. Go ask him yourself if you want more details.'

'All right, all right, I was just saying,' Elizabeth said.

Jill glanced up to the veranda where she could see Simone reading a book. 'I just love the fact that she doesn't seem to be trying so hard to be upbeat all the time.'

Matt nodded. 'Yeah, she's finally relaxing and just letting things happen. I think we've surprised her with the fact that we can take care of things ourselves. Speaking of that, what's for dinner tonight girls?'

After draping her towel around her shoulders, Jill said, 'I think it's your turn to decide. Liz and I are always coming up with stuff.'

'Yeah, true enough, but it is your thing.'

Elizabeth folded her arms. 'Thinking up dinner ideas is *our* thing? Let me guess, because we're females?'

'No, I didn't mean that. I just meant you're more creative than me, you've got better imaginations and more sophisticated tastes.'

'Yeah, right,' Jill said. 'Consider this an opportunity to improve your creativity and sophistication. And it can't be another barbeque either; we need to branch out a bit.'

Picking up the surfboard, Matt motioned the girls to come with him. 'Fine, I'll decide when we get to the shops. You guys have to come with me though. We can go to Woolworths at Rosethorn and get something exotic.'

'Exotic my eye. You just love hooning around in Mum's car you big revhead,' Elizabeth said.

Matt tried not to smile. 'That's Mr Revhead to you and I don't hoon, I just make use of the fine features of a luxury, European car.'

'And show off to any girls you might see along the way,' Jill added.

'You ladies are a full of great gags today. The question remains, however, are we going or not?'

The girls looked at each other and shrugged, but gave in easily. It was nice of Matt to take them surfing and they didn't mind the daily food run. Feeling less stressed than they had in a long time, the siblings walked up the beach together.

• • • • •

Liam brought his own board along for the lesson the next morning. Simone looked at it fearfully when they got to their regular spot. 'You're not going to try and make me ride that one, are you?' she asked. 'I can barely stay on the big one.'

'No, I'm going to come out with you. The swell is pretty decent today and I want you to really get comfortable paddling into the face of the waves.'

'So, you won't be on the board with me this time?'

'No, but I'll be beside you. You're ready to go it alone Mrs Ryan.'

Am I? Simone wondered. I've gone it alone for the past year and still don't feel like I'm really coping. Still, Liam was so patient with me yesterday. I really need to give it a try.

The first wave splashed right in her face, but she shook off the water and kept paddling. When she encountered the second and third waves, she remembered to lift her torso off the board.

When the sixth wave she encountered knocked her off, she let her feet seek out the sandy bottom before floundering her way back to the surface. Liam was sitting astride his board beaming like a proud parent as she clambered back onto the board.

'Hey, you did it!'

Simone smiled back wearily. 'I still didn't like it though.'

'Ah, you don't have to like it yet, but you will. Once you get the hang of it, you'll love it.'

They chatted easily as they walked back to the house. Simone carried the smaller board and Liam the big one. She found him so easy to talk to. *It's because he didn't know me before,* she realised. *He's not comparing this cardboard cut-out version to what everybody else remembers* – the confident, outgoing Simone whose charmed life extended in front of her like the fabled yellow brick road.

A young woman walking her dog gave Simone an envious glance. 'I wish my boyfriend would take me surfing,' she said.

As soon as she was out of earshot, they both laughed. 'I think the glare must have affected her eyesight.' Simone shook her head and smiled.

'Hey, come on, you do look very young. In fact you must have been a child bride.'

'Not quite, but nineteen does sound very young to me now. Not that I regretted it though,' she said. 'Andrew was the only man I ever wanted to be with.'

'Hey it's whatever works for you. If you meet the love of your life when you're young, why not get married?'

'Some people say that they lose themselves when they're part of a couple. I never thought that and I'm still struggling to see myself as a single person.'

'Maybe it just has to be a gradual process. You didn't see yourself as a surfer a few days ago, but you're getting into the groove of it.'

'That I can cope with, enjoy even. I just don't want to be single,' Simone said. 'I don't want to have to forge a new identity for myself, plan a life for my family by myself. It's the pits, Liam.'

He gave her a look of genuine sympathy. 'Yeah, it must be,' he agreed.

That evening Liam insisted on treating everyone to fish and chips and he and the girls walked down to pick it up. Simone and Matt played Three-Thirteen on the veranda while they waited.

'I wish they'd hurry up,' Matt said fifteen minutes later as he examined his cards. 'I'm starving and the smell from those beach barbeques isn't helping. What is it about fried sausages and onions that gets your tastebuds hopping?'

'I don't know, but I agree it's a very appetising aroma,' Simone agreed as she picked up Matt's discarded ace. 'Everyone says they do fantastic fish and chips over there so I presume that means there's a queue. Besides the caravan park is starting to fill up a bit, I've noticed a few cars pulling in there today loaded up with gear.'

'Yeah, there are some interstate numberplates too. For such a small place, it gets its share of tourists.'

'It's a lovely caravan park,' Simone said, trying to decide whether to stick with hearts or go for clubs. 'I had a walk through one day and was really impressed. I guess if you're into camping or caravanning and you find a nice spot you probably come back year after year.'

'Yeah true enough. I still say we've got the pick of the accommodation though.'

'Oh yes, that goes without saying.' Realising it had been a mistake to switch to clubs, Simone decided to try for diamonds. She also changed the subject.

'You don't mind that Liam is teaching me to surf, do you?'

'No, not at all. Should I?'

'No, no. I just wanted to make sure. I mean if you really wanted to do it or anything, I'm sure he'd understand.'

Matt shook his head. 'We'd probably kill each other out there. I think Liam's got the right personality for the job, he doesn't let things get on top of him.'

'I'll say. No matter what happens, he just patiently keeps on going. Nothing seems to faze him. Does he ever get worked up about anything?'

'Rarely. He's a real free spirit, but sensible when he needs to be.'

'That's good to know, should you ever decide to do anything too crazy.'

Matt studied his cards for a moment. 'You're enjoying the lessons though, right? You just seem more like your old self, now you've been doing them.'

'Yes, I am enjoying it.' Simone smiled. She knew how closely the kids watched her, willing her to move forward.

'Cool.'

Picking up the ten of diamonds Simone added it to her cards and laid them flat on the table. 'That's another round to me,' she said with a grin, just as Liam and the girls appeared up the front stairs.

· · · · ·

'You know I could definitely get used to this.' Simone dabbed her mouth with a napkin and smiled as they sat around the dining room table the next day. 'I mean, I honestly do enjoy cooking, but it's always nice to have someone else serve you up a meal.'

'I'd just like to say that lunch today was my suggestion,' said Matt, reaching over to grab the last club sandwich.

'Well, I'm suitably impressed,' Simone replied. 'And what has inspired you to become more interested in meal preparation?'

'The girls made me,' Matt said. 'But it's been kind of interesting. I never noticed those recipe cards in the supermarket before.'

'Well, they don't usually have them in the junk food aisle,' Jill said.

Matt gave her a withering glance. 'You girls really crack me up sometimes. Maybe I won't drive you over to Rosethorn after all.'

Jill shrugged. 'Okay, we'll go on the bus. It goes right to the shopping centre.'

'Yeah, yeah all right,' Matt backtracked hastily, not wanting to pass up the opportunity to go for a cruise in the Beamer. 'Hurry up and do the dishes Liz so we can get going.'

'Yes sir.' Elizabeth gave a mock salute as she started clearing the plates.

Once the kids left, Simone retired to the veranda to read the *Woman's Day*. Princess Diana is so beautiful, she thought as she studied

129

the cover picture. I'm sure she'll be one of those women who is still stunning in her sixties and seventies.

When the phone rang half an hour later she was startled out of an afternoon snooze.

'Hello Darling,' her mother said when she picked up the receiver.

'Hi Mum,' Simone replied, stifling a yawn.

They chatted for a while before her mother said excitedly, 'You'll never guess who's getting married?'

'Uncle Reg?'

'Tsk, Simone you love to make fun of me sometimes. Somehow, I think having made it to seventy-seven as a bachelor he's not going to opt for marriage now. No, it's your cousin Alicia, *Ms* career woman herself,' her mother said. Alicia was the same age as Simone but their lives had taken very different paths. Alicia was a stockbroker who had never before shown the slightest interest in getting married or having children, much to the consternation of her extended family.

'Well, that's nice,' Simone said, surprised at what a jolt the news gave her. She liked Alicia, although they weren't close, and she *was* happy for her, wasn't she? She listened as her mother eagerly filled her in and did her best to sound interested and excited, although her own emotions were in turmoil.

She stayed sitting on the couch after she hung up the phone. I'm jealous, Simone thought to herself. What kind of person does that make me? Alicia deserves to be happy, to have the kind of love I had.

Simone looked at the phone number she had copied down but made no move to pick up the receiver again. I will ring and congratulate Alicia, she thought, but not just yet. I'll need to work up to it.

Simone mentioned the phone call to Liam as they made their way along the beach that afternoon. She'd come to look forward to the chats they had on the way there and back. He just let her talk, without trying to fix her problems.

'I hate seeing happy couples now,' she admitted. 'They represent everything I've lost.'

'Well that's a pretty normal human reaction. It doesn't make you evil or selfish, it just means you want what they've got.'

'Oh Liam, you're very good for my self-esteem. Have there always been this many of them?' she asked, motioning with her hands to indicate the people around them.

Liam glanced at the teenaged couple in front of them, the elderly couple behind them and the thirty-something's coming towards them. All were holding hands. 'Yeah, I think so. You just never noticed them before because you were one of the gang. Now you're the outsider.'

'Do you think the feeling will ever go away?' Simone wondered out loud.

'I don't know.'

They eased back into a comfortable silence as they approached their lesson spot. It was part of the ritual now. Whatever they'd been discussing was put aside when they hit the water.

• • • • •

Simone was getting to know some of the regulars who made their way up and down the shoreline with her each morning. There was the tiny, birdlike woman who wore the same terry towelling beach robe every day, the reed-thin distinguished-looking man with the Maltese terrier, and the overweight young woman who shuffled slowly but surely a little further each morning, her face red with exertion. Simone never spoke to any of them, she just nodded and smiled and they did the same.

We're all doing beach walk therapy, she thought, as she wandered into the water and let it rush around her ankles.

The walks had become the foundation of her day, as had the surfing lessons. Although she couldn't believe it, she was actually starting to enjoy them and admitted it to Liam while they prepared for the morning lesson.

'Told ya,' he said.

Now they had paddling under control, Liam was attempting to ease Simone into an upright position. They practised the progression from lying down to crouching to standing on the sand, but she struggled to master it in the water, even though the waves were small and gentle that day. She toppled off the front end of the board, slid off the side and overbalanced off the back.

She draped herself over the board and rolled her eyes. 'I'm

honestly trying my hardest Liam,' she said. 'I just can't seem to get my balance. Maybe it's a sign that I'm just not cut out for this.'

Liam shook his head. 'Uh, uh you don't get to bow out that easily. Think how far you've already come in less than a week.' He hoisted himself over the board and sat astride the end of it. 'I will keep the board steady by sitting here. We don't even have to move yet. All you need to do is get from your tummy to your feet. Just make sure you stay in the middle or towards the front or you'll knock us both off the back.'

Simone looked at him doubtfully. 'What if I kick you or something?'

'I'll forgive you,' he assured her.

'Why are you so patient with me?'

'Because I know you really want to do this. Come on, off you go.'

Simone persevered. With Liam keeping the board steady she finally got the hang of crouching and got used to the feel of standing.

'It's pretty amazing, hey?' Liam said, as she stood for the fifteenth time.

'Yes, I've got to admit it is.' She smiled at Liam, but the expression froze on her face when Liam started thrashing his leg around in the water, a look of panic on his face.

'It's on my leg!' he yelled. He continued to thrash his leg around, which tipped the board violently and they both fell off. Simone was screaming when she hit the water and continued to do so once she came up again for air. She didn't know what had scared Liam, but a shark seemed like a good possibility. Forgetting all her newly acquired skills, she flailed helplessly in the water. She couldn't even see Liam, he was still under the water.

There was something touching her elbow! Simone let out a truly ear piercing scream and shook her arm violently. It took a moment to realise it was Liam's hand, trying to help her back onto the board.

'Liam, what's happening?' she cried. 'Are you all right?'

Liam guided her back to the board and they both took hold of it. Clearly embarrassed, he lifted his right hand out of the water and held up a thick piece of rope.

'I thought it was a sea snake,' he said. 'The way it coiled around my leg. I'm so sorry for scaring you like that.'

Simone studied him for a moment. 'It's a relief to know you're not utterly unflappable,' she said. 'I didn't think I'd ever see you lose your cool like that.'

'Well you weren't supposed to. My ego just took a big battering.'

'Don't worry, I won't tell the kids.'

'Thanks.'

Simone looked at him again and burst out laughing. 'I'm sorry Liam,' she gasped. 'But it was just so funny to see you thrashing around like that and falling off.'

Liam chuckled in reply. 'I'm sure it was. That would have been a great clip for the surfing instructor's video handbook.'

Simone kept laughing while Liam paddled them back to shore. She snickered a few more times as she picked up her towel and dried herself.

'You do realise you're crushing my self-esteem?' Liam gave a feigned hurt expression as they started walking back.

'Sorry, but oh that felt so good. I haven't laughed like that, well I couldn't say how long it's been. Definitely not since Andrew died. You see I feel like I'm being disloyal if I enjoy life without him being here. It's like if I don't feel sad for a really long time them I'm not honouring how much I loved him.'

'I can understand that.'

Simone stared at him. 'You can?'

'Well, yeah. Lots of things in life are measured and quantified in relation to something else. I'm not saying you should feel disloyal, but I can see why you do.'

'You're the first person I've said that to who didn't tell me to stop being silly.'

'There's nothing silly about acknowledging how you feel.'

'No, I guess there's not.'

· · · · ·

Simone's morning lesson the next day was particularly successful. The conditions were perfect and she managed to stand for dozens of waves. She wasn't standing for long, but the fact that she got herself upright was the biggest achievement.

'See what happens when you let go of your fear?' Liam said as they packed up.

'I actually do. I've never got that before.'

'All right then, we've tackled fear. What's next on the agenda?'

Simone busied herself drying off and having a drink before she answered. 'What about guilt?' she asked softly. 'Have you got any way to let go of that?'

Liam picked up the board and they started walking. 'Guilt?' he asked. 'What have you got to feel guilty about?'

'More than you think.'

'You can tell me Mrs Ryan.'

Simone veered away from the damp sand of the shoreline. 'I think I'll need to sit down to tell you this.'

Liam followed her up to the softer sand. 'Sure,' he said.

Simone found a patch of sand on the edge of the dune shaded by a bottlebrush tree. They sat down. She didn't speak for a moment and Liam didn't rush her.

'You know at first I tried to focus all my anger on the woman who caused the accident that killed Andrew,' she said eventually. 'She survived you know – just a few cuts and bruises and because the hospital was so close they could treat her heart quickly. I kept thinking about how she shouldn't have been driving if she had heart problems or that she must have been speeding or she should have pulled over sooner. I guess I got a bit obsessive about it because my sister got in contact with the woman before I had the chance to. It turned out she was a fit, healthy woman with no history of heart disease. She wasn't speeding and she said she desperately tried to steer off the road. Eventually I came to realise it really was a random accident and there was no point in me being angry at her.'

Liam nodded, although Simone realised he must be wondering what that had to do with her feeling guilty.

'Andrew was more of an early bird than me. He would get up and go swimming or running at the crack of dawn, but by the time he was having a shower I would get up and make his breakfast and lunch.'

Liam nodded again and waited for Simone to continue.

'The day of the accident I slept in. Andrew was up especially early because he had a meeting that morning. I remember hitting the snooze button and him kissing me goodbye when I was still in bed.'

Simone picked up a shell and cupped it in her hand, lost in the memory of that morning. 'He rang me when he started his lunchbreak. I heard the call waiting beep, but I was busy talking to my friend so I didn't answer it. I got the message on the answering machine later, the last time I heard his voice...' Simone paused a moment, willing herself not to cry.

'Once I stopped focusing on being angry at the woman, then the feelings I had been trying to suppress started to surface. I couldn't stop thinking about how two things I did put Andrew on that road at that moment. If I'd made his lunch he never would have gone out and if I'd answered the call and spoken to him it would have delayed him by five or ten minutes.'

Liam thought for a moment before he answered. 'You know Mrs Ryan, some things are just bigger than us and as much as we like to think we can control everything that goes on around us, we just can't.'

Simone was surprised by his answer. Usually he just let her talk, without offering an opinion. Before she had a chance to respond he spoke again.

'Have you considered that he could have eaten in the hospital cafeteria and never left the building? Or, even if he had taken his lunch, he might have gone out to buy a paper or a coffee or just to have a walk? We make a million decisions every day and each flows to another. There's way too many variables to take responsibility for the actions of someone else.'

Simone nodded, although she wasn't sure that she agreed with Liam. Pulling her towel tightly around her, she got to her feet and they headed back to the house.

· · · · ·

The room was familiar to her now. Simone was used to the firmness of the mattress, the way the sun came in the window and the way the floor creaked over near the window seat. Yet something felt different when she woke up the next morning.

She lay there for a while looking up at the high timber ceiling, trying to pinpoint what it was.

Five peaceful minutes passed before the thought struck her. It's me she realised. I feel different. Not dramatically different. It wasn't like the events of the past year had been a nightmare and she'd just woken up. But there was a shift in the heavy, dragging sensation inside her that she'd grown so used to.

The kids noticed it at breakfast.

'You look great today, Mum,' Jill said, as she served up scrambled eggs and grilled tomatoes.

Elizabeth eyed her carefully. 'Yeah, you do,' she agreed, setting down the toast. 'You look healthy again, not so washed out.'

Matt nodded too, although Simone knew he wouldn't notice if she shaved her head and starting wearing a caftan. He was definitely Andrew's son in *that* regard. Still, it was nice of him to be supportive.

'Where's Liam?' Simone asked.

'Slept in,' Matt mumbled, his mouth full.

'Oh, well maybe he won't be ready for the lesson this morning,' she said, surprised at how disappointed she was.

Matt shook his head. 'No, he said he'll be down soon.'

There was also something different about Liam that morning. It wasn't just the fact he hadn't shaved or that he hadn't talked much while they walked down the beach. He wasn't being moody, he just seemed listless. Even though he said the usual encouraging things and smiled occasionally as she practised, Simone could tell his heart just wasn't in it.

How ironic, she thought. Just when I've found some energy Liam seems to have lost his. I'll ask him if he's okay when we walk back.

Simone was paddling out when she noticed that Liam was distracted by something. She followed his gaze and saw two people swimming and frolicking in the surf about fifty metres away.

'What's wrong?' she asked.

'They're caught in the rip down there.'

Simone looked out again. A young woman was floating on her back and her male companion was ducking under the waves. 'Are you sure? They seem to be having fun.'

'They don't realise what's happening. They're right on the edge of that sandbank and the way they're drifting they're going to drop off it any second. See how the water is moving down near the rocks?'

'Yeah.'

'If they don't come in, they'll get carried over and knocked against them. Are you okay to get back in? I'm going to go out and get them.'

Simone waded back to shore and watched as Liam paddled over to the couple. She could see him gesturing with his hands and pointing at the rocks. The young man shook his head, but the woman draped herself over the board. Another seemingly heated discussion took place and then the young man attempted to swim back in. Liam sat and waited a few minutes as he thrashed around in the waves, then he moved over and had the young man drape himself over the board. He then paddled all three of them back to shore. Simone could hear the conversation as the three of them waded out of the water.

'You could have saved the heroics man, we were totally fine out there,' the light skinned, freckled young man said.

'You wouldn't have been in a few minutes, but you're welcome,' Liam replied.

The young woman was politer. 'Marty is a really good swimmer, but thanks anyway,' she said, apparently trying to appease her volatile looking boyfriend.

The Lifeguard four-wheel drive pulled up then and Jim Stewart climbed out.

'Everything okay?' he asked, looking around.

Marty put his hands up palms out. 'Oh yeah, superman here got his kicks dragging us in on his wimpy surfboard.'

Frowning fiercely, Jim eyeballed Marty. 'You're lucky he was here sonny and, might I remind you, that the consumption of alcohol on this beach is prohibited. I suggest you be on your way right now.'

Marty glared back insolently. 'Who's gonna make me?'

Crossing his arms, Jim intensified his stare and it was Marty who looked away first. 'Yeah, yeah, we were leaving anyway,' he said and stalked up towards the dunes, his girlfriend trotting along behind him.

Jim watched him walk away and then turned to Liam. 'Jim Stewart,' he said, extending his hand. 'Thanks for dragging him in.'

Liam reach over to shake Jim's hand. 'No problem. I'm Liam and this is Simone.'

'Nice to meet you both. That bloke is staying at the caravan park and we've had a few incidents with him,' Jim said. 'He jumped off the Crow's Nest the other day. He was lucky he didn't break his neck.'

'What's the Crow's Nest?' Simone asked.

Jim pointed to the southern cliff. 'See that rock ledge about half way up? It's a local dare spot.'

Gazing up at it, Simone shuddered. 'That's a huge drop. How could anybody contemplate leaping off there?'

'Plenty of people give it a try. There are big signs up but you can't protect people from their own stupidity.'

'I guess you can't,' Liam said.

Tilting his head to the side, Jim raised an eyebrow. 'You doing a sideline in surf lessons while you're up at the house?' he asked Liam. 'I've seen you down here a lot. Surf schools are supposed to register with the council and get a permit you know.'

Liam shook his head. 'No, not at all, Simone is a friend and it's strictly on the house.'

'Fair enough.' Jim motioned to the rapidly darkening sky. 'There's a bit of a downpour approaching. Hop in and I'll drive you back.'

The rain continued throughout the afternoon, so they had to miss the afternoon lesson. Simone had told the kids about Liam's rescue over lunch and he'd smiled at their praise, but still with the same distant expression she'd noticed earlier.

He'd been quiet all afternoon, reading a thick astronomy hardback from the bookshelf while the rest of them played cards and worked on one of the jigsaws.

'Hey buddy, it's your turn on kitchen patrol tonight,' Matt reminded him at four thirty. 'You have to come up with a meal idea, get the ingredients, cook it...'

'Oh right, yeah, sure.' Liam set his book down but didn't make any move to stand.

Jill looked up from the jigsaw. 'Liz and I will come with you Liam,' she said. 'I'm getting severe eye strain from this thing anyway.'

'Yeah, good idea. Are there any umbrellas around here?' Elizabeth asked.

'Take the car,' Simone said.

Liam's eyes widened. 'Are you sure?'

'Of course.'

'Gee I hope I don't get lost,' he said, with the first real smile Simone had seen all day. 'You know, I might have to circle the back streets a few times to get my bearings.'

'Yeah, you do that mate,' Matt said with a grin. 'It's a really sweet ride.'

Simone and Matt kept working on the jigsaw for a while, even though Matt was getting frustrated with it.

'This thing is just nuts,' he said, trying to jam a section of sky together. 'How are you supposed to find any kind of pattern when so many bits are all the same colour?'

'That's what the numbers on the back are for,' Simone said.

Matt moved onto another section. 'Yeah, but who wants to spend all that time turning every piece over? I don't get the point of it anyway, I mean you spend hours doing it and then you break it up and put it back in the box for the next sucker to drive themselves crazy with.'

'You're as bad as your dad. He couldn't see the point of them either.'

'Smart man, my father.'

Their eyes met for a moment and they shared a look that only two people bonded by grief can.

'We all miss him Mum,' Matt said. 'But I just don't think he'd want us to be sad for ever.'

'I know, Matty.' Simone smiled wistfully as she continued to sort pieces into piles.

They worked in silence for a few minutes.

'Is Liam all right?' Simone asked, as she moved the top right corner section into place.

'Are you kidding? After you gave him the keys to the Beamer I reckon he's in heaven about now.'

'Yes, I know that cheered him up, but don't you think he's been a bit out of sorts today?'

'Maybe a little. He gets like that occasionally. If you just give him space, he seems to work through it.'

'Don't you ever ask him what's wrong?'

Giving up on the puzzle, Matt leaned back against the couch.

'We're not women Mum, we don't spill our guts at the drop of a hat.'

'All right, I was just concerned, that's all.'

Matt stood up and stretched. 'I'll take him out for a drink later. That might help.'

• • • • •

The loud, insistent knock on the front door jolted Simone awake. Snapping on the bedside lamp she blinked in the sudden glare and peered at her travel clock. Twenty past two. Who was banging on the door at this hour?

It must be the boys. They'd gone to the pub and she'd told them the key would be under the bottom step. Obviously they'd forgotten or couldn't find it. Another series of sharp raps sounded as she climbed out of bed.

'All right, hold your horses,' she muttered, pulling on her bathrobe.

Elizabeth met her in the hallway. Her eyes were clouded with sleep and her hair frizzy and dishevelled. 'What's going on?' she asked, squinting against the glare of the hall light.

'The boys mustn't be able to find the key. I can't imagine where they've been until this hour, the pub closes at midnight.'

When Simone opened the door and saw the two blue uniforms, her knees buckled. 'No!' she cried, clutching at her chest.

It couldn't be true. She'd barely survived this nightmare the first time. She couldn't go through it again. Her heart started banging against her ribs so hard she thought it might explode.

'No!' she wailed again, collapsing against the doorframe, hugging her arms to her body. The younger policeman stepped forward, his light brown eyes watching her keenly. Of average height and slim build, he looked to be in his late twenties.

'Mrs Ryan?' he asked. 'Mrs Ryan, are you all right?'

He had a surprisingly deep voice, but a very calm, reassuring tone.

Elizabeth shoved the door right open. 'What happened to my brother?' she demanded, clinging onto Simone's arm desperately.

The policeman put his hand on her shoulder but Elizabeth shook it off. 'Just tell us!' she yelled. She was shivering violently even though the night was warm.

'Please calm down Miss Ryan, Mrs Ryan. We're still waiting for word about the rescue. We just came over to wait with you, because we thought someone might have come and told you and caused unnecessary panic.'

Simone was trembling so much she found it difficult to walk. Elizabeth led her over to one of the chairs and they both sat down.

'Where are they?' Elizabeth asked.

'Well they're still in the water. But the lifeguards are there, they've got a boat and everything…'

'Lifeguards?' Simone shrieked.

'Yes, we needed their expertise. We don't have the equipment, or the same skill level quite frankly.'

'WHAT HAPPENED?' Elizabeth yelled.

'I'm sorry Miss Ryan, I didn't get your name,' the policeman said.

'Elizabeth!'

'All right Elizabeth. My name is Senior Constable Patrick Elliot and my colleague over there is Sergeant David Wilson.' The older, bearded man nodded respectfully, but stayed standing near the door. Simone wondered why the more senior man wasn't doing the talking, but then turned her attention back to what Patrick was saying.

'We were called down to the southern cliff about an hour ago. There was a report of some young blokes jumping off the Crow's Nest. Do you know where that is?'

Simone nodded weakly.

'It's very dangerous, as you can imagine, particularly in the dark, and especially when there's a strong current like tonight. There was a gang of onlookers and not a very clear picture of what happened as yet. As I understand it somebody went in and was in trouble before he hit the water. Then somebody else went in to rescue him. We're not even sure how many people are in the water.'

'But Matt and Liam are in there?' Elizabeth asked.

Patrick nodded. 'Yes, we're pretty sure about that.'

Simone's heart was still pounding. She could feel the pulse in her neck vibrating violently. 'It was the middle of the afternoon last time,' she said dully. 'But I knew right away there was something wrong.'

Patrick showed no sign that he didn't know what she was talking about. 'You usually do,' he agreed.

'His friend Brian wanted to tell me, you see. He's a doctor too and was with him in the operating theatre when he died. The police let him come along with them. But to make it official *they* had to tell me. They were so young and even in the midst of those horrific few moments, I felt sorry for them, having to deliver news like that.'

Elizabeth thought she should try and explain. 'My dad was killed in an accident last year,' she said.

'Oh, I'm so sorry, so, so sorry,' Patrick said, reaching over and clasping Simone's hand. 'I know this waiting is torturous and I wish there was something I could do to make it easier for you.'

'Thank you, you're so kind,' Simone mumbled numbly.

The next twenty minutes inched forward with agonising slowness. The silence of the warm summer's night was suffocating, as if a giant blanket was draped over their heads. Simone realised she should invite the police inside, but held back. If they moved, it might shatter the desperate air of hope to which they were all clinging.

Everybody jumped when the radio in the police car squawked. Sergeant Wilson jogged down the steps and leaned into the car. He spoke for a few moments and then came back up shaking his head. 'Nothing new,' he said. 'It was just base checking in.'

Another five minutes crept past, punctuated only by the hooting of an owl and the scurrying footsteps of a possum in a nearby tree.

A wave of nausea hit Simone when a set of car headlights lit up the dark front yard. It was another police car.

'We had to call reinforcements in from Rosethorn,' Patrick explained. He reached over and clasped Simone's hand again. Elizabeth clenched the other hand, her grip as crushing as a vice. The tension in the air was beyond anything Simone had ever experienced before. The ten seconds the car sat there silently were an eternity.

Finally, a thick set, squat man with a rapidly receding hairline and a fleshy, red face climbed out of the squad car and slammed the door. Jamming his hat on, he wrenched the back door open and scowled as the three occupants filed out.

Matt and Liam averted their gaze as they walked up the stairs. Each had a blanket draped around them and both were soaking wet. Matt was wearing jeans, but Liam was clad only in boxer shorts. A piece of gauze littered with crimson splotches was taped across Matt's forehead.

The third man was wearing a wetsuit. It took Simone a moment to realise it was Jim, the lifeguard she and Liam had met earlier that day.

A deep moan escaped her lips. She was still too shaken up to speak. The relief was so profound, it was almost painful to breathe. Simone stumbled forward to embrace her son, not caring that he was cold and wet.

It wasn't until she got close that she smelt the alcohol fumes emanating from both of them and took in the glazed, incoherent expressions. 'You're drunk!' she screeched. 'Some stupid fool gets himself in trouble and you try and rescue him when you're drunk? Do you have any idea how dangerous that was?'

The third policeman shook his head. 'Ah no, it wasn't like that Madam,' he informed her. 'Mr Archer here was the ringleader of this whole fiasco. We have several witnesses both in the pub and up at the cliff who will attest to that. Matthew also jumped of his own free will, despite being warned not to when some of the onlookers realised how dangerous it was with the big swell coming in.'

Simone stared at Liam, struggling to comprehend that the patient, laid-back young man she had spent so much time with over the past week could do something so reckless and put her son in so much danger. She was trying to contain her anger before speaking when Elizabeth exploded into action.

Springing to her feet she shoved Liam hard in the chest. 'How could you?' she screamed. 'Our family is already torn since our dad died. I can't believe you could have killed my brother too!' She pushed him again and Liam stumbled backwards. He didn't speak. Jim steadied him and then gently turned Elizabeth around.

'Why don't you take care of Matt?' he said.

Elizabeth burst into tears. Simone gathered her in her arms and then moved over to enclose Matt as well. Ignoring how cold and wet he was, they huddled together as if they might never let go.

• • • • •

When Simone heard the kookaburras' morning chorus, she knew that daylight wasn't far away. How do they always know to wake just before the sun? she wondered.

Sure enough, the first light of day filtered through a crack in the curtains not long after. It must be about four thirty, Simone decided, and there's no point in me lying here when I'm not going to sleep.

Simone glanced over at Elizabeth, who was curled up beside her. She'd been inconsolable when they eventually got upstairs and had finally cried herself to sleep about an hour ago. Simone had lain there and held her, feeling numb as she comforted her precious daughter. It was times like these that she missed Andrew the most desperately.

Pulling the sheet up she tucked it around Elizabeth and kissed her head gently. She didn't stir and Simone eased quietly out of bed. Slipping her clothes on, she crept downstairs and out the front door.

The sun was a brilliant red ball on the clear blue horizon as Simone walked along. Despite the earliness of the hour she wasn't the only one pacing the sand. A young man jogged past, Crowded House blaring from a Walkman clipped onto his waistband. Two huge German Shepherds gambolled along in front of her, dragging a spry-looking elderly woman behind them.

The ache in Simone's muscles was just a distant memory now; the pain in her heart was so much more prominent. She'd held back again last night, feeling the tears well up but not letting them fall. It was force of habit now. She'd broken down completely on the night of Andrew's funeral and was so alarmed at how out of control she felt, that she hadn't let herself cry properly since.

It was only as she lay holding Elizabeth earlier that she realised what a release crying could be. She had literally felt her daughter's energy change as the stress and tension eased from her and had marvelled at how peacefully she slept.

Simone managed a smile for the dog woman as she passed by on her way back to the main beach. Is that what everybody did? Just put on a brave face and keep going? She scuffed through the soft sand onto the dunes and sat down.

Just cry Simone, she told herself. Your son could have died last night and you've barely shed a tear. You need to let the emotion out or it will poison you.

Eventually she succumbed, allowing single tears to roll down her cheeks as she stared at the sea and thought about Andrew and all the things she loved about him. Despite the tears, she smiled as she remembered how she had sent him out each morning looking immaculate, but he always looked dishevelled when he got home. How he was always spilling things on himself and could never do his own tie as neatly as she could. A sob caught in her throat as she remembered how they used to laugh about the fact he could neatly sew up his patients but couldn't sew on a button.

Don't wipe the tears away, she thought, let them fall.

Simone remembered how she and Andrew had sat at this very spot while the kids ran around on the sand and had planned the rest of their lives. Despite getting married young, they had never grown bored with each other and were confident they never would. It just hadn't occurred to them that one of them might die.

Once her brain registered she wasn't pulling herself up this time, Simone began to cry in earnest – great heaving sobs that racked her whole body and a volume of tears she could never remember shedding before.

Exhausted when the tears stopped flowing, Simone knew she must look frightful. Her face went bright red and her eyes swelled up when she cried. Her throat felt raw and her nose seemed to be twice its normal size. She was so glad nobody else had ventured this far down the beach to see her at her worst.

It was a sore and sorry Matthew who emerged onto the veranda at one thirty that afternoon. A thick graze extended across his forehead and there was an ugly purple and yellow bruise on his right shin. Three of the toes on his left foot were black and swollen. His eyes were bloodshot and his face was pale. Simone had heard him vomiting twice that morning.

A sob caught in her throat as she looked at him. Sure, he was an adult now and tall and strong, but he was still so young. So inexperienced at life. And she could have lost him because he made a stupid choice. She should yell at him for being so reckless, but she couldn't. Not now.

A tear leaked from Matt's right eye. 'I'm so sorry, Mum,' he sniffed.

Simone pulled him close and hugged him tight. 'I know you are Matty. But don't you ever, ever do anything like that again.'

'I won't.'

Eventually, he reluctantly revealed the details of the night before. 'We were just having a few drinks, you know, and these girls came in and seemed to take a bit of a shine to us. Somehow, we got onto Sambuca shots and Liam really hit them hard. I was pretty surprised, because he doesn't usually drink much at all. In fact I've never seen him drunk like that. He normally keeps an eye on me.'

'And I take it the girls encouraged you to keep going.'

'Yeah, you got it. By the time the pub closed we were really pi..., uh, drunk and the girls were looking for some further excitement. There were a few other young guys there too and Liam said we should jump off the Crow's Nest. He was all hyper and it got the rest of us revved up too.'

Simone shook her head. 'I just can't believe that's the same calm, level-headed young man I've trusted with my life out in the ocean all week.'

Matt shrugged. 'I couldn't believe it either, but with that amount of Sambuca in me, it sounded like a mighty fine idea. Anyway, it took us a while to walk up there and by then Liam seemed to calm down a bit. He looked down and said the ocean was too rough and we shouldn't do it. I think the other three guys were relieved to get out of it, but by then I was the one acting crazy. I said I was still doing it. Liam tried to talk me out of it and in the end tried to physically restrain me, but I pushed him aside and did it anyway.'

'Oh Matthew,' Simone murmured.

'As soon as I took off I knew it was a huge mistake. I was petrified. Don't ask me how I managed to avoid the rocks or even land feet first. Well, no, actually I reckon I know how.'

Simone looked at him.

'It was Dad,' Matt said softly.

'What?' Simone whispered.

'He was with me out there, he had to be. It's the only way I can explain not killing myself firstly on the jump and second when the swell washed me against the rocks.'

'Well, it's the kind of thing any father would do.'

'Anyway, the next thing I knew, Liam jumped in too, although he was a lot smarter about the way he jumped and where. He'd also had the bright idea to take his jeans off first. I soon discovered they aren't the greatest things to swim in.'

'So Liam went in to help you?'

'Yeah, totally. The other guys up the top told him not to, but I've got to tell you I was so glad to have him down there with me. I didn't even know which way was up but somehow he managed to get us around the worst of the rocks without getting too smashed up. Once we did that it wasn't quite so bad. I mean, we were still in the water, but it was calmer and there were a couple of places we could hold on.'

'Then the lifeguards came?'

'Yeah, they had a boat but it couldn't come right up to where we were so they had to tow us across. That Jim guy was pretty amazing, especially with me. I really started to panic and he calmed me down, then got me across to the boat.'

'Sounds like you had more than one guardian angel out there.'

'Yeah, without a doubt.' Matt paused for a moment and sighed wearily. 'Liam is going to leave. He's so cut up about this. He wants to talk to you first though.'

'I'm not sure I want to even see him Matthew.'

'Please Mum, you know he's a good guy. He saved me out there last night. He just made some really bad decisions and so did I.'

'All right, tell him to come down when he's ready.'

The afternoon was coolish and overcast and there weren't many people on the beach as Simone and Liam walked along. He'd suggested talking on the beach, rather than in the house, and Simone agreed it was a good idea. The awkward silence between them, and hostile vibes emanating from Simone, was a sharp contrast to the easy-going rapport they'd shared just the day before.

They walked past the patrolled area and found a spot to sit at the edge of the dunes.

It wasn't until then that Simone even looked at Liam. Unlike Matt he didn't seem to have any physical scars from the night before, except for the bloodshot eyes and deathly pallor. Despite her anger, Simone's heart went out to him. He looked wretched.

'First of all, I know this is of no consolation to you now, but I never intended Matt to do that jump. Just me and maybe the other guys. I've done that kind of thing before, so I knew the right way to jump and land and all that,' Liam said, eyes downcast.

'That may well be so, but it's ridiculously dangerous to do something like that at night *and* when you're drunk. The whole thing was just insane.' Simone shook her head and looked away.

'I know it; boy do I know it. I thought I could forget about what day it was, you know just go and have a few drinks and try and be normal. But then the girl appeared. She was so much like Deb, it just spun me out.' Liam propped his elbows on his knees and leaned forward. 'It spun me out so much that I started pouring Sambuca down my throat and regressed to some old behavioural patterns.'

'I'm sorry Liam, I'm not following you. What day was it and who is Deb?'

Liam sat back up, then reached down and wriggled the gold ring off his right ring finger. Wordlessly he handed it to Simone.

She took it with a puzzled glance.

'Read the inscription.'

Holding the ring up to the light, Simone examined the flowing script. "Liam and Debra 30-11-90" it read.

The penny dropped. 'It's a wedding ring,' she said, unable to keep the surprise out of her voice. 'And yesterday was the thirtieth of November, your anniversary.'

'Yes, it was,' Liam agreed softly. 'Although we never actually celebrated an anniversary together, we didn't get that far.'

'What happened?'

'She died,' he said.

Simone's hand flew to her mouth. Liam was just a baby himself, how on earth had he had time to be married and widowed?

Liam seemed to read her thoughts. 'I know I look young but I'm twenty-five.'

'Well, I just assumed you were around Matthew's age, but Liam back in 1990 you would have only been....'

'Twenty-one,' he finished. 'Two years older than you were. Deb was twenty-four. We met when I'd just finished high school. I decided

148

to take a year or two off to work before I started uni, so I could save up some money and maybe travel a bit. Even though nobody else in my family has been to uni, I'd had my heart set on meteorology for a long time.'

Simone hugged her knees to her chest and nodded. She knew how hard it was to delve into bittersweet memories.

'I got a job in a surf shop on the Gold Coast, which led to a job as a surfing instructor. Deb started working at that particular surf school the same day I did. We clicked from the moment we met.'

Liam picked up a stick and made a pattern in the sand. 'As it turned out, Deb was into anything crazy and adrenaline filled – skydiving, abseiling, mountain climbing, paragliding, kite surfing – and, being totally in love, I got interested in those things too. We had so much fun and life was just one big adventure. I guess I just put aside doing more study or anything remotely serious because there were too many other crazy things out there to do. We worked when we had to and lived constantly on the edge, looking for the next big challenge.'

'But you found time to get married?'

'Oh yeah, it was something we both wanted. Deb always said she would never have kids, but I intended to talk her around a few years down the track.'

A tiny crab scuttled across the sand and they both stared at it for a moment, transfixed by its efficient sideways movement.

Eventually Liam spoke again. 'Like Mr Ryan's, Deb's death was sudden and unexpected.'

Simone put her hand on Liam's arm. 'An accident?' she asked.

Liam shook his head. 'No, it wasn't, that was the irony of it all. Deb died in her sleep one Friday night from an aneurism. It turned out she had a weakness in a blood vessel in her brain. She was born with it and because of its position it was inoperable. She didn't find out about it until she was eighteen and decided that instead of taking it easy like the doctor's suggested, she was going to live every day to the full.'

'And you never knew about it?'

'No, she didn't tell anybody – not me, or her family. Only her doctor knew.'

'Liam, that's so sad. I had no idea…'

They both looked up as a shadow fell across where they were

sitting. Elizabeth stood there with her arms crossed, glaring at Liam.

'The police are here,' she said. 'They want to talk to you.'

Simone didn't get a chance to talk privately to Liam for the rest of that afternoon. The police stayed more than an hour, getting a statement and delivering a stern lecture. Simone almost cried with relief when she heard them say they wouldn't be pressing charges.

When the boys went to the police station to sign their statements, she sat and talked to the girls. Having heard all the details from her sister, Jill was just as angry at Liam and it was difficult to break through their brittle veneer.

'Girls you heard what Matty told the police, Liam didn't make him jump, he tried to stop him doing it.'

'Yeah, but it was his stupid idea in the first place. If he hadn't taken Matt down there he never would have thought of it,' Elizabeth said heatedly.

'Well, we don't know that for sure. Ultimately your brother made the choice to go there. Boys just do very stupid things sometimes,' Simone said.

'But why?' Jill asked.

Simone shrugged. 'I don't know for sure, Jill, but they don't talk about things like women do when they're upset. Instead they act out in different ways.'

'That's so dumb,' Elizabeth said, rolling her eyes. 'And hypocritical. Matt's always lecturing me about not drinking.'

'Really?' asked Simone.

'Yeah.'

'I'm glad to hear that. You don't drink do you?'

Elizabeth glared at her mother, clearly hurt. 'No, I don't.'

Simone put an arm around her shoulder. 'Sorry, I know you don't. You're right, it is dumb to take stupid risks, but human beings are very complex sometimes. Please don't be so hard on Liam. You've told him how you feel, so let's leave it there hey?'

Both girls folded their arms and pouted. 'We'll have to think about it,' Elizabeth said finally.

Jim was still on the beach when Simone got back from her walk. He nodded politely as she walked up to him. Simone nodded back, then reached over and hugged him.

'Well now, that's a nice way to end the day,' he said, a flush of red appearing on his cheeks.

Simone dropped her arms. 'I'm sorry Mr Stewart, that was a bit impulsive, but I'm just so grateful for what you did last night. I'm quite prepared to cover the cost of the rescue, in fact I insist on it.'

'You're very welcome, but saving lives is what my job is all about. We don't expect payment, a simple thanks is enough. However, if you really feel strongly about it, I'm sure the council would accept a donation to our equipment fund.'

'Consider it done.'

'The boys were down earlier to apologise. They seem like decent lads.'

'Yeah, they are when they haven't consumed their bodyweight in alcohol.'

Jim smiled. 'Well, I have to admit, I jumped off the Crow's Nest a few times in my youth. Never at night and not in that kind of swell, mind you, but I guess I can understand the young male reasoning that led them there.'

'There's a long story behind it all.'

'There usually is.'

Liam made himself scarce at dinner and after they finished eating Matt suggested they go to the movies to see *The Shawshank Redemption*.

Elizabeth and Jill were thrilled. They'd been clingy with Matt all afternoon and were chuffed he was offering to spend the evening with them.

'You'll come too won't you Mum?' Jill asked, as she stacked the dinner plates.

'No, thanks anyway. I saw the movie a few weeks ago with Aunty Marg, remember?'

'Oh, well, we don't have to go. You can't stay here by yourself.'

'Yes, I can. I'm so tired I'll be in bed very soon and I wouldn't want you to miss the chance to see such a wonderful movie. It's a really powerful story.'

The house was so quiet after they left that Simone wished she had gone after all. She turned the radio on, but couldn't get interested in the local talkback show. There were so many thoughts crowding her head, she didn't know how to begin sifting through them.

The knock on the front door made her jump in fright but she relaxed when she heard Liam's voice. 'It's just me Mrs Ryan. I'm going to grab my things and I can wait for the bus in the café.'

Simone ushered him inside. 'Don't be silly Liam, you don't have to leave. I want you to stay,' she said.

'No, I should go. I've wrecked everything.'

'I'm making us both a cup of tea and we can finish our talk.' Simone pushed Liam gently in the direction of the couch and headed into the kitchen.

At first they sat silently, drinking their tea. Simone felt macabre in a way, wanting to know the details of somebody else's tragedy, but she needed to know so she could understand. Finally, she broke the silence.

'Liam, I feel terrible that I've been unloading on you all week, while you've been carrying the same burden. And you never said a word.'

'I didn't want you to hold back. I was always going to tell you about me eventually.'

'Despite what happened last night, you're a real inspiration. You've obviously dealt with your grief and moved on. It gives me hope that maybe I can too.'

Liam raised his eyebrows and gave a hollow laugh. 'Oh, I dealt with it eventually, but believe me, I wreaked some havoc trying to run away from it. At least your way of coping isn't so self-destructive.'

'But you're so calm and laid back. You seem to know exactly where you're going.'

'I was married for nine months and was a widower two weeks after my twenty second birthday. After the initial shock of Deb's death subsided I went completely off the rails in the way most young males do. I started drinking heavily, taking stupid and very dangerous risks – like last night - and just bumming around with no purpose. I'm truly lucky I didn't kill myself or someone else with some of the stuff I did and I put my poor family through so much stress. They just didn't know how to help me.'

Simone nodded. 'You just want the ache to subside.'

'Yeah, that's it. Luckily someone finally got me to understand that

I wasn't going to get past it without going through it first.'

'A counsellor?'

Liam shook his head. 'One night I'd been out writing myself off as usual and just as I stumbled over to get into my car and drive home I got stopped by a policeman. After I gave him some attitude he took my keys, sat me in his patrol car and asked me to tell him why I thought I had the right to take other people's lives into my hands.'

Setting his cup down, Liam rubbed his jaw. 'So I let him have it. I told him what a bad hand I'd been dealt, how life wasn't fair and how nobody understood what I'd been through. He let me rant and rave and get all my anger out and then he drove me home without any kind of lecture. Then he rang the next day to see how I was. Of course I was hung over and gave him another serve about how life sucked. He didn't interject and tell me I was wrong, he just listened.'

Simone nodded, seeing the parallels in the relationship she had developed with Liam.

'Anyway, this cop Garry, his name was, turned out to be a pretty decent guy. He kept ringing me and listening to me, and whenever he saw me out at night he made sure I wasn't doing anything too stupid. The only thing he came down hard on me about was the drink driving. He told me my rego number was flagged and if I got caught, I'd be dealt with severely.'

'Did it stop you?'

'Yeah, it did actually. I really respected the guy and knew I'd be pretty lost without being able to drive. Anyway, one day I was reading the paper and saw this story about Garry. It turned out that he'd lost his wife, his father-in-law and his son in a car accident caused by a drunk driver.'

Simone clutched her hand to her chest. 'Oh, the poor man! You wonder how anybody ever gets past something like that.'

'Yeah,' Liam agreed. 'But that was the moment I realised I could do it too. As it turned out I saw him up at Point Danger that afternoon, you know near Coolangatta?'

'Yes, I've been there a few times.'

'I used to go up there a lot. I think the name appealed to my reckless spirit at that time. Anyhow I told him I saw the story and we talked for a long time. He told me the biggest hurdle he had to overcome was guilt. He thought as a policeman out on patrol he should have caught that guy before he did what he did.'

'So I'm not the only one then?'

'Not by a long way. It was one of my biggest hurdles too. In fact the other day when you told me about your guilt, I almost told you all this, just so you could understand.'

Simone leaned forward, tilting her head to the side.

'The night Deb died she wanted to go to a party, but I was tired and, to be honest, I was a bit sick of going out all the time. She was annoyed with me, so we had a quiet night in and went to bed early. The day of the funeral and for months afterwards I couldn't stop thinking that if we had been out somewhere, well first of all it might not have happened if she was awake or we could have got help, gone to hospital....'

'But Liam you didn't know – you couldn't have predicted what would happen. It might have happened later in the night when you were in bed anyway, or she could have been driving and caused an accident that killed you both or somebody else.' Simone stopped when she realised what she was saying. 'Oh, okay the light bulb just went on.'

Liam smiled sadly. 'Want to trade the millions of possibilities? As hard as it was, learning to accept that we actually control very little was my first big breakthrough.'

'Your first?'

'Uh huh. There is no one answer to resolving grief – just a series of steps towards acceptance.'

'What else did you do?'

'I read a lot of books and joined a support group. Deb's best friend even dragged me along to a yoga retreat.'

'Did it help?'

Liam shrugged. 'I honestly don't know. But it definitely didn't hurt. I was willing to give anything a try.'

'Unlike me.'

'It's never too late to start.'

'No, I suppose it's not.'

They sat in companionable silence for a few minutes, the ticking of the clock the only audible noise. Eventually Liam spoke again. 'I really think the most important thing in my recovery was having someone to talk to who understood. Don't you think it's made a difference to you?'

'Oh, absolutely. Matthew really got it right.'

'Huh?'

'Didn't he get you to come here and talk to me, to try and help?'

Liam shook his head. 'No, not at all, this was just a holiday for me. Matt and I have never really talked about how you're coping. I just picked up straight away that you were struggling, although you were doing your best to hide it.'

'It's that obvious?'

'Probably only to somebody who's been there. Your eyes had the wounded look I used to be confronted with every time I looked in the mirror.'

Simone furrowed her brow as a thought occurred to her. 'Matthew doesn't know any of this, does he?'

'No, none of my uni friends do. I needed to establish myself first, get back into a young, single guy's life without the people around me feeling sorry for me and treating me differently. I had to find my identity again without Deb.'

'Is it hard not to talk about her?'

'Yeah, it takes some effort, but I'm glad I did it this way.'

'I understand why, let's face it young men aren't renowned for their ability to express and discuss their emotional states.'

'Uh huh.'

Simone took Liam's hand in hers. 'You're amazing and I'll be forever grateful that you came into my life.'

'Just let others help you and you'll get there.'

It was still overcast the next morning but very humid as Simone and Liam walked along the beach. Between them, Simone and Matt had convinced Liam to stay and the girls had begun to thaw as well. Liam insisted they should finish the last of the surfing lessons.

Simone could feel herself sweating under her rash vest. 'Where's that sea breeze? The humidity must be about eighty percent.'

'Eighty-five actually, I checked the barometer before. Those low clouds are keeping all the hot air from escaping.'

Simone smiled. 'You sound like a weatherman already.'

'I wouldn't mind being on TV one day,' Liam admitted.

'So, you never lost your desire to be a meteorologist after all?' Simone asked. 'It's a big step to commit to years of study after being out in the workforce making money and leading the adventurous life you did.'

'No, I never lost the desire. Even amidst all the excitement and hype of the life Deb and I lived, it was a niggling little reality that I chose to ignore. But I would have had to face it again one way or another.'

Simone picked up a long stick and dragged it through the sand as they walked, creating a pattern. 'I guess we're both always going to wonder how things might have been aren't we?'

Liam nodded. 'Yep we are. To be truthful – and this has only come about after nearly three years of contemplation – I honestly don't know how things would have worked out for Deb and I if she had lived. Living that kind of life is great when you're young and carefree but I know I would have eventually wanted something more stable and solid and given her condition Deb just wouldn't have settled for that. We never properly discussed the more serious issues of life and I guess I will always feel a bit betrayed that she never told me, that she chose to make all the decisions about her life around something I knew nothing about.'

'Don't think too much about that Liam, you'll always have the memories of that time together, no matter what might have happened later.'

'Yeah I know. I grew to hate that saying about how it was better to have loved and lost than not to have loved at all, but I know now I would never trade those years with Deb for anything, despite the heartache of losing her.'

They walked in silence for a while before Simone spoke again. 'You're happy though, aren't you? You've found joy and meaning in your life again?'

'Yeah I have. Losing someone like we have will always be with us and we'll never get over it, but trust me if you work through it you can come out the other side and you will laugh and make plans and feel almost normal again one day.'

'I guess I just can't imagine that yet,' Simone said.

'Well, as you now know, I still have my moments, although fortunately not too often.' Liam held up his right hand and ran his thumb over the gold ring. 'I'm still working towards taking this off one day.'

Simone looked down at her engagement and wedding rings and shook her head. 'I can't imagine ever taking them off.'

'There's a lot of memories infused in them. It's all part of the grieving process.'

'It seems like I'm still right at the beginning.'

'Well, that's the thing to remember Mrs Ryan, there is no timetable for grief. Don't compare your experiences to someone else's. It will take you as long as it takes.'

'That's exactly what I've been doing with the kids.'

'Well, I remember you saying that the girls got a lot of help through their school and I know Matt....,' he hesitated for a moment, realising he may be betraying a confidence.

'It's all right, I know he had a few sessions with a psychiatrist who was an old friend of Andrew's.'

'Yeah, he said that. Sorry I just didn't know if he'd told you or not.'

'Well, he didn't actually, but he's never learned to clean his pockets out before putting his clothes in the wash and I found the appointment card one day. I didn't mind, I was just glad he was doing something constructive.'

'So, you see the value of getting help, but you've just been battling on alone and then beating yourself up for not being as far along in the grieving process as your kids.'

'I don't know why I've resisted for so long, I think it's part of the control thing I've wrapped myself up in. I am going to do something, now I've realised it's not that scary.'

'The worst thing that can happen has already happened and you survived. You'll make it.'

'What can I ever do to thank you for nudging me out of that dark corner I was hiding in?'

'You don't have to do anything. Just keep moving on as best you can and if you see someone else who's struggling, help them.'

Simone enjoyed seeing the daily message that appeared on the noticeboard outside the quaint, Methodist church. It was a tiny structure, but very lovingly maintained with a beautiful rose garden out the front. Her mother was Methodist, her father Presbyterian and she had attended both churches while growing up, although not that often as her parents weren't religious.

She had never seen anybody out there arranging the letters but a new message appeared each day without fail. Today it said, "Count Your Blessings." She saw it as she walked down to the shop to get milk.

On impulse she stopped and went over to sit on the bench that was in the middle of the rose garden. She'd always loved flowers, roses in particular. She grew three different varieties in her own garden.

After sitting and admiring the beautiful blooms for a few minutes she focused her attention on the tiny wooden building in front of her. It had been a long time since she'd been near a church - the day of Andrew's funeral to be exact. He had come from a Catholic family and given that he was much more devout than her, she'd had no objection to them being married in his church or the children being baptised there. She had often attended Mass with them, but felt no desire to convert.

In those shell-shocked first weeks after Andrew's death, Simone had asked his sister Kathryn to take the girls to church with her family. While she was spiritually numb, she wanted the kids to gain strength and comfort from their religion, and they had. Like she had told Liam, the girls' school had been especially supportive. Simone had been surprised, but thankful at the way Matt, too, had seemed to find depth in the faith that he had previously been fairly casual about. It touched her the way he spoke confidently about Andrew being around them, something she still wasn't sure about.

Tentatively Simone walked through the open front door of the church and sat down at the back. There was a woman at the front arranging flowers, but otherwise the church was empty. Simone was enveloped by the peaceful stillness and felt a faint stirring in her soul. The message outside came to her mind again and she took a moment to do what it suggested. She and the kids were healthy, financially secure and they loved each other. She'd had a wonderful, happy marriage of almost twenty years, which seemed a lifetime compared with Liam's experience. It was a good place to start from.

Before she left, Simone felt she should make some attempt to pray. Closing her eyes, she whispered, 'I'll never understand why he had to go, but thank you for the time we had him. Thank you for our wonderful children. Please help me find myself again.'

It seemed inadequate, but Simone thought God might understand she was only just starting to live again and it was going to take a while to get back on track.

Simone was so taken with the roses that she sat back on the bench outside for a while. Liam spotted her as he walked back from town and came over to sit beside her.

'What's next Liam? Are you going to tell me now that I have to get back out there, go nightclubbing, have a series of one night stands and get back in the dating scene?'

'I don't know how the kids would feel about that,' Liam said with a grin. 'Unless you really want to, of course.'

'Oh, heavens no Liam. I couldn't think of anything worse.'

'Do you know what my second breakthrough was?'

Simone shook her head.

'Finding a new focus and doing something just for me that expended a lot of energy.

'Kind of like me learning to surf this past week?'

'Yeah, it was just a warm up to show you that anything's possible.'

'What, you mean I'm not a contender for the world title?'

They both laughed.

Simone sighed. 'I guess I'm not really sure what I want.'

'Trust me if you think about it enough you'll come up with something.'

'I take it you did?'

'Deb's parents had one of those insurance policies for her and when the payment was finalised they insisted that I take the money. They're nice people and they felt that as her husband it belonged to me. It wasn't a huge sum, but it was enough to give me a few options I wouldn't have had otherwise, especially considering I hadn't worked for months.'

'Pennies from heaven hey?'

Liam nodded. 'I've always loved hiking but Deb hated it. She was such an adrenaline junkie that walking for hours on end was just too slow for her. So I spent six weeks tramping around the South Island of New Zealand and I did the Overland Track down in Tassie. I met lots of great people, saw some amazing scenery and got my fitness back. Then I came home and started uni.'

'I think you're braver when you're younger.'

'Mrs Ryan, you're still young. Your kids don't need you as much now and you've got no financial problems. The world's your oyster.'

'I just never imagined my life would take this path.'

'I didn't either but it did and here we are. You *can* do it.'

Simone sighed wistfully. 'I hope so.'

Late that afternoon Simone felt nervous when she saw the small cheer squad assembled on the sand to watch her demonstrate her surfing skills. They were her children and while that may laugh with her, surely they wouldn't laugh at her. Or so she hoped.

Fortunately the swell was only average that day. As she paddled out Simone focused only on what she was doing and not on the bigger things that learning to surf had unveiled within her. She didn't care that riding a long board was considered by some to be the easy way out, it was the fact that she was even in the water that was important.

Simone had been in the water for about fifteen minutes when she saw the biggest wave of the afternoon coming. Her first instinct was to hang back and wait for a smaller one. None of the kids would think any less of her for it. But then she realised she had to give it a shot, even if she did wipe out.

I'm actually a bit excited, Simone realised as she started paddling. I'm still nervous, but I'm definitely excited.

As she had learned over the course of the week, there was something amazing about standing on a surfboard and riding a wave, no matter how much of an amateur you were. Pushing herself tentatively up to standing position, Simone planted her feet the way Liam had shown her. When she managed to stay on the board as the wave carried her forward, Simone couldn't help but raise her hands above her head in triumph.

I get it Andrew, she thought as the wave continued to carry her towards the shore. I finally understand why you liked to do this so much.

Simone could see all the kids on the sand and Liam standing in the shallows waving to her. And then as clear as the picture she could see before her, she heard Andrew's voice saying, 'That's the way, Simone,' which had been his favourite words of encouragement to her.

It was then Simone knew she had started to turn the corner.

The kids decided that a gourmet feast was in order for their last night in the house. Simone wasn't sure if it was by chance or by planning on their behalf that she and Liam were assigned to do the chopping and marinading while they walked into town to get the rest of the supplies.

'So, do you think Andrew would be proud of my new-found surfing skills?' Simone asked. 'Well, I guess that's a bit of a hard question, you didn't know him.'

Liam paused for a moment. 'Well, I did, actually,' he said.

'But you and Matthew didn't meet until this past year.'

'That's true, but I didn't meet him through Matt. When I was eighteen I collided with a surfboard fin and sliced my foot pretty badly. There were nerves and tendons involved so they were going to send me to Brisbane for specialised surgery. As luck would have it there was a group of surgeons on the Gold Coast at a conference and when my GP rang to ask advice about which hospital I should be sent to, one of the doctors volunteered to do the surgery that night. His name was Dr Ryan.'

Simone nodded. 'I remember that. Andrew told me about it. He said what a nice boy you were.'

Liam smiled. 'I guess I fooled him hey?'

They both laughed.

'He was so kind and reassuring and my parents were so grateful because he didn't charge for the surgery, even though it was done in a private hospital. He took care of the hospital bill and even sympathised with it being a surfing injury because he was a waxhead too.'

'I don't think people believed him when he said that, he just didn't have the look.'

'I must admit I was surprised. Anyway, my GP told me I should be very grateful that such a skilled surgeon fixed my foot. He said it was the best tendon repair he'd ever seen, given how mangled it was.

Dr Ryan came back specially to see me twice and gave me his home phone number. He said if the foot ever gave me problems I should ring him. It didn't, it healed perfectly.' Liam lifted his right foot to reveal three faint scars.

Tears prickled Simone's eyes, but she didn't let them fall. 'He was a wonderful man.'

Liam nodded. 'You're right, he was. When I first met Matt, I was struck with déjà vu because some of his facial expressions, his eyes and his voice reminded me of someone. It bugged me for a few days and it wasn't until I heard his surname that I put two and two together. It was so sad to hear that he died.'

Simone poured the marinade into a glass bowl. Liam got the beef strips out of the fridge. 'In answer to your earlier question, yes, he would be very proud,' he said.

Simone didn't mind that she woke with the kookaburras on their final morning. Wandering over to the window, she pulled the curtains open and took in the pre-dawn vista of a Queensland summers day.

Her father called it the grey light before daylight and said it was the most beautiful time of day. Looking out the window, she had to agree. Her parents had been worried about her; they would be so pleased to see the holiday had done her some good.

Simone walked down to the beach and sat on the sand in the beautiful dawn to watch the sun rise. Liam was right; she was going to have to go through her grief to eventually come to terms with it. But at the same time, she felt like a weight had been lifted from her shoulders.

Someone had said to her once that help can often come from the most unexpected source and she had lived that truth. Going back home did not seem so scary now and although she wasn't ready to acknowledge it completely, Simone had rediscovered hope for the future and a belief she could live an amazing life despite her great loss. For that she was truly grateful.

Tom

1997

*J*om McKay dismissed his grade eight Physical Education class and smiled wryly as they scurried away. Ten minutes ago, they'd assured him they couldn't jog four laps of the oval, but now that it was time to go home they were up and running. He took his time packing up the ageing athletics equipment and locked it in the sports shed before heading over to the staff room.

Rummaging in the fridge for his extra sandwich, Tom exhaled loudly when he remembered it was his turn for afternoon detention. After grabbing a stack of maths tests that needed marking, he spooned some coffee into his mug and stuck it under the tap on the urn.

Gullyview High School's Deputy Principal, Janice Brown, bustled into the staffroom. She extracted a can of Pepsi Max from the fridge and a straw from the bench in one fluid movement before turning to Tom. 'The thermostat is playing up on that again,' she warned. 'We've requested a new one, but…'

'As long as it's at least lukewarm it'll do. Please tell me you have a nice easy afternoon lined up for me.'

'It's the usual suspects I'm afraid – Chris, Jeffrey, Aiden as well as two senior boys and a few grade ten girls.'

'You're too kind, Mrs Brown. What's the essay topic?'

Janice popped open her soft drink and stuck the straw in. 'How I can make this school a better place,' she deadpanned before taking a long draught.

Tom shook his head. 'Well aren't I the lucky one today?'

The small demountable classroom that hosted detention had mismatched furniture and no ceiling fans. With the outside temperature in the low thirties, the badly ventilated room was stifling. Tom used brute strength to wrestle open the sliding window on the west side, where the sun was beating in.

One of the girls stared at him. 'That window has been stuck for sooo long,' she said, brushing her thick fringe out of her eyes. 'I don't think you're meant to open it.'

'Yeah, good luck getting it closed again,' Jeffrey Topper snickered.

'Just get on with your essays, thanks,' said Tom, inwardly conceding Jeffrey had made a good point.

Twenty minutes later Tom placed another test on the completed pile and lay his pen down on the desk scarred with graffiti, scratches and gouge marks. "Gullyview is a HOLE!" was scrawled in marking pen across the bottom corner. You've got that right, Tom thought. Then he felt a stab of disloyalty. No, disadvantaged was the correct description, and, he *had* volunteered to come out to Western Queensland for his first teaching post. Growing up in Coolangatta, he just hadn't realised how different life would be.

The first thing he'd had to get used to was being seen as an outsider.

'I've never had a surfer on my staff before,' Principal Karl Sullivan had told Tom at the end of his first week.

Tom was surprised to be pigeonholed so quickly. 'It's not like I'm wearing board shorts or calling everybody "dude",' he replied a little defensively. 'And just for the record, I've never had a ponytail.'

Karl smiled. 'I think it's the blond hair and blue eyes…and the diver's watch and maybe the Quicksilver stickers and surfboard racks on your car…'

'And the freckles, right?'

'Well, maybe,' Karl conceded. He paused for a moment before adding, 'and, of course, it is listed as a hobby on your resume.'

Tom's face reddened. 'Oh, yeah, so it is. But I still get the feeling that I'm not getting taken seriously around here.'

Karl chuckled softly. 'Tom, I'm afraid that sometimes the arrival of someone who is young and enthusiastic is seen as a threat by those who are insecure about themselves and their abilities. I know Gullyview High doesn't rate in the top ten wish list of graduate teachers' first postings, but if you put in some hard work you'll make a great foundation for your teaching career.'

Stretching back in his uncomfortable plastic chair, Tom extended his legs under the desk. At just under two metres tall, he was used to furniture that didn't cater for his height. He glanced around the room. Chris Lane, Aiden West and Jeffrey Topper were the problem children of grade nine. As the grade nine co-ordinator, that made them *his* problem children. Disruptive in class and troublemakers in the playground they were regulars at detention. As the year drew to a close, he couldn't help but dwell on how little an impact he'd had on the conduct of any of them.

'Don't even think about it Jeffrey,' Tom cautioned, as he saw the boy about to flick a rubber band across the room. Jeffrey shot him an innocent look and picked up his pen. With his curly red hair and freckled complexion, he carried off the innocent look with aplomb. Although the other two boys were physical opposites - Aiden very tall and well-built and Chris slight and shorter than average – they, in contrast to Jeffrey, had perfected the look that spelled out bad attitude.

When the clock hands reached three forty-five, the ten students were up and out of their seats within seconds.

'Okay, you can go. Hand in your essays on the way out, thanks,' Tom said.

The students filed past and threw pieces of paper in his direction. Most of them had only written half a page or less. Gathering the essays together, Tom shoved them and the maths tests into his backpack. Then he went over to tackle the window.

Although he jogged the short distance between school and the local pool, Tom was still five minutes late for his coaching session. Hurrying through the wonky, rusting turnstile his chest swelled a little at the sight of the students sitting on the edge of the pool. Most of them could barely make one lap when they started and now they were easily doing three-kilometre sessions.

'Hey guys,' he greeted them. 'Good to see you're all on time even if I'm not.'

'Hi Mr McKay,' they chorused.

Tom raised his eyebrows. 'I take it you did your stretches while you were waiting?'

A series of collective groans greeted this suggestion.

'Come on, just get it over with, you know why we need to do them.'

Tom shook his head as the group of fifteen stood up to stretch. They may have come a long way, but they were still kids and always eager to avoid unnecessary work. Leaving them to it for a moment, he reached into the equipment cage behind him and grabbed a stack of kickboards.

'All right two hundred kick then four hundred freestyle for warm up,' he said, handing out kickboards as they finished stretching.

The kids started swimming and Tom allowed himself a moment's breathing space as he put together a session in his head. He'd left in such a hurry he'd forgotten his training book. Some of his teaching colleagues couldn't understand why he put in the extra hours to run the swimming club, but for him it wasn't a burden. Working as a swimming instructor and coach had paid his way through uni, but he now found it just as rewarding as a volunteer.

After waving his students off, Tom got changed and dived into lane six. The coolness of the water was an immediate relief from the heat of the day and he swam the entire first length underwater. He loved to swim. No matter how he was feeling, being in the water and getting into the rhythm of swimming always helped him shut out the outside world, for a while at least.

Ninety minutes later, Tom cruised leisurely through his warm down laps, his strong, smooth stroke not wavering until he glided to the wall to end his four-kilometre session. Roger, the pool owner, gave him a wave as he rolled up a lane rope, and squatted down for a minute to have a chat.

'Are you sure you don't want me to time you? I reckon you could be a serious competitor in the one hundred butterfly.'

Tom pulled off his goggles and leaned against the pool wall. 'Nah, I don't think so. I'm just a PE teacher who likes to swim.'

'Well I don't often see people putting in the kind of sessions you do and it's great for the kids to be doing something constructive instead of just hanging around and getting into mischief.'

'Don't I know it? I just wish I could get more of them interested.' Setting up a school swimming club had been his first extra-curricular project the previous year and getting it to this stage had taken a lot of effort.

'I really am sorry we can't pay you for all your hard work.'

'Honestly mate, I don't care about the money. They're not still talking about shutting you down, are they?'

'Not for this summer at least. But unless we can get some money together for maintenance over winter, well, who knows?'

Hoisting himself out of the water, Tom picked up his towel and rubbed his hair. 'Man, they can't do that! Gullyview needs this place.'

'Yeah, you said it. We'll work it out somehow.' Roger finished coiling the lane rope and put it inside the equipment shed. Locking the door, he turned to face Tom again. 'My boy Ricky is really looking forward to the grade nine camp. It sounds like it's going to be fun.'

'Yeah, it should be,' said Tom as he slipped his shirt on. 'I'm pretty excited myself. It's a great way to finish off the year.'

Roger smiled wistfully. 'Half your luck. I'll see you around Tom,' he said with a farewell wave.

'Yeah, mate, see you.'

• • • • •

Karl caught up with Tom in the staff room later that week. 'How's it going with the three amigos?' he asked, as they sat at a table drinking coffee before school.

Tom's sigh said it all. 'Not great,' he admitted. 'In fact I'm a bit concerned about taking them on camp.'

'Yes, I've been considering that as well,' said Karl. 'I realise their detention record is appalling, but beyond that they haven't done anything too outrageous, have they?'

'No, not really. It's not like they're out stealing cars or plotting to burn down the school. It's their attitude that stinks.'

'And that can be a tough thing to correct.'

'Uh huh,' Tom agreed, taking his last swallow of coffee. 'Individually they're manageable but together they bring out the worst in each other.'

'Chris is the ringleader, right?'

'Yeah. He's the stirrer, then when things get heated he lets Aiden do all the punching.'

'So, Aiden doesn't incite trouble on his own then?'

'No, not really, he's pretty firmly under Chris's thumb even though he's bigger. He's sullen too, which is enough to put the other kids offside.'

Karl took another mouthful of coffee. 'So where does Jeffrey fit?'

'He's got the smart mouth and I reckon he thinks up most of the pranks. If he'd just apply that creative energy to his schoolwork he'd be top of the class.'

The shrill ring of the first bell ended their conversation. Tom strode over to the sink and gave his cup a quick rinse under the cold tap. 'So, will we let them go to camp?' he asked, as he dried his hands on his shorts.

Karl walked over to wash his own cup. 'Leave it with me Tom, we'll see what we can work out.'

After lunch the following Friday, Karl donned his hat and set off on his daily stroll. Although it was officially sports afternoon, there was little activity around the school. Most of the seniors had begged off, saying they needed to study for their upcoming exams. Judging by the hum of conversation and laughter coming from the classroom they'd gathered in, there was precious little study being done. Still, it was Friday afternoon and they were teenagers after all. No harm in letting them enjoy their last weeks in the insulated school environment, before they had to face the real world.

A half-hearted cricket game was underway on one end of the top oval, while a lacklustre netball match limped along down the other. Most of the girls who'd elected the sport were gossiping on the nearby grassy bank, while the players on the court giggled and mucked around. The two supervising teachers stood talking in the middle of the oval, calling out the occasional instruction, but not paying very close attention.

Heading down to the lower oval Karl saw the first real signs of energy being expended. Two volleyball games were underway, with six aside on each. Although the nets were sagging and there was more dirt than grass underfoot, the kids were actually throwing themselves into the games with enthusiasm. Karl smiled as he watched Tom simultaneously referee both games.

'All right court one, that's eleven to seven, Gavin you're serving, Angus try a spike next time, Susie remember your team gets three hits, you don't have to do it all yourself. Now court two you're seven to four...'

Karl felt exhausted watching him. He couldn't ever remember having that much energy, even at Tom's age. His youngest staff member had no real clue what a positive impact he'd had on the school since he'd been there. With his sporting background, he could have applied for a specialised coaching job in any of the prestigious private schools, so Karl was very grateful he'd joined the graduate placement queue instead.

In truth, he had initially wondered whether a serious athlete like Tom would cope with the day to day minutiae of school life in a disadvantaged area – the politics, the lack of resources, the general apathy of students and parents alike and having to teach outside his area of expertise – but he had. And that was why Karl had nominated him for the special project to finish off the year.

He felt a bit mean in a way. Tom was really looking forward to camp and would be disappointed that he couldn't go. But opportunities like this seldom came along and there was no doubt in his mind that Tom was the right man for the job.

• • • • •

The travel agent had raved about the beauty of the coastal road leading into Sunset Point and Tom wasn't disappointed. As his old Land Cruiser negotiated the gentle curves at the foot of the cliff that bordered the south end of the town, Tom stole his first glimpse of the sea. There was nothing quite like the sight of breaking waves in the sunshine and he had to keep reminding himself that this wasn't just a fun, carefree sojourn.

Chris, Aiden and Jeffrey had treated the proposal with suspicion when Tom and Karl first outlined it. They only agreed to participate after being told their other option was to attend school and assist the janitor with the end-of-year clean up.

Minor panic set in as Tom turned onto Blue Pacific Boulevard. He'd never heard of this particular trial program for behavioural management until Karl mentioned it to him and hadn't even started reading the thick tome that set out the guidelines. It had only arrived in the mail yesterday. He was required to submit a report at the end with detailed notes of his experiences. What if he was the only supervising teacher who didn't have a successful outcome? How would that impact his career?

Janice the deputy didn't hold out much hope of a good result. 'It sounds to me like you're rewarding bad behaviour,' she had said at the weekly staff meeting. Several of Tom's other colleagues had nodded their agreement.

'Yeah, who wouldn't like a two-week beach holiday?' said Carol, the art teacher.

Privately Tom agreed with them, but he couldn't very well admit that.

'The cornerstone of this program is removing kids with a bad attitude from their everyday environment,' Karl explained patiently. 'The more appealing the setting, the more likely a good result.'

Well, the setting was top notch, Tom acknowledged as he drove along the ocean front, so it looked like the rest was up to him.

The boys had slept for the last two hours of the drive and not one of them stirred when Tom pulled into the driveway of the beach house. Climbing out of the car, Tom stretched and rolled his neck several times, unsure if the stiffness was due to the long drive or tension. Walking over to the edge of the yard he took in the view and smiled. *Now* he was back in his comfort zone.

Bounding back to the car, Tom flung open the two back doors. 'Wakey, wakey guys, we're here!'

He ignored the bleary-eyed, glowering looks that came his way as he opened the rear door and unpacked the luggage. Eventually the boys roused themselves enough to stumble out of the car. When they began walking over towards the house, Tom cleared his throat loudly until they turned around.

Casting his eyes to the back of the car he said, 'I believe this is your gear guys. Sorry, we don't have a concierge service here.'

Hefting his own bag onto his shoulder, he walked over to unlock the door.

Once upstairs, Tom claimed his room and directed the boys down the hallway. 'Three boys, three rooms,' he said, 'you guys can take it from here.'

'Bags the end one,' Chris yelled, running down the hall with the other two in pursuit.

Rolling his eyes, Tom retreated into his room. It was no surprise that Chris wanted to be as far away from his as possible. While none of them were friendly towards him, there was a distinctly hostile vibe from Chris that was unnerving.

Hefting his bag onto the bed Tom pulled out the thick bound document entitled *Mellish/Whitson Trial Program For Behavioural Management.* Considering they were already here, he'd better get up to speed on what the program was about.

Ten pages in, he tried to ignore the knot of anxiety forming in his gut. According to the précis, the program focused heavily on self-direction for the students, within the framework of basic rules (which in this case was a zero-tolerance policy for disobedience). So, while they still had to do what he told them, the idea was to give them a lot of leeway.

The other main focus was "frank and open discussion" which he was also expected to participate in. He laughed out loud at some of the suggested topics and at the idea of he and the boys sitting down to some kind of group therapy session.

Hi, my name is Tom. I have size thirteen feet. I feel like a fish out of water in Gullyview. I think having freckles makes me look like a teenager and that's why people don't take me seriously. I have a knack of dating women who are completely wrong for me.

Yeah, right!

Sighing, he tossed the guidelines aside and dumped the contents of his bag on the bed. This was going to be a very long two weeks.

Tom was standing by the window looking longingly at the waves when Chris appeared at his door. Tawny haired, fine-featured and with a complexion as yet untouched by teenage acne, he was a good-looking kid. But when Chris glared his grey-green eyes cut like a laser.

'What are we supposed to call you while we're here? Uncle Tommy?'

Sensing the death stare Tom only glanced at Chris briefly before turning his attention back out the window. 'Mr McKay will be just fine. Or Sir, if you like.'

Chris leaned against the doorjamb. 'So why do you get the big room and the double bed? Is your girlfriend coming?'

'I get it because I'm the grown up. And no, I don't have a girlfriend at the moment.'

'What about the redhead with the sports car?'

Tom kept his face impassive. He had learnt very quickly that a teacher in a small town had little privacy, even on weekends or holidays. Wherever you went, there was always a familiar face, ready to take note of what you were doing and who you were with. The relationship in question had been brief (weren't they all?) and he thought they had moved in circles outside the local high school crowd. Apparently they had been spotted somewhere, obviously in her car.

'She dumped you, didn't she?' said Chris.

Jeez, Tom thought, kids today are *way* too astute. Dumped was an understatement but he wasn't telling Chris that. 'No, it was a mutual thing and none of your business, anyway. Did you guys sort the rooms out?'

'Yeah.'

Stepping away from the window, Tom pulled off his sweaty driving shirt and put on a clean one. 'Well if you're settled in, there's shopping to be done. I don't know about you but I'm starving.' He slid on his shoes and grabbed his wallet. 'You can give up on the dirty looks. I'm not leaving you here alone and we've got to eat. So get a move on.'

Shopping was a disaster. In the interest of promoting self-direction, Tom drove them to the large Woolworths supermarket at Rosethorn to provide plenty of food options, but it didn't help much. Besides junk food, the boys were unwilling to make any suggestions about what they wanted to eat, but quick to complain when he selected something they didn't like. They slouched around after Tom and concentrated mainly on sneaking inappropriate things into the trolley.

Tom managed to pull out the women's underwear, Huggies nappies, denture cleaner and the can of Pal Extra Chunky before they got to the checkout. But he didn't notice the home pregnancy test until the checkout operator scanned it. All three boys burst out laughing, causing the teenaged girl – whose name badge read Annie - to pause and look at them.

Chris motioned with his eyes towards Tom. 'That's why he's so on edge,' he said in a stage whisper.

Glaring fiercely at the boys, Tom reached over and snatched the tester out of the bag. 'I'm sorry could we please cancel this?' he said, through clenched teeth.

The boys continued to laugh among themselves and nudge each other as Annie scanned the rest of their order. With his broad-shouldered, muscular build, Tom liked to think he came across as imposing, but the boys didn't seem even slightly intimidated as he stood there with his arms folded and his face a stony mask.

'He's our prison warden,' Jeffrey said to Annie. 'We're just on day release.'

Her eyes widened and she gave Tom a nervous glance.

Exhaling sharply, Tom shook his head. 'Just ignore them,' he advised.

When they finally made it outside, it was dark with drizzling rain. While they were packing the car, it started to pour. The fifteen-minute drive back was silent and Tom wondered what they were going to do for the afternoon cooped up inside the house.

Crash!

The unmistakable sound of breaking glass echoed through the lounge room startling Tom, who had been immersed in the Mellish/Whitson guidelines. Looking up, he was dismayed to see a large hole in one of the ornate leadlight windows. He'd sent the boys onto the veranda to play handball, thinking they couldn't cause much damage out there. So much for that idea.

The young woman at the real estate office was efficient and friendly, but Tom could tell by the intake of breath on the other end of the phone that there was a problem. 'A downstairs window you say?' she asked.

'Yes, the one nearest the front door.'

'Well the leadlight ones take a few days to get replaced due to the specialised design. I can send the handyman around to board it up for you in the meantime. And I'm afraid there's an insurance excess because, of course, they're more expensive than regular glass.'

'Right, that's fine,' Tom said, knowing she was just doing her job.

An hour later and fifty dollars poorer, his earlier visions of shooting the breeze on the veranda, cooking a barbeque and laying down some ground rules in a "firm but friendly" manner (as per the guidelines) had disappeared. In fact, the more Tom read, the uneasier he became about just how he was going to manage this whole situation. His nerves were already shot after a mere few hours.

Amazingly the rain began to clear by quarter to six and Tom half-heartedly suggested the boys take the Frisbee down to the park adjacent to the beach. Surprisingly they showed some enthusiasm for the idea, although they made it clear that four was a crowd.

'Okay, you guys behave yourselves, alright? I can see you from here,' Tom said, as he saw the boys off at the back door.

Chris gave a military style salute that prompted a snicker from Jeffrey and Aiden as they headed down the back steps. 'We'll be on our very best behaviour, *Sir*,' he smirked.

Tom sank onto a canvas deckchair and closed his eyes.

The Gullyview Hotel's lone pool table was housed in a dingy, back corner of the pub. With torn felt scarred with cigarette burns and stained with beer, it had definitely seen better days. So, the boys were amazed when they set eyes upon the games area at the surf club. They stared in wonder at the brightly lit modern room that boasted four new-looking pool tables.

'Not bad, hey?' Tom said.

Jeffrey nodded eagerly and was about to say something when he caught Chris's warning look. 'It's okay,' he mumbled.

Tom rolled his eyes. 'Don't knock me over with enthusiasm. We could just go back to the house instead.'

'Well, if we're here, we may as well play,' Chris said. 'By ourselves.'

'All right, fine. But I've got to stay in here with you.' Tom reached into his pocket and retrieved a handful of one and two dollar coins. 'Knock yourselves out,' he said, dumping them on the table.

Settling onto a chair along the back wall, Tom yawned. So much for Mellish/Whitson's idea to use a fun activity to build an easy rapport with his charges, he thought sourly. They get to have fun and I have to sit by myself. What a great two weeks this is going to be.

Chris broke, scattering the balls in all directions. 'This could turn out better than we thought,' he said with a sly smile.

Jeffrey nodded. 'Yeah. I didn't realise we'd get to play pool, or have pizza – although I don't know why got you extra anchovies. They're gross,' he said, making a face. 'It took ages to pick them off.'

'Duh, Tommy doesn't like them.' Chris smacked his palm on his forehead.

'Oh, right.'

'Did you sneak into his room?' Chris asked Aiden, handing him his cue.

Aiden ran a hand through his spiky brown hair. 'I didn't get very long,' he said, his deep blue eyes darting nervously in Tom's direction, 'but I short sheeted his bed and knotted his shoelaces together.'

Chris nodded. 'Cool. We need to think up some better stuff though, to really make him sorry he brought us on *special* camp.'

'I don't think it was his idea.' Jeffrey lined up his shot. 'He doesn't seem that happy about being here either.'

'Commandant Karl probably *made* him come,' Chris said. 'That makes it much more interesting.' He took the cue back from Aiden. 'Did you find anything incriminating in his room, like booze or dope or something?'

Aiden was offended by this suggestion. 'Nuh, I didn't go through his stuff or anything. I'm not a snoop.'

'He's too straight for that anyway,' Chris scoffed.

'Yeah I reckon. There was some book about behavioural management on his bed, but I didn't get time to look at it.'

'Only he'd be dumb enough to think some book's gonna make us into good little boys,' Chris said.

They all snickered.

'What about the zero-tolerance thing that Mr Sullivan went on about?' Jeffrey wondered.

Chris motioned with his eyes to where Tom was leaning against the wall, his eyes drooping as he fought to stay awake. 'He's already sleeping on the job. I don't think we have to worry about that at all.'

The beach conditions were perfect the next morning. There wasn't a cloud in the sky and the gentle, rolling swell was just right to ease Tom back into surfing after an extended break. It was only quarter past five and the beach was practically empty. He grinned as he waded into the water and launched himself onto his board. Man, I've missed this, he thought, as his arms sliced cleanly through the cool, clear water.

Riding his first wave felt like coming home. The world seems like a totally different place from this vantage point, Tom decided as he got to his feet and glided along a wave face. Okay, so maybe I didn't get off to such a great start yesterday, but today is a blank canvas. Jumping off his board, he let the next wave wash over the top of him before surfacing again.

Paddling back out, Tom sat astride his board for a moment as two dolphins frolicked in the distance. Shifting his gaze back to shore, he glanced up at the house where his three charges were still dead to the world. I love Sunset Point, he decided, and I reckon things are going to work out just fine.

Tom's positive outlook took its first hit when he headed into the bathroom to have a shower. Opening the vanity unit, he noticed his navy blue toiletry bag had been substituted for a gaudy pink and yellow floral one.

'Very funny,' he murmured as he peered inside and took stock of the contents – a bottle of extra-strong anti-dandruff shampoo, a pink women's razor, a tube of toothpaste especially for severe bad breath and a bottle of cheap perfume that made his eyes water when he accidentally knocked the lid off.

'Ugh,' he said, waving his hand to dispense the fumes.

Still, as annoying as it was to have to replace all his stuff, this was a pretty mild kind of prank. Sorry boys, you're going to have to do a bit better than that to get a reaction from me, he decided, heading back to his room to get his wallet.

The next hit came later that morning. Typical teenagers, Chris, Aiden and Jeffrey were serious about their sleep. It was almost ten thirty by the time they appeared downstairs, freshly showered and reeking of Tom's missing deodorant.

Don't comment, Tom thought. They're just trying to bug you. Having ploughed through another three sections of Mellish/Whitson, he was ready to have their first structured discussion and didn't want to get off on the wrong foot.

Waiting until they finished their breakfast, Tom cornered them as they tried to escape back upstairs. 'Okay guys,' he said, seating himself at one end of the dining room table, 'pull up a pew.'

'What?' asked Jeffrey.

'Sit down.'

Not surprisingly, they congregated down the other end. It was a large table that could comfortably seat eight, so the distance was definitely a statement. Tom debated moving closer, but decided not to bother. Two years of teaching had bestowed him with the ability to project his voice.

'Right,' he began, doing his best to sound positive and enthusiastic. 'The purpose of this meeting is to talk about some…. uh, stuff.' Great start Tom, he thought, you got right to the point.

'What kind of *stuff*?' asked Jeffrey suspiciously.

Tom shrugged. 'Anything, really. Maybe there's something you guys want to talk about.'

Three blank expressions was the only response.

'Right,' he said again, glancing down at his notes. Deciding they were nowhere near exchanging confidences, Tom had edited the suggested list of questions down to inoffensive topics. 'So,' he began brightly, 'My middle name is Owen, so my initials are actually T.O.M.'

Only Jeffrey reacted. 'Oh, so it's like your name,' he said, then stopped when he noticed the still bland expressions of the others.

'Yeah,' Tom agreed wearily. That piece of trivia was always a good conversation starter. This was going to be like pulling teeth.

Fifteen minutes later the only information Tom had managed to elicit was that the boys hated school, thought Gullyview was a dump but marginally better than the neighbouring Porterville and that, in their opinion, Jeffrey was the star of the rugby league team. As team coach Tom had to agree. The kid could really play.

Hoping to maintain the conversational momentum this last topic had generated, Tom moved onto another of the more personal questions. 'Any of you guys have nicknames?' he asked. 'My mates call me Macca.'

Chris feigned a yawn. 'You mustn't hear it much then.'

Jeffrey and Aiden smirked.

Keeping his face neutral, Tom decided to press on. 'Ha ha. So, you guys always refer to each other by your correct names then?'

The boys exchanged grins.

'Yes?' Tom raised his eyebrows.

Jeffrey shook his head. 'Uh, I don't think we should tell you.'

Tom cast his mind back to the guidelines. Engage them, they suggested, show interest in what they find amusing. 'Come on, you can tell me.'

Jeffrey sniggered.

'Go on, tell him,' Chris said.

Jeffrey looked at the other two again before speaking. 'Well, sometimes Chris and I call each other wan....'

Tom held up his hand. 'I guess that was a stupid question.'

'This whole conversation is stupid,' Chris said.

More smirking and nudging followed. Jeffrey made a face. 'Can we *please* go now?'

Tom folded his arms and stared straight ahead. 'Yeah, you can go.'

Having somehow heard about the skateboard park at the southern end of town, the boys elected to go there for the afternoon. Upon returning home they retreated upstairs, leaving Tom alone in the lounge room, feeling like an uncool parent waiting outside a school dance.

Sick of sitting in silence, he turned on the radio. Boy, this thing is a museum piece, he thought as he fiddled with the old-fashioned dial. He smiled when he came across the broadcast of the one-day cricket test from The Gabba, hearing his grandfather's voice in his head. 'Forget about the idiot box Thomas,' he always said. 'A cricket game is much better on the wireless.'

Pop's right, he thought, as he listened to the energetic commentary. This is pretty cool. Extending the foot rest on the recliner he settled back to listen.

At seven o'clock the boys came downstairs, plonked themselves on the couch and looked expectantly at the dining room table. Tom continued to listen to the sports roundup on the radio, ignoring the pointed glances. If they wanted to eat they could self-direct into the kitchen, he decided. The food kitty couldn't afford any more take away.

Finally Jeffrey broke the impasse. 'Uh, Mr McKay, we're really hungry. When's dinner?'

Tom turned the radio off. 'Dinner is whenever you want it to be.'

'Okay, we'd like it now,' Jeffrey said.

'Fair enough, let's go into the kitchen and get started.'

'All of us?' Jeffrey asked.

'Yes, all of us. It's a big kitchen, we'll fit.'

'But none of us know how to cook, and we don't even want to cook.' Jeffrey crossed his arms.

Tom held up his hands, palms out. 'Hey, if you don't want to cook, then don't cook. But just so you know, the only way you'll get a hot meal is if you help prepare it.'

Tom snapped the footrest down, stood and walked casually into the kitchen. He started whistling as he peered into the fridge. He didn't know how to cook when he was fourteen either, but they didn't need to know that.

Appearing in the kitchen ten minutes later, Jeffrey leaned against the bench with his arms folded. 'You can't *starve* us.'

Tom flipped his steak. 'The kitchen is full of food Jeff, help yourselves.'

Jeffrey retreated without another word.

Having discovered Jenga on the games shelf, the boys began a game and ignored Tom as he sat at the table and ate his meal.

Half an hour later the three of them went into the kitchen and made a great production of opening a tin of baked beans. After a few staged arguments and several loud comments that they couldn't work out how to heat them up, they ate them cold from the tin.

Tom knew he was being tested and, despite the boys' best efforts to bait him into saying something, he stayed quiet. He didn't utter a word when they prepared themselves thickly-spread peanut butter sandwiches or when they poured a quarter of the bottle of chocolate topping each onto their ice cream.

Choose your battles, he thought, as he read the sports pages in the paper. Don't let them know they're rattling you.

Waiting until the boys had left the kitchen, Tom went in to make himself a coffee. Taking in the mess they had left behind, he closed his eyes and took a deep breath. Don't react, he chanted softly, as he poured boiling water on the instant Nescafe and stirred in two teaspoons of sugar. Picking up his drink, he headed back into the lounge room and made himself comfortable on the recliner. Still involved in their Jenga battle, the boys didn't look up.

Well done, Tom, I think you're winning this round, he thought, picking up the paper again. It was only when he took his first mouthful of coffee that Tom's resolve slipped. 'Ugh,' he moaned, grimacing. Stomping back into the kitchen, he tipped the horrid tasting brew into the sink. Hearty laughter rang out as spat out the remnants and rinsed his mouth.

'Yeah, ha, ha,' he said, as he emerged back into the lounge room. 'Salt in the sugar basin, that's really original.'

A fresh round of laughter erupted. Clenching his fists, Tom retreated onto the veranda to simmer down - which gave the boys the perfect opportunity to sneak upstairs and sprinkle sand in his bed.

• • • • •

So many elements went into the perfect tube ride – a suitable stretch of coastline, the right offshore wind, being in the ideal location in the water and having the necessary level of experience. The following morning was one of those occasions when all the elements came together seamlessly.

It was another perfect late spring day when Tom emerged onto the beach. He was just wading into the water when a group of three men holding surfboards approached him. 'Hey mate, you look like you know your way around a decent surf break,' a guy about his own age said.

'Yeah, I do,' Tom replied.

'Well, if you don't mind jumping off the rocks, head out past the lighthouse. You can always get a pretty decent ride out there, but it's really pumping today with that wind.'

'Thanks for the heads up.' Tom gave a friendly wave, then walked back out of the water and headed north.

Fifteen minutes later, he was in heaven. The Sunset Point shoreline extended between the rocky outcrop on which the lighthouse was perched and the southern cliff. Both offered it protection from the larger swell. Out beyond those boundaries, Tom could feel the power of the open ocean.

Clambering back onto the rocks for the fifth time, he scrambled along the uneven surface, making his way back to the jump off point.

Tom sensed the amazing wave before he saw it and wasted no time leaping back into the water and paddling furiously. His arms burned with exertion as cool water splashed over him, but he kept up the frenzied pace. Amazingly he was going to have this beauty all to himself.

Feeling the wave carry him forward, he jumped to his feet and rode it for a few seconds. It was only when it began to break that he saw the barrel forming. Grinning from ear to ear, Tom positioned himself in the hollow section of the wave and began to journey through it.

He was in the green room!

Words could never adequately describe those few perfect seconds of being surrounded by water, while gliding along a wave. Nothing could touch you in there. Not Gullyview, or the boys or Mellish/Whitson's guidelines. It was like being in suspended animation.

Inevitably it had to end. Although he did his best to exit cleanly, Tom wiped out before he made it back out onto the open wave face. He stayed under the water a few seconds before bursting through the surface, a grin still plastered on his face.

A tube ride was never long enough, but while it lasted there was no place on earth like it.

The mellow feeling had all but passed by the time Tom got the boys together for another discussion at midday. After another late night playing pool, they didn't emerge until after eleven. By then he'd already read *The Sunday Mail* from cover to cover, washed his sandy sheets, straightened up the lounge room and finally trudged through the last section of M/W.

This time Tom parked himself in the middle of the table, which forced the boys to sit opposite him. It was the only way they could sit together but avoid at least one of them sitting beside him. Having got nowhere with the personal info discussion, he'd decided to move on to a specific behavioural issue.

When they were finally seated, he started playing with the object in his hand, rolling it back and forth with his thumb. When that got no reaction, he grasped it between his thumb and forefinger and swung it back and forth. So caught up in looking anywhere but at him, it took the boys a while to notice what he was holding. Tom had to hide a smile when he saw Jeffrey nudge Aiden, who in turn nudged Chris and then all three sets of eyes focused on his hand. Finally Jeffrey spoke.

'Uh, what's that Mr McKay?' he asked in a feigned casual tone.

Tom lay it down on the table. 'Oh, I think you know Jeff.'

'Ah, now I see, it's a lighter.'

Tom picked the lighter up again and flicked it to life, letting the flame dance for a moment before taking his thumb away from the button. Act casual, the guidelines said. If you don't make it such a big deal, it takes away the element of defiance in the behaviour. Having never lit a cigarette in his life, it had taken fifteen minutes of practice to get the action right.

Chris spoke next. 'So why have *you* got a lighter?'

'I was hoping to bum a smoke.'

Aiden and Chris managed to keep a straight face but Jeffrey couldn't. 'Yeah, right,' he laughed.

'What? Are you saying I'm not cool enough to smoke?' Tom asked, flicking the lighter on again. Unfortunately he tilted it too much and the flame grazed his knuckle. 'Ow!' he yelped, dropping it on the table.

This time the other two joined in Jeffrey's laughter.

Tom knew he'd lost the round, but pressed on regardless. 'So, which one of you guys lost your lighter?'

No reaction. He saw the slightest eye movement from Jeffrey, but nothing he could act on. Damn. He'd obviously picked the wrong colour when he bought it at the shop that morning.

Another twenty minutes of fruitless conversation followed. Seeing that none of them would even admit to smoking, getting them to explain why they felt the need to do it was futile. Two days in and he was losing ground rapidly. Whoever Mellish and Whitson were, they'd obviously never sat down with fourteen-year-old boys and had this type of pointless exchange.

Despite the smug looks from across the table, Tom had one last stab at gaining the upper hand. 'So, if none of you smoke, why do you have nicotine stains on your fingers?' he asked. None of them actually did, but he was already on the ropes. Why not have the last word?

Still no response, but at least he had the satisfaction of seeing each of them surreptitiously studying their hands before he stood and left the table.

The second day of self-direction was about as successful as the first, Tom decided that evening as he sat on a recliner flicking through a surfing magazine. Like yesterday Chris, Aiden and Jeffrey had lounged around, leaving the house only to go back to the skate park. They hadn't even set foot on the beach yet. At this rate the two weeks would be up without any progress whatsoever.

Convinced the cooking boycott would last much longer, Tom was amazed when Jeffrey appeared in the kitchen as he started his meal preparations. 'You here to help?' he asked.

Jeffrey nodded.

Tom handed him an onion and a chopping board. 'I'm going to throw a few snags on the barbie and you've gotta have onions to go with it.'

'Yeah, good idea,' Jeffrey agreed.

Eying him curiously, Tom wondered what had prompted the attitude change. He continued to watch for the next few minutes as Jeffrey diligently did everything asked of him. You're too suspicious Tom, he chided himself. Maybe the kid is just hungry.

Tom was even more surprised when Chris and Aiden sat down at the table to eat their peanut butter sandwiches with him and Jeffrey. There's something not quite right about this, he thought, with a slight sense of unease.

Jeffrey jumped up from the table and returned a minute later with the tomato sauce.

'Good thinking Jeff.' Tom smiled as he slathered a huge dollop on his bread, before piling on some onions and then a sausage.

The intense heat hit him like a bolt of lightning.

It began a couple of seconds after his first bite and travelled along his tongue and down his throat like a river of molten lava.

His mouth was on fire!

'Aaahhh!' Tom yelled, before spitting his food out. It didn't help. In fact the temperature in his mouth seemed to intensify. His eyes began to water. He started coughing. Sweat formed on his brow. Desperately, Tom reached for his water glass and drained it in one frenzied gulp. Still no respite. In fact, he was sure that steam must be escaping from his ears.

Amidst his severe discomfort, Tom vaguely registered the boys doubled over with laughter as they sat on the opposite side of the table. Too late he noticed that Jeffrey's food was bereft of any kind of condiment.

'What IS that?' he gasped, reaching for the plastic squeeze bottle.

'Tomato sauce,' Jeffrey guffawed.

'Like hell it is,' Tom wheezed, frantically reaching for Aiden's water glass and draining it as well. The bottle said Heinz Tomato Sauce all right but there wasn't a hint of tomato in what he'd just swallowed.

Sweat was running down Tom's face now and dripping onto his t-shirt. He picked up the edge of the tablecloth and used it to mop his brow, while racking his brain to remember what you were supposed to drink to neutralise the effects of spicy foods. Finally it came to him. Milk!

Staggering into the kitchen, Tom flung open the fridge, his eyes widening when he saw the empty space in the door. Where the bloody hell was the milk? How many times did he have to tell the kids to put it back in the fridge?

Tom's eyes darted around the kitchen, finally settling on the blue and white carton sitting open on the bench, right beside an empty jar of Extra Hot Chilli and Jalapeno salsa. Upending the carton, he gulped down several mouthfuls, wincing at the warm, slightly sour taste.

Eventually, after a large bowl of ice-cream, the heat began to dissipate and Tom started to cool down as well. Glad he'd stayed in the kitchen, he thought about what he'd read in the guidelines that morning. Reason with the kids if they try and get under your skin. Explain why you don't like their negative behaviour. It wasn't what his gut was telling him to do, but then again, yelling at them wouldn't have any impact either, and he figured that force-feeding them the left-over salsa wasn't really an option, as tempting as it may be.

In any case, they'd disappeared upstairs by the time he re-emerged, obviously guessing it might be a good idea to take cover.

Proud of how calm he was when he headed upstairs later to go to bed, Tom fought to stay composed when he came across the slimy strands of seaweed on his towel. Marching into his room, he pulled back the bedcovers and made sure there was no sand or anything else lurking there.

They've finally left my bed alone, he thought as he climbed between the sheets. I guess they put so much energy towards the sauce prank they didn't have time tonight. Reaching across to plump his pillows, his heart almost stopped when he saw the long, brown snake coiled up underneath the one on the right.

'Oooh shiiit!' Tom shouted, banging his arm hard on the wooden headboard and stubbing three of his toes on the floor as he leapt out of bed. He'd hated snakes ever since encountering an aggressive red-bellied black under his house when he was eight.

Stay calm, he thought frantically. Make no sudden moves. Edge quietly away and get the hell out of the room.

It was only when he crept closer to the door that he heard the muffled laughter outside and realised they'd got him, again.

Right! he decided as he stomped back over to his bed. Enough of this malarkey! Grabbing the offending fake reptile, he hurled it out his bedroom window with great ferocity.

It was time for Mr McKay to take charge.

• • • • •

The high-pitched shriek of the alarm penetrated deep into Tom's brain when it burst into life at four am. Still in the vestiges of a deep sleep, he thought for a moment that the boys must be playing another trick on him. Fumbling groggily in the dark, he thumped the bedside table five times before finally making contact with the off button.

Tom was just settling back to sleep, when he remembered he'd set the alarm himself. Using all his reserves of willpower, he rolled out of bed and forced himself upright. Pulling his clothes on, he stumbled into the bathroom and splashed cold water on his face. Catching a glimpse of his reflection in the mirror he was pleased to see he looked more awake than he felt.

Stomping down the hallway a few minutes later, Tom banged on each bedroom door. 'Rise and shine boys! Rise and shine!'

When that approach got no response, he poked his head into Jeffrey's room and turned on the light.

Jeffrey pulled the covers over his head. 'It's the middle of the night.'

'No, it isn't - it's ten past four and dawn is not far away,' Tom replied brightly, banging on the wall again. He targeted Jeffrey first, as his room was closest.

'We're not getting up, it's too early.'

'Then we'll get packed up and be back at school before morning-tea time. Either way you'll have to get out of bed.'

Jeffrey pulled the covers back and sat up, squinting in the light. 'What? Why would you take us back to school?'

'Zero tolerance Jeff, as Mr Sullivan explained before we left. If you disobey me it's all over, whether it's a big crime or a small one. You've got ten minutes to be downstairs.'

The protests started the moment they pulled into the car park at the base of the southern cliff.

'We can't climb a cliff,' Jeffrey whined.

'It's too dark to see,' Aiden added.

Chris just sat there with his arms folded. 'I'll wait here,' he said.

Tom swivelled to face the back seat. 'Out!' he ordered.

It was a well-designed walking path that curved around the cliff, with only a few difficult stages. Tom tuned out the complaints as he walked briskly along the track. He was enjoying the physical challenge. If the boys hadn't been there, he would have run parts of it.

They made it to the top just as the first light of day appeared over the horizon. The boys were amazed to see several other people clustered on the rocky platform.

'Who in their right mind does this kind of stuff?' Jeffrey asked.

'Weirdos,' grumbled Aiden.

'Come on. Are you telling me that there wasn't something satisfying about doing that climb and then being here to watch one of nature's most amazing shows?'

All three boys shook their heads and sat down. Tom rolled his eyes. 'Sorry, I forgot you can't admit to liking something so wholesome. Ah well, I guess we could try the north track next time, it goes straight up the other side there', he said, pointing. 'About 600 steps.'

Jeffrey paled. 'It's just too early to get excited. But the sunrise is good,' he said, turning his attention to the flaming orange ball now visible above the water.

'Yeah, not bad at all,' said Tom.

While Chris and Aiden parked themselves on the couch as soon as they as they got inside, Jeffrey followed Tom towards the kitchen. Chris and Aiden exchanged surprised glances.

'Hey Topper, what are ya doing?' Chris hissed.

Jeffrey paused and turned around. 'Duh, cooking breakfast,' he said. 'Didn't you hear Mr McKay say he's making bacon and eggs *and* French toast? I'm starving.'

'We're not cooking remember?' Chris reminded him.

'Well you guys aren't, but I helped him last night, remember? My boycott is over.'

Chris shook his head. 'That was just to set up the sauce, idiot.'

Jeffrey hesitated, looking first at Chris and then towards the kitchen where the sounds of bacon frying could be heard. 'But that's not how a boycott works. Once you give in, you give in.' He glanced over at Aiden for support, but only got a shrug in reply.

Chris glared at him. 'Don't do it!'

'But I'm *really* hungry.'

'Then eat some more baked beans.'

The enticing aroma of cooking bacon began to drift into the lounge room. Tom stuck his head around the door. 'Hey, what's keeping you Jeff? I could use some help in here.'

Jeffrey didn't need much convincing. Ignoring Chris's glower, he murmured, 'I hate baked beans,' and walked into the kitchen.

It was a quiet breakfast. Chris and Aiden sat down one end of the table to eat their cereal and toast. Obviously in the bad books, Jeffrey sat in the middle. With the memory of the salsa still fresh in his mind, Tom chose the other end, to eliminate the possibility of any food tampering.

Once they'd finished eating Tom produced a piece of paper and a pen. 'Okay guys, it's time to draw up a chore chart.'

Ignoring the hostile glares that came his way he explained what had to be done each day to keep the house liveable.

'You're not going to make us clean our rooms as well, are you?'

Jeffrey moaned.

'No. That's up to you guys. You can have a rotting compost pile of dirty clothes a mile high in there if you want – but the dishes, bathroom and downstairs are non-negotiable.'

Chris eyeballed him. 'So where are your chores, *Mr McKay*?'

'I will do the washing, clean the veranda and maintain the food supplies.'

The boys were silent for a moment, eyeing each other glumly.

'And we have to start this *now*?' Jeffrey asked, eyeing the mess in the kitchen he'd helped to create.

Tom nodded.

Eventually, after an extended rock/paper/scissors contest, Chris and Jeffrey slouched into the kitchen to tackle the dishes. Aiden was incensed when Tom handed him the broom. 'But you swept the floor yesterday,' he said.

'Yeah, and we'll do it again tomorrow. The downside of being this close to the beach is that you can't escape the sand.'

Zero tolerance was a great thing, Tom decided, as Aiden grudgingly snatched the broom and he went outside to straighten up the veranda.

The mood was grim in the bathroom an hour later. Jeffrey and Aiden were making a half-hearted attempt to clean up while Chris sat on the floor, leaning against the wall. 'It's that book he's reading,' he said. 'It's got to be.'

'You don't reckon it was because of the snake?' Jeffrey asked, using Tom's towel to wipe a puddle of water off the floor.

Chris shook his head. 'Nah, he's too embarrassed to even mention that. It's got to be the book.'

Aiden wiped a glob of toothpaste off the sink with his t-shirt. 'But what can we do about it?'

'Well, we've got to get the book obviously,' Chris said.

'But how?' Jeffrey wondered.

'Well Aiden's the only one who knows what it looks like. So, I guess it's going to be his job.' Chris smiled insincerely at his friend.

'Oh no, I'm not going in his room again,' Aiden protested. 'Haven't you noticed how he watches us really closely now? It's too

190

risky.'

'He can't watch us every single moment,' Chris assured him. 'As soon as the coast is clear that book is going to go mysteriously missing.'

The heat was intense that afternoon, so they headed down to the beach as soon as their substantial lunch had settled. Aiden had caved in and helped with preparation when he realised hamburgers were on the menu, although Chris had stood firm.

Jeffrey and Aiden headed right for the waves, but Chris hung back. Tom watched as he spread his towel in the shade of the lifeguard tower and sat down.

'Not coming in?' he asked, dropping his own towel on top of the untidy heap the other boys had made.

Chris shook his head. 'Swimming is for girls.'

'Each to their own,' Tom replied easily. 'Come and join us if you get too hot.' After wading through the shallows, he dolphin dived smoothly through the smaller waves and swam out to the breakers. The coolness of the water was refreshing under the heat of the sun and he relaxed instantly as the motion of the waves bobbed him up and down.

After about ten minutes, some bigger sets started rolling in and Tom glanced around to see where the boys were. They were country kids after all and weren't used to swimming in the ocean. He spotted Aiden in the shallows. He was patting a dog that a young boy was holding on a leash. He scanned the sand but still couldn't see Jeffrey. A frisson of alarm hit.

When Tom had delivered the surf safety lecture earlier, Jeffrey had rolled his eyes and assured him he was a good swimmer. What was he thinking, taking a fourteen-year-old boy at his word? A boy who was full of false bravado at that.

Tom's heart began to pound. He moved closer to shore and studied all the wet heads bobbing up and down. Being such a hot day the patrolled area was packed. Jeffrey's bright red hair and matching red rash vest should have made him easily visible, yet there was no trace of him.

Tom took another quick glance at the sand. Chris was lying on his towel now and Aiden was still playing with the dog. No Jeffrey.

Wading to shore, Tom stood in the shallows to get a better view of the shoreline. Shading his eyes with both hands, he looked to the north, then the south. There he was! Jeffrey was afloat and didn't seem to be panicking, but a rip was pulling him further out by the second. Adrenalin surged as Tom ran further down the water's edge and then out into the waves.

Jeffrey frowned as Tom approached him. 'It's not time to go in yet,' he said. 'We've only been here for a little while.'

'You're outside the flags Jeff; go back to shore and into the patrolled area like I told you to.'

'Okay, fine.' Throwing Tom a withering glance, Jeffrey started swimming towards the beach. It didn't take long for him to realise he was going nowhere fast. Stopping for a moment, he looked over at Tom. 'I'm stuck,' he said, panic creeping into his voice. 'The water is pushing me backwards.' Gamely he struck out again, and then came up coughing after copping a mouthful of water.

Tom swam closer. 'You didn't listen when I was talking about rips. You can't go directly back to shore; you have to swim out of it first. Head over this way and then in.'

Intent on changing direction, Jeffrey didn't notice the huge wave rolling in, nor did he hear Tom's warning to dive under. Surfacing in the white wash a few seconds later, Jeffrey started thrashing around. 'I'm sinking! I can't stay up!' he yelled.

Knowing another big wave would finish the set, Tom headed towards him as fast as he could. 'Duck under Jeff,' he shouted as the next wave thundered in.

Taking a breath, Jeffrey submerged but was barely able to stay afloat when they both surfaced. He reached out and tried to grab Tom as soon as he got within striking distance. 'Help me, Mr McKay!' he pleaded.

Tom backed away slightly. 'I'm going to help you mate, but you need to stop panicking. If you grab me, you'll take us both under. We're right now, there's a lull, so I'm going to tow you across, all right?'

Seeing the waves ease off, Jeffrey calmed down, allowing Tom to assist him out of the pull of the rip and back to where he could touch the bottom. Pale faced, he walked the rest of the way back to the shore. 'I think I'll go sit with Chris for a while,' he mumbled.

'Okay, go ahead but remember you have to stay between the flags when you're in the water.'

Jeffrey nodded and walked away. Tom watched him go, feeling both relieved that he was all right and annoyed that he hadn't bothered to thank him. As Tom stood there, a lifeguard came up beside him.

'Jim Stewart,' the man said, extending his hand. 'I'm in charge around here and just wanted to say that was a good save. I'm always impressed when someone can do an old-school tow without the aid of a tube.'

'Thanks,' Tom replied. 'I'm Tom McKay,' he said, reaching over to shake Jim's hand, noticing that the other man was of similar height to him. It wasn't often that he spoke to someone without having to look down.

'Looks like you've had a bit of experience then?'

'Yeah, you could say that. I started nippers when I was five and patrolling at thirteen. I can't remember a time I wasn't involved in surf lifesaving.'

'Are you a patrol captain yet?'

'Yeah, I have been for a few years now.'

'Which beach?'

'Coolangatta.'

Jim nodded. 'Just on the right side of the border, hey?'

'Oh yeah, I'm a Queenslander all right,' Tom said.

'The kid was lucky you were watching him.' Taking a closer look at Tom, Jim nodded. 'You're staying up at the house with the juvenile delinquents, right?'

'That's overstating it a bit. I'm doing some behavioural management.'

'They're from out bush somewhere, aren't they?'

'Yeah, Gullyview, it's about four hours west.'

'That's a bit of a drive to do patrol.'

Tom laughed. 'Yeah, well, I do a few swaps to make up my hours in the school holidays. My brother and I share the PC duties.'

'Sounds like a good compromise.'

'Yeah, it is. I didn't want to have to give it up while I'm out in the wild west.'

Jim scanned the water for a moment before speaking again. 'I thought country kids were well behaved, being so far away from the evils of the big cities.'

'Well, Gullyview used to be a booming place once, but when the mine closed it left a big economic hole, so there's high unemployment, lack of resources - the usual social problems.'

'They're not going to cause any trouble around here, are they?'

'Not if I can help it. It's their attitudes I'm working on, they're not going to terrorise the town.'

Trying not to be obvious Tom looked over to the tower and was relieved to see Chris and Jeffrey sitting on their towels minding their own business.

'Not a peep out of him so far, but I've been watching.'

'I can assure you, any trouble and we'll be heading home.'

The boys were not happy when they realised they wouldn't be going to the surf club every night to play pool. Tom knew he'd made a mistake in setting that precedent on the first two nights. He tried to tune out their nagging as they sat in the lounge room after dinner that night.

'There's nothing to do without a TV,' whined Jeffrey, 'and we all really like pool.'

'You guys have cleaned me out - two bucks a game starts to add up when you play for three hours a night.' Tom picked up the free community newspaper and started reading an article about fundraising efforts for a proposed bowls club. Glancing up to see three sullen faces staring at him he said, 'Well, if you're prepared to spend your cigarette money, we can go.'

Only Jeffrey flinched, but quickly recovered. 'We don't smoke,' he said.

'The Wiggles Movie is playing at the cinema,' Tom suggested.

Jeffrey was highly insulted by this remark. 'That's not even funny.'

'Sorry, I forgot you guys have such a sophisticated sense of humour. I mean all your pranks, they're *much* more mature.'

The boys eyed each other and smirked. Tom went back to the newspaper. Once he finished reading, Tom looked up at the games shelf. 'How about a game of Scrabble or Trivial Pursuit or Pictionary?'

The silence was deafening.

'Cards?' Tom said, walking over and picking up a deck. He noticed a mild flicker of interest from Jeffrey, but knew it would take time before any of them stopped pouting. Oh well, there's no reason I can't do something, he decided, emptying the cards out of their box.

Jeffrey wandered over after a while. 'What are you playing?' he asked, examining the stacks of cards lined up on the table.

Tom scratched his head, searching in vain for another possible move. 'Solitaire.'

'You mean like the computer game?' Jeffrey was astonished. 'Did somebody work out how to play it with real cards?'

Tom chuckled. 'Other way around Jeff. Believe it or not, people were playing this with real cards long before the first PC was invented.'

'But what do you do when you can't win?'

'Watch and learn.' Tom scooped up the cards, shuffled and re-dealt. Jeffrey found another deck of cards on the shelf and after getting directions began playing at the other end of the table. After a while Tom suggested they play Gin Rummy.

Jeffrey's head snapped up. 'Is that a drinking game?'

'No, I'm afraid not, but it is fun,' Tom said. 'Come on I'll show you.'

Jeffrey learnt the rules quickly. After a couple of rounds, he started winning games, which reinforced Tom's view that the kid had a sharp brain that just needed to be channelled in the right direction.

Jeffrey burrowed under his pillow when Tom flung his door open at six thirty the next morning. 'Couldn't we wait until, like, seven thirty?' he pleaded.

'Nope. You know the drill Jeff, you've got ten minutes.' Tom felt he was being generous letting them sleep in this long. He'd already been for a surf and had a pre-breakfast snack, and was enjoying sliding into the summer morning routine he had grown up with.

Tom immediately noticed the flat tyre on his car when they walked down the front steps. 'How peculiar,' he said sarcastically. 'I wonder how that could have happened.' He eyed each boy closely, but got no reaction from any of them. 'Just as well we don't need the car this morning,' he said, pasting on a fake smile.

The boys followed him despondently as he strode into town but brightened when they arrived at the bicycle hire shop.

'Cool,' Jeffrey said.

Aiden and Chris didn't say anything, but Tom could tell they liked the idea as well.

An attractive young woman appeared in the office seconds after the melodic ping on the door announced their arrival. Her name badge read Naomi. 'Morning guys!' she said, with an infectious grin.

Tom's eyes lit up. 'Hi,' he replied, returning the smile. This was an unexpectedly nice start to the day. When he'd rung to make the reservation, he'd spoken to a cranky-sounding older man with a hacking smoker's cough.

Naomi consulted the open diary on the counter. 'You're the school kids, right? Dad said your teacher rang, in fact I thought he was coming with you.'

All three boys burst out laughing.

'I *am* the teacher,' Tom said, feeling his face redden. 'My name's Tom.'

Naomi's hand flew to her mouth. 'Oh, I'm sorry. You just look really young…and your hat…'

Tom reached up and ripped off his Gullyview High cap, smoothing down his hair the best he could.

'Right,' said Naomi as she reached for a clipboard with a form on it. 'I just need some ID and a signature down the bottom of the page.'

Pulling out his wallet, Tom removed his licence and slid it across the counter. Naomi looked up and smiled, then looked up again. Tom shot her back a lazy grin.

'Okay, do you have a local contact number?' Naomi asked, glancing up at Tom again and making some kind of signal with her eyes.

Ah, that's a clever way to get my number without being obvious Tom thought. Sure, I can play along. 'Uh, I don't know it off hand, but we're staying at the Beach House.'

'Oh, no problem then.' Naomi brushed her hair off her forehead and tilted her head slightly to the right.

Tom raised his eyebrows in reply, trying to convey that he was flattered by the attention but not in a position to flirt back.

'All right, just head out the back there and I'll be right with you.'

Tom shepherded the boys into the storage room that housed several rows of helmets as well as the bikes themselves. Naomi joined them about a minute later, pressing a folded piece of paper into Tom's hand as she walked past. 'Your *receipt*,' she said.

Wow, she's really keen, thought Tom. She's already got my number and now she's giving me hers as well. Waiting until the boys were caught up in choosing their bikes he unfolded the piece of paper.

"You have lipstick on your forehead," it read. Mortified, Tom made his way back into the office and peered at his reflection in the mirror hanging near the door. He did indeed have a thick red stripe of lipstick smeared across his forehead. Flipping his cap over, he ran his finger around the rim, not surprised to feel a thick, waxy residue. Jamming it on his head, he strode back into the other room.

Right, this was going to be one bike ride those boys wouldn't forget!

Chris, Aiden and Jeffrey could barely keep up with Tom as he flew around the flat sections of Sunset Point, but followed him eagerly enough, determined to showcase their own bike-riding skills.

They were much less keen, however, to tackle the hilly north section of the town. They baulked as Tom turned into Wave Crest Avenue, one of the steepest streets.

Chris's face was red and sweaty as he rolled to a stop and crossed his arms. 'We're not riding up there!' he declared.

'Okay, then we'll head home after breakfast,' Tom replied, as he turned his bike around.

'You can't send us home because we can't do something.' Chris scowled and stared over at Tom. 'That's discrimination.'

Tom met his gaze. 'No, but I can if you won't at least try to do it.'

Jeffrey was still trying to catch his breath. 'All right, we'll try,' he panted, 'right guys?'

'I don't know, I think going home sounds good about now,' Chris said.

'Yeah,' Aiden echoed.

Tom stood his ground. 'Up to you.'

The boys talked in a huddle for a few minutes but eventually agreed to go.

Famished after the ride, Tom bounded up the front steps and unlocked the door. Holding it open, he watched in amusement as the boys staggered inside and collapsed on the couch. Retreating into the kitchen, he opened the fridge and shook his head at the sight of the almost empty orange juice bottle. Downing the remains in one gulp he walked back through the lounge room towards the front door. 'Just going to get some more OJ,' he said.

The boys didn't even look up.

Jogging over to the shop and back only took a couple of minutes and, while Tom didn't intentionally sneak back up the steps, his charges obviously hadn't heard him return as they talked inside.

'I've got a headache from that stupid helmet,' Aiden grumbled.

'My legs are dead!' Jeffrey moaned. 'And I've got blisters on both feet.'

'Yeah, well it's all your fault we had to do the hills,' Chris said.

'*My* fault?' Jeffrey said. 'I thought you said it was because of the book.'

'Well, the book obviously suggested some stuff, but *you* gave in to Tommy way too easily, just like yesterday. That zero-tolerance stuff doesn't mean anything. He's all talk.'

'No, I reckon he really means it,' Jeffrey replied. 'I think he was pretty mad about the lipstick.'

Despite their discomfort, all three boys laughed. 'Yeah, did you see the way he was standing there trying to impress that chick, not having a clue how stupid he looked? He's such a *loser*,' Chris said.

Outside, Tom blushed at the memory, glad he'd thought to leave his hat on while he went to the shop.

'Yeah, maybe he is, but I don't think he's kidding,' Jeffrey said.

'He's not going to give up a two-week holiday to go back early and make himself look bad,' Chris assured his friend. 'He's a dickhead but he's not that stupid.'

'Teacher's aren't stupid Chris, they have to go to uni and everything,' Jeffrey said. 'Don't you reckon Aiden?'

'Maybe,' Aiden hedged.

'Trust me, he's stupid,' Chris replied. 'He's just a *P.E.* teacher. How hard is it to teach kids to play games? I just want to punch his dumb, ugly face sometimes.'

Tom raised his eyebrows, wondering yet again why Chris disliked him so strongly. Karl had assured him he was being paranoid, but Tom had always sensed a deep, personal hostility from the kid right from their first meeting.

'Come on, Chris, don't do anything crazy, we don't want to go back to school, right Aiden?'

'Yeah, that would *really* suck,' Aiden agreed.

'I'm telling you he won't make us go back.'

Having heard enough for now, Tom snuck around to the back door and banged it loudly as he walked in. 'Right, what are we cooking today guys? Omelettes or pancakes?'

Jeffrey and Aiden hesitated. Tom caught the pointed look Chris gave them, but hunger won out in the end.

'Can we have both?' asked Jeffrey.

'Sure, why not?' Tom said.

Once the kitchen clean-up was over Tom directed the boys outside. Ignoring the folded arms and bored looks he asked, 'So, who knows how to change a tyre?'

'None of us do.' Jeffrey spoke for all of them.

'Good, then it will be a new experience for you all,' Tom said, as he detached the spare tyre from the rear door.

'You can't prove we let down the tyre,' Chris said.

'No, I can't,' Tom agreed as he pulled out his tool kit. 'I'm not even accusing you of it. I just think this would be a good skill to learn, living out in the bush as you do.'

'But this is a big car,' said Jeffrey. 'And we don't know what to do.'

'The principle is the same for any car. I'll walk you through it.'

Jeffrey and Aiden came over but Chris remained where he was. Tom showed no reaction. Instead he got out the jack and showed Jeffrey and Aiden how to work it. Both boys worked diligently while Chris scowled in the background. Jeffrey was chuffed when he undid the first wheel nut. 'Sometimes my dad can't even do that on the first go,' he said, sweat running down his face as he moved onto the next one.

Tom stifled a smile, deciding not to mention he'd loosened the nuts while the boys were cleaning up the kitchen.

Once they got the spare on and started putting the wheel nuts back on, Tom brought his surfboard down from the veranda and laid it on the grass.

'What are you doing, Mr McKay?' Jeffrey asked, as Aiden tightened the first nut.

'Just starting to get packed.'

'Packed? But why? We changed the tyre.'

'Yeah, you and Aiden did, but your mate over there didn't.'

'But that's not fair,' Aiden put in.

'No, it's not. You guys did the right thing and he didn't.'

'Well, we're not finished yet,' Jeffrey said, 'there's still time for Chris to help.' Turning around, he glared meaningfully at his friend. '*Come on*,' he mouthed.

Chris didn't move.

Tom sauntered over to the Hill's Hoist and began unpegging the wet washing. He watched out of the corner of his eye as both Jeffrey and Aiden pleaded with Chris to help them. The boy still hadn't moved when Tom walked back over and dumped the basket of clothes next to his board. Taking the wheel brace from Aiden he said, 'I'll finish this while you guys go and get your stuff together.'

'You're bluffing,' Chris mumbled.

Tom attached the wheel brace to the next nut and heaved it to the right. 'I can assure you I'm not. In fact, I'm kind of glad. I get to go to camp after all. You guys will be the ones scrubbing graffiti off the lockers and shovelling manure on the new garden beds.'

'Come on, Chris,' Aiden pleaded.

'He really means it, Chris!' Jeffrey said.

Finally, there came a flicker of movement. Avoiding Tom's gaze, Chris sidled over to join his friends. Tom held out the wheel brace and Chris snatched it from his grasp.

'Good on you, Chris.' Tom stepped back to let them finish the job.

Pumping the flat tyre back up with the hand pump almost sent the boys to the point of physical collapse. So much so that when it got to lunch time, even Chris could no longer hold out on his cooking boycott. Tom couldn't believe it when he appeared in the kitchen a few minutes after the others.

'There's only so many sandwiches and cold baked beans you can eat, hey Christopher?' he said.

Chris gave one of his trademark death stares in response.

Undeterred, Tom handed him a chopping board and a capsicum. 'We're making kebabs. Just cut it into bite sized pieces and put it in the bowl.'

Chris glared at Tom again, apparently tossing up whether he really *was* hungry enough to concede this particular point in their power struggle. Tom ignored the look as he busied himself getting the barbeque implements together.

Eventually Chris picked up the capsicum and started slicing.

Chris still wouldn't go in the water when they went to the beach that afternoon. He watched Aiden and Jeffrey throw a tennis ball to each other in the shallows but made no move to join them.

He still didn't come over when Jeffrey and Aiden grew bored with the tennis ball and started throwing wet sand at each other. Tom, who been watching the boys as he bodysurfed, made his way back to shore. He was sure Jim wouldn't approve of that kind of behaviour. As Tom splashed through the shallows Aiden and Jeffrey ran back over to Chris. Tom stood on the sand and watched as they tried to convince their friend to come down to the water. Chris kept shaking his head until the other boys picked him up by his wrists and ankles and carried him towards the water.

Chris fought them valiantly, wriggling violently in their grasp. It was only when the boys passed by Tom that he saw the expression on Chris's face. The kid was petrified. Tom grabbed Jeffrey's arm. 'Put him down,' he said.

'We're just having fun,' Jeffrey mumbled, but lowered Chris's legs onto the sand. Aiden let go of his arms. Avoiding the gaze of his friends, Chris stomped back to the towels. Aiden and Jeffrey exchanged a quizzical glance then headed back into the water.

Tom followed Chris closely and sat down next to him, ignoring his hostile stare. 'I can teach you to swim you know,' he said.

Tom caught a quick flicker of emotion in Chris's eyes but then the usual coldness returned. 'I don't want to swim!'

'It's okay to be scared sometimes.'

'I'm not scared.'

Tom slicked his wet hair back. 'You know sometimes it takes much less energy to attempt something you're afraid of than it does to maintain your image.'

Chris just stared straight ahead so eventually Tom stood up and walked back to the water's edge. As he stood there watching the other two boys in the ocean Jim came and stood alongside him.

'Everything all right?' he asked

'Yeah, it's about as good as it's going to get for now. But, you know, this whole thing is making me paranoid. I feel like everyone is looking at me today.'

Jim nodded thoughtfully and then reached behind Tom's back. Puzzled, Tom glanced over his shoulder as he felt something being peeled off his rashie. Jim stifled a smile as he handed Tom a wide piece of masking tape emblazoned with the words **"I'M RETARDED!!"** in thick, red Nikko pen.

Scrunching it into a ball Tom forced a sarcastic smile. 'Who'd be a teacher, hey?'

Jim just smiled sympathetically in reply.

Even though they had only started playing Frisbee to temporarily escape Tom's close supervision, the boys had come to enjoy their daily game in the park, although they didn't admit that to Tom.

'Come on, Topper, stop throwing like a girl,' Chris mocked, as he dove down to catch the low-flying disc later that afternoon. 'We'll have to put a sign on *your* back tomorrow.'

'You better not,' Jeffrey said, relieved that Chris wasn't holding a grudge about what had happened earlier. 'That was a great throw; you just left it too late to catch it.'

Chris flung the Frisbee over towards Aiden. 'Whatever you reckon. Did you see the way everybody was looking at Tommy's back and laughing? How funny was that? He had no idea what was going on.'

Jeff laughed. 'Yeah, it was a crack up. He couldn't work out why people were staring at him.'

'The loser probably thought they were *admiring* him.' Chris ducked out of the way as Aiden tossed the Frisbee especially hard, right at head level. 'Hey! What was *that* for?'

Aiden shrugged. 'Nothing.'

'Yeah it was. What's eating you?'

'I just don't reckon we should have done that.'

'Why not? You thought the sign was a great idea last night.'

'It's not the sign, it's what it said. You're making fun of people who aren't normal.'

'So?' Chris replied.

'Well they can't help having something wrong with them. Sometimes they're just born like that or they have an accident or something.'

Jeffrey looked on nervously. Aiden never stood up to Chris, even though he was physically much stronger than him. Taking a deep breath, he braced for a tussle of some kind, but amazingly it didn't happen.

While Chris stared hard at Aiden for several moments, he didn't say a word. Instead he picked up the Frisbee and flung it, hard, in the direction of the beach, before stalking back towards the house.

Aiden and Jeffrey looked at each other and shrugged, before Aiden too headed back towards the house.

'Yeah, don't worry *I'll* get the Frisbee,' Jeffrey muttered as he jogged back down onto the sand.

• • • • •

Jim was setting up the red and yellow flags the next morning when Tom walked out of the water after his morning surf.

'So how goes things in the juvenile detention centre?' he asked as he expertly ground the first flag into the sand. 'You seem to be holding your own.'

'Yeah, I guess so.' Tom stopped, setting the end of his board down.

Jim looked at him. 'You seem to keep them under control all right when they're down here. Isn't that what you want?'

'Yep, it is. But they're only toeing the line because we're on a zero-tolerance policy, not because they really want to or because they actually respect me.'

'Zero tolerance? Isn't that what that Giuliani bloke did in New York?'

Tom nodded.

'And you reckon that's the way to manage them?'

'To be honest, I don't know. It's working for the moment at least.'

'I know you're not allowed to admit it these days, but there was something to be said for a good clip around the ear or a boot up the backside. I learnt my lesson many times as a result of that kind of punishment.' Jim walked further down the beach with the other flag.

Tom lifted his board and walked with him. 'You know my swimming coach used to make me swim four hundred metres butterfly if I was late for training. His theory was that most kids hate butterfly because it's hard, so four hundred is murder.'

Jim positioned the second flag and stamped on the sand around its base, ensuring it was secure. 'So, I guess you made it on time for training.'

'No, not really. I discovered I had a natural ability for butterfly and, pretty soon, four hundred metres wasn't much of a challenge. My lack of punctuality actually made me a state champion at the age of ten.'

'I'm not sure of your point.'

'Kids adapt. They work out how to get what they want with the least compromise on their part.'

Jim did a quick scan of the water. 'In my experience, kids who constantly act up usually have a reason behind it somewhere. You've just got to work out what it is.'

'Then I'd better make plans to stay for another year.'

Jeffrey was the first to appear downstairs, still in his pyjamas and with his curly hair awry. He hesitated on the bottom step, glancing first at the chiming clock on the shelf and then over at Tom, seated at the dining table. Tom looked up briefly and smiled. 'Morning Jeff.'

'Yeah, hi.'

'Something wrong?' Tom asked, looking up again from the pile of papers in front of him.

'It's eight forty-five.'

'It is indeed.'

'What happened to dawn patrol?'

'Change of pace today. Don't worry, I've still got something planned for later.'

Jeffrey had obviously told the others there was something on the agenda for that morning, as they all hung around the lounge room after breakfast, instead of retreating rapidly, as they usually did.

Tom let them wait for a while, well aware that he needed to be unpredictable if he wanted to stay one step ahead. When he did finally put them out of their misery, he almost laughed out loud at the outraged expressions flung his way.

'It's a *maths test*,' Jeffrey exclaimed in complete disbelief, holding the stapled pieces of paper by two fingers at arm's length, as if they were drenched in something particularly unpleasant.

'Bingo,' Tom replied.

'I *hate* maths!' Aiden growled.

Tom was shocked to hear Aiden voice such a strong opinion off his own bat. He usually just echoed whatever Chris said. 'Most kids do,' he agreed. 'But you've got to learn to live with it.' Truth was he'd never particularly liked maths either and had never planned to teach it. But, he had discovered, one of the realities of rural schools was that if there wasn't a trained teacher in a particular subject, somebody else got drafted into it. And, the newest staff member inevitably got the least popular offerings.

'And, if we don't do it?' Chris asked.

'We'll be back at school in time for you to do rubbish pick up.'

Jeffrey was still scowling. 'But school work is over for the year. Camp is supposed to be fun.'

'None of you guys passed this test, you were too busy flicking spit balls around the room. We're going to do a variation of it each day until you get at least fifty percent. If you need some help, just ask.'

Three surly faces glared back at him. He held his hands up, palms out. 'That's the way it is guys. You've got an hour starting now.'

When Tom stood up to open the rest of the windows, the boys' eyes met briefly. 'We've got to find that book,' Chris mouthed.

Aiden and Jeffrey nodded their agreement.

Ravenous after expending so much mental energy, the boys headed straight to the kitchen as soon as they'd finished their tests. 'Aw, there's no biscuits left!' Jeffrey said.

'Are you guys kidding me?' Tom asked, sticking his head into the kitchen. 'There were five packets the other day.'

'We get hungry,' Jeffrey said.

Tom was about to protest, then stopped. Whatever their attitude problems may be, they were still growing boys, always on the prowl for food. He could understand that. 'All right, I'll duck over to the shop and grab some more.'

He was just about to cross the road when he realised he'd forgotten his wallet. Sighing, he retraced his steps back to the house and let himself in the front door.

Jeffrey's eyes widened. 'Oh, Mr McKay, what are you doing back?'

Tom looked at him intently. The kid hadn't moved from the couch, but he certainly looked guilty about something. Glancing around the room and seeing no evidence of anything amiss, he decided not to worry about it. 'I forgot my wallet.'

'Oh, okay. Is it in your room? I'll get it for you,' Jeffrey offered eagerly. Much too eagerly.

Very suspicious now, Tom looked at him again. 'No that's all right, I can manage. Thanks anyway.'

Jeffrey jumped to his feet. 'You know, it doesn't matter about the biscuits,' he stammered. 'We're not hungry anymore. Why don't you have a cup of coffee?'

Tom shook his head. 'No thanks Jeff. I think I might just head upstairs.'

Treading lightly up the stairs, Tom tiptoed along the hallway and pushed his bedroom door open. Aiden was so busy rifling through the things on the desk, it took him a few seconds to look up. When he saw Tom standing there, he almost jumped out of his skin.

'U-u-u-h,' he stuttered.

Tom walked over towards him. 'Looking for something?'

Aiden studied the floor and shook his head.

'What are you doing in my room, then?'

Aiden's eyes were still downcast. He shrugged wordlessly. Although not a great deal smaller in size, he shrank away from Tom's reprimand. Without the support of the other two, Aiden was introverted, timid almost. He had none of Chris's defiance, nor Jeffrey's quick answers. *He's not sullen, he's shy*, Tom suddenly realised.

'Whose idea was it to come in here?'

Aiden still wouldn't look at him. 'Mine,' he whispered.

Tom knew he could come down hard on him. He'd caught him red-handed at something that breached the house rules. But he didn't want to go down that road, because he knew he'd be punishing the wrong kid.

Knowing that he was intimidating him, Tom took a step backwards. 'All right Aiden, I'm in a good mood today so I'm going to cut you some slack. But if I catch you in here again, you'll be going home and so will you mates – understood?'

Aiden glanced up briefly and nodded. Then he bolted from the room.

Surprised but pleased when the boys joined in a volleyball competition in the park that afternoon, Tom took the opportunity to swim out to the lighthouse and back. It had been months since he'd done an ocean swim and he enjoyed every moment of the two-kilometre course. With the volleyball still in progress when he got back, Tom spread out his towel and lay on the beach. It was late afternoon and the sun had begun its western descent, but he still found it very therapeutic to lie on the sand and listen to the waves.

When Tom opened his eyes and sat up, he could see the lifeguards were packing up around him. Jim nodded to him from the tower and then, a few minutes later, wandered over.

'Thought we were going to have to wake you up,' he said.

'Just trying to de-stress,' Tom replied.

Jim looked at Tom a little disdainfully as if stress was a weakness he didn't tolerate. 'That ginger curly haired kid you've got with you, is he Warren Topper's boy?'

'Uh, yeah, he is.'

'I thought so. His old man was a top footballer. Could have gone all the way in the big leagues, if he'd had the opportunities the kids get today. His other son just got signed with one of the Sydney clubs for next year.'

'Yeah, I heard. Jeffrey's a great player too, although he missed a lot of this season.'

'Injury prone, is he?'

'No, too many detentions. Three in a row and you miss a game – let's just say he sat out more than he played.' Tom looked at Jim curiously. 'How did you pick him out?'

'Back about twenty-five years ago, a group of kids from out west got sent here for a week in their holidays. It was a Rotary program or something to give the bush kids a look at the ocean. Anyway, Warren came out one year, but he wasn't the least bit interested in the ocean. All he cared about was that he was missing pre-season training back home. He used to go and run laps at the sportsground and practice kicking while the other kids went swimming. I always remembered him and the boy is his spitting image.'

Tom nodded politely and stood up, but Jim wasn't finished.

'Got to wonder what's wrong with kids today. His old man would have killed for an opportunity to play professionally and if Jeffrey is anything like his brother he'll get it all handed to him on a platter. So, what's his caper?'

Tom exhaled loudly. 'I wish I knew.'

Tom was reading the paper when the boys emerged from the kitchen clean up after dinner that night.

'I take it we're not going to play pool?' Jeffrey asked.

Tom shook his head. 'We couldn't go anyway. It's tournament night tonight.'

'Can we play Gin Rummy again?'

Tom nodded, careful not to look too pleased. 'Sure. You guys want to play as well?'

Chris and Aiden ignored the question.

'I'll take that as a no,' Tom said, reaching over to the shelf and picking up a deck of cards.

This boy is really starting to grow on me, Tom thought as he watched Jeffrey earnestly studying his cards, plotting his next move. He's actually a nice kid underneath the smart alec façade and, like Jim said, he's probably going to have some major opportunities that the rest of his schoolmates could only dream of. Why deliberately sabotage it?

'So, I guess your brother is happy that the whole Super League thing has been sorted out?' Tom said.

Jeffrey's eyes didn't leave his cards. 'Hmmm,' he agreed.

Tom threw down his Queen of hearts. 'I don't know about you, but to me it just didn't feel the same this year with the two comps running.'

'My dad hated it.' Jeffrey pounced on Tom's discarded card.

'Just think, your brother might get to play Origin in a couple of years. How cool would it be to see him in a maroon jersey?'

'Pretty cool, I guess,' Jeffrey mumbled, still focused on his cards.

He really doesn't like talking about this, Tom realised. It must be hard to constantly hear people rave about your brother, but then again, he could be just as successful if he'd only try.

Aiden wandered into the kitchen then, supposedly to get a drink. He dawdled back into the lounge room, looking longingly at the cards.

'Would you like to play?' Tom asked, not taking his eyes off his cards.

'Nah, I only play poker.'

Tom was momentarily distracted as Jeffrey laid down seven hearts and triumphantly announced 'gin'. Shaking his head, he gathered up the cards and prepared to shuffle them. 'I'm game for some poker, how about you Jeff?'

Jeffrey nodded eagerly.

'Cool,' Tom said. 'There's even a set of poker chips in the cupboard over there.'

Aiden blanched, but realised he'd backed himself into a corner. 'Yeah, okay I'm in.'

Tom got the chips and the other deck of cards and started shuffling them. 'What do you want to play – Five card stud? Texas Hold 'Em?'

Aiden shrugged. 'Whatever.'

Working hard to keep his voice casual Tom said, 'Poker is better with at least four players if possible.'

Fortunately Jeffrey took the baton. 'Come on Chris, we need someone else.'

Surprisingly, Chris came over and sat at the table. Tom began to deal the cards. Jeffrey didn't know how to play and Aiden obviously didn't either, so he gave detailed instructions and played an open hand to begin with. Chris could play so he and Tom dominated the early rounds, but Jeffrey soon began to understand the rules and got competitive. Even Aiden, who was clearly out of his depth to begin with, stuck with it and proved to have the best poker face of the three.

For the first time, Tom felt like he was bonding with the boys at some level. But he also knew one false move would reverse the momentum. So, he just went with the flow. When he called it a night at eleven o'clock, he knew that the boys had enjoyed themselves, although he didn't dare say that out loud.

Heading upstairs to bed, he couldn't help but smile.

• • • • •

It wasn't until the next afternoon that Tom had a sudden realisation about Jeffrey. While the boys played their daily game of Frisbee in the park, Tom ventured into the surf. The thought struck him while he was sitting astride his board waiting for the next decent set of waves.

Later as he walked back to shore he could see the boys talking in a huddle. They seemed amicable enough, but then he noticed Jeffrey shaking his head, apparently disagreeing with something. He continued to walk up the beach, hoping to surprise them and maybe overhear at least part of the conversation, but, like bloodhounds, they sensed his presence and aborted their discussion before he was within earshot.

Thinking on his feet Tom said, 'Hey Jeffrey, turn the shower on for me, will you?'

The other boys kept walking while Jeffrey trudged over and turned the tap on, holding the broken button in so the water would continue to flow while Tom rinsed off his board. Handing the board to Jeffrey, he stood under the shower himself for a minute, thinking of how he could best approach the conversation he wanted to have.

'Did Chris want you to do something you're not supposed to?' he asked, as they walked back to the house.

Jeffrey looked at him but gave nothing away. 'Nuh, what makes you think that?'

'You were disagreeing with him.'

Jeffrey shrugged as if to say that it was none of Tom's business and they walked in silence for a while.

'Jeff, you don't have to do what Chris tells you. You're a smart kid, you can think for yourself.'

'Smart kids don't get sent to *special* camp.'

'On the contrary, a smart kid who has worked out a way to avoid something he doesn't like might very well end up there. Then he's got an excuse for not doing what everyone tells him he should do, or, more importantly, *expects* him to do.'

Jeffrey smoothed his unruly hair back and stared at Tom for a moment. 'I don't know what you're talking about Mr McKay,' he mumbled, and jogged across the yard and up the steps.

Jeffrey was sullen and moody throughout dinner that night, refusing to be engaged in any kind of conversation. His refusal to be drawn into his usual role put the other boys on the back foot and they too ate mainly in silence.

Later that evening, Tom went out to sit on the veranda, as he did every night. Settling back on his favourite deck chair, he got a real fright when he saw another figure on one of the other chairs. 'Far out Jeff, you almost gave me a heart attack. How long have you been out here?'

'A while.'

'You want to talk about something?'

Jeffrey nodded slowly, but didn't speak for a moment. 'I hate it,' he said finally.

'You hate what?'

'I hate rugby league. I think it's boring and pointless and the rules are stupid.'

'So I figured. That's what the attitude is all about right? A way out.'

'I s'pose so.'

'Jeff, it's okay to hate it. I'm a pretty big fan myself, especially the Origin games and the test matches. But it's not for everyone. I despise hockey but my three brothers love it.'

'Yeah, but I bet you can tell them you hate it and they don't go mental.'

Tom nodded. 'Yeah they don't particularly care that I don't like it. You reckon your brother and dad would get mad if you told them?'

'I've tried to say it, but I can't. People don't understand, they think if you're good at something then you should love it. I'm only good at it because all my life I've done drills, and been told the rules, and had to watch millions of games on video, being told what's right and what's wrong. Every day, Dad makes me practise in the back yard.'

'Jeffrey, sometimes parents can get a bit over zealous in what they want for their kids, they want them to have the things that they didn't have. Your father didn't get the chance to make it big, but he wants you to have that opportunity. I think you're right, it will be hard for him to accept and understand that you don't want to be a professional footy player, but it will be worse if you keep going the way you're going to avoid it. You'll have to tell him sometime.'

Jeffrey shook his head. 'You don't know my dad. He thinks anything except footy is for sissies.'

'You're right Jeffrey, I don't know your father, but he seems like a good guy. Sometimes we have to do things we don't want to do and that may even mean disappointing people we love, but in the end, you have to live your own life.'

Jeffrey frowned. 'But you've told me that I shouldn't keep misbehaving.'

'That's right you shouldn't. Living your own life doesn't mean that you shouldn't respect your parents and your family and do your very best at school, but you have to do what makes you happy too. Your dad will get over it, especially when you show him that you can succeed in your own chosen field, just like your brother does in football.'

'But I don't know what my chosen field is.'

'You don't have to know that yet. Just find something constructive to do that doesn't involve football.'

Tom was up at five the next morning, following his usual routine of surfing and a pre-breakfast snack. He couldn't think of a better way to greet the day and wished the boys shared his enthusiasm.

Jeffrey didn't even bother protesting when Tom marched into his room at six o'clock and pulled the curtains open.

'What now?' he groaned, rolling over to hide his face from the sunlight flooding in through the window.

'Just a nice, relaxing beach walk.'

'But the beach isn't even open this early.'

'Trust me Jeff the beach is always open. Well, except in extreme weather conditions.'

'But the flags won't be up yet.'

'That's a good point and I'm glad you now get the importance of the patrolled area, but we're not going in the water yet. There's plenty more kilometres of beach to explore besides our little patch down here.'

The boys were amazed to see so many people walking along the shoreline. In all fairness, Tom realised it must be a foreign concept to them, living so far from the ocean. Gullyview wasn't the kind of place where people went for long walks, just for the fun of it.

Even though the tide was out, leaving a wide expanse of damp, firm sand to walk on, Chris insisted on trudging through the soft sand up near the dunes. He really doesn't trust the others not to try and chuck him in again, Tom thought, wondering how he had slipped through the system and missed learning to swim. He strode over to Jeffrey, who had realised it was easier to walk on the wet sand and had distanced himself a bit from the other two.

'Did Chris go swimming at school?' he asked, knowing that Gullyview Primary had an aquatics program for the upper grades.

'No, he's got a problem with his ears. They get infected or something.'

'Right,' Tom replied, guessing that the ear excuse was a good cover story.

Jeffrey looked over at Tom. 'How far are we going to walk Mr McKay?' he asked.

'Just up to the cliff.'

'The cliff way up there? You mean the one we climbed the other day? The one we drove to?' Jeffrey's jaw dropped.

'Yeah, it's not that far. Tell you what I'll race you guys up there, then we'll get finished quicker.'

'No way!'

Tom wasn't naïve enough to believe in miraculous behavioural turnarounds, but he could see the outward change in Jeffrey's demeanour that day. Most noticeable was the way he began to openly enjoy himself at least some of the time, instead of keeping up the façade of disinterest the other two persisted with. He was also willing to share an occasional friendly conversation with Tom.

'You know before you came to our school I always thought freckles went away when you grew up,' Jeffrey said that night as they set up Pictionary. He had finally given in and agreed to play. Chris and Aiden were playing Jenga on the floor.

Tom smiled wryly. 'Hate to break it to you buddy, but we're stuck with them for life. You'll probably hold them at bay a bit if you make sure you always load up on the sunscreen.'

'That's what Mum tells me all the time.'

'Adults do have the occasional flash of insight you know.'

Jeffrey wasn't convinced. He shook his head and they started playing.

An hour later, Jeffrey looked critically at Tom's attempt at drawing a Shetland pony. 'Ah Mr McKay, now I understand why you never became an art teacher.'

Tom turned the piece of paper around, attempting to hold it at its most flattering angle. 'Come on Jeff, I think you're being a bit harsh. To me it screams Shetland pony.'

Jeffrey shook his head and laughed. 'Yeah, okay it does sort of look like an animal, but it's more like a giraffe cut off at the knees.'

Tom laughed. 'Well, there goes my dream of my own art exhibition. What do you reckon we'll call it a draw, no pun intended.'

'Okay.'

Glancing around the room, Tom noticed a pile of abandoned Jenga pieces but no sign of the other boys. 'Where did Chris and Aiden go?'

Jeffrey began packing up the game. 'They've probably gone out to have a s.., uh stars to look at the stars.'

Tom narrowed his eyes. 'Look at the stars hey? I don't know how you guys afford cigarettes, they're not cheap.'

'I didn't say anything about smoking. We can't buy smokes because you need ID now.'

'And I'm sure that stops you from getting your hands on them through other means.'

'So, are you saying that you never smoked when you were a kid?'

Tom nodded. 'Cigarettes stunt your growth you know.'

'No, they don't. Aiden's almost as tall as you.'

'But I thought none of you guys smoked?'

Jeffrey's face glowed crimson when he realised his gaffe. 'I just meant…,' he stammered. 'Well he might have had a few, like, last year.'

Tom let him hang for a moment, and then cut him a break. 'I honestly didn't smoke Jeff and you guys shouldn't either, it's really bad for your health. Besides, I was a competitive swimmer, so I needed my lungs to work at full capacity.'

'So why didn't you go to the Olympics or something?'

'Because I wanted to be a teacher more than an athlete,' Tom said, hoping his answer sounded convincing.

Jeffrey raised his eyebrows and put the game back on the shelf. 'I think the Olympics would have been more exciting.'

'Yeah, maybe, but then I would have missed out on coming here with you guys.'

Jeffrey just raised his eyebrows and left the room, leaving Tom sitting at the table.

Chris and Aiden were indeed outside sneaking a cigarette, although Aiden was much jumpier than usual. He crouched down low near the side veranda and flinched every time he heard the slightest noise.

'Why don't you just relax?' Chris said impatiently. 'Tommy's not going to bust us. He's too busy hanging out with his new pal Jeffrey.'

'They're not really pals, he's just trying to get on his good side.'

'No, they're pals. If you'd got the book it probably wouldn't have happened.'

'I told you, I'm not going in his room again. Besides, he's probably already read the book, so it wouldn't matter if we got it or not.'

'Sounds like you want to be pals too.'

Aiden sighed. 'We don't have to be pals, but I reckon it would be easier if we got along with him. He's not really *that* bad. Poker is kind of fun.'

Chris shook his head. 'I might have known you two would wimp out. Fine, be pals with him if you want, but I'm not gonna.' With that he tossed his cigarette butt on the ground and stormed back around the front of the house.

Aiden put his own cigarette out and stomped on Chris's butt as well, before picking them up and dropping them in the wheelie bin on his way back inside.

Happy to be making some headway with Jeffrey, the next day Tom untied the extra surfboards from his car roof racks and lined them up on the veranda, waiting for a reaction. He'd be pretty annoyed if there wasn't some kind of interest, given he'd made a mad dash home a fortnight ago to pick the boards up. Undertaking the sixteen-hour return trip in one day was not for the faint hearted.

Tom made a show of checking each surfboard over, although he knew they were all in good order. Then he started waxing them. He was halfway through the first one when Jeffrey appeared.

'They're the biggest surfboards I've ever seen,' he said.

'They're called long boards. They're much easier to stand and balance on until you get the hang of things.'

'I've never been surfing before,' Jeffrey said.

Tom didn't take his eyes off the board he was waxing slowly and methodically. 'There's always a first time and the waves are just right for a beginner today.'

Jeffrey nodded. 'I've seen girls do it so it can't be too hard.'

'Come on Jeff, let's not be sexist. I know plenty of girls who are amazing surfers.'

'Yeah, yeah.'

'Well, are you willing to give it a go? Just remember that you have to be prepared to take a few spills, when you're learning. It's not quite as easy as it looks. When you're riding a wave though, there's nothing quite like it.'

Jeffrey took a closer look at the boards. 'There *is* a fair bit of room to stand on,' he said. Tom just raised his eyebrows and started waxing the next board. Jeffrey stood watching for a while longer and disappeared inside.

Tom was surprised when Aiden announced over lunch that he would like to go surfing as well. Having become good at concealing little smiles when he had a victory, he just kept eating and replied casually. 'Cool. But you guys have to do exactly as I say once we're in the water. If you muck around or don't follow my instruction, that's it.'

The standard look of disapproval crossed their faces, but both boys nodded. Mentally Tom punched his hand in the air, but physically he just smiled and kept eating his lunch.

The surfing lesson was a success. After reluctantly practicing the basic moves on the sand, they progressed to the water. Like Tom had said, the waves were just right for beginners and were also breaking a fair way from shore, which gave them plenty of room to practice.

At first the boys were frustrated and annoyed when they realised surfing was much harder than it looked. It was hard to maintain an image of being a cool guy, when you had to be physically helped up onto your board.

'All right Jeff, this time concentrate hard on staying in the middle of the board, you're just overbalancing a bit,' Tom said as he held the board steady while Jeffrey got into position. 'Okay, go, go,' he said, pushing the board forward, smiling, as Jeffrey managed to stand up.

Aiden was getting frustrated. 'Why aren't we going along the waves sideways like those guys?' he asked, pointing to some of the other surfers.

Tom motioned for him to duck as a large wave approached and then draped himself over the end of Aiden's board when they resurfaced. 'It's like anything Aiden, you've got to crawl before you can walk. You're not quite up to carving just yet. You guys are both doing well for a first lesson.'

Aiden looked marginally happier at this announcement and positioned himself for his next attempt. He was more cautious than Jeffrey, but determined to keep up with him and made a good attempt at standing on the next wave.

After two and a half hours, Tom suggested they go in. He could see that the boys were flagging and he was a bit weary too. Besides, the volleyball comp was winding up and he didn't want to leave Chris unsupervised. He followed Aiden and Jeffrey back to shore as they attempted to cruise in on their boards. They both fell off, but picked themselves and their boards up and waded out of the water, trying their very best to look like surfing pros.

Tom walked a little way behind them as they crossed the sand to the house but he could hear their excited conversation.

'Man, did you see when I nearly hit that rock, I thought I was dead!' was Jeffrey's version of coming within four metres of a small rocky outcrop.

'What about that monster wave I got even though McFreckle told me not to?' was Aiden's embellished recreation of when Tom had said 'wait for the next one' but he had gone anyway, purely by accident, with terror etched on his face all the way in.

McFreckle, hey? Tom thought. He wouldn't be revealing that to any of his own mates or it just might catch on.

Hearing the clatter of the surfboards on the wooden veranda, Tom ran the last few metres to the house and caught the boys before they disappeared inside. 'Hey guys, you use them, you put them away,' he said and even the belligerent looks he got in response weren't enough to dampen the positive vibe. With a bit of luck, they might just all survive this behaviour management program after all.

• • • • •

The resounding bang of the back door echoed through the silent house, jolting Tom awake. Instantly alert, he shot upright, his eyes darting around the pitch-black room while his ears strained for further sound. His heart jumped to his throat when he heard the sound of pounding footsteps along the veranda and one of the boys yelling, 'No! No!'

Leaping out of bed, Tom flung his door open and immediately noticed light spilling from Chris's room. Moving rapidly down the hallway, his eyes widened at the scene before him. Chris's bedclothes were in complete disarray, the top sheet in a mound on the floor and the bottom one untucked at the bottom end, exposing the bare mattress. The pillow, half removed from the pillowcase, had been tossed onto the spare bed. Chris's suitcase lay open on the floor, its contents strewn to all four corners of the room.

Truly frightened, Tom hastily checked on Aiden and Jeffrey and was relieved to find them both sound asleep. Tom flew down the stairs, his heart hammering. Flicking on the light in the lounge room, he was relieved to find no signs of a struggle, but still no sign of Chris.

Tom wasn't surprised to find the back door unlocked. Stepping onto the veranda he snapped the light on, illuminating the backyard. But there was still no sign of the boy and no clue where he had gone. Tom loped down the stairs, shivering a little in the stiff ocean breeze.

'Chris, where are you?' he called, running around the side of the house and almost stepping on one of the three cane toads congregating near the downpipe. They hopped back into the shadows as he made his way around to the front.

Cupping his hands around his mouth, Tom called Chris's name again. Pausing a moment, he listened, his ears gradually tuning in to the sounds of the night. He could hear the pounding of the surf, as well as the rhythmic *skit-skit* sound of the sprinkler system in the park, but that was all.

Tom exhaled sharply, at a loss what to do. Wherever Chris was he couldn't have gotten far. There'd been no sound of a car. His four-wheel drive was fitted with floodlights for the dark, outback roads, if he went for a cruise in that, he should come across the kid pretty fast.

Jogging up the stairs to get his keys, Tom almost missed the huddled figure leaning against the house wall. If his eyes hadn't been accustomed to the dark, he would have gone right past him.

'Jeez Chris, didn't you hear me calling you?' he asked, his heart still banging in his chest. 'What are you doing?'

'Go Away!' Chris hissed.

Tom leant back against the railing for a moment, feeling completely out of his depth. Chris was clearly upset about something, but there was no way he was going to confide in him about it. 'Look Chris, if you just go back inside we can…'

'Piss Off!'

With his nerves already on edge, the sound of the door opening caused Tom to jump in fright. 'Who's that?' he snapped.

'It's me, Jeffrey. I saw Chris wasn't in his room and I thought he might have had a nightmare.'

'Nightmare?' Tom asked.

'Yeah, sometimes he has these really bad dreams and…' Before Jeffrey could say anything further, a blur of movement shoved him further down the veranda. 'Don't say anything to *him*!' Chris warned.

'All right, it's okay Chris,' Jeffrey said, putting a reassuring hand on his friend's shoulder.

Chris shook it off. 'I didn't have a nightmare. It was hot inside and I just wanted some air.'

Tom exhaled wearily. If anything the night was a little on the cool side. 'Okay, if you don't want to talk about it, that's fine. But you guys both need to go back to bed.'

'Okay we're going, right Chris?' Jeffrey said, holding the door open for his mate.

Chris hesitated for a second, then stormed back inside, slamming the door in Tom's face.

Tom had taught Jeffrey to play chess and was secretly relieved it was the one thing he could still confidently beat him at. As quick as Jeffrey was to pick things up, he hadn't caught on to all the intricacies of the game as yet.

'Watch your king,' he cautioned as they sat playing late the next morning. Chris and Aiden were in the back yard attempting some kind of record as to how many times they could throw and catch a tennis ball without dropping it, and it was keeping them surprisingly quiet.

'Oh, yeah, that's a bad idea,' Jeffrey agreed, leaving the piece he was about to move where it was and examining the board carefully.

Tom decided to use the lull in the game to see if he could coax some information out of Jeffrey. 'How long have you and Chris been friends?' he asked casually.

'Since pre-school,' Jeffrey replied, still deliberating over his next move.

'And did you give your pre-school teacher as much grief as you've given me?'

Either Jeffrey didn't realise he was being grilled, or he had decided to let his guard down a bit. 'We haven't always been in trouble,' he said, eventually moving one of his bishops. 'I used to look out for Chris, you know, because he was always so small.'

'Really?' Tom tried not to sound too interested as he considered his next move.

'Yeah, it's kind of weird when I think about it now. He never got into trouble at school until we were in grade five. We had this teacher who was super strict and for some reason Chris just decided to do everything that Mr Wilson told us not to.'

'Was this when his dad left?' Tom asked, thinking he might finally be on to something.

Jeffrey shook his head. 'No, he left when Chris was really little. I don't think he even remembers him that well.'

'Right.'

They played in silence for another few minutes before Tom spoke again.

'Does he have the nightmares very often?'

Jeffrey shrugged. 'I don't really know. He never talks about it or anything, I just heard his mum telling my mum one day.'

'They must be pretty scary, to make him rip his room apart like that.'

Jeffrey stared at Tom. 'His room was already like that before last night.'

'Oh, right.' Tom shook his head. Idiot, he thought, realising what had initially freaked him out last night was just teenage messiness.

Jeffrey seemed to realise he might be saying too much and withdrew, choosing not to volunteer any further information.

Not wanting to put Jeffrey in an awkward position with his friend, Tom likewise backed off. He finished the game with a couple more carefully considered moves. While Jeffrey packed up the board and put it back on the shelf, Tom sat contemplating what he'd learnt. Although interesting, it didn't put him much further ahead in understanding Chris. With a sigh, he got up and headed out onto the veranda.

• • • • •

Tic-toc. Tic-toc. Tic-toc.

Tom had never noticed how loud the clock above the radio sounded before. The boys were out in the yard kicking a ball around, so the house was abnormally quiet. He'd thought it would be a good opportunity to get his notes in order, but instead he was procrastinating.

The clock struck three, startling him. He glanced back down at his scant notes. Having not done an assignment since uni, he was finding the written component of this experiment hard going.

He'd been having second thoughts about overthrowing Mellish/Whitson. While he still believed their program was impractical and generally unworkable, he *was* going to have to submit a report about his experiences. He hated to let Karl down after he'd put so much trust in him. Maybe he could skew his findings somehow to support the program?

The sound of yelling in the back yard broke into his thoughts. He ignored it for a moment, but then realised it was more than minor disagreement. Throwing his pen down, Tom strode out onto the veranda and down the back stairs, his eyes widening at the scene before him.

Aiden had twisted Chris's arm behind his back and was violently shoving him in the shoulder, while apparently accusing him of something. Chris was yelling, both in pain and fear, while Jeffrey was screaming at Aiden to back off.

Tom was astounded. In all the playground stoushes he'd see Aiden involved in, he'd never touched Chris. He *always* deferred to him. Tom would have been much less surprised to see him in a tussle with Jeffrey.

Jeffrey stepped back as soon as he saw Tom approach, but Aiden either didn't see Tom or didn't care, as he continued to yell and shove Chris.

Although Aiden was tall and well-built for his age, Tom still had a ten-centimetre height advantage and weighed at least fifteen kilograms more. Taking a deep breath, he stepped into the fray and managed to separate the two boys. Pushing Chris away from immediate danger, he restrained Aiden by holding both his arms behind his back. It was no easy feat, as the boy struggled hard against his grasp and continued to yell at Chris. 'You hurt him,' he seemed to be saying.

Now out of harm's way, Chris shook his head violently and yelled back, 'I didn't! It didn't even hit him.'

Tom turned to Jeffrey for an unbiased view of the situation. He paused for a moment, but then spoke. 'You know that stray dog that's been hanging around?'

Tom nodded.

'Well, Chris tried to scare it away by throwing a rock at it.'

Tom raised his eyebrows at Chris. 'Well?'

Chris's face reddened. 'Yeah, I threw the rock, but I didn't hit him.'

'Liar!' Aiden screamed, attempting once again to shake his arms free.

Still restraining Aiden, Tom said, 'You two go inside and stay there until I say so.'

The boys paused for a moment, but on realising Tom was in no mood to be argued with they walked across the yard and into the house.

Leading Aiden to the opposite corner of the yard Tom released him, not knowing what kind of reaction to expect. To his surprise the boy slumped down onto the ground with no argument and buried his face in his hands. Tom sat down on the ground next to him.

'You want to tell me why you're so upset?'

When Aiden attempted to reply, Tom could tell that he was fighting against a stutter that he had never heard before.

'C-c-c-chris was l-l-l-l-laughing when he threw that rock.'

Tom thought for a moment before responding, deciding not to mention the stutter at that point. 'Okay maybe he was. But I know the dog chased him yesterday and looked like he might bite him.'

'N-n-n-n-o he wouldn't have. He was just playing.'

'All right, I agree Chris shouldn't have been cruel to an animal, but he's not a violent kid. Let's face it, you're much more violent than him.'

'N-n-n-not to dogs.'

Tom nodded slowly, choosing his words carefully. 'Want to tell me why a kid who cares so much about animals is always so happy to beat up his fellow humans?'

Aiden looked straight ahead and took several deep breaths. When he spoke again, his stutter had gone.

'You've got to get them before they get you.'

'Them being the other kids?'

Aiden nodded. 'When I was a little kid I stuttered really bad. I hated school because all the kids teased me. What made it worse was that Dad kept getting transferred for work and we kept moving schools. As soon as I made a friend we had to leave and I'd have to start all over again. I used to get beaten up all the time for being the new kid with the stutter. The other kids called me retarded.'

Tom nodded, trying to swallow the lump he could feel forming in his throat. Despite hearing and seeing firsthand the cruel things that kids did to each other, it was never easy to hear just how difficult school life was for some children.

'Oscar, my dog, was the only thing that made life bearable. I'd go home from school and he'd be waiting for me. As soon as he ran up to me things never seemed quite so bad. He was the best dog.'

Aiden took another deep breath before continuing. 'High school was even worse. One day some kids knocked me off my bike and my ankle got hurt pretty bad. I had to stay in hospital for weeks and have rehab for a few months. One of the physio guys told me I should go to the gym and get strong. I'd always been pretty skinny and I never thought I could do that. The social worker at the hospital also got me into a program to help my stutter and arranged for me to have the rest of the year off school as long as I repeated grade eight the next year.'

Tom nodded encouragingly. 'Okay, I'm with you so far.'

'I got right into the gym work and I also had a growth spurt and got pretty tall.' Aiden said. 'One day I met a boxing coach at the gym and he offered to give me a few lessons. The thing that stuck most in my mind was when he said, "Get them before they get you."'

Aiden paused again before finishing the story. 'Then Dad got transferred and we moved to Gullyview just before the start of school the next year. I really didn't want to move again and, even worse, Oscar got run over our first week there.'

'That must have been hard?'

Aiden's lower lip wobbled. 'Yeah,' he agreed, wiping his eyes with the heel of his palm. Eventually regaining his composure, he continued. 'On my first day of school I was so nervous my stutter came back. So, I decided not to talk unless I had to. I thought I could just stay in the background and be invisible.'

'Did it work?'

'No. At lunchtime this grade ten boy gave me a hard time and I just stood there like an idiot until Chris came over and told me to hit him.' Aiden shrugged. 'So I did. I couldn't believe it when the kid backed right off. It made me realise that being bigger and stronger than everyone gives you some respect, even if you are the new kid.'

'And you found a new friend?'

'Yeah, well two new friends including Jeffrey. I'd never had that before. When I started hanging out with them nobody knew I was really the shy kid with the stutter.'

'Okay, I understand how important it is to have friends, but didn't it bother you that started getting into so much trouble?'

Aiden shrugged again. 'It did a bit, but it's better than being bullied and beaten up every day.'

'But you use violence yourself Aiden, isn't that hypocritical?'

Aiden shook his head. 'I'm not a bully. I don't touch kids who stay out of my way or who are weaker or smaller. I only go after the ones who give me or my mates a hard time.'

Tom nodded again, feeling some empathy for the boy. 'And thanks to Chris you have no shortage of combatants.'

'Yeah, I guess so.'

Tom made a steeple with his fingers and considered his words before replying. 'Here's the thing Aiden, two wrongs don't make a right. You suffered at the hands of people who used violence against you for no good reason and you hated it. I hear what you're saying about only being violent towards those who deserve it, but, in the end, you are acting in the same way that your bullies acted towards you.'

Aiden shook his head. 'Not really.'

'Yeah, you are,' Tom reiterated. 'Mate, if you just stayed away from the other troublemakers you wouldn't have to use violence. Wouldn't school life be easier without the regular scuffles?'

Aiden sighed deeply. 'Maybe,' he muttered.

Tom stood up to go back inside. 'Just think about it,' he said.

• • • • •

At the end of each surfing lesson, Tom would go into shore and observe from the sand, letting the boys practice their skills without his constant instructions. As he sat watching them late that afternoon, Jim approached him.

'I've got to give it to you son, they're coming along well on those big boats.'

Tom laughed. 'Come now, let's have some respect for the long board. I'll have them on regular boards in a couple more days.'

Jim gave a half smile. 'Yeah, they're not all bad I suppose. I had a go on one myself once back in the sixties.'

They watched the boys a bit longer, then Jim spoke again. 'You reckon they'd behave themselves out on a sailboat? One of the sailing club members is going out tomorrow with his son and he could use some crew. It's a pretty decent boat.'

Tom's face lit up and then fell. 'I'd love to take them out, but Chris won't go and I can't leave him here.'

'He's the one who can't swim?'

'How'd you know that?'

'I wasn't much of a scholar, Tom, but I can still put two and two together. The boy is terrified of the water.'

'Yep, I know. Won't let me teach him to swim though.'

'Well, he's got an image to maintain. Does he like loud music?'

'Sure, what kid doesn't?'

'There's a band coming to play at the surf club tomorrow night. Not my idea of entertainment, but it brings in a good profit. They could use some help to set up, which could keep Chris occupied for the day.'

'Sounds good, I'm just not sure he'll do it, though.'

'Leave it to me. If I get a yes, I'll tell Terry to expect you down at the harbour by eight in the morning.'

'Okay, you've got a deal.'

Tom had no idea how Jim coerced Chris into a day's work as a roadie, but the fact he did meant that he and the others got to go out on the boat. He enjoyed brushing up on his own sailing skills and was pleased to see how quickly the boys picked up the basic tasks as well.

The absence of Chris made a noticeable difference to the demeanour of Jeffrey and Aiden, and Tom was torn between being grateful that Chris hadn't come and frustrated that he hadn't made any impact on his bad attitude. In the end, he decided to leave all thoughts of Chris on the shore and just enjoy being out on the water.

As he watched the boys reel in a good-sized fish under Terry's expert eye, he wished he had a video camera to capture the moment so he could submit it with his report. His stomach knotted briefly as it always did when he thought about his report. He still wasn't quite sure how he was going to approach it yet.

'I've never caught a fish before,' Jeffrey said. 'It's really cool.'

'You haven't quite caught him yet,' Terry replied. 'Keep reeling there or you might lose him.'

Aiden, who did have some fishing experience, took over the winding.

'I can't believe Chris is missing this,' Jeffrey said, watching eagerly as Aiden gave one last tug and landed the fish on the deck.

'I don't think he likes fishing.' Aiden picked up the wriggling fish by the tail and carefully removed the hook.

'Yeah, I think it's a bit mundane for Chris,' Tom said. Jeffrey and Aiden didn't respond to that statement, which didn't surprise him. Chris was still their friend and their loyalty was to him, naturally enough, even though the balance of power had shifted. Not wanting to upset the rapport he had built up over the course of the day, Tom left the boys on the stern and followed Terry to the hatch.

'I'll be honest, I wasn't sure how this would go today,' Terry said, pouring himself and Tom a glass of orange juice.

'Me either. I'm glad they proved us both wrong though.'

'Yeah, they seem like nice kids and they've still got that wide-eyed wonder about doing something new and fun.'

'That's true. You know for all their street smarts, they're just country kids who haven't really experienced much of the world yet.'

Both men were startled when the boat began to rock back and forth fifteen minutes later. They could hear footsteps on the deck and then Terry's son Ian saying, 'Hey, no running! What are you doing?'

Tom rolled his eyes. 'We spoke too soon.'

The sound of Aiden's voice came down into the hatch. 'Mr McKay? Mr McKay, where are you?'

Tom climbed up the steps and stuck his head out. 'What is it?' he asked. 'Can't you guys take it easy for just a while?'

Aiden grabbed him by the arm. 'Mr McKay, you've got to come quick. Jeff's in the water.'

'What?'

'We were just mucking around down there, he was trying to see if he could climb around the edge of the lifeboat. He almost did it too, then he slipped off.'

Tom leapt up the last two steps and scrambled along the deck. 'He's wearing his life jacket, right?' he asked.

'Um, no,' Aiden said. 'It was really hot in the sun and Jeff decided to take his off.'

'Are you kidding me?' Tom bellowed. 'What did I tell you guys about safety?'

Aiden shrugged miserably and handed Tom the discarded life jacket.

Tom dragged his shirt over his head, clipped his own life jacket on and firmly attached the spare jacket for Jeffrey. Just when he was thinking he'd actually made some inroads with him, he went and pulled a stunt like this.

Climbing over the railing Tom leapt out into the water as far as he could. His stress level immediately skyrocketed once he felt the strength of the current and recalled Terry's graphic stories about recent shark sightings in the area. Although only a few minutes had passed, Jeffrey had already drifted quite a distance. He head was still above water, but Tom could tell by his frantic arm movements that he was panicking. 'H-E-L-P!' he yelled desperately.

'Stay calm, Jeff!' Tom yelled back, but knew the kid probably wouldn't hear him. Putting his head down he struck out desperately towards the figure in the distance. It was an uphill battle. Although Tom was swimming as fast as he could, Jeffrey continued to drift further away. Stopping for a second, Tom was alarmed to see his head dip under the water.

A fresh surge of adrenalin kicked in. Tom recalled his swimming coach's words when he'd wanted him to swim faster. "Imagine there's a shark nipping at your feet." Well, I might not have to imagine too hard, Tom thought grimly. Putting his head back down he powered on.

Finally, he came within grasping distance of the flailing figure. His surf lifesaving experience had taught him that once someone started going under, there was a narrow window of opportunity before their last desperate surge of energy deserted them. He could see that Jeffrey was right on that precipice as his head disappeared under the water yet again.

Reaching over, Tom grabbed hold of the boy's t-shirt and hauled him back to the surface. Coughing and spluttering, Jeffrey was too weak to even speak. He just started to cry.

'It's all right,' Tom reassured him, 'I've got you.' Unclipping the extra life jacket, he helped Jeffrey put it on. 'You're fine, buddy,' Tom said. 'The life jacket will hold you up now, but I'm going to hang onto your arm so we stick together.'

Jeffrey just nodded numbly.

Tom kept up a meaningless stream of conversation, while monitoring Jeffrey's physical state, as they waited for Terry to turn the boat around.

Finally back on board, it suddenly hit Tom what a close call they'd just had. Still buzzing with adrenaline, he was ready to let Jeffrey have it as they sat dripping wet and exhausted on the deck, trying to catch their breath.

Deathly pale and still teary after his ordeal, Jeffrey spoke before Tom had a chance to. 'I'm really sorry, Mr McKay, it was a dumb thing to do.'

He sounded so sincere that Tom couldn't tear strips off him as he had intended. 'Yeah, it was dumb, Jeff, you've got to think about consequences more.'

Jeffrey nodded silently. 'Thanks for saving me again, that's two times now.'

'You're welcome, but let's not make it three.'

Chris was still hard at work helping to sort a tangle of electrical cords and assorted band equipment when Tom walked into the main bar of the surf club at six o'clock. He stared in wonder at the scene before him. A compliant Chris, working as part of a team, was smiling as he talked to one of the band members, who had a dangerous looking spike embedded in his chin.

He was snapped out of his reverie when a familiar voice said, 'Can I buy you a beer?'

Tom turned and looked over to where Jim was sitting at the bar, still in his uniform. Shaking his head, he walked over and perched on the stool alongside Jim. 'As tempting as that sounds, I'm technically on the job non-stop at the moment so I'll have to pass, but thanks.'

Jim nodded. 'Fair enough. How was your day?'

'It was awesome, to borrow an expression from the kids. Beautiful boat and Terry is a good guy.' Tom decided not the mention the boy overboard incident. No doubt Jim would hear about it soon enough.

'Yeah, he is. I thought you'd have a great day out there.'

Tom glanced over at Chris. 'Dare I ask how it went back here on land? I took it as a good sign that we didn't get a Mayday call on the boat to come and pick him up.'

'He's been good as gold. Well, they came back from lunch reeking of smoke and he might have snuck a swig or two of beer, but apart from that, nothing to report.'

Tom nodded glumly. There was yet another indication that it was him personally that Chris objected to so strongly. Then again, even Chris probably wouldn't dare disobey Jim. He was one of those people whose very presence and body language demanded respect. Tom himself was a bit nervous of him. No doubt Chris could sense that he just might get a clip around the ear from him, if he didn't do as he was told.

'He's still giving you trouble, is he?'

'Yeah, he is. I've really got somewhere with the other two, but Chris is another story.'

Jim took the last mouthful of his beer. 'Don't throw in the towel just yet, you've still got a bit of time up your sleeve,' he said as he put his glass on the bar and nodded goodbye.

Buoyed by Jim's positive report about Chris's behaviour, Tom greeted him with a smile when the set-up work was finished.

Chris scowled in response. 'I was hoping you might get shipwrecked out there,' he said. Tom sighed inwardly and shepherded him out of the bar area, feeling the positive mood gained over the course of the day leave him in an instant.

As they walked back to the house in silence, Tom thought about how the dynamics between the boys had changed over the past few days. Chris was no longer calling the shots and clearly wasn't happy about it. He'd taken to spending more time alone in his room and wouldn't even come onto the beach any more. Instead he sat up in the park listening to the Walkman that Tom pretended not to notice he'd brought along.

Tom had an uneasy feeling in the pit of his stomach when only Jeffrey and Aiden sat down to play poker that night. Chris hadn't played the previous night either. Refusing for a second night was not a good sign, mainly because the nightly poker game had become their most important bonding time. Jeffrey and Aiden didn't say anything, but Tom could sense that they were concerned about Chris's attitude as well.

· · · · ·

Tom slept badly that night and woke to the sound of pelting rain on the tin roof and against the windows. Great, he thought, as he noticed a puddle on the floor under the open window. He wasn't sure if he had the patience to keep the boys entertained inside all day.

At ten o'clock Tom glanced up from his reclined position on the couch, feeling like he was in a parallel universe. Chris had retreated to his room yet again, and the other boys were involved in an intense Jenga game, which involved a lot of extended silences as each considered their next move. They'd been at it for the past half hour, leaving him to read the paper in peace. In fact he was so relaxed, he might just have a ten minute power nap.

When Tom woke an hour later, the heavy rain had given way to a light drizzle and the house was quiet. Too quiet. Immediately suspicious, Tom sat bolt upright and looked around the lounge room. The Jenga pieces lay abandoned on the floor. There was no sign of the boys.

Thud.

The noise came from outside. It was followed by footsteps along the back part of the veranda and a yell from Jeffrey. 'Gotcha!'

More footsteps followed, then a screech of laughter. Once again it sounded like Jeffrey, but Tom couldn't be sure. Scrambling to his feet, he made his way over to the back screen door and flung it open, his jaw dropping at the scene before him. A carton of eggs lay open on the table, at least half of them missing. Yolk dripped down one of the windows. What Tom could only assume was flour was strewn underfoot along the length of the veranda and a pile of water bombs sat on one of the outdoor chairs. His can of shaving cream was balanced on top of the railing, a trail of white foam oozing out of the nozzle.

'You're so dead Topper!' Aiden yelled from some unseen location.

Another peal of Jeffrey's laughter rang out. 'You've got to get me first,' he challenged. A second later he appeared at the bottom of the steps. Covered in flour and soaking wet, he was also clutching a huge water pistol. Still laughing, he started up the steps, then froze, when he noticed Tom standing there.

Tom hesitated, torn between yelling at them for making such a mess, and turning a blind eye and letting them have fun. If only Jeffrey hadn't seen him, he could have snuck back into the house and stayed there until it was all over.

So caught up in trying to decide what to do, Tom didn't notice Aiden sneaking along the veranda on his left. He only caught the last-minute blur of action that resulted in an egg being cracked against his chest and what seemed like a bag of flour being dumped over his head.

Ten seconds of silence followed. Jeffrey stood rooted to the spot, as did Aiden, who now seemed unsure about what he had just done. Tom froze as well, ignoring the sticky mess that was dripping down onto his feet and resisting the urge to touch his hair. All right, now things had gone too far, he thought, thoroughly annoyed with himself for letting Aiden catch him unaware.

Jeffrey broke the impasse by lifting up the water pistol and spraying both Aiden and Tom. Aiden, in turn, picked up the shaving cream and sprayed it in the direction of Tom's head, before bolting down the stairs. This time Tom only hesitated a second before picking up two water bombs and aiming them expertly in the boys' direction. He then vaulted over the railing and chased them into the yard.

The melee only lasted a few minutes, but Tom couldn't remember the last time he'd had so much fun. Having stumbled onto the stash of flour bombs, he bombarded both boys mercilessly before briefly taking cover under the house. Being under there with dirt underfoot reminded him of his own childhood and the various games that had ended up with kids congregating under the house. He grinned as both Jeffrey and Aiden's feet moved past his line of vision. 'Where'd he go?' Jeffrey asked.

Tom froze when he heard a rustling noise over in the far corner. The downside of hiding out in a dark, cool place was the possibility of coming face to face with a rat, or, worse still, a snake. That thought was enough to send Tom back into the firing line. Emerging near the bottlebrush tree, he kept low as he made his way over behind his car.

'There he is!' yelled Aiden from the veranda. An egg sailed over in Tom's direction, missing him, but splattering across his windscreen.

Tom leapt to his feet. 'Hey! Don't pelt the car! It's murder getting egg yolk off.'

Jeffrey took the opportunity to throw another egg, which hit the front passenger window.

'Jeff!' Tom warned.

Realising he was pushing his luck, Jeffrey bombarded Aiden with the shaving cream again, before taking off down the stairs. Tom took the opportunity to pick up the bucket he'd left outside yesterday after washing his car. The heavy rain had quarter filled it and he took great delight in dumping the contents over Jeffrey's head.

It was only then that Tom heard the cough. Swivelling around, he noticed two things. The first was Chris standing in front of the house, smoking a cigarette. The second was Karl standing in the driveway, taking in the flour covered veranda, egg splattered windows and the dishevelled appearance of him and the boys with an unreadable expression on his face.

An hour later, Karl watched wistfully as Tom worked his way through an iced caramel sundae and a large slice of black forest cake. Oh, to be twenty-four again! The menu at the Sunset Café was very tempting, but with the results of his latest cholesterol test still fresh in his mind he'd stayed strong.

Taking a sip of his black coffee, Karl smiled kindly and said, 'Honestly, Tom, I wasn't trying to spy on you. This Principal's conference that I'm going to had the afternoon session cancelled at the last minute and I had a few hours to kill.'

'Yeah, but of all the days to come. I don't think that kind of conduct gets you nominated for teacher of the year.'

'Come on, Tom, it's not that bad. Now, if you'd been trashing the inside of the house and Chris had been smoking a *cigar* and knocking back a vodka martini, then you might be in strife.'

They both laughed.

Karl took another mouthful of coffee. 'Tom, I've always been a big believer in the old adage whatever happens on camp stays on camp, and, what better way is there to show you've built a rapport with the boys, than by having fun with them?'

'With two of them,' Tom said.

Karl nodded easily. 'Some kids take longer than others, according to Mellish/Whitson.'

Tom sighed heavily. 'Yeah, about those guidelines…'

'What do you reckon?' Karl asked. 'Is it the way forward? The answer to attitude problems in schools?'

'Well, uh, maybe…' Tom hedged. Glancing over at his boss, he tried to look nonchalant.

Karl took another sip of coffee. 'Well, come on, tell me all.'

Tom stared at the table for a moment, wondering yet again if there was some way he could skew his report to support the program.

'Tom?' Karl prompted.

Tom shook his head and sighed. 'I guess I may as well tell you now. I haven't followed the guidelines. I started to, but….'

'I know. I didn't think you would.'

Tom's eye's narrowed. 'Why would you assume that?'

'Because it's been proven in ninety percent of the other trial cases to be ineffective. Most reports suggest it's largely impractical, far too theoretical and aimed at individuals with a higher maturity level. They're scrapping it at the end of the year. In fact you are the last ever case study.'

'*What?*' Tom's face flushed red. 'You mean you let me do all this expecting me to fail?'

Karl held his hand out in a calming gesture. 'Who said anything about failing?'

'Why send us here if you already knew all this? So you could reinforce the fact I've still got a lot to learn?' Tom shoved his empty plate aside and shook his head.

'Tom, when you're an administrator, you learn ways to work the system. The funding for this program had already been allocated, so I figured we may as well use some of it of it. To protect the validity of the study, I couldn't tell you what I knew about it. Feel free to write an honest account of your experiences.'

'I still don't get why you sent me. I'm the least experienced staff member.'

'I chose you because I knew *you'd* find a way to make it work, despite the lousy guidelines.'

Tom took another spoonful of sundae and met Karl's gaze. 'Do you really mean that or are you just trying to bolster my self-esteem?'

'Of course I mean it. For two years I've watched you just get on with it, despite having a lot of obstacles in your path. One of the few things the guidelines got right was removing the kids from their normal environment to have the best chance of a positive impact. I figured if we got that bit right, you could do the rest.'

It took Tom a moment to process that statement. 'Thanks. That means a lot, coming from you.'

'You know me, Tom, credit where credit is due. But, really, how has it all gone?'

'Jeffrey and Aiden have responded well. But what can we do about Chris?'

'Unfortunately, Chris is one of those hard cases that the education system might never be able to correct.'

'So, what, we're supposed to just give up on him?'

Karl sighed. 'No, definitely not. I just mean, don't let it break your spirit if it doesn't work out. And don't think for a second I'll think any the less of you if you send him home early, if it means you'll do a better job on the other two.'

'Maybe you won't, but I would.'

Karl sat back and folded his arms. 'Why are you so hard on yourself son? I honestly believe you have a great career ahead of you in education, but you're going to have to start believing in yourself or you'll burn out before you're thirty.'

Tom stirred the remnants of his sundae and shrugged. 'I just want to be a good teacher. What's so bad about that?'

'Nothing, but you've got to understand you already *are* a good teacher. There's nothing wrong with wanting to be better but you've got to stop taking the knocks so personally, okay?'

'Yeah, okay.'

• • • • •

The boys were wary when Tom let them sleep until nine the next day. As much as they protested against the crack of dawn starts, at least that usually meant an easy morning after whatever activity they were drafted into. When Tom *didn't* come pounding on the door it usually meant something even worse, like school work.

'Everyone has passed the test now, right?' Jeffrey asked, after he swallowed his last bite of bacon and egg roll. While he had passed first go, it had taken Aiden and Chris two and three attempts respectively, but they'd eventually done it.

'Mmm,' Tom agreed, as he took another bite of his own roll.

'So, we don't have to do any more of them? No tables quiz or something?'

Tom shook his head.

Jeffrey still wasn't convinced. 'And we don't have to write lines or anything?'

'Well if you're that keen, I could rustle something up,' Tom said. 'An essay on Shakespeare or a science experiment maybe?'

'No! That's okay, I was just checking.'

Tom wiped his mouth with a serviette. 'Relax guys, there's no hidden agenda this morning. I've got something pretty cool planned, as long as you can get the house in shape in half an hour or less.'

He got the usual glares, but only as a token gesture. Jeffrey started clearing the plates and Aiden and Chris had a brief tussle over who would sweep the floor. It was the most sought after chore, being the least labour intensive. Eventually Aiden's size won out and he took custody of the broom. Chris trudged into the kitchen, where he and Jeffrey bickered about whose turn it was to wash versus dry.

Tom was relieved that Chris seemed to have come out of his self-imposed exile. If he'd headed back up to his room, they wouldn't have been able to go.

The boys did their best to hide their excitement when Tom told them to get in the car. Besides their shopping trip, it was the first time they'd ventured away from Sunset Point since they'd arrived. Truth be told he was excited too - it was going to be a great day.

Even Chris couldn't hide a smile when they pulled into the car park of the Hidden Gorge Flyover Park.

'This is the place where you get to ride those flying fox things,' Jeffrey said.

Tom nodded. 'Yep, that's it.' They'd all seen the billboards when they'd driven to Rosethorn on the first day and Tom had caught the longing looks the boys had exchanged. Even though Chris's attitude still needed some work, the other two deserved a fun day out and maybe it might even inspire him to follow their lead.

After Tom paid their admission, the boys scurried off to explore the lower section of the park. Having been there before, it didn't bother Tom too much when they abandoned him. He knew they would soon work their way through the lower adrenaline circuits and would need him for the next level, which required adult supervision. Besides, they'd be hungry before too long and he would be needed to bankroll lunch.

Unlike their climb up the southern cliff, the boys didn't complain once about the steep terrain they had to negotiate to reach the High Octane area, a series of zigzagging lines that extended across the picturesque Hidden Gorge.

'This is going to be so awesome!' Jeffrey declared.

'I wonder if you can go across backwards?' asked Aiden.

'Bet you guys won't keep your eyes open,' said Chris.

'Will so,' Jeffrey replied.

The boys continued their excited banter as they walked up the rest of the path and then climbed up the steps that led to the main take-off platform. Even though it was crowded with dozens of other thrill-seeking teenagers and adults, the staff worked with amazing efficiency. As they got close to the front of the queue, each person was fitted with a harness and assembled in four separate lines that gradually moved their way to the front of the platform.

Tom couldn't help but smile as he watched the boys talk animatedly amongst themselves. And, finally, he had elicited some kind of childlike reaction from Chris about something. There was a fourteen-year-old beyond the worldly ice-cool façade after all.

Thanks to his height, Tom could easily see the magnificent view of the swirling Archibald River rapids as he waited in line. They were in full force today, due to rain further upriver and made a stunning backdrop for the ride across.

Tom was so busy watching the water, that he didn't pay much attention to the commotion at first. It was only when he heard Jeffrey yell, 'Chris!' that he turned around.

Chris was shoving his way back through the waiting lines, seemingly in some kind of fury. 'Hey mate,' one of the staff members called, as the boy attempted to jostle his way through the bottleneck of waiting people. 'We need your harness back.' When Chris showed no indication that he'd heard, the young man grabbed one of the shoulder straps and hauled him backwards. Chris glared at him, but stood still long enough for the harness to be removed. He then took off again, ignoring the dirty looks he got as he pushed his way back down the steps.

Shaking his head in bewilderment, Tom called, 'Move onto the lookout and wait for me guys,' to the other two and shrugged himself out of his own harness. He then made his way back to the safety checkpoint, flinging his harness to the same young man who'd taken Chris's, and took off after him.

His height worked to his advantage once more as Tom made his way back down the path. Although it was crowded, he could see over enough heads to keep Chris in sight. It was a narrow walkway and several people gave annoyed looks when they saw two people making their way down the path. The descent was on the other side of the gorge.

Tom was almost upon Chris, when the boy suddenly veered off the walkway and started making his way through the shrubby bushland alongside the path.

'What the—?' Tom stopped too, bumping into a slightly built young man, as he tried to keep his eyes on Chris's fleeing form.

'Hey, watch it idiot!' the man snapped, apparently not bothered by Tom's size advantage.

'Sorry, I'm so sorry,' Tom called, making his own way into the bushland. Chris had found his way onto some kind of fire trail and, while the ground was clear enough to move along without stumbling, the surrounding trees and plants were overgrown. Low lying branches grazed Tom's shins and the higher ones slapped his arms and face.

'Chris, will you please stop!' he yelled, ducking under a low hanging vine.

No response, no indication the kid had even heard him. For someone who had never voluntarily participated in any kind of sporting activity, Chris could move. Tom was glad of his own level of fitness; somebody less so wouldn't have a chance to keep up with him.

Tom continued to chase him for another couple of minutes, hoping they wouldn't get lost. That was all he needed, for him and Chris to be stranded in the wilderness, after abandoning the other two boys in an area that required adult supervision. What a spectacular end to his brief teaching career *that* would be.

The terrain was getting rockier. Tom had to slow down so he didn't stumble on the stones underfoot. Clambering over a few small boulders, his stomach lurched when he came across the rocky outcrop Chris was perched on. The ground fell away dramatically on either side, dropping into a yawning chasm that looked deeper than the gorge below.

Tom had little hesitation about diving into the ocean or any other kind of waterway to rescue someone, no matter how bad the conditions were, but he had limited experience at rock climbing. He couldn't tell if the shelf of granite Chris was standing on was stable or even how far back it extended. From where he was standing, it seemed pretty precarious.

Chris faced Tom like a cornered animal – wild eyed and desperate. Sensing this, Tom stayed still and kept silent for several moments as he caught his breath. Without having to check his pulse, he knew his heart rate was increasing rather than slowing.

Stay calm, he thought. Don't freak the kid out. 'Looks like you've hit a dead-end Chris, why don't you come back down.'

'No!' Chris replied.

Despite the defiant tone, Tom could see the fear on Chris's face. It was like the day the other boys had tried to drag him into the ocean.

'Come on, just come down.'

'Go away!'

'No chance Chris. It's my job to look after you, I can't go away.'

A frill-necked lizard scurried onto the rock, startling both of them. Flinching, Chris took a step backwards, sending a shower of small stones over the edge of the precipice, echoing loudly as they fell.

'Don't move!' Tom yelled, feeling his blood pressure ratchet up another notch.

Apparently equally freaked out at Chris's presence, the lizard shot back down in the direction it had come, its long tail rustling in the undergrowth.

Knowing he had to act, Tom stepped gingerly onto the rocky ledge and grabbed Chris's arm. Only about half Tom's weight, the boy didn't offer much resistance and let himself be guided down off the rock. But once they were back on solid ground, he wrenched his arm free.

Tom faced him. 'You want to tell me what that was all about?'

Chris wouldn't meet his gaze. He shook his head vehemently and kicked at a spot on the ground.

'Seriously buddy, that was one crazy stunt. What's the problem?'

Chris eyeballed Tom. 'I'm-not-your-buddy!'

'All right we're clear on that, but it doesn't explain why you took off.'

Chris studied the ground, kicking it forcefully again. A small hollow was forming under his foot. Tom stayed silent for a moment, hoping the action might calm Chris down a bit.

'Come on, Chris,' he said eventually.

Chris's eyes didn't leave the ground. 'I didn't want to go on there,' he mumbled.

'That's fine. You know I wasn't forcing you to do it. You should have just told me you were scared. They have a tandem line. I could have gone across with you.'

'I wasn't scared and I don't want to go anywhere with you!'

'Okay, you hate me, that's obvious, but you could have gone with one of the other guys.'

Chris shook his head again. 'It's not just today, it's this whole stupid thing. I want to go home!'

'But there's only a few days to go. The other guys have done really well and it seems like a shame to go back early.'

'They can stay, I'll go back myself.'

Tom exhaled loudly. 'All right, Chris, we can talk about this, but let's go back to the house first.'

Chris didn't want to give in, but knew he had no other option. 'Fine,' he said eventually.

A truck rollover on the two-lane Sunset Road extended their return journey by over an hour. Although Jeffrey and Aiden talked a little, Chris remained silent. Sitting behind the wheel in a line of stationary traffic, with the heat of the afternoon sun beating in his window, Tom felt physically and mentally drained as he pondered yet again what he had missed with Chris. A pounding headache assaulted his left temple as Karl's words replayed in his head.

Unfortunately, Chris is one of those hard cases that the education system might never be able to correct.

Maybe Karl was right. Was there any point in spinning his wheels any longer, when it was obvious that while the tough but fair approach had sorted the others, it hadn't had any real impact on Chris.

Then again, Tom just couldn't bear to give up. This episode today hadn't been about bad behaviour or being disobedient, Chris was desperately trying to run away from something and some unknown element had tipped him over the edge up on that platform.

A cacophony of horn blasts brought Tom back to the present. The traffic controller had turned his stop sign to slow and was waving him through. Shaking his head, he turned the key in the ignition and drove forward.

Chris bolted straight up to his room when they got home. Tom sank wearily onto one of the recliners and motioned for the other boys to sit on the couch.

'Look guys, I'm not trying to get you to dob in your friend but do you have any idea what's going on with him? Anything I can help him with?'

Jeffrey shook his head. 'Honest Mr McKay, I don't know why he ran off. He usually likes stuff like that. Remember how he was the first one to finish the high ropes course at camp last year?'

Tom nodded thoughtfully. He'd forgotten about that.

'Do we have to go home?' Aiden asked.

'I'll have to see what I can sort out, I'm really not sure yet,' Tom said.

Jeffrey and Aiden nodded, both lost in their own thoughts.

'Can we still go play Frisbee?' Jeffrey asked. 'We'll stay up this end where you can see us.'

'Yeah, that's okay,' Tom said.

Once the boys left, he went up and knocked on Chris's door. 'Let me in Chris, we need to talk about some things.'

The silence was deafening.

He knocked again and twisted the doorknob. It was locked. 'Come on Chris, we didn't finish our conversation this afternoon.'

Still no response.

'All right, fine, stay in there and cool off if you need to. But we're going to have to talk at some point.'

Chris refused to come down for dinner and Aiden and Jeffrey retreated up to their rooms early as well. Tom could hear them knocking on Chris's door and Jeffrey pleading with him to let him in. After getting no response, they too gave it up.

Tom lay on the couch with his feet hanging over the edge, staring up at the high timber ceiling. It reminded him of his family home and he realised he would be back there in just over a week. He couldn't wait. It was going to be so relaxing to distance himself from Gullyview and its problems for the long Christmas holiday break.

The knock on the door startled him. Hauling himself to his feet, Tom peered through the screen and recoiled in surprise when he saw Jim standing there, with Chris. Wrenching the door open, he stared at them.

Reading his puzzled look, Jim spoke. 'You know the tree just outside that end room? If you're daring enough, you can climb out the window, shimmy along that small patch of roofing iron and grab onto one of the top branches.'

Tom continued to stare at Chris, the irony of the whole fiasco that afternoon racing through his head. The second story of the house was high and grabbing a tree branch from up there was much more dangerous than going on a thrill ride with full safety gear. Once again, the kid had him stumped.

'He was down at the bar in the surf club, trying to get someone to buy him a drink,' Jim said.

Tom could only shake his head. 'I'm really sorry about that. As far as I knew he was upstairs.'

Jim nodded. 'Not your fault, son, and I got him out of there before anyone suggested calling the police. You might want to review that zero-tolerance policy, though.'

'Yeah, I know.'

Tom ignored the death stare as he locked the windows in Chris's room and pocketed the key. Turning to face him again he said, 'You want to tell me what the hell that was all about?'

'I told you I wanted to go home. All this time you're banging on about your zero-tolerance policy, so I thought I'd really test it out. You're full of it, just like I thought. Why didn't you just ring Commandant Karl and get him to come and pick me up?'

'Because it's late, Chris. It's a four-hour drive on dark, two-lane roads with a huge roving kangaroo population. I'm sure that even you wouldn't want Mr Sullivan to put himself in danger and drive up tonight.' Tom hoped Chris wouldn't remember that Karl was actually close by at his conference.

Chris just looked right through him.

'We'll talk about it tomorrow, Chris,' Tom said wearily, closing the door on his way out.

It was almost midnight when Tom bedded down on the couch. Despite the window locking, he didn't trust Chris not to try some other crazy stunt. At least if he slept down here, he might hear him if he tried to sneak out.

He was dozing lightly when the sound of footsteps on the stairs woke him at quarter to three. Lying still, Tom listened as they continued across behind the couch and past the kitchen. Then there was the grating sound of the back door being opened. Untangling himself from the bedclothes, Tom eased off the couch and tiptoed out onto the veranda.

Chris didn't look particularly surprised to see him, nor did he attempt to put out his cigarette or hide the packet that was sitting on the table. Tom eyed them for a second, but decided to sidestep that particular issue for the moment.

'Whoa, it's Mr Super Teacher,' Chris mocked. 'Worked any miracles today? Straightened out any bad kids?'

Tom sat down on a lounger. 'You know you could have gotten so much out of this whole experience, Chris. It was an opportunity to sort yourself out, away from all the problems of home. I've really tried to help you.'

'I don't need your help, *Macca*.'

'Why not? What's so bad about letting someone help you?'

'Who says you know anything about helping people.'

'Look, Chris, I know there's fear under all this. If you'd let me teach you to swim you....'

Something in Chris seemed to snap and he jumped to his feet with eyes flashing. 'What is it with you and swimming? Just because some kids join your stupid little club it doesn't make you some kind of hero you know.'

Tom stood up as well and leaned against the railing. 'I never professed to be any kind of hero, I was just trying to do something constructive. I wanted to show kids who didn't seem to care much about anything that if you have something positive to put your energy towards then you can achieve more than you ever realise.'

'I don't want to learn anything from *you*!'

Tom gave an exaggerated shrug and extended his hands in front of him. 'Chris, I know you're trying to run away from something but I can't figure out what. Your Mum seems like a nice lady and your brother is a good kid. You seem to have enough to eat and a roof over your head. Whatever your problem is, we can sort it out.'

'Sort it out?' spat Chris. 'Sort it out? Some things can't be sorted out, especially when people drag you places you don't want to go and try and make you do things you don't want to do.'

'Chris, you gave no indication you didn't want to go there today. You were genuinely excited until we got up on that platform. I know it was a big drop and the water was loud, but...,' Tom stopped abruptly as a thought stuck him. 'Ahhh, I get it. It was the water that spooked you, wasn't it?'

Chris didn't reply.

'You didn't realise the lines were over water because the lower bit wasn't.' Tom shook his head, wondering why he hadn't picked up on that before. 'It's not swimming per se, it's *water* that you're scared of.'

Chris stared straight ahead.

'Talk to me, Chris.'

Still no response. They stood in silence for a few minutes, the sound of the surf the only audible noise. Chris lit another cigarette. Tom pointedly waved the smoke away but didn't comment.

'You know what? I can swim, I just choose not to go in the water,' Chris said eventually.

'And why is that Chris?'

'Why is that? You want to know why I don't want to go anywhere near the water?' Chris said, his eyes flinted and angry.

Tom remained still and nodded his head slowly. Chris picked up a small rock that had found its way onto the veranda and threw it with great velocity into the yard below.

'You've been to the swimming hole on the Gullyview River, right?'

'Yeah, a few times.'

'I used to go there all the time with the other kids who lived in my street.'

'Okay.'

'I was a good swimmer, really good for a little kid.' Chris threw his cigarette butt down and stared straight ahead. Just to be doing something Tom took a step over and ground it out with his heel.

'So, what happened at the river, Chris?' Tom asked gently.

'It was the day after I turned ten. We'd had a lot of rain so the river was flowing really fast. It made the swimming hole really deep and the current made it swirl like a whirlpool.' Chris paused and shook his head, as if trying to erase an unwanted thought. 'I asked Mum if I could go and she said no, that it was too dangerous.'

'But you went anyway?'

Chris nodded. 'I asked Nathan the kid next door to go with me. He was older than me, maybe twelve or thirteen, and he was always doing crazy stuff. He thought it was an awesome idea. When we got there the water was churning through and I realised it was too scary for me. But Nathan decided to go in and I egged him on to do it.'

Chris paced in a small circle for a few seconds and banged the veranda railing with his hand. 'He jumped in and for a while he was having a great time, spinning around like he was on a ride or something. Then this other older kid, Brett, came along. He was about seventeen and a real cool guy. He thought it was pretty amazing that Nathan had the guts to go in and he dared him to jump over the waterfall. I didn't think it was a very good idea but I didn't say anything or try to stop him.'

'He jumped off twice without a problem but on his third go he got sucked under and swept further down the river. We ran after him, but he was too far away from the edge. I was only little; I couldn't do anything to help him.' Chris put his hands on his forehead and bowed his head. 'Finally, he got caught on this tree branch. We climbed down there and Brett pulled him out…' Chris's voice cracked and he shook his head. 'He was alive, but we could tell he was badly hurt.'

'Did he survive?' Tom asked gently.

Chris nodded. 'Yeah, he did but he ended up in a wheelchair. I went to visit him in hospital in Rockhampton once. His family had to move there so he could be close to his doctor.'

Tom was at a loss to know what to say. 'You poor kid,' he said.

Chris composed himself again. 'You mean you *bad* kid, you *horrible* kid.'

Tom shook his head. 'No, I don't. Why would I say that? It was a terrible accident.'

'I got him to go there, I dared him to jump in.'

'It was still his choice to do it.'

'Yeah, well we left him there. We could see some people coming to look at the floodwater and Brett and I just ran away and let them find him. We didn't tell anyone we'd even been there.'

Tom felt very inadequate standing on the veranda in a pair of boxer shorts and a t-shirt in the cool, pre-dawn air. 'Chris, I'm sorry. The whole swimming thing must have been so hard for you and I've been pushing it.' He shrugged helplessly, not sure what else he could say.

'I thought we should tell someone what happened,' Chris mumbled. 'I went to Brett's house later that afternoon and told him that. He said we should go back down to the river and talk about it. Once we got there he picked me up and threw me in the water. The current wasn't as strong, but it was still flowing pretty fast. I was grabbing onto the side, but Brett kept kicking my hands away.'

'You poor kid,' Tom said again.

'He kept yelling at me that we couldn't tell anybody, then he used his foot to push my head under the water. I thought I was going to die! But eventually he pulled me out and told me I knew what would happen if I didn't keep my mouth shut.'

Chris shook his head violently and then crumbled against the wall of the house, like he was on the verge of collapsing. Concerned, Tom moved a step closer to him but Chris pushed him away and swiped away the tears that were running down his face.

'I can't forget it,' he kept repeating as he flailed his arms against the wall of the house. 'That's why I have nightmares. And when I think about Nathan being like that, it just makes me…'

Concerned he might hurt himself Tom grabbed the boy and held his arm around his chest, while Chris attempted to claw him off. It took all Tom's strength to keep his arm there, even though Chris didn't look particularly strong. After struggling for a while, Chris eventually gave in and let himself be sat down, while he continued to sob. Unsure of what he should do, Tom acted on instinct and put his arm around Chris's shoulder while his body convulsed.

Eventually, Chris pulled away and curled himself into a ball on the sun lounger. Tom silently sat down on the other lounger and they remained there until the first light of dawn appeared across the water.

• • • • •

Jeffrey and Aiden could sense something was up the next morning when they came down to an empty kitchen. Tom was *always* up early. Not sure what was going on, they made themselves some breakfast and were sitting at the table eating when Tom came down.

'Hey boys,' he said, with a forced smile, before heading into the kitchen.

They looked at each other in surprise, taking in the uncombed hair, red eyes and stubble. They'd never seen Tom unshaven before, even when they'd used up all his shaving cream the other day.

'Do you reckon he's been drinking?' Jeffrey whispered.

Aiden shrugged. 'Maybe. He looks kind of hung over.'

They stopped talking when Tom emerged with a bowl of cereal. Jeffrey was going to offer him a hair of the dog but thought better of it. Instead he said, 'Do you want me to make you a cup of coffee?'

Tom smiled gratefully. 'Thanks Jeffrey, two sugars please.'

Aiden eyed him cautiously before asking, 'Is Chris okay? He still wouldn't come down.'

Tom took a spoonful of Vita-Brits before replying. 'Yeah, he's okay, but I think he needs some space at the moment.'

Both boys nodded, happy enough to take Tom's advice and leave Chris alone for the time being.

'Uh, are we still allowed to go to the skate show this morning?' Jeffrey asked.

Tom nodded. 'Yeah, sure. Get ready and I'll take you down.'

Chris emerged just after eleven o'clock and Tom stayed on the veranda while he ate breakfast, not yet sure how to handle whatever came next. When he finally joined Tom outside, they eyed each other warily. It was one thing to be privy to somebody's deepest secrets in the wee small hours of the morning, but quite another to face them in the light of day, knowing that they knew.

'You get some sleep?' Tom asked.

Chris nodded.

'Are you okay?'

Exhaling, Chris nodded again. 'Yeah. But you can't tell anyone.'

'I promise I won't tell anyone. But you need to talk more about it Chris, and sort it out in your head.'

'What's there to sort out? I ruined his life.'

'No, you didn't. You just happened to be there when he made a reckless decision. He was older than you remember?'

'Yeah, but he was just a kid too.'

'Did Brett keep hassling you?'

'For a while. He'd just look at me in this real mean way and that was enough to scare me stupid. He moved away about a year later and I thought then that I should say something, but I didn't have the guts to.'

'I can understand that. The longer these things go on, the harder it is to speak up.'

Chris went back inside. Tom picked up the previous day's paper but didn't read much before he felt himself nodding off. It was only the bang of the door that alerted him when Chris came back outside. Shaking himself awake, Tom rubbed his bleary eyes and looked down onto the beach while he waited for Chris to speak.

'I can't go to the beach anymore, being that close to the water is just making me crazy. If you want me to go home, then I'll go.'

'No, you don't have to go. We can work around it.' Tom paused for a moment. 'Why did you agree to come here in the first place?' he asked. 'You must have known it would be really hard.'

'What choice did I have? The other guys wanted to come and I wasn't going to be stuck at school by myself.'

Tom sighed. 'For what it's worth Chris I'm sorry, I really am. I had no idea what was going on with you.'

Chris nodded slowly in reply and went back up to his room, where he stayed for the remainder of the day.

• • • • •

The waves were non-existent the next morning, so Tom decided to go for a swim instead of surfing. He was just wading into the water when Jim jogged over. 'You going out to the lighthouse?' he asked.

'Yeah, I need a good stretch out today.'

'Mind if I join you?'

Tom shook his head.

They dived into the water and made their way north to the lighthouse. He's really fit for an older guy, Tom thought, as Jim matched him almost stroke for stroke.

They paused for a breather when they reached the rocks surrounding the lighthouse.

'It's good to have a challenging pace to match,' Jim said. 'I reckon you were trying to shake me off for a bit there.'

'Yeah, I soon realised that was a waste of my energy. All bets are off for the return leg, though.'

'All right, challenge accepted.'

They both smiled but made no move to head back.

'Are you okay, son?' Jim asked. 'Did you get Chris sorted out the other night?'

'Kind of. I've come to realise that dealing with kids and their problems isn't always black and white. There's some pretty big shades of grey you have to look out for.'

'I don't envy you that job, Tom. I reckon I just wouldn't have the patience. You're good at it, though. I really mean that.'

'Thanks.'

Jim just nodded and dived back in the water. Not wanting to lose any ground, Tom followed close behind.

Tom's eyes widened when he walked back up to the house and saw

Chris sitting on the veranda. Hanging his towel over the railing, he remained standing, as he faced Chris. 'Good morning,' he said.

'Yeah,' Chris replied.

'You want to talk about something?'

Chris gave a hollow laugh. 'Why do people always say that?'

'Because it's the way problems get solved.'

'You can't solve my problem. Whatever I do, Nathan is still going to be in a wheelchair.'

'All right, that's true. Problems or situations don't always go away or get solved, but there are ways to learn to live with them.'

'How can I learn to live with this?'

'I'll be honest Chris, I don't know exactly. But I do know it involves talking about it.'

'What if I don't?'

'Then you'll continue on the downward spiral that you're on and will end up selling yourself way short. You're just a kid Chris, you've got your whole life ahead of you. It can be a good life if you let it.'

'Why did it have to happen to me?'

'Because life isn't fair. Some people just get dealt worse cards than others and there's no rhyme or reason to it. You can wonder about that your whole life and never have an answer. Or you can just work with what you've got.'

'But I don't even know who can help me.'

'We can work something out. The most important thing is to ask.'

Averting his gaze, Chris nodded slowly. 'I'll think about it.'

• • • • •

Karl had mentioned that he was going to drop in again on his way back to Gullyview, so Tom wasn't surprised when he knocked on the door that afternoon. They sat on the veranda and talked while the boys played volleyball in the yard.

Karl listened thoughtfully as Tom gave him an edited version of what had happened with Chris. 'It's going to take a lot of untangling to really get him sorted out,' Tom said. 'I promised I wouldn't tell the specifics, but he's been through a major trauma and needs professional help.'

'Yes, but you've made a move in the right direction. That's far more than anyone else has done for him.'

Tom just nodded as he kept watching the boys play in the yard.

'What's driving you Tom? Why do you find it so hard to accept praise when it's due to you?'

Tom didn't answer for a moment. 'I've always been a bit of a cruiser, you know?' he said finally. 'All through school I was picked for just about every sports team and lots of people told me I had the makings of a professional athlete. I came pretty close to getting a start on the professional surfing circuit and I deferred my teaching degree for a year to train full time in the hope of making the ninety-two Olympic swimming team. Obviously I didn't, but I came *really* close.'

'That doesn't surprise me, but there's no shame in not making it you know.'

'Yeah, I do know. It seemed to bother other people more than me. My coach used to tell me that I had more than enough talent to be a champion, but I just didn't go the extra mile that *winners* do.'

'Why didn't you?' Karl asked.

Tom shrugged. 'I realised I'm one of those people who compete to train rather than the other way around. I love just being in the water and churning out laps. Sure, I like to go fast and better my own best times, but racing at the big events kind of left me cold.'

'Good on you for making that choice.'

'Thanks, but a lot of people view it as a weakness if you don't have that single-minded determination to make it to the top. Sometimes it makes you question the decisions you've made.'

'All right, do you regret not doing either of those things? You're still young enough to go after them if you really want it. Sydney 2000 is just around the corner.'

'No, I don't regret it. I love teaching, but I feel like I've got to do at least as well at it as I would have as an Olympic swimmer or a pro surfer to prove to everyone and to myself I guess that this wasn't the easy road.'

Karl chuckled softly. 'We both know there's nothing easy about teaching.'

'Yep, you got that right.'

'I've already said it Tom, you are *really* good at your job, but you're never going to prove it to some people and nor should you have to. Being an educator is not like winning an Olympic medal or a world surfing title where you're going to get a moment of glory with plenty of accolades to follow. It's an ongoing journey where you have to acknowledge your own success because most of the people around you just won't notice it.'

'So, in a nutshell, you're telling me to give myself a pat on the back.'

Karl smiled. 'Yes, that's about it.'

As Jeffrey waded into the water that afternoon, clutching his surfboard he said, 'I never even thought about surfing before, now I'm going to miss it heaps when I go home.' He looked over at Tom. 'You must miss it heaps seeing that you're so good at it.'

'I do,' Tom said.

Jeffrey leant down to fasten his leg rope. 'You're not going to stay at our school for too long, are you? You're only there because you have to be.'

Tom shook his head. 'I don't see it quite like that. I'll admit I'm not a real country boy, but it doesn't mean that I'm not learning and gaining valuable experience by being out at Gullyview. I'll be around for another year to keep an eye on you guys.'

Throwing his board down Tom lowered himself onto it and started paddling out. 'Come on boys, boards down, let's get out there!'

Since Karl's first visit, Tom had made more of an effort to get his notes in order. He spent a half hour or so each night recording the day's events while the boys cleaned up the kitchen.

Needing to catch up on the big events of the last two days, Tom was still hard at work when his charges meandered back into the lounge room that evening. Expecting them to look to him for entertainment, Tom was surprised when Jeffrey dragged Scrabble off the shelf and the three of them sat down at the dining table to play.

Careful not to show any surprise, Tom remained sitting on the recliner and continued writing. Smiling to himself he resisted the urge to jump up and cheer. This was progress! Judging by the laughter coming from their direction the boys were having some good old-fashioned fun.

Determined not to upset the applecart, Tom worked away for another twenty minutes before heading into the kitchen for a coffee. Caught up in their game, the boys didn't notice him wandering over in their direction. It was only when he came right up to the table that Jeffrey looked up.

'Uh, Mr McKay,' he stammered, his pale face reddening.

Glancing down at the board and the colourful selection of expletives upon it, Tom resisted the urge to smile. 'Who's winning?' he asked.

'Um, well we're not really keeping score,' Jeffrey said, 'we're just mucking around, you know.'

'Yeah, I know,' Tom replied. 'But just so you know, there is only one t in snot, you're missing the r in bastard and smart arse is two words not one. You seem to have all the four letter ones right though.'

'Right,' Jeffrey murmured.

Shaking his head, Tom headed into the kitchen and held back his laughter until it could be hidden by the sound of the kettle boiling.

• • • • •

Early the next afternoon, Tom was attempting to use his very basic handyman skills to reattach the handle that had fallen off the cutlery drawer. They were leaving the next morning and Tom wanted to make sure the house was perfectly in order when they departed.

'Fu…ar out!' Tom threw the screwdriver down, as the screw went in crooked yet again. It was an old-fashioned round handle attached with a single screw and Tom was ready to admit defeat.

Having felt another presence in the room he looked up to see Chris leaning against the door frame, arms crossed. While they weren't exactly best buddies, they had managed to develop a bit of a rapport over the past two days.

Walking over to the toolbox on the table Chris rummaged around and handed Tom a different kind of screw. 'It's just as well you don't teach manual arts; those kind of handles need a longer screw.'

'Yeah, I knew that,' Tom said, embarrassed to have been corrected by a fourteen-year-old but delighted at the same time that they had moved to the point of having productive conversations.

Chris opened the fridge, picked up the orange juice and took a swig straight from the bottle. He watched as Tom finally reattached the handle successfully. 'What does Commandant Karl think about your great success in sorting out the *naughty* kids?' he asked.

Tom put the tools back in the box and closed the lid. '*Mr Sullivan* is very happy to hear that you have all done so well. He's a reasonable guy Chris, you start behaving yourself he'll get right off your case.'

Chris put the juice back in the fridge and shrugged. 'Yeah, we'll see,' he mumbled.

It was hard to believe it was their last night at the house. Tom was torn between being relieved it was over and wishing they had a few more days to just enjoy themselves. He glanced into the kitchen as he set up the barbeque. While he wouldn't say that the boys had the makings of gourmet chefs, they were doing a pretty decent job getting the food ready. But it was just as well he'd always been a big believer in the ten second rule, he thought, as he noticed Aiden dusting off a hamburger roll that had fallen on the floor.

He smiled as his mind flashed back to the first night he'd tried to get the three of them to cook. You've done okay, Tom, he thought.

They ate out on the veranda, enjoying the warm summer night.

'So, are you guys glad you came along instead of doing janitor duty?' Tom asked, as they ate their way through the mountain of barbequed food.

'Yeah, course we are,' said Jeffrey, looking to his two friends for support.

Aiden waited a moment before nodding. 'It's been interesting.'

Tom raised his eyebrows at Chris, who would only go as far as giving a shrug. But he had a hint of a smile on his face, something Tom had come to recognise as high praise.

'You guys are really lucky, you know. Not many kids in any school get this kind of opportunity.'

Chris met Tom's gaze. 'I guess that means you're lucky too. Not many teachers get a chance to take three kids on school camp instead of fifty.'

'Well, it did beat sleeping in a cabin on a bunk bed and eating dodgy camp food,' Tom agreed.

'Yeah, remember that cold mashed potato last year?' Jeffrey groaned. 'Talk about gross!'

'But at least we didn't have to cook it ourselves,' said Chris.

'You'll thank me for teaching you to cook one day, Christopher,' Tom assured him.

'Yeah, we should all take home-ec next year,' Jeffrey laughed.

'I know you guys don't believe me, but a good education is so important. Promise me you'll at least think about making more of an effort next year.'

The boys didn't agree, exactly, but they didn't dismiss the suggestion either, which Tom could only take as a sign of real progress.

Seeing it was their last night, Tom agreed to a few games of pool at the surf club. Jeffrey offered to be his partner and they had several closely fought matches, each team winning twice.

For their last game, Aiden suggested a three versus one contest. If they won Tom had to clean the bathroom (their most hated chore) before they left the next morning. If Tom won, he could choose his own reward. He said he'd think about it while they played.

It came down to the wire. They each had one ball left, although the eleven ball (Tom's) was in a seemingly impossible position to win off, while the boys was almost too easy.

Jeffrey rubbed his hands together. 'We're gonna watch you scrub the toilet,' he taunted.

Tom didn't flinch. After adjusting the angle of his cue several times, he slammed it hard against the cue ball, which ricocheted against eleven and sent six spinning perilously close to the centre pocket before bouncing back off the side. The green ball gathered steam as it traversed back across the table bumping into eleven with just enough momentum to send it to the right corner pocket.

'Nooo waaay!' the boys howled.

Tom raised his hands in triumph. 'Oh yeah!' he gloated, before knocking the eight ball easily into the centre pocket to finish the game. 'And that's why *I'm* the teacher,' he couldn't resist adding, as he lay his cue along the side of the table.

'It was a pretty wicked shot,' Aiden said.

Eventually Jeffrey asked Tom what reward he'd like. Taking the boy aside, Tom told him. Jeffrey stared at him. 'Is that what you *really* want?' he asked.

Tom nodded.

Gathering the others into a huddle, Jeffrey outlined what they had to do. Chris and Aiden rolled their eyes but eventually turned back to face Tom, along with Jeffrey. After much nudging and eye rolling they finally mumbled something unintelligible.

Tom gave them a withering glance. 'Come on, guys, I need to be able to hear it.'

Looking at each other again, the boys shook their heads, but eventually spoke again. 'Mr McKay is totally awesome!'

Tom grinned in response, amazed that the simple sentence brought a lump to his throat.

Tom was too keyed up to sleep much that night. After tossing and turning for a couple of hours he got out of bed and went down to sit on the veranda.

He'd been out there a while when he heard somebody open the door and walk outside. Chris didn't notice him sitting there so Tom didn't speak or move. He just sat silently as Chris lit up a cigarette and took a couple of puffs before realising that he wasn't alone.

'Jeez! You scared the life out of me,' Chris stammered, after jumping violently in fright.

Tom motioned to the cigarette. 'This is a non-smoking zone, remember?'

'Yeah, yeah, fine.' Chris stubbed out the cigarette.

It struck Tom then how young and innocent Chris looked in the moonlight, despite the traumas he had endured.

Chris folded his arms. 'I hated you heaps, you know.'

'No? Really?' Tom feigned a shocked expression. 'I got the message all right, I just didn't know why.'

'You remind me so much of Brett. He was big and tall like you, he had blond hair and lots of freckles.'

'Foiled by the freckles yet again,' Tom mumbled.

'What?'

Tom waved his hand to show it didn't matter. 'Never mind.'

Chris stared into the distance. 'You know, you're the only person who actually asked me what I was trying to escape from. Nobody else seemed to understand or care.'

'I've just come to realise that kids don't act up without a reason,' Tom said. 'You were a tough nut to crack though, I nearly gave up.'

Chris waited a moment before replying. 'You're the first person who didn't.'

They sat there in silence for another few minutes before Chris went back inside. Tom could hear Chris's bedroom door close and him getting into bed. Only then did he let the tears fall down his face.

Clare

2000

*C*lare Crawford fixed a smile on her face as she approached the empty table and tried to ignore the impatient foot tapping and pointed glances of the couple standing next to it.

'About time,' said the young woman to her older male companion. 'You have to wait for it to be cleared or else they'll just ignore you. I can't stand sitting near other people's dirty crockery.'

'Yes,' he agreed. 'I don't know what's happened to decent service these days. You have to wait for everything.'

How about what's happened to basic good manners, Clare thought, stacking the dirty plates and cups. It was obvious the staff were run off their feet and the couple had only been waiting about two minutes.

She grimaced when her fingers brushed against the wad of chewing gum on the menu holder. 'Charming,' she muttered. Picking it off with one of the used napkins, she threw it in the bin and quickly sprayed the table, then wiped it down. Once the couple was seated, Clare smiled and greeted them. She then handed them menus, recited the specials and rushed over to clear another recently vacated table.

Clare was relieved when her shift was over at eight. While she loved the energy and pace of St Kilda, waitressing in one of its busiest café's was exhausting at times.

'Aw, you're not going are you, CC?' her friend and workmate Ellie moaned when she saw her taking off her apron. 'How'd you get out of the close?'

Clare folded the apron and put it in her bag. 'I've done three this week, last night I didn't get home until after eleven.'

'Half your luck,' Ellie said, as she put a muffin into the microwave. 'I reckon we'll be here until midnight tonight. I suppose you're heading out on the town?'

'Nah, my back is aching from carrying trays and I've got a blister from these shoes. A hot bath is the only thing on my agenda tonight,' Clare said, slinging her bag over her shoulder.

Ellie laughed. 'Haven't you heard about the medicinal properties of tequila shots?'

Clare smiled and waved goodbye. As much as she enjoyed a night out, she really was too tired tonight.

It was only a short walk to the tram stop. Clare dawdled along, enjoying the brightness of the late November evening. Lots of people were out and about and a carefree vibe filled the air. Uni was out for the long summer break and seemed a million miles away. Nobody at the cafe cared if you had made the Dean's list three semesters running, they just wanted their coffee served fast.

Clare yawned as she let herself into the silent kitchen of her family's home in Kew. Her parents and younger sister had left two days earlier to fly to her uncle's remote property near the small settlement of Pittibarra, in Western Australia. He was hosting a family reunion for Christmas. While her parents and sister were staying for a few weeks, she couldn't get much time off and was flying over closer to Christmas.

Unused to the house being so quiet, Clare turned on the stereo and put the chicken lasagne she had charmed out of the chef into the microwave. After pouring herself a glass of flavoured mineral water, Clare retrieved the *Cleo* from her bag and headed out to the balcony to enjoy the sunset.

• • • • •

Peter Kilsyth removed his reading glasses and rubbed his eyes, before swivelling around to take in the panorama of Sydney Harbour. Having the best office, with undoubtedly the best view, was one of the perks of being senior partner at Kilsyth, Angus and Jones Architects. Peter watched a Manly ferry chug its way across the blue water and debated whether or not to stay and finish the plans he was working on. Another hour would probably get them done, but it was almost six and he longed to be outside, enjoying the beautiful late spring evening. Lillian, his wife, was at a fashion show with some friends, so the evening was his own. A good walk would be just the thing to clear out the cobwebs.

As he strolled towards the parking garage to drop off his briefcase and jacket, he heard, 'Dad, wait up.' Turning around, Peter saw his son Michael making his way along the crowded footpath. How does that work? he wondered. There were probably dozens of men walking along the street who could answer to the title of dad, yet instinctively he knew it was *his* son who had called out. He waited while Michael approached, glad for the unexpected chance to catch up.

Michael was still in his work clothes and carrying a backpack. 'It's

262

not like you to leave before six,' he said. 'I thought I'd have time to read the paper while I waited for you to finish. I was hoping we could go for a drink.'

'Sure, a drink would be great. I decided to take an early mark today,' Peter replied. 'You want to put your stuff in the car? We could go for a wander first.'

Father and son walked companionably along Circular Quay and over to the Opera House. There were lots of tourists around, as well as people in formal wear heading to evening performances.

'It's busy out tonight,' Michael said. 'Everyone is finally getting over their post-Olympics depression.'

Smiling wistfully, Peter nodded. 'Yeah, life goes on. It was an amazing two weeks and it definitely reminded us just what a beautiful city we live in.' Peter never tired of the scenery of his hometown and often walked the streets or along the waterfront, in his lunch hour, just to take it all in.

They found an alfresco table at a small wine bar. Before they had a chance to speak, a waitress appeared with an order pad. 'What can I get you?' she asked.

Surprised at the speed of the service, Peter had to think for a moment. 'Oh, uh, two beers, thanks.'

Perching himself on the high stool, Michael grinned. 'What if I wanted a cocktail instead?'

'Then I'd say it's your shout.'

They both smiled. Despite repeatedly offering, Michael was never allowed to pay for drinks when they met.

'Well, what exciting news have you got for me today?' Peter asked.

Michael ran his hands through his hair. 'I always go first. How about you tell me what's happening with you and Mum?'

Peter smiled, happy, as always, to be in the company of his son. 'Okay, let's see. First of all, I got one of those new Nokia 3310s.'

Michael nodded. 'They're a cool phone.'

'Yeah, amazing technology. The aerial is built in.' Peter paused for a moment while the waitress put their drinks on the table. 'Thanks,' he said.

Michael took a sip of his beer. 'All right, what else?'

'Well, the renovations at home are set to begin next week, your mother has decided she wants to keep the Mercedes after all and we've taken on two new associates at work.'

'Business must be booming then.'

'Well, I don't know about booming, but it's very steady,' Peter said, taking a mouthful of his own beer. 'Now come on, I know you've got something to say. How's your work been?'

'Great, really good. We removed a kidney tumour from a Great Dane today.'

'We?'

'I got to assist. I'm fine with the ordinary stuff, but that kind of surgery can be pretty delicate and I must admit it got a bit hairy for a while. One of the blood vessels ruptured and it took us a while to control the bleeding. He came through though and should make a full recovery.'

Peter shook his head in wonder. 'My son, the vet,' he said proudly. 'Remove a tumour, set a broken leg, treat kennel cough – all in a day's work, hey?'

'Yeah. I couldn't imagine doing anything else, even though first year was so tough. I'm glad you and Mum made me stick it out.'

'We never doubted you'd get there,' said Peter. 'You loved animals from birth, even though you never had a pet of your own.'

'Well there were all those strays I kept rescuing. And the wounded wildlife. You were always very good about letting me keep them in the shed.'

'Let's face it we both knew the house was off limits.'

'Except, of course, the time I snuck the three-legged dog into my room.'

They looked at each other and burst into laughter. 'Ah Mike,' Peter stammered, trying to regain his composure. 'To my dying day, I'll never forget the look on your mother's face when we woke to the sight of that mutt lying between us. I swear she levitated right out of bed.'

Michael wiped tears of laughter from his eyes. 'Well, we heard for months about the fleas and the fact that he wasn't housebroken.'

'I tell you what, Mike, you, me and that dog almost ended up as flatmates after that escapade. As it was, it cost a fortune to replace the carpet.'

They grinned at each other again.

Michael took another sip of beer. 'I guess it's time for my news.'

'I knew you had something to tell me.'

'I just got offered a six-month work exchange in Canada. The other guy pulled out so it's all very last minute. In fact, I have to leave on the fifth so I'll be away for Christmas.'

• • • • •

Peter didn't hold back the tears as he hugged his only child tightly at the airport departure gate two weeks later. He was excited for him and pleased that Michael was taking the opportunity to travel, but he would miss him terribly, especially at Christmas. Michael couldn't hold back a few tears of his own.

'Your mother really wasn't well, she was disappointed she couldn't come out to see you off,' Peter said.

'I know,' Michael sniffed.

'She does love you as much as I do Mike, she's just not great with emotional stuff.'

Michael broke the embrace and wiped his eyes with the back of his hand. 'Dad, it's okay. Mum is Mum.' Michael spoke without rancour. All his life his father had been the more affectionate parent – the one who kissed him better when he hurt himself, who hugged him when he was upset and who got up to tend to him during the night when he was sick or had a nightmare. He had long ago accepted his mother's emotional aloofness and they were still close.

Peter handed Michael his handkerchief. 'You kids today never think you'll need one of these.'

Michael took the hanky and gave his father another quick hug. 'Thanks Dad, I'll call you when I arrive and thanks for the money too.'

'Spend it wisely. We'll miss you more than you know.' Peter smiled sadly as he watched Michael disappear through the gate.

• • • • •

On the morning of her flight to Western Australia, Clare sat at the kitchen table drinking tea and debating whether or not to go shopping in the city. I really shouldn't, she thought. I have packing to finish and chores to do. It will be so busy in town this close to Christmas.

But, I really want those shoes from DJ's, she thought, and Myer has a sale on too. Besides, I haven't seen the Christmas decorations yet and that's a must to get into the festive spirit. Looking at the clock, Clare saw that it was only eight thirty. If I go in now, she reasoned, I'll still have plenty of time to get ready when I get home.

Standing in a queue in the Myer cosmetics section four hours later, Clare began to feel a bit concerned. She even considered abandoning her planned purchases. But they're forty percent off, she reminded herself, and I've waited ten minutes already. It's a waste if I pull out now.

Clare tried to conceal her impatience when the saleswoman couldn't find the product code on the L'Oréal set and called for assistance. When the cash register roll jammed and needed replacing she could literally feel her blood pressure rising. Clare sat on the edge of her seat on the tram ride home, willing it to go faster. When it did finally reach her stop, she jumped off and power walked home, not caring how ridiculous she must look with her packages flapping along beside her.

Glancing at the dirty dishes in the sink, the un-vacuumed floor and the pile of unsorted washing on the couch, Clare took a deep breath. 'Okay, prioritise,' she said aloud, in an effort to calm herself. The dishes, vacuuming and washing would just have to stay there. Racing around the house like a whirlwind, she threw a random assortment of things higgledy-piggledy into a bag, changed her clothes and made sure all the windows and doors were locked. Realising she didn't have time to make the necessary connections for the sky bus, Clare phoned for a taxi. She was very relieved when it arrived only a few minutes later.

Wow, I can't believe I made it, she thought as the cab wove its way through the busy afternoon traffic. No, I probably shouldn't have gone shopping, but I did get the stuff I wanted and I should get to the airport just in the nick of time. I really shouldn't cut things so close, Clare conceded as she looked out the window at the grey, overcast sky. It causes too much unnecessary stress.

Engrossed in her thoughts, she didn't pay any attention to the chatter on the taxi's two-way radio. It took her a moment to realise the driver was speaking to her.

'Sorry, what did you say?' Clare asked.

'You're not in too much of a hurry, are you?' he said. 'There's been a truck rollover on the freeway and it's down to one lane. It could take us a while to get there.'

When Clare finally made it to departures and checked the board, she saw that her flight had long taken off. Having already accepted that she wouldn't make it and knowing there was no point getting upset, she went over to the ticket counter to reschedule her flight.

The young woman at the desk was helpful but blunt. 'I'm afraid there's no way you can get to Pittibarra by Christmas.'

Clare's mouth dropped open. 'But can't I just get on the next flight to Perth? Isn't there one at eight tomorrow morning?'

'We can get you to Perth or Darwin for that matter, but the flights to Pittibarra are only once a fortnight and you needed to leave tonight to make the connection. Unfortunately, Perth or Darwin wouldn't be much good to you anyway because the roads to Pittibarra are flooded this time of year – flying in is your only option.'

· · · · ·

Peter had the windscreen wipers on maximum and the lights on high beam, but still struggled to see very far in front of him as he negotiated the dark, two-lane road. It was bucketing down and showed no signs of easing off.

'Do we have to have the air-conditioning on?' Lillian asked. 'It's freezing in here.'

'Sorry Lil, but it's the only way to stop the windscreen fogging up.'

'I knew we'd have problems going with a less reputable hire car company, I did warn you about it.'

'Well, it was this or nothing. Because we booked so late everything else was taken.' The five-year-old Camry was perfectly adequate but Peter didn't even try to convince Lillian. When she was being disagreeable she would argue that black was white.

'I'm beginning to wonder if it's all worth the effort, with our flight being so late and then having to wait so long for our bags. Not to mention the weather. So much for the glorious Queensland sunshine.'

267

Peter didn't bother pointing out that a Queensland Christmas was actually Lillian's idea or that the tropical thunderstorm would pass over soon enough. Well used to Lillian's moodiness, he knew when to withdraw from a conversation that would end as an unwinnable argument.

When Peter finally saw the sign for the turn-off to Sunset Point, he smiled in relief. 'There we go, it's only ten kilometres away,' he said, as he indicated left and turned onto another two-lane road.

'Well hopefully we won't get hypothermia before we arrive,' Lillian replied grimly.

Peter sighed internally, a sigh that seemed to reach into the depths of his soul. At the age of fifty-four, he often wondered how his life had ended up like this. To an outside observer, he and Lillian had it all. His architectural firm was one of the most respected in Sydney. They lived in a beautiful waterfront home that he had designed himself. Michael was a wonderful, loving son who had never caused them a moment of worry. So why this feeling of discontent?

When they hit the coastal road that hugged a sweeping cliff, Peter knew they were almost there, thanks to the precise directions from the travel agent. With Michael overseas and their home in the throes of renovation, a luxury beach getaway up in Queensland had sounded like a good idea. Lillian had organised it all with her usual efficiency. And now their holiday was underway.

• • • • •

Emma White stared out the window of the overnight bus, surprised at the amount of traffic on the highway. Where was everybody going at this hour of the night? Hearing a little whimper, she turned to her three-year-old daughter Lucy, and adjusted her blanket, ensuring she was covered. The air-conditioning was quite cold. Across the aisle six-year-old Ben was also curled up asleep under a blanket, worn out from excitement about the adventure ahead.

They were going on a holiday, their first ever. It still seemed too good to be true. At first Emma had been against the idea because she didn't like accepting charity. But her social worker had eventually convinced her to go

She felt guilty when she lied about having no family. She did have a family – parents, two sisters and a brother. But she could never expect them to forgive her for what she'd done and it was just easier to pretend they didn't exist. Opening her bag, Emma looked at the Christmas card addressed to her family. She sent one every year, but never gave a return address or any news. She just signed it. She would post this one when they stopped in Brisbane. Maybe they would throw it away unopened, but at least they would know she was okay.

Trying to get comfortable by leaning against the window, Emma looked wistfully at the gold ring she still wore. With hindsight, she could see all the pitfalls and mistakes she had made so clearly, but she really had been in love when the kids were born. She thought that Tim was happy too. She never imagined she would end up fleeing their home to keep them safe or that they would be reliant on welfare.

An old woman on her way to the toilet in the rear of the bus smiled kindly. 'What a beautiful little girl you have,' she said.

Emma managed a smile in return. 'Thanks.'

Stroking Lucy's soft blonde hair, she took a deep breath and made a decision. This holiday was going to be fun. They would enjoy themselves for two weeks and then she would go back to the family crisis centre and have them help her find a small town where they could go and start again. It was time to take control of her life.

• • • • •

Ron Jackson didn't spend long packing before he left his small farming community in Western Queensland. He didn't need much, just a few changes of clothes, a couple of books and his fishing rods.

Every year at Christmas, Ron took a holiday. He chose places where he could be alone and the day could pass without him having to acknowledge it. This year he was going to the beach for some serious fishing. It was one of life's pleasures for him and he could happily indulge in it for hours at a time. Ron worked long hours as a station hand and looked forward to a decent break, where he could keep to himself without any expectation from people to join in Christmas festivities. He'd even managed to get himself a lift over to the coast with his mate George, a long-haul truck driver.

When he saw George's lights approach, Ron picked up his gear, locked the door of his worker's cottage and walked out to the road to climb aboard.

At first the two men chatted easily, about how their rugby league teams had fared that year and what they thought of the latest additions to the national cricket team. But then George became more serious.

'Any jobs going out in your place?' he asked.

'Oh, there's usually something around, if you know who to ask. Why, you giving up the road?'

George's sigh seemed to reach his toes. 'Maybe,' he mumbled. 'Janice is really starting to nag me, wants to get married and have babies.'

'Do you want that?'

'I don't know, mate. It feels like someone is putting a harness on me. I like the freedom to take off for days at a time and drink as much as I like when I'm away.'

'Well, you know what they say, marriage and the whole domestic thing is a prison sentence. You've gotta decide if you want to submit yourself to it or not.'

'I can't say I don't envy you mate, you've got the life of Riley. Off fishing for Christmas, you can forget the whole big drama while I'm off to Janice's parents to face more nagging.'

'I can hear the cell keys rattling now my friend.'

After travelling for almost two hours, Ron closed his eyes and pretended to sleep. Part of him felt guilty for giving his younger friend such negative advice. But another part argued that he was saving George a lot of pain. Ron's own marriage had lasted five years and produced a beautiful daughter named Sylvia. He was working as a labourer in Townsville then and loved nothing more than coming home to his family after a hard day's work. His unhappy childhood had taught Ron to be wary of good things that came his way, but, at the age of twenty-seven, he truly believed he had it all.

Ron could still clearly remember the day he came home to an empty house and a short note on the kitchen table. His wife had left him for someone else, taking four-year-old Sylvia with her. In the sixteen years since, Ron hadn't heard one word from either of them.

This incident reinforced the lessons learnt in his childhood and he had resolved, yet again, to be wary of allowing good things into his life. So, no, Ron didn't feel guilty for trying to save George from heartache. He was just being a mate.

• • • • •

Sinking down into seat 37E, Clare sighed with relief. It was only after she jammed her carry-on bag under the seat in front, snapped her seat belt closed, and pulled the strap to tighten it, that Clare allowed herself to relax.

'Just made it, hey?' The woman beside her smiled.

'Yeah, it was a bit tight,' Clare agreed, watching the flight attendants move briskly along the aisle, shutting overhead bins in preparation for take-off.

The woman smiled again and turned back to her magazine. Clare picked up the safety card and studied it briefly, not really paying attention to it. She was still too flustered after the drama of the past few hours.

It was going to be strange spending Christmas without her family, but at least she had come up with a contingency plan. A few weeks ago, Clare's friend Joanne had mentioned that her family were renting a beach house in Queensland for the Christmas break. Clare had written down the address and stuck it in her purse, so she could send Jo a Christmas card. Clare felt a bit bad arriving unannounced, but she was sure Joanne's family would understand her predicament.

The voice over the intercom interrupted Clare's thoughts. 'Once again, sorry for the delay, ladies and gentlemen. We have been cleared for take-off in ten minutes and should be landing in Brisbane at about eleven thirty-five. Thank you for your patience and thank you for flying Ansett.'

Clare didn't care what time they got there. She was just happy she didn't have to spend Christmas at home, alone.

Used to the later sunrise time in Melbourne, Clare was surprised how light it was at quarter to five, when she arrived at the Roma Street Transit Centre. She'd picked up a timetable at the motel and knew there was a bus leaving at six. The rotund, middle-aged man at the ticket counter was surprisingly chipper for such an early hour in the morning.

'Let's see now..., you want to go to Sunset Point, yes, you're in luck, we have one seat left. You don't mind the back, do you?'

'I'll take anything.'

'You're easy to please,' he said, with a wink.

Clare smiled wearily in reply. Although excited about securing a ticket, she was still upset at the thought of being separated from her family at Christmas, for the first time ever. Her two older brothers were both married with children. They had gone to Pittibarra as well. She would miss them all a lot.

The cashier slid her ticket across the counter. 'There you go. Enjoy your trip and have a great Christmas,' he said cheerily.

His enthusiasm was infectious and Clare smiled in return. 'Thank you, I will,' she said, determined that she would.

By the time she got off the bus in Sunset Point, Clare knew how dishevelled she must look. Somehow she had lost the padlock key for her bag, so was still in the clothes she'd left home in. The subsequent flight, sleep and bus ride had rendered them very wrinkled. She also had a tomato sauce stain on her t-shirt from the breakfast burger she had eaten at their last stop. Having no access to her hairbrush, which was also in her bag, Clare's wavy, shoulder-length, auburn hair had gone frizzy and at least half of it had escaped from the plait it had been in when she boarded the bus. A quick look in the bus side mirror confirmed that her lip gloss was long gone, her mascara had smudged and her green eyes were red with substantial bags under them. Looking good Clare, she thought.

A bead of sweat ran down her face. 'Is it always this humid?' she asked the man standing next to her, as they waited for their luggage.

He laughed. 'I'm from Cairns. This feels positively dry to me.' Seeing her alarmed look, he said, 'Just keep on the beach side and the breeze will take care of you.'

Clare took a long drink from her water bottle. 'Thanks, I'll remember that.'

After retrieving her luggage, she downed the rest of her water and headed into town to ask directions.

Captivated by the charm of Sunset Point and the beauty of its coastline, Clare was in high spirits as she walked along Blue Pacific Boulevard. She was going to have a great Christmas after all, she could just feel it.

A rusting Valiant with bald tyres and a dinged in passenger door pulled up alongside her. The smoke pouring from the exhaust matched the smoke trailing off the cigarette dangling out of the driver's mouth. 'Need a lift?' he yelled over the roar of the engine.

Clare looked him over. He was wearing a grubby white t-shirt, had a bad comb-over hairstyle and was missing several teeth. Yet, she knew the offer was genuine. She smiled politely. 'Thanks so much for offering. But it's just up the road here.'

The man nodded. 'Ah, you're at the Beach House. I saw some people arriving there last night. Friends of yours, I suppose?'

Clare nodded. 'Yes, they're not expecting me. So it's probably best that I walk in. Thanks anyway.'

The man nodded. 'No worries, love,' he said, peeling off in a cloud of exhaust.

Clare coughed and waved the fumes away with her hand. It was nice to know the locals were so friendly. Her eyes widened when she turned into the driveway of number forty-five. What a great house! I think I'm going to love Christmas in Queensland, Clare decided, as she bounced up the front stairs and rapped jauntily on the door.

Excited about surprising Joanne, Clare was taken aback when an unfamiliar man stepped onto the veranda. Tall and slim with greying hair and warm brown eyes, he had a friendly face, but he wasn't Joanne's father. Ah, Clare thought, this must be Joanne's uncle. She'd mentioned he'd be joining them here.

Dropping her bag, she tucked a lock of hair behind her ear and smiled broadly. 'Let me guess … Uncle Henry, right?'

The man smiled politely but hesitantly. 'Uh, no.'

Clare's stomach plummeted when she peered inside and saw a group of strangers. An attractive, middle-aged woman with subtly tinted short, brown hair and designer label clothes sat at one end of the table. Two seats down, a stocky, muscular man, whose black hair was fashioned in a military style crew cut, was staring at his hands. A thin young woman with a pale complexion and shoulder-length strawberry-blonde hair rounded out the group. Sitting at the far end of the table, she was holding a little girl on her lap and a young boy stood beside her. Clare looked back at the man on the veranda. 'Can I ask who you are?'

'My name is Peter Kilsyth. And you are?'

'Clare. Clare Crawford. I'm a friend of Joanne's.'

'Joanne?'

Clare's heart lurched. 'Joanne Martin?' she said. 'You don't know the Martins?'

Peter shook his head.

'Okay,' Clare said slowly. 'I thought they were staying here. I came here to visit my friend.'

Peter shrugged. 'Sorry, never heard of them.'

'What's going on, Peter?' asked an impatient female voice from inside.

'Um, it seems we've got another visitor,' he replied.

'You've got to be joking!'

Peter held the door open. 'You'd better come in,' he said wearily.

Once inside Peter made the introductions. 'My wife Lillian,' he said motioning to the older woman. Flawlessly made up, her green eyes held no warmth. She nodded curtly and glared at her husband, before turning her attention to her perfectly manicured nails.

Peter kept going with the introductions. 'This is Ron and Emma and the kids are Ben and Lucy.'

Clare smiled warmly, but her friendliness wasn't reciprocated. Ron's hazel eyes barely met her gaze before staring back down at his calloused, work-roughened hands and Emma was too busy trying to settle her kids to give more than a brief, strained smile. Lucy started whimpering, burying her head in Emma's shoulder and Ben began kicking the chair leg.

'Who's that strange lady?' he whined.

Why am I the strange one? Clare thought. These people are in an amazing holiday house on a beautiful beach, yet they're sitting inside around a table looking like they're about to walk the plank.

Ben intensified his chair kicking. 'I don't like this holiday anymore Mum,' he said in a tone guaranteed to set any adult's nerves on edge. 'We're not having any fun like you said.'

What a little charmer he is, thought Clare. But then she took in

Emma's harassed demeanour and reconsidered. Kids always react badly to stress, she reasoned, and I'm sure I do look strange. I'm sweaty, my hair is a giant frizz ball and I've got tomato sauce smeared over my shirt.

'Do you mind if I use the phone?' she asked. 'I'll see if I can sort this out.'

Peter gestured to the small table where the phone sat. 'Go right ahead.'

Clare stared at the rotary dial for a moment. She hadn't seen an old phone like this for years. Gosh, this really brings back memories, she thought, as she listened to the whirring noise the dial made for each number. After the last number clicked through, the whirring was immediately replaced by the abrupt beeping of an engaged signal. Perfect! Clare thought. Oh well, I guess I'm going to have to make some conversation here, seeing that nobody else is. Fixing a smile on her face, she turned back around to face the curious little group.

Peter looked at her expectantly.

'It's engaged,' Clare said. 'I'll try again in a minute. I guess I must have got my wires crossed. I was sure Jo's family were coming here for Christmas.'

'Well they could turn up yet,' Peter said. 'Some people leave their phone off the hook when they go away.'

Ron looked positively horrified at the idea, as did Lillian. 'There's no way anybody else is coming through this front door,' she said grimly.

Clare decided to be direct. 'So how do you guys all know each other anyway?' she asked. Going by body language these people didn't even want to be in the same room together, let alone on a group holiday.

'We don't!' said Lillian.

Clare looked over at the only friendly face in the vicinity. 'What's going on, then?' she asked Peter.

Peter rolled his eyes. 'It's a *really* long story,' he warned.

Seating herself on the couch, Clare smiled. 'They're always the most interesting.'

When they pulled into the driveway of the majestic old house Peter loved it upon sight but at the same time he braced for a very different reaction from Lillian. She took in the surroundings, folded her arms and made no move to get out of the car. Peter undid his seatbelt and reached for the door handle. 'I'll just get the umbrella out of the boot, I've parked as close as I can to the front door.'

'Peter, this is a timber shack,' Lillian said. 'This isn't what the travel agent booked us.'

Peter sighed wearily and held out the piece of paper with the address printed on it. 'Yes, it is, see, it says 45 Blue Pacific Boulevard,' he replied. 'Come on Lil, it's eight o'clock on a Friday night, so we can't do anything now, anyway. Let's go inside and relax, I'm sure it won't be that bad.'

Dashing out into the rain, Peter grabbed the large golf umbrella, retrieved the keys from the mailbox, opened the front door and turned on the lights. Then he splashed back to the car and opened Lillian's door, carefully positioning the umbrella to shelter her from the downpour. Ignoring the rain soaking into his clothes, Peter escorted Lillian to the door, before heading back outside to unpack the luggage.

Peter immediately felt at home in the comfortable, old-fashioned interior of the house and did his best to ignore the pout on Lillian's face, as she sat on the couch drinking the cup of tea he had made for her. Drying his hair with a towel, he nodded wearily as she told him how she was going to ring the travel agent first thing in the morning and have them moved somewhere else. Trying not to be obvious about it, Peter peered up at the high ceilings and marvelled at the magnificent workmanship in the classic old Queenslander. They just didn't make houses like this anymore.

'Peter, are you listening to me?' Lillian asked.

'Yes, Lil, we're not staying. I heard you.'

When Lillian finally went to have a shower, Peter took the opportunity to have a look around the house. He may as well, considering their time here was so limited. It was hard to explain to people who weren't interested in architecture, just how amazing old timber houses like this one were. Built in a time when there were no power tools, just manual labour, it exuded such an aura of building skill and craftsmanship.

Peter took in the hardwood floors, the tongue and groove walls and the breezeways above each doorway. He knew the stumps the house was set on ensured adequate ventilation by allowing air to circulate under the floorboards. It was too bad they wouldn't be here to appreciate the pleasant respite from the Queensland summer heat.

Jogging up the stairs Peter looked in each spacious bedroom and watched the rain splash against the beautiful leadlight windows. He could hear it pounding on *the tin roof. Was there any more delightful sound during a summer storm? Hearing the shower stop, he retreated back downstairs and out onto the veranda, the crowning glory of the house. Lillian could go to bed in a huff if she liked, but he was going to sit here a while and take it all in.*

When Peter woke up, it took him a moment to work out where he was. The room was unfamiliar and he could hear the ocean. Lillian's side of the bed was empty. His eyes focused slowly and it all came back to him. Peter stretched out on the comfortable Queen sized bed and wondered what the day would bring. He was perfectly happy to stay at the Beach House; in fact, it was exactly the kind of place he would have chosen himself. But he knew Lillian was not likely to be easily won over by its simple charm.

Walking down the stairs Peter could see Lillian sitting on the couch. She had the phone up to her ear and a notepad and pen on her lap. Hearing his footsteps, she turned around and rolled her eyes. 'I'm on hold, again,' she said crossly. 'It seems that nobody is prepared to take responsibility for the mistake.'

Peter nodded in a way that he hoped conveyed sympathy and went into the kitchen. Selecting an oversized mug from the cupboard, he spooned in coffee and sugar and flicked on the kettle.

'Do you want a coffee Lil?' he called.

'No, I've had my breakfast. I've been up for two hours, trying to get this sorted.'

Ignoring the loaded comment, Peter wandered out onto the veranda and sat down, captivated by the beauty of the summer's morning. The angry grey clouds and high winds of the day before had been replaced with a cloudless blue sky and a balmy breeze. The beach was already a mass of umbrellas and sun tents and the patrolled section of the water was packed. The tide was out leaving a wide expanse of white sand, with the damp section glistening in the sun. Peter sat there drinking his coffee, peacefully, until Lillian joined him. The look on her face was enough, but he was going to hear the whole story anyway.

'That's the last time I'll be using that travel agency. They've botched the whole thing up and the best they can do is tell me that the girl who booked it is on holidays, so they can't verify anything with her.'

'Well, that's fair enough, isn't it? Everyone has to take their holidays sometime.'

Lillian folded her arms. 'Yes, but the other people in the office should be able to sort out her mistakes. If something is described as a beautiful beachfront property it should be that.'

Peter shrugged and ignored the barb, well aware that Lillian was spoiling for a fight. When she realised he wasn't going to bite, she continued, 'The manager tried to pull some strings and get us into one of the villas at the resort.'

'The one just north of here?'

'Yes, it's supposed to be very nice – much more our kind of place. But no, we can't go there, it's fully booked,' she said sarcastically.

'Well, it is Christmas.'

'Yes, a Christmas we're going to have to spend in a rustic beach shack.'

'Well, it's not really a shack...' Peter began. How could she even say that? It was so much more than a shack.

Lillian ignored that comment. 'There are absolutely no flights available until after Christmas and, as you know, the hire car is getting picked up this morning. I tried to extend our time but they refused.'

'Well, like I told you, we were lucky to get it for the time we did. All of their cars are booked solid until the middle of January.'

Lillian began massaging her temples. 'This whole thing is turning into a nightmare and it's giving me a migraine. I rang a few more resorts further up the coast but they're all fully booked too. What are we going to do Peter? This is not supposed to be happening.'

Peter tried not to look as pleased as he felt. 'Well, staying here isn't the end of the world. It's a beautiful spot and the house isn't that bad. It's nice and peaceful and it will give us a chance to relax and unwind.'

'Of course you'd say that. Don't you ever get tired of looking on the bright side of everything? What's the point of having money if you can't stay somewhere nice when you're on holiday? You infuriate me sometimes, Peter!'

Lillian stomped inside and up the stairs. Knowing it would be several hours before she started speaking to him again, Peter decided to take a walk.

The southern end of the beach was much less crowded. Peter walked slowly along the water's edge, savouring the feeling of sand between his toes and the sun on his back as he contemplated just how this holiday was going to turn out. The lead up to Christmas at home was always a whirl of parties and seafood lunches that Lillian seemed to thrive on. Their own drinks party was always held the weekend before and had become one of "the" social events of the Christmas season. Somehow, Peter didn't think that anybody in Sunset Point would be hosting anything like that. Not that he minded – it would be nice to take things quietly for a change – but Lillian was not going to cope so well.

Then, there was Christmas day. Without Michael – who had always been the centre of their world – there would be a gaping hole in their Christmas celebrations. In some ways the resort might have been a good option, probably offering a formal Christmas lunch which they could have attended to help give the day some shape. Maybe they could go anyway, he would look into it.

Peter stopped for a moment and sat down on the soft sand. The sun was hot and he was glad of his hat and sunglasses. He watched the gentle rhythm of the waves rolling into shore and looked out at the horizon, wishing that the prospect of spending Christmas day alone with his wife of twenty-seven years was more appealing.

Glancing at his watch, Peter realised he should be getting back before the sun got too hot. Dusting the sand off his shorts, he walked back to the water's edge and let the waves run over his feet. It was warmer than the water in Sydney and very inviting. With a bit of luck, he might even have a swim before the day was out.

• • • • •

Emma was puzzled when she arrived at the house and saw a car in the driveway. She opened the mailbox and peered inside. No key. A knot developed in her stomach. She had just enough cash for necessities and their return bus tickets weren't valid until their pre-booked date. They literally had nowhere else to go. Holding Lucy on her hip and Ben by the hand, she walked up the front stairs and timidly knocked on the door.

Two hours later, Peter hung up the phone and let his breath out slowly. Everybody he'd spoken to over the past hour had been helpful and apologetic. But none of them had been able to fix the problem.

Lillian glared at him. 'Well?' she demanded.

'Apparently, there has been a temp working in the real estate office and she got things a bit muddled. She has let the house as share accommodation, so technically we are both right in being here. Unfortunately, there's not a lot that they can do about it now because there's nothing else that they can offer us locally. That means if you would prefer to cancel, they will give you your money back.'

Emma shook her head. 'No, we'll have to stay. We came on the bus and the return tickets aren't until the twenty-seventh. I'm sorry if that's a problem.'

'Don't be silly it's not your fault.' Peter smiled kindly. 'Take your things upstairs and get settled into one of the spare rooms. It's a big house with lots of *space, so I'm sure we can work something out.'*

Emma nodded gratefully to Peter, but carefully avoided the frosty gaze of Lillian, who was clearly not happy with the situation. Apart from a barely polite greeting, she hadn't spoken to Emma since she arrived.

Relieved that things seemed to be under control she took the kids upstairs and chose the room farthest away from the main bedroom so she wouldn't be in Peter and Lillian's way. It was a nice big room, so they could entertain themselves in there if they needed to. As Emma dropped their meagre belongings on the floor, Ben jumped up onto one of the four-poster beds and bounced excitedly. 'Are we on our holiday now Mum?' he asked with a grin.

Emma nodded and smiled in return. 'Yes, we are.'

• • • • •

The dusty roads of Western Queensland gradually gave way to the greener vegetation of the coast and Ron began to feel excited. It was years since he had been near the ocean. In his impoverished childhood, there had been rare trips to the beach, and he could remember the sheer wonder of having a whole day to play in the water and on the clean white sand. It was one of the few happy childhood memories he had.

It was late morning when they arrived at Sunset Point. George was running behind schedule, so Ron insisted that he drop him off on the outskirts of town. Judging by the size of the place, it wouldn't be a long walk to the house and it would give him chance to stretch his legs before settling down for some serious fishing.

He climbed down from the cabin and gave George a goodbye wave. 'Thanks for the lift, mate. Have a good trip.'

George waved in return. 'No worries, I enjoyed the company. I hope the fish bite.'

Ron hefted his bag over his shoulder, took his rods into his hand and started walking in the direction of the beach.

Several people smiled and nodded a greeting as he strolled along, but didn't stop and chat. That suited Ron perfectly. He liked civility without the complication of getting to know people too well. He was sure he fit right in with his fishing rods. To the locals and other holidaymakers, he was just another angler on a Christmas fishing trip.

A customer in the butcher's shop happily gave directions and it didn't take Ron long to find Blue Pacific Boulevard. He began to whistle as he walked towards number forty-five.

Walking up the driveway, Ron was puzzled to see the front door of the house open. Dropping his bag, he pulled the receipt out of his pocket. Yes, it was the right house and he had the dates correct. So why were there people standing on the veranda and children running around the yard?

Ron shook his head. He'd spent more than twelve hours on the road and now, in a seemingly ironic Christmas twist, there was no room at the inn. Swearing under his breath, he picked up his bag and set off towards the place that was supposed to be his refuge from the madness of Christmas. Somebody up in the house had better have a good explanation.

· · · · ·

Despite how complicated and stressful things had become over the past twenty-four hours, Peter felt calm and in control as they all sat around the dining room table. Circumstances had thrust him into the role of mediator and leader and he had risen to the challenge, even if finding a solution was proving very difficult.

He genuinely liked both Emma and Ron, even though he had only just met them. They were just as much victims in this whole mess as he and Lillian; the only difference was that he and Lillian had arrived first. Personally, he thought they should all make the best of it and stay. Technically they all had the right to be there.

Looking around the table he wasn't sure if that would be possible. Lillian was filing her nails, so as to avoid eye contact with anybody. Ron was flustered and obviously annoyed that his plans had been disrupted. Emma looked scared and kept apologising, as she seemed to think that the whole mix up was somehow her fault. Keeping calm and businesslike Peter formulated a contingency plan.

'Okay, Ron, can you go down to the bus depot and ask them to check if there are any vacant seats over the next few days? You go down the main street and turn left at the roundabout.'

Ron nodded and got up from the table.

'Emma, you take the kids outside to play and I'll make a few more phone calls. We'll meet back here in about an hour.'

Emma took Ben and Lucy by the hand and led them outside, relieved that she hadn't been given a job to do, as she knew she wasn't very good at solving problems like this one.

Lillian picked up her copy of Vogue and went upstairs to lie down.

· · · · ·

When Peter finished speaking, Clare was wide eyed. 'Wow, it's all a bit complicated then, isn't it?'

Peter nodded wearily. 'We were just having a bit of a council of war when you knocked on the door,' he said.

Clare went back over to the phone. 'I'll just try again,' she said. This time the number rang and was answered by Joanne herself. After a brief conversation, punctuated by her friend's laughter, Clare said goodbye and hung up. Feeling foolish, she turned to face the table.

'It would appear that I've jumped the gun a bit. Jo's family isn't coming until after Christmas. It looks like I'll have to grab the next bus back to Brisbane.'

'The next bus with spare seats leaves on the twenty seventh,' Ron answered glumly.

'Hire a car maybe?'

Peter half smiled. 'None available until the thirteenth of January.'

'There's no train nearby?'

Ron shook his head. 'There's a station about half an hour away, but the tilt train is booked solid until New Year's Eve.'

'Maybe I can book in somewhere else?'

This time Lillian spoke. 'Everything is taken. Believe me I've tried to make other arrangements,' she said, her pinched expression conveying how unimpressed she was. She took in Clare's dishevelled appearance and made it clear that she didn't think much of her.

But Clare was long past caring what people thought of her and put a bright smile on her face. 'Well, it looks like we're all roomies then. I'll chip in some rent.'

Cautiously, the group all looked at each other. This was the truth they'd been dancing around all day and Clare was the only one forthright enough to come out and say it. It wasn't the Christmas that any of them had planned or foreseen. But it was the Christmas they were stuck with whether they liked it or not.

Clare picked up her bag from outside the door and surveyed the bottom floor. 'It's a great house, so rustic. Is there another spare room or will I be bunking on the couch?'

Peter motioned towards the staircase. 'There's another room, it's the second one along.'

Clare nodded and started up the stairs. Halfway up she stopped, turned around and smiled. 'Hey, don't look so worried everybody, we're going to get on great.'

Ron stayed sitting at the table for a moment after the others dispersed. Yeah, I'm *sure* we're going to get on great, he thought. That Clare girl must be delusional. This was supposed to be his time to enjoy some peace and quiet and now he was caught up in a household of *women*, including Lady Muck herself. Peter didn't seem like a bad bloke, but he was obviously firmly under the thumb. He couldn't understand why any man lived like that.

Down at the bus station he'd practically begged for a seat, *any* seat to get him out of here, but it was to no avail. The young woman at the ticket window just shook her head and showed him the cancellation list, that already had twenty-three names on it.

Oh well, I'm just going to have to spend every daylight hour I can with my line in the water, Ron decided. In fact, now that this meeting was over, he was going to go for a wander and find himself a decent fishing spot. After all this, he was going to need it.

Lillian gestured for Peter to follow her onto the veranda. 'Peter this is not going to work,' she warned. 'We can't be expected to share our accommodations with small children, a socially inept fisherman and some chirpy drama student. It just isn't done.'

Peter looked at her. 'How do you know Clare's a drama student?'

Sighing impatiently, Lillian said, 'Didn't you hear her on the phone? She was talking about living the student life. She's also wearing a university t-shirt that says, "Drama students have class." It wasn't that hard to work out.'

'Well it's neither here nor there what she studies, she seems like a really nice girl.'

'I don't care how nice she seems, she's still a stranger as are the others. You have to do something, Peter!'

'I can't Lil. We've all got as much right to be here as each other. We've all paid a share of the rent and we have genuinely tried all the other avenues we can think of. It's a big house and there's lots of room – we'll just have to get used to keeping out of each other's way.' Secretly he was looking forward to the prospect of spending time with people from outside their normal social circle.

'Well, that's a typically male thing to say! Not everybody is as easy-going as you Peter, some of us like a bit of personal space. I can't believe we're going to be stuck here and that *you* can't do something about it.'

Peter threw his hands up in exasperation. 'Sorry Lillian, I guess you forgot to pack my magic wand,' he said.

Lillian stormed back inside and up to her room.

Emma was getting the kids ready to go down to the beach when she heard Clare's door open. She had warmed to Clare right away. So friendly and down to earth, she was the kind of person Emma would like to be. Clare went to uni and wasn't afraid to do and say things that Emma was too timid to consider. Sighing, she helped Lucy put on her sun shirt. As much as she loved her children, getting pregnant at seventeen had limited her in many ways. She hoped Clare wouldn't think she was unfriendly after their initial meeting. The kids were usually so good, but of course they had to pick their moment to act up. Clare must have wondered what she had walked into.

Having found her padlock key in her handbag, Clare changed into shorts and a clean shirt. She stopped by Emma's room to say hello. 'Isn't this an amazing house?'

Emma nodded, relieved at Clare's warm manner. 'I've never stayed so close to the beach before. The waves are incredible.'

Surveying the two excited children, Clare smiled. 'You've got gorgeous kids, you must feel so proud of them.'

'Yeah, I do. They never give me much trouble.'

'I'm just going down to the shops. Do you want anything?'

'No thanks, I think we're okay.'

'Okay, I'll see you a bit later then.' Clare left the room with a smile.

Emma sat down on the bed for a minute. It was so nice to hear somebody say something positive about her kids. Usually people just felt sorry for her. She was looking forward to spending time with Clare. All in all, this might not end up so bad after all. Peter was such a nice man although she wasn't sure about Ron yet. Lillian was pretty frosty, but surely she could keep out of her way. As much as Emma had been looking forward to the holiday, it would have been a bit lonely with just her and the kids. Now she had some people to share Christmas with and she was excited.

When Clare got back from town in the late afternoon, a thunderstorm was just about to break. Happy to make it back before the rain started, she soon realised that it might be nicer to brave the storm, given how strained things were inside. Annoyed that his first fishing session had been interrupted, Ron was reading the paper on the couch. Emma was playing blocks with her children on the floor, urging them to stay quiet. Peter was attempting to tune in the ancient radio to hear the news, and Lillian sat at the dining table, leafing through *Marie Clare*.

Walking inside, Clare dumped the two bulging garbage bags she was carrying on the floor, then dragged a rectangular box through the doorway. Without saying a word, she managed to pique the curiosity of everybody in the room. Peter asked if she needed a hand, Ron eyed the bags curiously and even Lillian snuck a glance, to see what was going on.

Ben jumped up and opened one of the bags. 'Look Mummy, it's Santa!'

'No Ben that's not yours,' Emma said, pulling him back.

Putting her hands on her hips, Clare examined the room. 'Okay housemates, where's the best place for the Christmas tree?' she asked.

Everybody seemed taken aback by the question.

'We can't all stay here for Christmas without a tree or decorations,' Clare announced. 'I found all this in the storage cupboard down the end of the veranda. All right, we'll let the men put the tree together and us girls, oh, and you too, Ben, can do the decorations.'

She gave the directions in such a casual yet firm way that nobody could think of a reason to disagree. Ron, who had been planning to say that he never celebrated Christmas, found himself in the throes of assembling the plastic tree. Emma, who was always cautioning her kids not to touch things that didn't belong to them, let them unpack the decorations with reckless abandon. Even Lillian, who attempted to distance herself from the whole project, wasn't hard hearted enough to ignore Lucy, who took the older woman's hand and led her to where the decorations were. Peter did a double take when he saw his wife unravelling tinsel and helping Lucy unpack ornaments from their box.

Emma supervised the kids and decorated the top of the tree once it was up, while Clare directed the men to hang decorations in various locations around the room. Lillian refrained from helping with the setup, but, she sat on the couch and watched, as the room took shape. She didn't smile, but neither did she look completely displeased. As the thunderstorm raged outside and darkness fell, the Beach House took on a very Christmassy atmosphere.

'She's a beautiful little girl, isn't she?' Peter said as he knotted his tie an hour later. He and Lillian were in their room dressing for an evening out at Leo's restaurant. It was a peace offering on his behalf after their little spat earlier.

Lillian made a face as she fluffed her hair and examined her new linen sundress in the full-length mirror. 'Be that as it may she's still illegitimate.'

Peter frowned as he put his wallet in his back pocket. 'That's not Lucy's fault, she's three years old. Besides, people don't even use that word anymore.'

Lillian adjusted her pearls and sprayed on some perfume. 'That type grow up fast enough. No doubt she'll end up just like her mother.'

Peter didn't respond to that comment, recognising it as a stepping-stone to a debate that could last for hours. Sighing, he looked out the window at the moon on the water and mentally counted to ten. He was glad that Clare was staying, knowing that she would be good company for Emma. After Lillian's less than warm welcome, she must have wondered what she was in store for.

Lillian gave her hair a quick spray and picked up her handbag. 'Well, shall we go?'

'Yes, Lil, let's go.'

Ron had gone to the pub, so it was just Emma, Clare and the kids at home for dinner. Emma had brought a few groceries with her for immediate use and planned to get some more the next day. She was a careful shopper and was used to managing on a meagre budget. Clare hadn't thought to buy herself groceries when she'd gone to town earlier and was feeling hungry. She wandered into the kitchen as Emma opened a tin of baked beans.

Perching herself on the bench, Clare grinned. 'Tell you what. You fix the kids up with the beans and I'll get us a pizza. There's a shop just near the caravan park, so I can walk down.'

Emma's eyes lit up for a second and then fell. 'No, I can't. I mean, I don't have very much money. Beans are boring but they're cheap.'

'No, I insist. It's my treat to celebrate having Lillian out of the house for the night.'

Emma considered for a minute, then smiled. 'Okay. I can't remember the last time I had pizza and it is nice not to be walking on eggshells. She's a bit of a Nasty Nell isn't she?'

Clare laughed. 'Yeah, definitely. It's not so much what she says but the facial expressions and body language that tell the story. There's a definite lack of warmth there.'

'Peter's a sweetheart though.'

'Yeah, he is. It will be nice to get to know him better.'

As she served the beans into bowls for the kids, Emma said, 'Can we get garlic bread with the pizza?'

'Of course we can! My theory is if you're going to eat unhealthily, then go all out. Besides, you obviously don't have to worry about your weight, lucky thing.'

Emma smiled and looked down at her thin, lanky frame. 'No, I don't. But neither would you,' she said, taking in Clare's tall, athletic build.

'Well, not really, but I'm always referred to as a *strong looking* girl which is a polite way of saying I'm not dainty like my mother and little sister.'

'Well, people think I'm about twelve until they see the kids, then they think I'm the babysitter.'

Both girls laughed, each delighted they had found a new friend.

Later when the kids were in bed, Clare and Emma played Scrabble.

'Kiwi,' said Clare, as she arranged her tiles. 'Just like you.'

Emma looked up in surprise. 'Can you still pick my accent?' she asked. 'Most people can't.'

'Yeah, it's not strong but you can hear it in certain words like *swumming*,' she teased.

'It's you Aussies who say it wrong.'

Shaking her head, Clare wrote down her score. 'How long have you been here?'

Emma studied her letters. 'About seven years.'

'What made your family move here?'

Emma was quiet for a moment before she replied. 'My family didn't move, just me.'

'Wow, that's a big move to make alone.'

'Well, I came with my boyfriend, my now ex-boyfriend. I guess you could say I ran away, considering I was only sixteen.'

Clare couldn't hide her surprise. 'Wow. How did you manage to leave the country?'

'I had a passport from a school trip to Fiji and Tim knew someone in Customs. It was surprisingly easy.'

'How did your family take it?'

'I guess they were devastated. I left a note, but I made out we were going to Auckland so they wouldn't try and look for me over here.'

Clare shook her head. 'Gee, I'm afraid my life is very boring by comparison. Didn't you get on with your family?' she asked gently.

'Yes, I did, honestly,' Emma said. 'It was just that Tim had this effect on me, he could talk me into doing anything. He was nineteen then and when he told me he was coming over here, I couldn't stand the thought of not being with him.'

'But things didn't work out long term?'

'To cut a long and very involved story short, it was fun for the first year, when the kids came it was harder, but we did okay until he discovered drugs. After that, it went downhill at warp speed.'

'You poor thing. I'm sorry, I shouldn't ask so many questions.'

'No, really, it's okay. It's a relief to tell someone and we're doing all right.'

'Emma you've got two great kids, you're all fit and healthy. I'd say you're doing better than all right.'

While Clare and Emma had become firm friends in the short time they had known each other, there was still a distinctly strained atmosphere at breakfast the next morning. Lillian, who was dressed immaculately with full make up, made it clear she disapproved of the two younger women coming downstairs in their pyjamas by giving several pointed glances in their direction. Peter attempted to cover the tension by keeping plenty of light-hearted chitchat going. Ron hardly said a word and kept his head buried in the paper, although he did keep sneaking glances at the children when he thought nobody was watching.

After Clare finished her toast, she produced a piece of paper and a pen. 'Okay everyone, we'd better get our shopping list sorted out,' she said, taking a sip of tea.

Everybody looked at her as if she had suggested they run a marathon.

'Shopping?' they all repeated.

'Yes, shopping, you know, so we can eat. Christmas is just over a week away and we haven't planned the menu for that, let alone the rest of our meals. I don't think any of us would like to live on Chinese takeaway or pizza for that long.'

Lillian recoiled, as if in shock at the idea. 'Oh, I don't think that will be suitable at all. I'm sure we all have different tastes and then there's the children to consider.'

Ron glanced up briefly from the paper. 'I'm not much of a cook so I'm used to just pleasing me.'

Clare waved away their concerns. 'Come on, let's all live a little. I'm sure between us we can come up with meals that we all like. Besides, I'm a pretty good cook. My brother is a chef and he's taught me almost everything he knows. As for the kids, Emma's already got their stuff sorted out, so that's not a problem.'

Looking up again, Clare gave a hearty smile. 'All right let's go round the table. Each person name something they like and we'll get a general consensus whether the rest of us like it too. There's got to be some middle ground between us.'

Fifteen minutes later, Clare had come up with a menu for the coming days and was busy finalising a list. Lillian had made the task as hard as possible, but eventually agreed to several different meals. Peter volunteered to go shopping with Clare, which apparently annoyed Lillian. Clare invited Lillian along too, but she refused and retreated to her room. Ron looked relieved when the whole discussion was over and disappeared with his fishing gear. Emma approached Clare after the others had left the room.

'Clare, it's a wonderful idea but I can't afford to chip in. I'll just get some pasta and instant noodles for me.'

'Don't be silly,' Clare replied. 'Peter's already offered to pay your share and he would be very offended if you refused.' /

Emma's mouth dropped open. 'Clare, I can't let him do that! I just met him and it's not his responsibility.'

Clare swept her hair into a messy ponytail and put on her University of Melbourne cap. 'Emma, he's loaded and he's generous. You shouldn't be afraid to accept gifts given with kindness and good intent.'

'Well, all right then, if you put it like that. But I still feel funny about it.'

After taking Ben and Lucy down to the playground in the caravan park for two hours, Emma was ready for lunch when they got back to the house. Opening the fridge, her eyes widened, as she took in the huge selection of food inside, including a Christmas ham. Noticing Clare sitting reading on the veranda, she went out to say hello.

Clare looked up from her book. 'Have you been in that little second hand bookstore?'

'No, I just walked past yesterday.'

'It's amazing. There's a huge range of books and it's so nicely organised. I bought a bagful of novels.'

'You have had a busy morning. I can't believe you could get so much food from that tiny supermarket.'

Clare laughed. 'Oh, no, we soon realised our shopping list was a bit ambitious for Four Square. We took the bus over to Rosethorn. There's a great shopping centre over there with a big Safeway.'

'A what?'

'Sorry, I mean Woolworths. I'm not sure why Victoria has a different name for the same supermarket chain.'

Emma was still amazed. 'And you managed to carry all that back on the bus?'

'No, Peter insisted on treating us to a taxi. He's a real laugh when you get him by himself. We had a nice morning.'

'Well, I can't say the same for Lillian. It was a very silent morning here in the house.'

Clare closed her book and lay back on the lounger. 'Yes, I noticed we weren't welcomed home with open arms. Oh well, now we've got some nice food, let's make a decent lunch.'

Emma scrubbed the potatoes with gusto, as she helped Clare prepare dinner that evening. She couldn't remember the last time she'd had so much fun. She and Clare had taken the kids to the beach for the afternoon and had had a ball swimming, building sand castles and playing on the boogie boards that Clare had found in the storage cupboard.

So used to being solely responsible for her kids, Emma had forgotten how nice it was to have adult company, when she played with them. Ben and Lucy also loved having somebody new to play with. Especially somebody like Clare, who was completely prepared to go along with whatever they were doing. She'd barely flinched when Lucy dumped a bucket of sand on her head.

'You should have seen some of the role plays I've had to do at uni,' she had said, shaking her hair. 'Getting sand on your head is actually quite tame by comparison.'

'Wow, I could never do that,' said Emma. 'I hate being the centre of attention and having people watch me. If I had to get up in front of the class, I always forgot what I was supposed to say.'

'Well, you get used to it in my course. If you don't do it, you don't pass.'

Emma thought again just how confident and accomplished Clare was and hoped that some of it would rub off on her before the holiday was over.

'Hey Em, did you see how many fish Ron brought back?' Clare said, as she cut up some carrot sticks for the kids.

'Yeah, it was a real haul, he's obviously no amateur.' Emma glanced out to the veranda. Ben had been glued to Ron's side since he arrived back from fishing and was watching him intently as he cleaned and scaled his catch. Although Emma couldn't catch what was being said, she could hear Ben's excited chatter, and Ron's deep voice, so they must be having a conversation. She often worried about the lack of male role models in her son's life, so having a type of grandfather figure, even if it was temporary, was a good thing.

Emma finished the potatoes, then looked into the lounge room to check on Lucy. To her amazement, her daughter was perched beside Lillian on the couch, watching in fascination as she worked on an embroidery picture. Lucy was a shy child who took a long time to warm to strangers. Clare had won her over with her extraverted personality, but Emma couldn't fathom why she was so drawn to Lillian's frosty demeanour.

Ben bounded into the kitchen with a plastic container of fish fillets. 'Hey Mum, look at all the fish Ron caught. He said we can eat it for dinner.'

Emma rescued the fish before Ben upended it and smiled her thanks at Ron, who was hovering just near the kitchen door.

'Wow Ron, we'll have to subtract this from the food kitty,' Clare said. 'Is that whiting?'

'Uh huh. There's a lot of it around here. There's also some cod.'

'Cool, thanks!' Clare said. 'Dinner won't be too long.'

Ron smiled shyly and eased away back onto the veranda.

Emma looked into the lounge again to find Lillian reading Lucy a story. She nudged Clare and motioned for her to look. Clare raised her eyebrows in surprise. When Peter walked in the door a few seconds later, he did a double take. The only one who didn't seem amazed was Lucy, who was listening to her favourite story with the rapt attention of a three-year-old.

Emma taught Clare how to play the card game SPIT that night, after the kids were asleep. The game quickly became spirited, with both girls guilty of shoving the other's hand out of the way to get their own card to the desired pile.

Wiping tears of laughter from her eyes, Clare smiled. 'Okay, you won that one, but I'm still disputing the first one.'

'No way, I won them both,' Emma insisted, packing up the cards.

Clare folded her arms. 'Cheaters never prosper, but I'll forgive you on this occasion. Hot chocolate?'

'Yes, that would be lovely.'

The two young women sat on the veranda and sipped their drinks, enjoying the magical display of stars in the night sky.

Clare gazed down towards the surf club. 'Those Christmas lights they've got strung up in the trees down there look great.'

'Yeah, they do. I'll have to take the kids down to have a look one night.'

They sat in companionable silence for a while, enjoying the peace of the summer's night. Emma savoured each sip of her drink. 'You are a master of hot chocolate,' she said.

'Thanks. One of the many skills waitressing has bestowed on me.'

Emma sighed. 'I wish I had some skills.'

'Are you kidding? You've got two kids. Mothers are the masters at multi-tasking.'

'No really, I wish I'd had a job of some kind. I'm nearly twenty-four and I've never done anything daring.'

Clare stared at her. 'Daring? A schoolgirl who runs away to another country with her dashing boyfriend? Who is brave enough to leave him when things go wrong and who has single-handedly raised two great little kids? What's not daring about that?'

'With hindsight, it wasn't daring it was stupid,' said Emma. 'I love Ben and Lucy and I'd never trade them for anything, but I just wish I'd finished school before I met Tim.'

Clare placed her empty cup on the table and stretched out on the lounger. 'I guess we're all insecure no matter what we've achieved. I'm having lots of second thoughts about my chosen career.'

Knowing actors could be sensitive about their performances, Emma paused for a moment before replying. 'Did you get a bad review?'

'It was a bit worse than that. I don't know, you grow up believing you know exactly what you want to do. So, you go and study and try and put those skills into practice, but then you get a bit over confident...' Clare's voice trailed off.

Emma rubbed her arms as the sea breeze picked up. 'Was it bad stage fright?'

Clare looked at Emma before speaking again, wondering how she had come to that conclusion. Although she knew Emma's story, Clare had disclosed very little about her own life. 'Not exactly, more like I got booed off the stage.' She shivered a little.

'Clare, I think you are amazing and you'll work it out.'

'I hope so.' Sighing softly, Clare picked up the cups and they went inside.

Ron was up at the crack of dawn. He wanted to get in some serious fishing while the conditions were so good. He also wanted to avoid breakfast with the others. Ron hadn't been around women for so long; especially young women, and he felt conspicuously out of place. While he couldn't escape the evening meal, he could be out of the way at breakfast and lunch, when possible.

Walking into the dark, silent kitchen, Ron reminded himself that he didn't need people around him. He was a loner and quite happy that way. Fishing was his passion. It was uncomplicated and undemanding. That was what he came for and that was what he was going to spend his holiday doing. Flicking on the light, Ron stuck two pieces of bread in the toaster and filled the kettle. Waiting while the water boiled, Ron looked out at the water, transfixed by the beauty of the emerging sun. Although he saw many sunrises out on the land, it was completely different on the water.

Once the water boiled, it didn't take long to make his breakfast. Spreading butter and honey on his toast, Ron took a sip of tea as he stood at the kitchen bench. Making a face, he stuck another teabag in his mug. He was used to strong billy tea and found teabags bland in comparison. Feeling a presence, Ron turned around and saw Ben standing inside the doorway, watching him intently.

'What are you doing up at this hour, young man?' he asked.

'I just wanted to see what you were doing. Are you going fishing again?'

Taking another mouthful of tea, Ron nodded. 'Yes, I am. It's a good time to go, early in the morning.'

'Even when it's still dark?'

'It's not really dark, have a look outside – can you see the sun coming up?'

Ben ran eagerly over to the window and peered outside. 'Yeah! I can see it over the water.'

'It's a special time of day, sunrise.'

'You know, I'd like to go fishing one day.'

'You'll have to tell your mum.'

Ben shook his head. 'She's a girl, so she doesn't know anything about it. I'll have to wait until I'm big enough to go by myself.'

Ron tried to ignore the emotions that welled inside him at these words. 'We'll check with your mum, and if she says okay, you can come with me sometime.'

Ben's smile engulfed his whole face. 'Really? Could I really come? That would be the biggest treat, ever.'

Ron nodded. 'Yes, you can really come. Now you be a good boy and go back to bed for a bit.'

Ben scampered off, like a person who had been promised the world, and Ron couldn't help but smile to himself as he ate his toast.

When Emma and Clare took the kids down to the beach that afternoon, Peter was already in the water.

'Do you think we'll see Lillian down here splashing around too?' Emma asked, dumping the bag of beach toys and the towels onto the sand.

Both girls dissolved into laughter at the thought. Clare arranged her towel carefully and sat down. 'Somehow, I don't think so. She doesn't seem like the swimming in the ocean type.'

'Why do you reckon she came on a holiday to the beach then?'

'I think she was expecting a resort with a pool where she could just look at the ocean without having to go there. Peter loves it, though.'

Looking at to where Peter was bodysurfing to his heart's content, Emma nodded. 'He's definitely having fun and we are going to do the same. Come on kids, let's go for a paddle.'

An hour later Clare finally freed her feet from the mountain of sand Ben had buried them under.

'Aw, Clare,' he wailed.

Clare stood up and brushed the sand off her legs. 'As much as I love having my limbs buried, I think it's time for an ice cream. The truck is just coming up the road.' She grabbed some money and set off across the crowded beach, with Ben tagging along behind her.

Emma and Lucy were working on their own sand creation. Using the selection of sand moulds, they had constructed a multi-towered castle, complete with a pointed turret in the centre. 'There we go Lucy Lou, how does that look?' Emma asked, as she smoothed the sand on the right edge.

Lucy clapped her hands in excitement. 'Cinderella!' she exclaimed.

'Mmm,' said Emma. 'I was thinking more Sleeping Beauty, but I guess any fairy tale would fit.' She stood up to stretch. Her knees were stiff after being on her haunches for so long. What a great way to spend an afternoon, she thought happily, gazing around the packed patrolled area. It's so nice to be on holidays.

Caught up in her musing, Emma didn't see the Frisbee coming straight at her. She got a shock when it struck her on the cheek. More stunned than injured, it took a moment to work out what happened.

'I'm so sorry!' cried a teenage girl in a red bikini. 'Are you okay?'

'Yeah, I'm fine. Don't worry about it,' Emma replied, rubbing her cheek.

'Are you sure? You don't want me to get some ice or something?'

Emma shook her head, surprised at the girl's politeness. 'Really, I'm okay. I should have been paying attention to what was going on around me.'

'I told the guys not to throw it so hard. I'm going to make them move a bit further down where there's not so many people. Sorry again.'

Emma smiled. 'I'm fine, I promise,' she assured the girl. 'Go and enjoy your game.'

Watching the girl make her way back over to her friends, Emma sighed. It was hard to remember being that young and carefree. Dropping her gaze, she turned around to check on Lucy.

She wasn't there.

An arrow of fear pierced Emma's heart. 'Lucy!' she screamed, looking frantically around her.

The girl was back. 'Hey, what's wrong?' she asked.

Emma's heart lurched into a violent rhythm. 'My little girl!' she cried. 'She's missing!'

'Oh no, it's all my fault!' the girl said. 'I'll go get some help.'

Emma shoved her way through the crowds of people relaxing on the sand, completely oblivious when she stepped on somebody's feet and then knocked over a sand castle. A boy of about five burst into tears. 'You're a bad lady!' he yelled, as he surveyed the ruins of his fortress. His mother's glare was wasted on Emma as she kept moving, searching frantically for any sign of Lucy. Due to its protected shoreline, Sunset Point had a large patrolled swimming area and the crowds on the sand extended beyond that area. There were so many places she could be.

Maybe she was in the water! Surely not, thought Emma. Lucy was timid in the ocean and only splashed in the shallows if she or Clare was with her. But kids were so unpredictable. Lucy rarely let her mother out of her sight and must be petrified to be on her own. If she thought Emma was swimming, she might venture into the waves.

Oh, please, don't let anything happen to her! Emma prayed frantically. I know I've made a mess of my life, but her and Ben are the only thing I've done right.

The girl was back, dragging a lifeguard behind her. Emma burst into tears at the sight of him. He put a calming hand on her shoulder. 'Try not to panic, love,' he said kindly. 'My name is Jim and we're going to find your little girl, alright?'

Huge sobs wracked Emma's thin body. 'She c-c-c-an't swim,' she stammered. 'She's so l-l-l-little.'

Jim was patient, but brisk. 'How old is she?'

'Three.'

'Hair colour?'

'B-b-blonde,' Emma sniffed.

'What's she wearing?'

'It's p-p-pink. It's one of those, you know those...' Emma waved her hands in frustration, unable to articulate her thoughts.

'Sunsuits?' said the girl. 'With the sleeves and the legs? Zip up the back?'

Emma nodded emphatically, tears still spilling down her cheeks.

'Okay,' said Jim, 'We'll get right onto it.'

'Oh, she's wearing a h-h-hat,' sniffled Emma. 'One of those swimming hats with the flap on the back. It's g-g-got Dorothy the Dinosaur on it.'

'All right.' Bringing the two-way radio he was holding up to his mouth, Jim spoke into it, urgently. More urgently than Emma would have liked. This really is an emergency, she realised. He knows what can happen to lost kids at the beach. 'Get the clubbies onto it too,' she heard him say. 'We want every available body looking.'

Emma let out a primal moan at the mention of the word body.

Jim leant down to meet Emma's gaze. 'I know it's hard love, but please stay here. It makes our job so much easier if we know at least where you are. She might make her way back to you too. Kids are smarter than we think sometimes.' Turning to the girl he said, 'Can you help us look?'

She nodded.

'Right, off you go.' Placing his hand on Emma's shoulder again he said, 'I'm going to look as well.'

Emma nodded numbly and rubbed the goose bumps on her arms. How can I have goose bumps? she thought. It's thirty degrees!

'Is there anyone I can get for you before I go?' asked Jim.

Emma gazed around helplessly. Where were Clare and Peter when she needed them? Looking up past the grassed area she could see the queue for the ice-cream truck snaking along the road. Clare was too far away to see her. As for Peter, she'd seen him head off for a walk a while before. He could be anywhere along the shoreline. Wordlessly, Emma shook her head.

'We'll find her.' Jim squeezed her shoulder gently before jogging down to the water's edge.

Emma watched as two other lifeguards and three surf lifesavers began moving briskly through the crowd both on the sand and in the water. The girl in the red bikini ran along the shoreline, talking to each person she met and gesturing with her hands.

The tap on her shoulder startled her. Emma jumped in fright.

'Sorry darling, I didn't mean to scare you,' said a plump middle-aged woman. Decked out in a long-sleeved caftan-like beach cover-up, a wide-brimmed straw hat and Cancer Council wrap-around sunglasses, she looked like a walking advertisement for the Slip, Slop, Slap campaign. Emma stared at her dully.

'Here, I've got a chair. Sit down,' the woman said kindly.

Emma shook her head. 'I can't,' she said. 'I need to be able to see everything.'

The woman nodded. 'Of course. Oh, you poor love! Is there anything worse than your child missing around any kind of water? The statistics for drowning these days, just dreadful.' She shook her head. 'My neighbour's cousin, well, her niece drowned in the local river. Her parents just took their eyes off her for a few seconds...'

A younger woman with a baby on her hip nudged the woman

sharply. 'Not helping, Mum,' she hissed through clenched teeth.

Jim jogged past, talking into the two way again. 'Give it another ten and then we'll get the coppers in,' he said. 'You've got to be so careful with abductions these days…'

Emma started crying again, hysterically this time. The police! Oh God, it must be looking pretty bad. 'I can't lose her!' she cried. 'She's all I've got, her and Ben!'

The younger woman handed the baby to her mother and took Emma's hand. 'Here, we'll walk a bit closer to the water and see what's happening,' she said.

Her body still convulsing with sobs, Emma let herself be led along by the woman, whose name she didn't even know. In the space of a few minutes her world had imploded. She'd heard it said that your life can change in an instant, but had never understood the concept until right then.

Although heartened to see the lifeguards and surf lifesavers searching so frantically, Emma felt a sense of hopelessness. There were so many people, so many…

Because her eyes were blurred with tears, Emma thought she must be hallucinating when she saw the tiny figure in pink, about twenty metres along the shoreline, being dragged along by an older girl. 'Lucy?' she shrieked. Emma had never moved as fast as she did in that moment. Wrenching her hand from the young woman's, she ran to the water's edge, just as the freakily powerful wave knocked her baby off her feet.

Jostling her way through the crowd, Emma was so distressed, it took her a moment to focus on the familiar figure wading out of the water, carrying Lucy. 'Peter, oh, Peter, thank you!' she cried, taking her screaming daughter into her arms.

Peter put a consoling hand on Emma's shoulder. 'She's okay. I don't think she even swallowed any water. She's just stunned.'

The feeling of relief was indescribable. Emma finally felt like she was getting air into her lungs again.

A female surf lifesaver in a yellow and red shirt came running over. 'This was the little lost one?' she asked.

Emma nodded. 'Yeah,' was all she could manage to say, as she comforted her still crying baby.

299

The tall blonde teenager patted Peter on the back. 'Nice save, Grandad. Are you trying to take over my job?'

Peter smiled humbly not bothering to correct her.

'I'll let the others know,' the lifesaver said. 'I'm so glad she's okay.'

'Thank you so much,' Emma said shakily. 'Please tell everyone thanks.'

The girl nodded. 'No worries.'

Peter shepherded Emma back up to where their belongings were. 'Here, sit down,' he said, spreading the towels back out. Emma did as he said, cuddling Lucy close. Quiet now, she seemed unharmed by the incident.

Emma stared at Peter. 'I don't get how you just magically appeared,' she said, shaking her head.

Peter sat down alongside her. 'I was walking back up when I thought I saw Lucy playing with that little girl in one of those sun tents. I couldn't work out where you were and then, when I saw the girls heading down to the water, I took off after them. I haven't run that fast in years,' he said.

'I'm such a bad mother! I shouldn't have taken my eyes off her, even for a second.'

'You're not a bad mum, Emma. Every parent has moments like that. It's harder for you because you have to do all the watching yourself.'

'You know, if you had told me when I was fifteen that I was going to be a single mother before I turned twenty-one, I would have laughed. Sometimes, you end up in places that you just don't plan to be.'

'You're right, Emma,' said Peter. 'Look, I'm sorry that Lillian hasn't been very friendly. She's just not great at mixing with people she doesn't know well.'

Emma smiled politely, knowing how hard it must be for Peter to apologise on Lillian's behalf. 'Don't worry about it, I'll just stay out of her way. I hope you weren't embarrassed when the lifesaver thought you were Lucy's grandad. I mean, you don't look old or anything.'

'There's much worse things you can be accused of than being somebody's grandfather,' said Peter. 'I'm looking forward to being called Grandad one day.'

'Well, I know you'll do a great job,' Emma replied, although she just couldn't picture Lillian as a doting grandmother.

They both looked up as a shadow fell over them. Ben and Clare had arrived back, laden with ice-creams and napkins.

Clare rolled her eyes dramatically. 'Talk about a wait! I was afraid you guys might have packed up and gone home.' Handing everyone an ice-cream she plonked herself back on her towel.

'So, did we miss anything exciting?'

Clare pressed Peter and Ron into service manning the barbeque that night while she and Emma prepared the salads and vegetables. They slipped into their usual easy-going chitchat while they worked companionably in the kitchen.

'What do you reckon an architect from Double Bay and a station hand from the outback have to talk about?' Emma pondered as she peeled a carrot. She could see the two men talking, as they each drank a beer and occasionally turned the meat.

'People usually find a common ground somewhere. When I took the onions out before they were talking about cars, you know petrol versus diesel, that kind of riveting stuff.'

'I guess it's as interesting to them as shopping and fashion is to us.'

'Yeah, fair comment. I'm just jaded after growing up with two older brothers.'

'My brother is younger. He reckoned there was too much girl stuff in our house.' Emma smiled wistfully.

Lillian arrived downstairs then. She had gone to Rosethorn to get her hair done and have a facial that afternoon. When she got home, she retreated to her room for a lie down. Now, she sat primly on the couch and peered out onto the veranda, where the barbeque was exuding some aromatic smells.

Clare nudged Emma and whispered, 'No, that's okay, Lillian, you sit down and have a rest, we'll finish up here.'

Emma had to bite her lip to stop from laughing. She was just opening the fridge door, when she saw Lucy climb up onto the couch and sit beside Lillian. Taken aback, Lillian sat back a little.

Inching closer, Lucy said, 'I felled in the water.'

Lillian's face softened. 'Did you, dear? That's no good, is it?'

Lucy shook her head. 'The ice-cream made me feel better,' she said.

'Did it now? Well, ice-cream can make you feel good.'

Noticing Emma's preoccupation, Clare turned her attention to the lounge room as well.

Ben appeared next to the couch. 'She's still scared of the water. I'm not 'cause I'm six. But she's only little.'

Lucy had moved even closer to Lillian. 'I'm a big girl now.'

Lillian smiled kindly.

Clare and Emma exchanged an amazed glance. 'There you go, she can smile after all,' Clare whispered.

'Yes, you are a big girl. A big, brave girl,' Lillian said.

Lucy's face beamed at this announcement. 'Can you read me a story?' she asked.

'All right, just one before we eat.'

Lucy scampered off to retrieve her book and Lillian turned around to see what was happening in the kitchen. Caught in their spying, Clare and Emma frantically tried to look busy. Clare re-tossed Emma's beautifully arranged salad and Emma started peeling another carrot, even though they had plenty. They didn't dare look into the lounge room again.

· · · · ·

Clare made bacon and eggs for breakfast the next morning, which went down well with all the housemates.

'Great idea Clare,' Peter said, as he reached for another piece of toast. 'You just can't beat a cooked breakfast, especially when you're on holidays.'

'I usually have my eggs scrambled.' Lillian pouted, but slid a fried egg onto her plate anyway.

Ron just nodded and kept eating.

'So, what did you get up to last night, Ron?' Clare asked, determined to drag him into the conversation. 'Did you discover some hidden nightlife here in Sunset Point?'

Ron shook his head. 'No, just a quiet game of pool at the surf club.'

'Oh, cool, I didn't know they had tables there. I love playing pool.' Clare smiled across the table.

'Me too,' said Emma. 'I'm actually pretty good.'

After breakfast, Peter helped Clare and Emma stack the dishes. 'I'll wash up,' he said, 'Then I'll take the kids down to the playground for a while, if you'd like to have a game of pool.'

The girls didn't need any further encouragement and headed straight over to the modern brick building that was right on the beachfront. The poolroom had floor to ceiling windows, so they could see both the water and the playground.

Clare broke and managed to sink two balls as well. 'Looks like I'm smalls,' she said and took her next shot, which wasn't as successful. They chatted and laughed as they played their first two games, with Emma winning the first and Clare the second.

'My brother taught me that winning shot,' Clare said, 'but he regretted it when I started beating him occasionally. Another?'

'Yeah,' replied Emma. 'Oh, only if it doesn't cost too much.'

Clare fed some more coins into the slot. 'It won't break me.'

Emma looked down at the playground while Clare set the balls up. 'Do you think kids miss out by not having grandparents and aunts and uncles?' she asked, watching Peter push Ben and Lucy on the swings.

'That's hard to say,' Clare said, carefully lifting the rack. 'Ideally if you have extended family, then it's a great thing. No matter what they say, family bonds are the strongest. I couldn't imagine not knowing my niece and nephews.' Seeing Emma's troubled expression, she spoke again. 'It's not always possible, though.'

Emma sank the orange five ball and lined up her next shot. 'It's just that Peter is so good with them. I mean, we've been happy, just the three of us, since I left Tim, but now I see how it would be nice for them to have their own grandad and grandma.'

'Do your parents know you've got kids?'

Emma shook her head. 'I did something so horrible, Clare, I just left and put them through all that heartache. They could never forgive me for that.'

'I don't know, Em, it could take some time but I think they might.' Clare concentrated on her next shot and ended up sinking one of Emma's balls. 'Maybe you could give them a call?'

'I can't,' Emma said. 'I'm not brave like you. I couldn't stand it if they hung up on me.' She looked out the window again and saw Peter and the kids heading back.

Clare gave her new friend a hug. 'We're all brave in different ways.'

Two men were waiting for the table, so they finished the game without saying much more and went down to meet Peter.

The house was quiet that afternoon. Clare and Emma had taken the kids to town to see a nativity play put on by the local drama group. Ron was still out fishing. Peter waited until Lillian was relaxing on the couch, reading her book before he started banging around in the kitchen. Just for effect he had the small roasting pan out on the bench, as well as two small saucepans and the bluntest knife.

It only took five minutes to get her attention. 'Peter, what are you doing?' she asked. 'I'm trying to read.' Setting her book down, Lillian walked over and stood in the doorway of the kitchen.

Peter looked up from the recipe book he had randomly pulled off the kitchen shelf. 'Sorry Lil, maybe you can go out onto the veranda. I'm just getting dinner sorted out. I thought I'd do the lamb roast.'

Lillian folded her arms and stared at her husband. '*You're* cooking a lamb roast?'

'Yep, I thought I'd give it a bash. Poor Clare is exhausted, so I said I'd give her a hand.'

'She doesn't seem exhausted to me and she did offer to do the cooking.'

'She's trying to be nice, it doesn't mean we should take advantage of her generosity.' Peter removed the leg of lamb from the fridge and attempted to jam it into the too-small roasting pan. Out of the corner of his eye he could see that Lillian was itching to correct him, but wasn't quite ready to give in. 'Hmmm, there's no room for the vegetables, maybe I can just boil them in the saucepan,' he said.

'You can't serve roast lamb with boiled vegetables, it's not the way it's done.'

'I'm sure everyone will understand. We're all just trying to muck in here.'

Lillian rolled her eyes. 'To think we could be up at the resort now, with an on-site restaurant.'

'Maybe I should just ask Clare to do it,' said Peter. 'She seems to be able to turn her hand to just about anything.'

Lillian walked over to the cupboard and took out the large roasting pan. 'Young women today don't know how to cook roasts properly, they're not exotic enough apparently. They only want to do quirky, complicated dishes with outlandish ingredients,' she said, as she took some potatoes from the bag on the bench.

'Well maybe Clare could give you a hand when she gets back.'

Lillian ran water in the sink to wash the potatoes. 'Just give me space, Peter, I'll do it myself. It will be easier that way. So much for a quiet afternoon of reading.'

Peter picked up his own book from the dining room table and slipped out onto the veranda. He grinned to himself as he settled into the squatter's chair, listening to the sounds of Lillian preparing the meal, but, then, as he thought more about it, his smile faded. Yes, he had won the battle, he had manipulated Lillian into doing what he wanted her to, but it was a hollow victory. Why couldn't he have just asked her, or why couldn't she have just offered? Why did everything these days have to be weighed up and arranged around Lillian's moods? And, why had he become one of those people who put up with anything for the sake of a quiet life?

The lamb roast was a big hit. Lillian can really cook, Clare thought as she relished a bite of the beautifully cooked meat and crisp roast vegetables. So why had she acted like she couldn't boil water?

Clare snuck a glance across the table at the older woman. Lillian didn't look like she'd spent the afternoon in the kitchen. Her hair and makeup were perfect and there were no stains on her clothes or chips in her nail polish. Clare had always assumed that wealthy people had hired help to do their cooking and cleaning, but maybe that was a bit of a generalisation.

Ron was enjoying the meal so much that he couldn't stop complimenting Lillian. 'I can't remember the last time I had a home cooked roast like this one,' he said, between mouthfuls. 'I mean, they do a roast at the local pub and it's nice enough, but nothing like this.'

Lillian gave a small nod and a half smile. 'Thank you, I'm glad you're enjoying it,' she said, obviously in the mood to be magnanimous.

'I haven't had gravy this nice since Mum died,' he added, reaching for the jug again.

Peter was enjoying the meal too. While Lillian wasn't exactly the life and soul of the party, she was engaging in at least some conversation with the others, which was a step forward. It was nice not to have to make all the effort to keep mealtime small talk going. I'm almost relaxed, he realised as he took a sip of wine. Maybe, just maybe the rest of this holiday might turn out okay.

The rest of the meal passed by pleasantly and they all enjoyed the lemon meringue pie that Peter had picked up at the Sunset Café.

I can't believe we're actually lingering around the evening meal, thought Clare, as she half listened to Peter and Ron talk about fishing lures. Usually we're finished and scattered in our various directions immediately after the last bite has been taken.

'Coffee anyone?' she asked, hoping to stretch this unprecedented camaraderie a bit further.

'Yes, thanks,' the other four agreed.

'I'll help,' offered Emma, as she gathered up some plates to take in the kitchen. Stacking them in the sink, she turned to look at Clare. 'Did some aliens land here today without me realising?' she asked.

'Possibly,' said Clare. 'Having both Lillian and Ron talking at the dinner table was pretty bizarre.'

'I'll say. And they actually talked to each other!'

'Well, they say the way to a man's heart is through his stomach.' Clare smiled as she spooned coffee into five mugs. 'The barista in me hates to use instant, but it's the best I can do.'

The atmosphere at breakfast the next morning was not so convivial. Ron was annoyed because a group of yobbos had invaded his favourite fishing spot, Ben and Lucy squabbled over the toy in the Cornflakes packet and Lillian complained about the loose board in the upstairs hallway.

'It's so difficult to get a good night's sleep when you hear every movement outside your door,' she said to Peter, but loudly enough for everybody to hear. 'That's the problem with having your room right near the bathroom, it's a bad design flaw.'

Peter sighed wearily. 'People were probably still using chamber pots when this house was built, so traffic to the bathroom at night wasn't an issue,' he said, with no attempt at humour.

The thought of Lillian emptying a chamber pot was enough to cause Clare to let out a chuckle, despite biting her lip and desperately trying to hold it in. She started giggling in earnest when Emma glanced at her quizzically across the table.

'Hey, why are you laughing Clare?' Ben asked.

The others looked at her expectantly.

'Yes, come on, share the joke,' said Peter.

Clare took a deep breath to compose herself. 'It's really not that funny,' she said, struggling to keep a straight face. 'I have a weird sense of humour sometimes and having brothers I've been exposed to a lot of toilet humour. The mention of chamber pots set me off, that's all.'

'It's hardly appropriate breakfast conversation,' Lillian said, 'and it doesn't solve the problem.' Setting her cutlery down neatly on her plate, she frowned at Clare.

'I'll swap rooms if you like.' Clare snickered again, still not over her burst of mirth.

Lillian gave her a withering glance.

'Just a suggestion,' said Clare, with another little chuckle.

After they finished eating Emma helped Clare with the dishes. 'I see lemon lips is back,' she said, picking up a bowl to dry.

'I'll say,' said Clare. 'Our pleasant dinner was obviously a blip on the radar.'

'Yeah, I thought it was too good to last.'

'Well, I think I'm to blame for the creaky board last night. Coffee at night is like a diuretic for me. I thought I was being quiet though.'

Emma giggled. 'Snap! It must be the caffeine.'

Clare laughed too. 'I'm surprised we didn't meet in the hallway.' She let the water out of the sink and they headed upstairs to get changed.

'What does Lillian want Peter to do anyway?' asked Emma, as they climbed the stairs. 'Re-lay the flooring?'

'Probably,' Clare replied and then stopped short when they reached the top of the stairs. There was Peter with a toolbox on the floor beside him and a plank of wood in his hand.

Seeing their alarmed looks he smiled. 'I know you're supposed to tell the real estate agent when there's a problem, but the builder in me can't go past a simple thing like fixing a loose board, well two loose boards actually.'

'Builder?' asked Emma. 'I thought you were an architect.'

Peter held up a second floorboard and removed the nail from it. 'I am, but I was a builder first. My dad was a builder and my brothers and I started working part-time with him when we were about ten. By the time each of us had graduated from university we had put in enough hours to have served a full apprenticeship.'

'Did you get paid?' asked Clare.

'Oh yes, it was all by the book. It was how we put ourselves through university.'

'And you didn't mind doing it?' asked Emma.

'No, I liked it. We did everything by hand in those days and that's where I learned to love buildings – their design and structure, the craftsmanship that went into each one.' He shrugged. 'If I hadn't been able to study architecture I think I would have been happy enough to work as a builder.'

'That's career satisfaction for you.' Clare smiled. 'Did you teach your son the trade as well?'

Peter's face displayed the look of pride it always did when he talked about Michael. 'Not exactly, I mean I didn't make him do his apprenticeship but I've taught him a lot. He knows how to put a wall frame together and hang a door.'

Their conversation was interrupted by the sounds of another quarrel between Ben and Lucy. 'We'll leave you to it,' Emma said, hurrying off in the direction of her room. Clare headed for the bathroom, while it was free.

Ron found another fishing spot and Peter and Lillian went shopping in Rosethorn, leaving only Clare, Emma and the kids for lunch. Feeling spontaneous, they packed the picnic basket, grabbed a blanket and headed to the grassy park just off the beach.

'Ah, this is the life.' Clare spread a handful of cheese and onion chips between two slices of soft, white bread and surveyed the waves rolling in gently along the shoreline, under a cloudless blue sky. The beach was packed and they shared the park with dozens of other people also enjoying picnics and barbeques. It was a true lazy summer holiday atmosphere and seemed a world away from the normal hustle and bustle of Christmas.

Emma cut the crusts off Lucy's sandwich and poured each of the kids a drink. 'Yeah, I'll say. Picnics are so much fun and it's been so long since I've been on one. Somehow I don't think Lillian would have come along, do you?'

'Uh, no, I think not. You wonder how she and Peter ever got together don't you? I mean, they must have had pretty different backgrounds if he had to work his way through uni. She obviously had a privileged upbringing.'

'Maybe she didn't meet him until he was a successful architect?'

'Good point, I'm pretty sure he's a few years older than her. She's hard going today, hopefully after a day out in the big smoke she might be a bit more pleasant tonight.'

Emma finished making her own sandwich. 'I hate to be a party pooper, but I'm predicting that she won't.'

Emma must have ESP, Clare decided as she served herself some more rice to go with the stir-fry they were eating for dinner. Lillian's mood hadn't improved during the day and, as yet, she hadn't spoken at all during the meal. Seated at the end of the table, she had turned her chair slightly askew, facing the empty space to her right, rather than Peter to her left.

'Oh, by the way Clare, we had the same taxi driver on the way back,' Peter said. 'He's actually from Melbourne, originally. We had a good-natured Sydney versus Melbourne debate. He claims the traffic moves better in Melbourne.'

'It definitely does,' Clare replied. 'Of course, I'm sure you don't notice how bad Sydney's traffic really is, when you drive a Mercedes.'

Peter shook his head. 'Uh uh, Lillian drives the Mercedes, I drive a Subaru.'

Clare decided to be brave. 'What do you think, Lillian?'

'I really wouldn't know.' Lillian scrunched her serviette and placed it on her plate. 'I don't care for Melbourne at all and I have no intention of ever driving there.'

Clare ignored the barb. Glancing at Emma, she rolled her eyes.

Lemon lips had been putting it mildly.

'You've got your kids well trained Emma,' Peter said, in an obvious attempt to change the subject. 'They go down to bed right on seven without any rigmarole. Lots of parents today seem to let their children stay up until all hours.'

'Well I have to do it for my own sanity,' Emma replied. 'Otherwise I don't get a minute to myself. They've had their moments, though. Ben, in particular, used to be a terrible sleeper when he was little and then he'd be awake at the crack of dawn. Some mornings I would just lie there and think, please don't wake up, please don't wake up!'

'Yes, our son was an early riser too wasn't he Lil?' said Peter.

Lillian stared the tablecloth, acting like she hadn't heard.

'I'd be like that some mornings too, especially on weekends. I would think, just another half hour, please give me another half an hour to sleep.'

Clare couldn't help but notice the change in Lillian's demeanour. While she'd started the meal out apparently trying to distance herself from the conversation, and the people at the table, she was now sitting ramrod straight. Red spots stained her cheeks. Picking up the serviette from her plate, Lillian proceeded to shred it into strips.

Concerned at what she was seeing, Clare tried to steer the conversation away from Lillian. 'I guess you don't have anyone to pass the buck to, though, do you, Em? If the kids are up, so are you.'

'Yeah, that's single motherhood for you,' Emma said.

Folding her arms hard against her body, Lillian glared at Emma. 'It's a bit late to be complaining about it now. Why didn't you get married, when you got pregnant? You wouldn't be in this situation now if you had.'

Everybody at the table looked up in shock. Emma recoiled as if she had been slapped.

Peter's mouth dropped open. 'Lillian!' he exclaimed. 'You can't speak to Emma like that.'

'Why not? It's the truth, isn't it? We never had this problem years ago, when single motherhood wasn't tolerated.'

Peter's face was red now. Gripping the table hard, he leapt to his feet. 'Lillian, stop it! This is not the time or place for this conversation.'

Lillian ignored him. 'Oh, heaven forbid if you have an opinion these days. Society would have many less problems if there weren't so many single parent families.'

Peter leant down so he was face to face with his wife. 'Lillian, we are leaving the table now,' he said. 'I'm not going to sit here listening to you insult people who have done nothing but be nice to you.'

'Oh, yes, Saint Peter,' she sneered. 'You would never offend anybody, would you?'

'Not deliberately,' Peter replied, gesturing with his head towards the stairs.

Lillian stared at him for a moment, then shoved her chair back. With one last glance at Emma, she got to her feet and strode towards the stairs. Peter followed close behind.

The other housemates listened as Peter and Lillian's footsteps echoed up the stairs, then moved into their room. The door slammed, then the muffled sound of raised voices could be heard. Still shocked, Clare, Ron and Emma just looked at each other.

'Wow, that was awkward,' Clare said. 'Are you okay Em? She really laid into you for no apparent reason.'

Emma nodded. 'Yes, I'm fine. It's not the first time I've had that kind of abuse. You have to develop a thick skin and ignore it.'

Clare reached out and gave her hand a squeeze. 'It still doesn't make it okay. You do realise this is Lillian's problem, not yours?'

'I know. It's weird how she suddenly turned though, isn't it?'

'Yeah, I don't know what set her off.' Clare shrugged.

Ron looked as if he would rather be anywhere else than right there. 'I'll do the dishes,' he said and moved off into the kitchen.

Clare started clearing the table. 'Let's take these in and I'll make us some hot chocolate,' she said. 'Then we can sit outside for a while and wait for the storm to pass.'

Clare went to bed early but couldn't sleep. She finished one novel and started another, but eventually she closed the book and got out of bed. Tiptoeing along the hall she made her way downstairs to get a drink of water.

There was a small arc of light coming from the lounge room. Someone must have left the lamp on. It wasn't until she got closer that Clare saw Peter sitting on the couch with a glass in his hand and a bottle of Johnnie Walker Black Label Scotch on the coffee table in front of him.

Seeing her alarmed look, Peter shook his head. 'Don't worry, I'm not going to drink it all. I just needed something a bit stronger than the leftover chardonnay.'

'Fair enough. It was a pretty intense mealtime conversation.'

'She wasn't always like this you know,' Peter said softly, taking a sip of his drink.

Coming in closer, Clare sat on a recliner. 'Who, Lillian?'

'Yes, Lillian,' said Peter. 'She was so quiet when I first met her, very self-contained.'

'Still waters run deep.'

'Yeah, I realised that. It took a long time for her to talk to me, but when she finally did, it was like the floodgates opened. We used to have these amazing conversations that could last for hours.'

'Well, they say communication is key for a successful relationship.'

'I don't know when we stopped talking like that.' Peter stared at his glass for a moment before taking another small sip. 'People think she's just a stereotypical wealthy, spoiled woman who creates tension because she's bored. You think that, don't you?'

'Well, uh, no, not exactly….' Clare hedged.

Peter swirled the scotch around in his glass. 'Sorry, you don't have to answer that. I know she puts that across and I just don't understand why, because there is so much more to her.'

'I'm sure there is. I had no idea she was such a great cook.'

'Yes, she is, among other things.' Peter hunched forward and rubbed his eyes. 'You know that saying - behind every successful man, stands a capable woman?'

Clare nodded.

'That's Lillian. I've never had to lift a finger around the house and she's always been very supportive of my career. I remember the first high profile contract I had. The day before the plans needed to be presented I just froze with self-doubt. She sat up all night with me, made me endless cups of coffee and told me I could do it.'

'Wow,' was all Clare could think to say.

'We had a very happy marriage to begin with. She's just never been great with expressing emotion or affection. She's not much of a hugger and she never cries.'

'Really?'

'Yeah. I was the one who shed all the tears at Michael's milestone events. I must admit I could never understand why she didn't want to hug him more, or have him sit on her lap or snuggle up in bed with him, but I realised that was just her way and I've never doubted how much she loves him.'

'And you didn't want more children?'

Peter took another sip. 'It just didn't happen. I do sometimes wonder if things might have been different if we had – you know, Lillian might have learned to be more affectionate and tolerant,' he said. 'I would have loved three or four children.'

'It's hard to understand why the people who want children can't always have them.'

They sat in silence for a minute. The only sound was the crashing of the surf in the distance.

'I hate to think that it's money that has made her a different person, but that's the only thing I can come up with,' Peter said. 'My business only really took off when one of my designs got noticed by the right person about ten years ago. In a short space of time my income tripled, we got to build our dream house and adopt a while new lifestyle.'

'And Lillian changed when that happened?'

'Well, I think she did. She just seemed to thrive on the whole upper class social scene. At first I didn't mind, I enjoyed being able to give her anything she wanted because she had done so much for me.'

'And now?'

'I still love being able to provide so well for her, but it's gotten to the point where I feel like nothing will ever be enough and I can't help remembering how much happier we were when we had less. I'd honestly trade it all in if I could make Lillian happy again.'

'You can't make someone else happy, Peter.'

Exhaling, Peter nodded slowly. 'I don't know about that.' Leaning forward, he poured another small measure of scotch into his glass. 'I'm sure you're all wondering why I put up with it, why I stay with her.'

'Peter, it's really none of our business.'

'It's all right, I want to tell you.'

Stifling a yawn, Clare nodded. 'Okay.'

'First and foremost, I'm not perfect either. I worked long hours for many years and I didn't always cope with the pressure that well,' Peter said, indicating the scotch bottle. 'But, more importantly, I'm still with her because I love her. Despite all the drama, I know her better than anyone else and I still see glimpses of the woman I married.'

'That sounds like a very valid reason to stay together.'

'Some days it does, but, on nights like tonight, I think I just don't know if I can do it anymore.' Setting his glass down on the coffee table, Peter leaned back on the couch and closed his eyes. 'Go back to bed Clare, I'll be all right in a while.'

'Are you sure? I don't mind sitting with you.'

Peter shook his head. 'The night cap has helped, I'll head up to bed soon too.'

'All right, good night then.' Clare stood up and headed for the stairs.

'Yes, good night.'

Peter was late for breakfast the next morning and the stress of the night before was clearly etched on his face. I wonder if he slept at all, Clare thought, as she buttered her toast.

'I'm so sorry about last night Emma,' he said, when he sat down. 'I don't know what gets into Lillian sometimes.'

'It's okay, Peter,' Emma replied. 'It wasn't your fault.'

Peter reached for the cornflakes. 'It's not okay at all, but thank you for being so tolerant.' He didn't say why Lillian wasn't at breakfast and nobody liked to ask.

It was a quiet morning in the house. Ron was fishing as usual, Clare was finishing the last of her Christmas cards and Emma kept the kids busy making some Christmas decorations for their room. Lillian did not emerge, but Peter went in and out of their room several times and each time the muffled sound of raised voices could be heard.

Lillian finally appeared at lunchtime, subdued, and clearly unhappy about facing everyone. Glancing over at Peter she exhaled loudly before speaking. 'I apologise for my behaviour last night. It was inappropriate meal time conversation and very bad manners on my behalf.' Lillian looked over at Peter again and he angled his head towards Emma. 'Especially to you, Emma,' she said.

'That's all right,' Ron, Clare and Emma murmured, relieved to have it out of the way. Nodding stiffly, Lillian sat down at the table. Peter still didn't look very happy and Clare could guess why. As apologies went, it hadn't been a particularly heartfelt one. Lillian had said the bare minimum to quantify an apology and hadn't actually said that she didn't mean her words last night. Neither had she said "sorry", instead hiding behind the more generic "I apologise".

Clare snuck a glance over at Lillian and thought about what Peter had said the night before. She was a complex woman for sure, but more than anything, Clare knew she was very unhappy. But, like an alcoholic, she had to admit she had a problem before anybody could help her.

Things were still very strained between Peter and Lillian that evening. Even though he was far too polite to involve the others in their dispute, it was clear by their body language and lack of communication that all was not well. Peter didn't try and draw her into the conversation like he usually did, nor did he speak much himself.

Ron wasn't perturbed by the lack of conversation. He just ate his meal in silence, apparently working on the theory the faster he finished the sooner he could escape.

Thank goodness for Emma, Clare thought as their eyes met across the table and they exchanged a weary glance, if she wasn't here I think I would have packed up and camped on the beach.

Clare sighed gratefully when she came down for breakfast the next morning and found Peter and Ron deep in a conversation about boat engines. Well, that's an improvement on last night, she thought. Both men looked up and smiled and Clare felt her heart lift a bit.

She poured milk over her Sports Plus and pondered the day ahead. Ron was taking Ben fishing and Peter and Emma were tagging along. That left her, Lucy and Lillian on the home front. Clare planned to start the Christmas food preparation and freeze it until the day. Lillian was yet to put in an appearance. Clare didn't expect any help from her, even though Lillian had demonstrated she more than capable of giving it.

By ten o'clock the house was quiet. Lucy was absorbed in drawing pictures with the crayons that Clare had bought for her and Lillian was

315

ensconced on the couch, leafing through the Christmas edition *Women's Weekly*. Clare toyed with the idea of asking her for advice about glazing the ham, but given the circumstances of the last couple of days, decided it wasn't worth the bother.

Clare worked contentedly for an hour and then realised that she was out of onions. 'Damn,' she said, dropping her knife. It was ridiculous to feel nervous about asking such a simple question, but she did. Exhaling loudly, she walked into the lounge room, before she lost her nerve. 'Lillian, could you please watch Lucy for a few minutes so I can go down to the shop and get a few more onions?' she asked, in her nicest voice.

Lillian gave a blank look in response. Clare bit her tongue and tried to keep her frustration in check. Oh yes, Lillian, I can see that you're flat out there, I'm sorry I shouldn't have asked, she wanted to yell. After waiting for thirty seconds and getting no response, Clare shook her head. 'Fine, I'll take her with me,' she said, stomping back in the kitchen to wash her hands.

There was a sound of movement from the lounge room and Lillian appeared in the doorway, her designer resort shorts and linen shirt still immaculate and wrinkle free. 'I didn't say I wouldn't look after her,' she said.

Clare rinsed her hands under the tap and dried them on a hand towel. 'Thank you,' she said, then grabbed her purse and walked out the door before Lillian changed her mind.

The quick walk to Four Square was a nice break from the oppressive silence of the house. Look at that sky! Clare thought, momentarily transfixed by the deep shade of blue. A light, balmy breeze blew gently, just enough to take the sting out of the midday heat. There were lots of people in town and all the shopfronts had been decorated in a festive way. Clare couldn't help noticing what a contrast the laid back, yet exciting, atmosphere was to the frantic pre-Christmas pace of Melbourne. The little supermarket was packed and she had to elbow her way through the crowd to grab the last three onions.

Lillian was starting to wear her down, Clare realised, as she strolled slowly back towards the house. She prided herself on her ability to get along with anybody and to ignore anti-social behaviour in others. But, here she was, getting annoyed and tense from just being around Lillian. No matter what Peter said about the person behind the mask, Clare was finding it hard to see beyond Lillian's apparent enjoyment of being difficult.

The sound of a child screaming shattered the peacefulness of the summer's day. Wow that kid had got a good set of lungs on them, Clare thought, as one ear-piercing shriek after another rang out. I hope they're all right. Some children just had a knack of getting themselves into scrapes. Emma was so lucky with her two, especially timid little Lucy.

It was only as Clare got closer to the house that the realisation hit her. Oh no, that *is* Lucy!

Clare started running. She'd never heard her scream like that. Something must be horribly wrong and it was all her fault. Emma had trusted her to mind her precious child and she'd let her down. She should never have deferred that responsibility onto someone else.

By the time Clare raced up the driveway, her heart was pounding. Bolting up the stairs, she shoved the door open, dreading what she might find. It took a moment for her eyes to adjust from the bright sunlight to the relative darkness of the house. Clare's hand flew to her mouth when she saw Lucy lying on the floor, with what seemed like oceans of blood running down her face, seeping into her snowy blonde hair and dripping down onto her pale pink t-shirt.

Lillian stood beside her, wringing her hands desperately, but making no move to touch her. Tears rolled down her cheeks.

Kneeling down beside Lucy, Clare took a deep breath. 'What happened?' she asked Lillian, trying to keep the panic out of her voice.

Lillian's response came in ragged gasps. 'I was just on the phone for a moment … I didn't see … I didn't notice she came over here … she fell and hit her head on the edge of the coffee table.'

Clare gently examined Lucy's head and found a deep cut up near her hairline. She grabbed a handful of tissues from the box on the coffee table and wiped away as much blood as she could. She then applied pressure to the wound and gathered Lucy in her arms.

'You're okay Luce, you've just cut your head,' she said softly. 'If you stop crying, it won't bleed so much.'

Lucy clung to her, but started to calm down.

'Lillian listen to me,' said Clare. 'The man staying in the house on the corner is a doctor. I met him in the shop one day. He's out sitting on his veranda now. Could you please go and get him?'

Lillian stood rooted to the spot, tears still slipping down her cheeks.

'Lillian!' Clare snapped.

It was the jolt that the older woman needed and she did as Clare instructed.

It wasn't as bad as it looked. It was a deep cut, but a clean one, and it only needed two stitches. After it was all over, Lucy sat happily on Clare's knee on the veranda and ate a frosty fruit.

After thanking the doctor and waving him off, Clare instructed Lillian to sit down. 'Are you all right?' she asked.

Lillian stiffened. 'Yes, why wouldn't I be?'

'Well, you were very upset before, which was why Lucy got a bit hysterical. Kids react to that…,'

Lillian stared at Clare, raising an eyebrow. 'I have raised a child Clare, which you haven't done as yet, so I don't need your advice.'

'I know that. I'm not criticising, I was just wondering why you found it so upsetting.'

'It's been a long time since Michael was so young,' Lillian replied. 'And I've never been good around blood. Besides all that, it's always worse when it's someone else's child you're responsible for.'

'Okay, then. As long as you're sure that's all that was upsetting you.'

'Well, no, it's not all that is upsetting me. I'm stuck in an old house with strangers at Christmas. It's all very stressful.'

'Look Lillian, none of us planned to be spending Christmas this way, but the rest of us are dealing with it and trying to get along,' Clare said. 'You, on the other hand, are doing your best to make things as difficult as possible. We're all walking on eggshells around you.'

Lillian's eyes blazed, but then she glanced at Lucy and dropped her gaze. 'Am I really that difficult to live with?' she asked.

'Yes, quite frankly.'

Shaking her head, Lillian stood up and left the veranda without another word.

Clare fed Lucy and put her down for a sleep, then had some lunch herself and continued to prepare the Christmas food. She was making stuffing and humming to herself when Lillian appeared once again.

'I apologise for not watching Lucy better,' she said stiffly. 'Whatever you think of me you must know I would never want a child to be hurt.'

Clare looked up from the bench. 'Of course I know that and I'm not blaming you for the accident. Kids fall over, it happens. It could have just as easily happened while I was watching her.'

'Yes, I suppose it could have,' Lillian replied. 'I know you all think I'm not very pleasant, but I was looking forward to this holiday and to have it spoilt by some travel agent's incompetence is frustrating.'

'Lillian, it's not about the travel agent.'

'What do you mean?'

'You're laying blame on somebody else for something, that in the greater scheme of things, is pretty superficial. I'm just wondering why you're so unhappy.'

'I didn't say I was unhappy.'

Clare turned her attention back to the stuffing. 'I've got an idea why you are.'

Folding her arms, Lillian arched an eyebrow. 'Oh really? Do tell.'

'I think that although you enjoy the results of Peter's success you actually feel overshadowed by it. By being difficult, you make yourself the centre of attention, that way people take notice of you.'

Lillian shook her head. 'Oh, no, no, no you're very wrong. This has nothing to do with Peter, nothing at all.'

'So, there is something, then?'

Lillian realised she had backed herself into a corner. 'No, I didn't say that. I just mean...'

'Yes?' Clare prompted.

'Why do you even care?'

'Like I just said, I think you're very unhappy. I know you don't like me, but I'd like to help you, if I can.'

'I don't dislike you personally, Clare,' Lillian said softly. 'You just remind me of a very difficult time in my life.'

'How so?'

'Well you're from Melbourne, Kew specifically.'

'Yes, that's right, but what's so bad about that?'

'Nothing as such, oh, it's a long story. It happened a long time ago…' Lillian's voice trailed off. Walking over to the kettle, she filled it, then plugged it in.

Clare kept working on the stuffing while Lillian put a tea bag in a mug, then poured the water in. It wasn't until she took her first sip that she looked at Clare again. 'I'm sorry, I didn't ask you if you'd like a tea.'

'I'm fine, thanks.'

'You think I grew up wealthy, don't you?' Lillian asked, seemingly off on a different tangent.

'Clare hesitated. She *had* initially thought that, but Peter's comment about money changing Lillian meant she mustn't have. She couldn't reveal that now, though.

'Uh, yeah,' she said.

Lillian shook her head. 'Pete is the one who came from money, well, compared to me anyway. He's the one who went to a private school and grew up on the North Shore.'

Clare eyed Lillian curiously, more surprised to hear her use the shortened version of Peter's name than to learn of his background. 'But he said his father was a builder.'

'Yes, that's true, his father was a builder – a very astute man who worked hard and reaped the rewards from the post war building boom. Because he was self-made, he expected his sons to be as well.'

'Oh, okay.'

'I grew up in the western suburbs and, like most girls those days, I left school at fifteen. My first job was at the local dry-cleaners.'

Clare nodded, but kept working.

'After a couple of years, I did a secretarial course and got an office job in the city. I'm sure it sounds very mundane to young women these days, but, back then, it was a big deal. It was a whole new world for me.'

'I understand, Lillian. My mother was the same.'

'Through my job, I met a very wealthy, powerful businessman. I'll just call him Tony. He was married, of course, but that didn't stop him from pursuing me. Eventually I became his mistress.'

Clare's eyes widened. That wasn't what she'd expected to hear.

'Oh, it was all glorious and fun, for a while,' Lillian said, nursing her mug. 'There were clandestine meetings, weekends away, promises of undying love and him leaving his wife. I thought I loved him at the time, although I'm not sure if it was genuinely love, or just a sense of accomplishment that Lillian Nixon, from the wrong side of the tracks, caught the eye of somebody so important.'

'As you might expect, the whole thing ended badly. Very badly,' said Lillian. 'His private secretary confronted me one day after I left work. Tony was running for a federal seat and she told me very bluntly that she hadn't worked behind the scenes for the past twenty years to get him into politics to have any kind of scandal hanging over him. I was banished to the Melbourne office, immediately. Tony, of course, made himself scarce until I was safely out of the way. I never spoke to him again.'

'That's why you don't like Melbourne, then?'

Lillian nodded absently.

'All right. I understand that must have been an upsetting thing to live through, but you're right, it *is* ancient history. If you don't mind me asking, why are you upset about it now?'

'Like I said, Tony was very a very powerful businessman and is still a federal politician. He presents himself very much as a morals crusader, a beacon of honesty and decency.'

Clare gave the stuffing a final mix, then transferred it to a Tupperware container. 'And you feel like he's betrayed the public? Gotten away with pretending to be somebody he's not?'

'No, it's not that. Heaven knows, he wouldn't be the first one. I don't know how closely you follow the news, but a about a year ago, a journalist published a book about a certain high profile businessman turned politician. He's been very careful not to name names, but it's fairly obvious who it's about.'

Clare's mouth dropped open. 'Oh! So Tony is—'

Closing her eyes, Lillian nodded. 'Yes, that's him. I'm not proud of it Clare, but it is what it is.'

'Wow. It is pretty big news. And I guess he's got a lot to lose given the way he's always parading his children and grandchildren around and boasting what a great marriage he has.'

'Yes, he does. You know what that journalist is like, always digging for dirt. I'm terrified he's going to uncover what happened with Tony and me. Peter doesn't know and I couldn't bear it if he found out.'

Clare had moved onto making shortbread. 'That's why you're so unhappy? You're stressed that it's all going to come out?' she asked, as she weighed the butter on an ancient set of kitchen scales.

Finishing her tea with one last swallow, Lillian took her mug to the sink and rinsed it. 'Yes, the uncertainty is unbearable. I hate what it's done to me. I've made Peter's life a misery too. I could live with the damage to my own reputation, but I just couldn't bear ruining everything Pete has worked for.'

'You don't think it would be better to just tell him? Prepare him for the possibility it might come out?'

Lillian shook her head emphatically. 'No! Definitely not. He's such a good person, he'd never understand how I could have had an affair with a married man.'

'But it was so long ago. You were so young…'

'No, Clare. I'm not telling him. I couldn't bear to lose him.'

'You do really love him, don't you?'

'Yes, I do. He's the kindest, most patient man I've ever met.'

'Do you ever tell him you love him?' Clare asked.

'Well, no, not as such. But he knows, of course he knows. When you've been married as long as we have, you can sense these things between you.'

'It's not the same though, is it? I mean he probably does *think* that you love him but I'm sure he doesn't know for certain if you don't say the words. It would probably smooth things over if you told him.'

'You don't know Pete as well as I do. He's angry with me about the other night and, while it can take a while for him to reach the end of his tether, once he's there he doesn't back down easily. Thank you for trying to help, Clare, but it will just have to sort itself out.'

Remembering Peter's comment the other night about not knowing if he could do it anymore, Clare had to bite her tongue from saying any more.

Careful not to look at Clare again, Lillian left the kitchen.

The events of that morning were told and retold when the others got home and Lucy managed to elicit more than her fair share of sympathetic hugs, lollies, and generally being spoilt. Ben told them if it had happened to him he would have been much braver and not cried at all. Emma reassured Clare that she didn't blame her in any way.

'Clare, kids are kids. She's fine now and you won't even see the scar.' Emma hugged Clare to show she wasn't upset.

At four o'clock Clare realised she should start thinking about dinner. 'I'm sorry, Ron,' she said, closing Lillian's *Women's Weekly* that she'd been reading, 'Lucy's incident overshadowed what happened with you guys. Did you catch enough to feed the masses?'

Looking up from the paper, Ron nodded. 'More than enough. Speaking of which, I'd better go and prepare it for you.' Getting to his feet, Ron gestured for Ben to come with him. 'Part of going fishing is cleaning and scaling the catch, so off we go,' he said.

Clare smiled as Ben scampered off after Ron, ready to do anything his new hero suggested. Her mind was a million miles away, as she made a salad to go with the fish. Lillian hadn't reappeared since their conversation. Peter had only gone upstairs briefly so she obviously hadn't attempted to mend any fences yet.

It had been such a weird day. Clare still couldn't quite believe what Lillian had told her. As an outsider to the situation, to Clare, it seemed obvious that telling Peter would be better than living with the fear of discovery. But, then again, Lillian had a point. Clare didn't know Peter as well as she did and maybe her fears were well founded. In any case, Clare now had a deeper understanding of Lillian, which hopefully might make the next week a lot easier to cope with.

Lillian didn't come down for dinner and Clare couldn't help noticing how relaxed everybody was in her absence. Although she had apologised for her outburst the other day, there was still an air of tension at each meal. Clare did her best to join in the light-hearted conversation, while she formulated a plan of action in her mind.

There was still an hour of daylight left so she insisted that Ron and Emma take the kids down to the beach to fly the kite that Ron had made. She assured them she would be down as soon as she finished the washing up. As she hoped Peter came in and helped her.

'Wasn't Lillian hungry?' she asked.

Peter picked up a plate to dry. 'She said she had a headache.'

'She was pretty upset about Lucy, I think she felt guilty even though it really was just an accident.'

'She was never good with blood; she used to worry about every little scrape Mike got and think that death was imminent.'

'Maybe she could use some sympathy.'

Peter's silence suggested it wouldn't be coming from him.

'Would you like me to make her something and you can take it up?' Clare asked, as she let the water out of the sink.

Peter shook his head. 'She can get herself something if she's hungry. I might just go for a walk into town and listen to the local jazz band, they're playing in the town square.'

'Are you sure?' Clare had hoped Peter would agree to the meal idea, which would at least put the two of them in the same room. Lillian really was skating on thin ice, she realised.

'Yes, sometimes it's just easier to stay out of her way. I'll see you later,' Peter said. He hung up his tea towel and walked through the lounge room and out the front door.

Clare poured herself a drink of juice, but thought that a hit of Peter's scotch might hit the spot better. Why am I getting so caught up in all this? she asked herself. It's really not my problem. I've told Lillian what I think she should do – I can't force her to tell him. And who could blame Peter for backing off? He doesn't know Lillian's secret.

'Ah, this is too hard,' she said, aloud. It's time to stop worrying about other people's issues and just have some fun. Clare gulped down her drink and went down to the beach to join the others.

Clare slept fitfully and woke at ten past five. Stretching in her bed, she decided to get up and go for a walk instead of just lying there. She'd been meaning to do it since she arrived, but had never managed to get up early enough. After dressing quietly, she tiptoed down the hall and stairs, taking care not to wake the others. As she walked through the lounge room she noticed Peter sleeping on the couch.

Oh dear, she thought as she slipped out the back door, not a good sign.

Clare walked slowly along the clean, white sand and tried to clear her head. She took in the beautiful morning, but the events of the previous soon day crowded her consciousness. While it would be easier to forget all about it, she knew she couldn't. She had invited Lillian to confide in her, so it wasn't right to back off just because it was more complicated than she had anticipated.

Clare walked down to the water's edge and let the water run over her feet. There had to be a way to get Peter and Lillian talking again.

It was a very frustrating morning for Clare. Lillian didn't join them for breakfast. Peter wasn't very communicative either. In response to Clare's enquiry about his and Lillian's plans for the day, Peter tersely informed her they were doing their own thing. He left the house soon after, so she took the opportunity to try and gently encourage Lillian to smooth things over with Peter. Unreceptive to further advice, she seemed to regret confiding in Clare the day before.

'You caught me at a weak moment yesterday, Clare,' she said. 'I don't need your advice, thank you. I know Peter better than you do. When he starts hitting the scotch, there's no reaching him.'

'All right Lillian, I was just trying to help. But can you please come down for lunch, at least?'

Sighing deeply, Lillian nodded. 'Okay.'

Clare's attempted manoeuvre to seat Peter and Lillian together at lunchtime was unknowingly foiled by Emma, who, seeking to ease the obvious tension, placed Lucy next to Lillian. When Peter and Ron left the house after lunch with fishing rods in tow, Clare put her plans on ice and joined Emma and the kids on the beach.

Clare patted the top of the sandcastle she and Ben had built and closed her eyes momentarily. Lack of sleep combined with stress was giving her a headache. She had tried to stave it off by drinking lots of water, but the end result was a full bladder as well as a pounding head. Unearthing her towel from the pile on the sand she called to Emma, 'I'm going to head back and have a nanna nap.'

'Sounds like a great idea,' Emma said. 'Off you go and enjoy some peace and quiet.'

As she trudged up the path towards the house, Clare noticed Peter standing on the side veranda. Maybe some time out fishing had left him in a better frame of mind?

She climbed halfway up the back steps but stopped when she heard the heated argument. Definitely not a good time for a chat, Clare decided. Knowing they had the house to themselves Peter and Lillian were really letting fly.

'I did apologise,' Lillian yelled.

'Not very sincerely,' Peter yelled back. He was still on the veranda and apparently Lillian was in the lounge room.

'Wouldn't it be great to be as perfect as you?' Lillian responded. 'You never have to apologise for saying the wrong thing.'

'I'm not claiming to be perfect, but it's not that hard to be polite.'

'Well how about you and your silent treatment? That's a very juvenile way to solve a problem, isn't it? And it makes other people uncomfortable when they know you're ignoring me.'

'No more uncomfortable than you insulting Emma at the table.'

'Oh, we're back to that again, are we? What about your drinking? That's a great way to sort things out. You still think I can't tell when you knock back half a bottle of scotch before bed. You're very transparent sometimes Peter.'

'I have never drunk half a bottle!'

'Close enough. I can smell you a mile away.'

'Yeah, well it's lucky I've been sleeping a mile away, isn't it?'

Oh boy, thought Clare. This could get really ugly and I don't want to witness it. About to retreat down the stairs, she realised Peter had moved further along the veranda. If she went down now, he would see her in the yard. What a perfect place to be trapped, she thought, right in the middle of someone else's argument.

The sound of raised voices was momentarily replaced by the scraping of furniture along the floor.

'Lillian what are you doing?' Peter asked.

'Not that it's any of your concern, but I'm going to straighten that picture frame. It's been driving me mad all week.'

'Lil don't stand on that chair,' Peter warned, 'you'll over-balance.'

'I'm can look after myself thank you.'

Seconds later Clare heard a loud crash and the sound of breaking glass. Then a scream from Lillian. Dropping her beach gear, she leapt up the last two stairs and rushed to the door. She could hear Lillian sobbing.

Clare took a step inside and, as her eyes adjusted to the relative darkness of the house, she saw a scene that almost brought tears to her own eyes. Amid the upturned chair and shards of broken glass from the picture frame, Peter was holding Lillian in a tender embrace, cradling her head on his shoulder.

'Did you hurt yourself?' he asked gently.

Lillian cried harder and clung to him desperately.

'Hey, hey it's all right,' Peter soothed, 'it's just a picture frame. I'll get another one. And I can fix the chair.'

Glad she hadn't been noticed, Clare eased back out the door and down the steps. Now she just had to find the nearest toilet before her bladder burst.

Clare loitered around the surf club for an hour and then headed back to the house.

'Hello, anybody home?' she called loudly, banging the back door behind her. She stood still and listened, but only silence greeted her. She breathed a sigh of relief, glad that she wouldn't have to skulk around outside any longer. Walking into the kitchen, she saw a note from Peter saying that he and Lillian had gone to the early bird seating at Leo's. Well, that sounds more positive, Clare thought, then smiled as a plan formed in her mind.

Although it was only five thirty, Clare hastily prepared a platter of sandwiches for an early dinner. Ron always returned around that time and she could see Emma and the kids walking up the path towards the house.

She swooped on them as soon as they came in the door. 'Hey, guess what? I'm shouting us all to the movies to see *Chicken Run*. It starts at six thirty so we'll have to hurry.'

Emma and the kids were excited at the news but Ron was perplexed when he walked in a couple of minutes later and had a pile of sandwiches thrust at him. He ate them without complaint, but when Emma and the kids went upstairs to get changed he voiced his dissent regarding the movie.

'It's a kid's movie,' he grumbled, as Clare tried to hurry him up to get ready.

'Yes, that's why we're taking the kids,' she said, almost bodily pushing him up the stairs.

For such a quiet and unassuming man, Ron could be surprisingly stubborn. 'But can't just you and Emma take them? I'd rather stay here and read the paper,' he said, his feet still firmly planted on the bottom step.

Closing her eyes, Clare pinched the bridge of her nose. 'Okay, Ron, you don't have to come to the movies with us. You can go to the pub, or to the RSL or the surf club. You can go anywhere you like, but please just leave the house. I think Peter and Lillian need some privacy.'

'Privacy?' Ron replied. 'They're barely speaking. I think she really did her dash the other night. He's been sleeping on the couch, you know.'

'Trust me on this, Ron, it's all sorted out. I just thought it might be nice if they had the house to themselves. It's their anniversary,' she ad-libbed desperately. 'That's why they've gone out to dinner.'

The penny dropped and Ron nodded. 'Oh, right, yep, I get 'ya. But how will they know when we're due back?'

'I'll leave a note.'

Now he was on board with Clare's plan, Ron didn't muck around. He was back downstairs, cleaned up and neatly dressed, in less than ten minutes. As they walked down the street towards the King George Hotel, Clare repeated her earlier offer.

'Honestly, you don't have to come to the movie, Ron. Like I said, there's always the pub.'

Ron didn't break his stride as they walked past the historic timber hotel, that was packed with revellers. 'Yeah, but who do I know at the pub?'

Christmas Eve dawned sunny and hot. Clare felt like she had run a marathon over the past couple of days, but it was a good kind of exhaustion and she was excited about the day ahead. Peter had been out for a walk and was whistling when he came in for breakfast. Clare and Ron exchanged a conspiratorial glance across the table and smiled to themselves.

After breakfast, Lillian came into the kitchen as Clare was making a final checklist of things she would need for the big meal the next day.

'Oh, Clare, I won't disturb you,' she said, turning on her heel to leave again.

'Don't be silly, Lillian,' Clare replied. 'I'm just making a list. Do what you need to do.'

Carefully avoiding eye contact with Clare, Lillian took a glass from the cabinet and filled it with water.

'It's all right, Lillian. I don't expect you to be my new best friend and confide in me about everything.'

Finishing her drink, Lillian turned to face Clare. 'I know. I just feel a bit exposed, knowing what you know about me. I can't believe I actually told you, I've never disclosed that to anyone.'

'It was the Cone of Silence, Lillian. Your secret is safe with me.'

'I know.'

'It looks like you and Peter patched things up?'

Lillian gave an exasperated look. 'Honestly, Clare, it was all very pointed, with the rest of you clearing out like that.'

Clare smiled. 'We just happened to be going to the movies.'

Lillian shook her head. 'I didn't know where to look at breakfast.' Making to leave the kitchen, she hesitated. 'You seem to know Lucy well, could you get her something for tomorrow, something beautiful? I'll just get you some money.'

Clare stuck the list on the fridge. 'It's all taken care of. Peter arranged it the other day.'

'Yes, well, that's Peter for you, generous *and* organised. I just didn't want her to miss out, she's such a sweet little thing.'

'She is. You've got yourself a real little admirer there, Lillian. You know what they say about kids being able to pick a kindred spirit.'

Expecting Lillian to smile at that comment, Clare was surprised when she shook her head. 'I very much doubt that Clare, I've got no experience with little girls. None at all.'

Peter wandered into the kitchen then. 'Oh, there you are Lil, are you ready to go into town?'

'Yes, I'm ready. I'll just go and get my bag.' Lillian headed up to her room.

Leaning against the bench, Peter folded his arms. 'I'm not sure what you did, but thank you.'

'You're welcome, but for what?' Clare did her best to look puzzled.

'Lillian actually told me she loved me. I can't tell you the last time she said that. Given this occurred after my conversation with you the other night, it doesn't take much to see a link there.'

'Peter, you know you can't *make* a person do or say something they don't want to.'

'Well, mere mortals can't, but you, Miss Crawford, seem to be able to work all kinds of miracles.'

Averting her gaze, Clare shook her head. 'I think miracle is kind of overstating it, Peter. Maybe it's just being away from your normal environment, the spirit of Christmas and all that.'

Peter stared at Clare for a moment. 'All right, I'll leave it there. But I do thank you, very sincerely.'

Lillian came back into the kitchen, looking perplexed. 'Why on earth did Ron just wish me a happy anniversary?'

Clare was surprised when Ron volunteered to walk down to the shops with her after lunch, to pick up the last-minute things they needed. He usually went fishing for most of the afternoon.

'Peter thinks you're a great girl,' Ron said shyly, as they headed down Blue Pacific Boulevard.

'Oh, Peter's a sweetheart, he's always saying nice things.'

'No, he really means it. He told me if his son was in the country he would have introduced you two, quick smart.'

Clare blushed. 'Ron, you're killing me! Thanks though.'

'You know, I've spent the last sixteen years avoiding women,' Ron said, as they walked, squinting in the afternoon sun. 'I stopped trusting them because I got this idea they were all sneaky and deceptive and out to make every bloke's life miserable.'

Clare nodded. 'That's understandable if you had a bad experience, but I have to defend my gender and say it's not true of all of us.'

Sliding his hands into his pockets, Ron nodded. 'I know. You see, when I first saw how Lillian behaved and how miserable she was making poor Peter, it reinforced everything I thought I knew. But then you appeared and it was like the light went on.'

'Yes, right,' Clare murmured, unsure where this conversation was headed. Suddenly struck by a bolt of panic, she almost gasped out loud. Surely Ron didn't fancy her? She knew it wasn't that unusual for men of his age to date younger women. But Ron was always so quiet – although they did say you had to watch the quiet ones! She was sure she hadn't done anything to encourage him, positive in fact. Oh, how do I get myself into these situations? she thought, as she waited for Ron to continue. And, more importantly, how am I going to get out of this one?

Oblivious to her panic, Ron smiled. 'Yep, meeting you, and Emma too, made me realise what I've been missing out on.'

Clare felt decidedly faint. She steered Ron towards Sunset Point's new Bowls Club, that was hosting its first Christmas mixed tournament that day. 'Let's stop for a quick drink, and a chat,' she said, wondering how on earth she could diffuse the bomb she was currently holding in her hands. Ron nodded eagerly and led her inside. And then, amidst the loud conversations and general hilarity of a tipsy pre-Christmas crowd, Ron told the story of his failed marriage and lost daughter. Clare was so relieved it had nothing to do with her, she had to stop herself from smiling several times. After the panic of a few minutes before, she felt this issue would be almost easy to solve.

'It *can* be hard to trust people,' she said, taking a sip of her gin and tonic. 'And yes, sometimes people you do trust will let you down. But if you just avoid people all together, then you're cutting off your nose to spite your face, aren't you?'

Ron took a slug of beer. 'I dunno. I do okay out on the land. It's very uncomplicated.'

'Yes, I'm sure you are doing okay, but wouldn't you like to do better than okay? Don't you get lonely?'

'Sure I do, but who doesn't? I just don't know if I could ever let a woman back into my life.'

Clare sighed. 'I'm not suggesting that you storm the dating agencies, Ron. Maybe you could just be open to the idea of being a bit more social, rather than locking yourself away. You could start by being more involved in things at the house. Can you do that?'

Ron scratched his chin thoughtfully. 'Yeah, I reckon I could.'

As the heat of the day gave way to the cooling breezes of late afternoon the occupants of the beach house got ready to celebrate. First, they had their own private drinks party on the veranda, while the children played in the yard. Lillian hadn't exactly transformed into a social butterfly, but Clare could see that she was making an effort to be pleasant, even if it might not be obvious to the others.

At seven o'clock it was time for carols by candlelight down on the beach. Clare was surprised when Ron readily agreed to go.

'My gran used to take us along,' he said. 'She had a beautiful voice.'

Clare glanced over at Peter and Lillian.

'We might just watch from here,' Peter said.

Clare considered taking Lucy aside and telling her to ask Lillian to come. It would probably do the trick. But, then again, she'd already pushed Lillian well out of her comfort zone and being involved in a group house activity might be a step too far. Besides, some more time alone for Peter and Lillian might be a better bet, anyway.

Gathering some blankets together, Clare, Ron, Emma and the kids set off down the pathway to the beach.

There was a large crowd at carols, thanks to the holidaymakers, and the atmosphere was wonderfully festive. Clare watched Ron singing heartily and pondered how much heartache he must have endured being denied access to his only child.

It was almost eleven o'clock when they walked back up to the house, with Ron and Clare carrying a sleeping child each. Peter was doing a jigsaw puzzle when they came in. 'I'm just trying to keep myself awake for midnight Mass,' he explained.

'Great, we can go together,' Clare said. She went into the kitchen to make everyone a cup of tea, as nobody seemed in any hurry to go to bed. She brought the drinks out and sank down gratefully on the couch.

Emma sat down next to her. 'Do you mind if I come? My family never went to church, but it seems like a nice thing to do at Christmas time.'

'Of course you can.'

'Oh, what am I thinking? I can't abandon my children.'

'They'll be okay Emma,' Ron said. 'I'm sure that Lillian and I can handle a couple of sleeping kids.'

'Thanks,' Emma said gratefully. 'It's the church on the hill isn't it? The one with the statue out the front and the funny name?'

'Yes that's the one. It's called Stella Maris. It means star of the sea, so it's pretty appropriate for a beachside town.'

While the adult occupants of the Beach House were keen to sleep in on Christmas morning, the children had other ideas. Awake at the crack of dawn, they raced down to see what was under the tree. Used to the lean Christmases of their past, they couldn't comprehend that so many of the brightly wrapped gifts were for them. Ben could read both his and Lucy's names and counted a sizable haul. The two children raced back upstairs and dragged Emma back downstairs with them. She also couldn't believe how kind Santa had been. She was even more amazed when Ben pointed out that some of the presents had her name on them.

Later, when everybody else had come down, Emma sobbed with gratitude in both Clare's and Peter's arms, as she knew they had been behind it all.

As the kids paraded around in their new clothes and played with their new toys, the unlikely group of housemates prepared a Christmas feast. While the men took care of the barbequing, Clare and Emma did all the indoor kitchen work. Although Lillian still didn't offer to help with the food preparations, she did create a beautifully decorated table, complete with party hats, bon-bons and elegantly folded napkins. There were endless compliments about the food and they all ate until they were stuffed.

After the obligatory afternoon nap to recover from overindulging at lunch, Ron suggested a game of cricket. Clare smiled to herself, thinking that Ron had really taken on her suggestion to involve himself more in house events.

Both Clare and Emma threw themselves into the game enthusiastically, giving the men a run for their money. Ben joined in as well, while Lucy and Lillian made daisy chains.

Finally, they all went down to the beach. Lillian was the only one who didn't venture into the sea, but everybody else had a marvellous time in the water. Ron was especially patient with Ben, carrying him out numerous times so he could ride the boogie board to shore. Peter showed Emma how to dive under a wave, something she had always been scared of. Clare and Lucy paddled happily in the shallows and played with the beach ball that Emma had found at the house.

After the kids were in bed asleep they played hearts. While Lillian wasn't officially part of the game, she sat with Peter and watched him play. Peter and Ron were enjoying a beer or three and Lillian was drinking champagne from one of the elegant flutes in the china cabinet. Clare and Emma just had a glass of wine each as neither of them were big drinkers. But they felt they were enjoying themselves just as much as their somewhat tipsy housemates.

On her third glass, Lillian went from giggly to wistful. She was the first to voice the thought that had been playing on their minds all day. 'Clare,' she said 'How did a drama student manage to create order in the horrendous situation we found ourselves in?'

'Come on Lillian, it wasn't horrendous,' said Clare. 'Unfortunate, maybe, or inconvenient, but not horrendous.'

'All right, not horrendous. But you still didn't answer my question.'

'Well, first of all, I'm not a drama student,' said Clare.

Lillian raised an eyebrow. 'All right, a drama graduate then?'

Clare shook her head. 'Uh, no. Not even close. What makes you say that?'

Peter, Lillian, Ron and Emma exchanged puzzled glances. Nobody had actually asked Clare, but they didn't think they'd needed to. Who was she if not a drama student?

Lillian held up a finger, as if to make a point. 'That shirt you were wearing with the slogan about drama students having class. Your cap says University of Melbourne. And you mentioned living the student life to your friend on the phone.'

Clare laughed. 'You all seriously thought I was a drama student?'

The housemates nodded.

Clare laughed again. 'You guys could never work for ASIO. A friend gave me the t-shirt. And, I did go to the University of Melbourne, hence the cap. As for the student life comment, I just meant that although I've graduated I still haven't gotten a *real job* yet,' she said, holding her fingers up to indicate inverted commas.

The others were still waiting for more. It was Emma who spoke this time. 'But when you talked about doing role plays – isn't that drama?'

Clare shook her head. 'No, that was something else. But now I know why you were talking about stage fright. I thought you were using metaphors.'

Emma shook her head. 'No, I barely remember what a metaphor

is,' she said.

Everybody laughed.

Determined to solve the mystery Emma spoke again. 'Come on Clare, if you're not a drama student, who are you, then?'

'I thought you might have guessed,' Clare said. 'I'm a psychologist. Well, I will be, when I finish the next part of my training.'

Everybody around the table exchanged knowing looks as the light bulbs went on. Yes, now it all made sense! Clare had sorted them all out in one way or another and had diffused a few potentially volatile situations. But, on the other hand, they all had a mental picture of a psychologist being older, much more serious and full of clichés and platitudes.

Lillian poured more champagne into her glass. 'So, why haven't you got a *real* job yet? Didn't you say you're working as a waitress?'

Clare nodded. 'I have been for the past year. I guess it's my turn to fess up now.'

Four sets of eyes looked at her expectantly.

'I've wanted to be a psychologist since I was about twelve,' said Clare. 'I was one of those annoying teenagers who knew exactly what they wanted to be and never wavered.'

Everybody nodded.

'I did well in my VCE and got into the University of Melbourne no problem. I loved the course, worked really hard and never doubted I had found my true vocation. Everybody told me I was a natural and I had no reason not to believe them.'

Pausing for a moment, Clare gathered her thoughts before speaking again. 'Because I was one of the top students in my course, I was offered an opportunity to undertake an internship. They're pretty hard to come by and it's a real feather in your cap when you apply for your supervised placement. I had specialised in teenage psychology and the internship was at a youth centre.

'So, I went in there, all guns blazing, completely sure I was going to take the world by storm.' Shaking her head, she stopped speaking.

'What happened?' Emma asked gently.

'I totally blew it. I thought I knew more than the people already working there and set about introducing all these new programs and trying to be best buddies with the kids.' She shook her head again. 'It was a disaster. So much so that they asked me to leave, because I just didn't listen to their advice.'

'And did that affect your academic record?' asked Peter.

'Oh, no, that was all fine. It was extra-curricular so that wasn't an issue. No, I just totally lost my confidence and couldn't even contemplate doing my supervised placement. I told the psych department I was taking some time off to travel and have been dodging their emails about my return date ever since.'

Ron surprised everybody by speaking then. 'It seems like a shame to waste all that study after just one setback.'

Clare nodded. 'You're right Ron. I've been thinking about it a lot since I've been here and when I was talking to Li..., uh, someone recently, I realised that I *can* be a good psychologist, but I need to learn the ropes properly first, which is what supervised placement is all about.'

Lillian gave Clare a sharp glance, alarmed at the thought her personal business might be disclosed and discussed among the group, but nobody else seemed to notice Clare's slip of the tongue.

Peter unknowingly rescued the situation. 'I think you've helped us all one way or another,' he said, giving Clare a meaningful glance, 'and I believe we're all very grateful. Right everyone?'

They all nodded.

Buoyed by the success of the day and relieved to finally tell everybody her true background, Clare drifted off to sleep happy. It had been so long since she'd let herself think about going back to psychology and now she'd made the decision, her heart was joyful. It was her true vocation and she was going to embrace it fully. Lillian had been a test, Clare decided. If she hadn't been able to get through to her, she would have probably closed the door on psychology all together.

Awoken by a raging thirst at four thirty, Clare willed herself to go back to sleep. After their early start yesterday, she'd planned a decent sleep in for Boxing Day, even remembering to close the curtains tightly so she wouldn't be woken by the sun. Feeling herself becoming more dehydrated by the second, however, Clare gave in ten minutes later and crept downstairs to get a drink.

She was surprised to find Lillian in the kitchen boiling the kettle.

Clare had never seen her downstairs before breakfast at eight. Dressed in an elegant pink silk nightie with a matching robe and slippers, Lillian's outfit contrasted sharply with Clare's singlet/boxer shorts/bare feet ensemble. Lillian's hair was flat and un-styled and her face looked pale and drawn without make up.

'Oh, Clare, you gave me a fright. I didn't think anybody else would be up at this hour,' Lillian said, patting her hair self-consciously and looking embarrassed to have been caught in her sleepwear.

'Me either. Are you going for a walk or something?'

Lillian shook her head gingerly. 'No, I'm trying to settle my stomach. I don't know why I over indulge in champagne, the end result is never pleasant.'

'Sit on the veranda and get some air, I'll bring your tea out,' Clare said, reaching for the teabags.

Lillian smiled gratefully and went outside. Clare made herself a cup as well and carried them expertly out on their saucers without spilling a drop. They didn't speak as they drank their tea, each of them lost in their own thoughts as they watched the sun rise. When Clare finished her tea, she put the cup and saucer down and gave Lillian a kind smile.

'So, how are you getting along?' she asked.

Lillian didn't answer immediately. She closed her eyes and put her fingers to her forehead. Clare thought she must be feeling sick. It took her a moment to realise that Lillian was fighting back tears. She went inside and retrieved a box of tissues. Lillian took one gratefully and dabbed at her eyes.

'I'm sorry to be so emotional,' sniffed Lillian. 'I just really miss Michael and I worry about him being so far away.'

Clare nodded, accepting the comment at face value. But, as the minutes passed, and Lillian struggled to compose herself, a realisation came to Clare. This was the third time she'd seen Lillian cry in the space of a few days, yet Peter had told her she never cried. Closing her eyes for a moment, several thoughts crowded Clare's mind and it took her a moment to process them. Some psychologist you are, she thought, you missed the big picture.

According to Lillian, it was the publication of the book that had made her unhappy and caused tension in her marriage, but that was only a year ago. In Peter's version of events, things had been going wrong a lot longer than that. Then, there was Lillian's reaction to Lucy's accident. She had seemed genuinely paralysed, unable to offer comfort to Lucy. Surely any mother, even one as emotionally reserved as Lillian, would instinctively react to calm a hysterical child? Finally, there was the Melbourne comment. Lillian had said, "You're from Melbourne, Kew specifically," yet had not offered any further explanation and Clare hadn't picked up on the significance of that statement.

Most of all, though, Clare suddenly realised that Lillian wasn't just unhappy, she was genuinely, deeply sad. The kind of sadness she had witnessed in other women Lillian's age, who had been living with a secret for a long time.

'You were pregnant, weren't you?' Clare said softly.

Lillian recoiled, her eyes like saucers, as she stared back at Clare.

'That's why Tony banished you to Melbourne. I know there used to be a private home for unmarried mothers in Kew. It's only a few streets from where I live. You were forced to adopt your baby out.'

Reaching for another tissue, Lillian dabbed her eyes again and blew her nose. 'You're half right,' she whispered.

Feeling like she should give Lillian a hug, but knowing it might not be well received, Clare patted her hand instead. 'Which half?' she asked.

'I *was* pregnant. I hadn't told Tony, but his secretary must have worked it out when she caught me throwing up on more than one occasion. She was a nosy old biddy, but Tony trusted her implicitly. No doubt she knew about our little dalliance.'

'Right.' Clare nodded. 'What happened in Melbourne, then?' she asked.

'I did move there, but I refused to work another day in that company. After I cashed the generous relocation cheque, I found a job as a live-in housekeeper for a wealthy, middle-aged widow named Mrs Astor. She lived in Kew.'

'And she treated you badly when she found out about the baby?'

Lillian shook her head. 'No, no, not at all. The opposite. She was my saviour. We talked endlessly about the best course of action and she supported me financially and emotionally when I decided to keep the baby. She insisted I stay living with her.'

Knowing how hard it must be for Lillian to tell her story, Clare kept her expression as neutral as possible.

'I had a little girl, Teresa. She was beautiful, exquisite. I couldn't believe you could feel such love for another human being. The eight weeks she was with me are like this gilded, sacred memory.'

Sensing what was coming, Clare could only nod.

'Then early one morning I went in to her cot and she wasn't breathing. She was so cold…,' Covering her face with both hands, Lillian began to sob.

This time Clare acted on instinct. Sliding across the outdoor couch, she gathered Lillian in a hug and held her as her body trembled. Several minutes passed before Clare felt like she could drop her arms and let Lillian compose herself. Eventually, she spoke again.

'It was a cot death. The pain I experienced after that was so great that I honestly thought I would die. Some days I didn't get out of bed and many nights before I went to sleep I hoped I wouldn't wake up. Eventually, after a few weeks, Mrs Astor gently coaxed me back into the land of the living and I realised that I could keep going, even though life seemed so pointless.' She shook her head. 'But I swore I would never love anyone that wholeheartedly ever again because I knew I might lose them.'

'So, you never had counselling or anything?' Clare asked gently.

'This was the sixties, Clare. People didn't get counselling back then, especially girls who had got themselves into trouble. No, when I got myself back together, I moved home. I never told anybody what happened, I didn't even keep a photograph of Teresa.'

'That's so sad, Lillian,' Clare said, blinking back her own tears.

Lillian dabbed her eyes and blew her nose. 'Initially I took a secretarial position at the local doctor's surgery and lived a very quiet life, while I tried to heal my broken heart. Then, a year later, I went to work at Kilsyth Constructions.'

'Ah, that was Peter's father.'

'Yes, that's right. It's lucky that Pete was so persistent, because I certainly wasn't looking for a boyfriend. I insisted that it had to be friendship only for several months.'

'But you fell in love?'

'We did. Pete was so different to Tony and I realised that was what real love was. As scared as I was about having another baby, I knew I wanted to marry him.' Lillian was calmer now, her voice almost normal again.

'My pregnancy with Michael was textbook perfect, but I was still terrified that something might go wrong. Even when he was born safely, I knew then and there that I could never have another child. The anxiety was too great.'

'Oh, right,' said Clare.

'I know it was a horrible thing to do, to go on the pill without Peter knowing, but I just couldn't tell him about Teresa.'

Clare nodded.

'I loved Michael just as deeply, but I was guarded with him. I couldn't let myself be affectionate like I had with Teresa. I had this idea if I didn't show my love for him too much then he wouldn't get taken away.'

'That's perfectly understandable, Lillian.'

'When Michael was younger and Pete was setting up his business, I kept myself very busy on purpose, so I just didn't have time to dwell on the pain. But when Mike got towards the end of high school, he didn't need me as much and I had far too much time on my hands. I couldn't stop thinking about what Teresa would be like and I began to regret not having any more children.'

'Oh, Lillian.'

'I even tried to get pregnant again about ten years ago, but it just didn't happen. So, I immersed myself in our new, affluent lifestyle to try and disguise the ache. Nothing can make it go away, though. Not having a beautiful house, a substantial household income, being invited to all the best social events or even having a wonderful husband and son. It's always there.'

'I can't imagine what it feels like.'

'I hope you never find out, Clare.'

'That's why Emma's comments upset you so much.'

Lillian nodded. 'Yes. Of course, it wasn't her fault, but that's what catches you off guard sometimes.'

'Not to go all psychologist on you, Lillian, but you have to remember that you haven't grieved properly. You've locked all this pain away and never dealt with it. There are ways to make it more bearable.'

'You think I should tell Peter, don't you?'

Clare nodded.

'That's your professional opinion, I suppose?'

'Yes, it is, but it's not up to me to force you to do anything, certainly not before you're ready. And, I absolutely don't pretend to know much about the kind of counselling you need. There are lots of very experienced practitioners out there, though, and you're in a position to get the help you need.'

'I wouldn't even know where to start.'

'I'll look into it for you and find some people who specialise in this area in Sydney. In the meantime, you can always talk to me if you need to. I really mean that.'

Lillian dabbed her eyes again. 'Thank you, Clare, you're very kind.'

Heading up to her room after Lillian's revelation, Clare climbed back into bed, but didn't sleep. At first her insecurities resurfaced, as she contemplated how she'd initially dismissed Lillian's prickly demeanour, not seeing the wounded soul beneath. But, after an hour of ruminating, Clare acknowledged that even a skilled practitioner wouldn't necessarily have worked it out. Having spent the last thirty years keeping a tight lid on her pain, Lillian held her cards very close to her chest. You're just a beginner, Clare, she reminded herself. Give yourself a break and do what you've got to do to get properly qualified. You can't start saving the world just yet.

Picking up the novel that Peter had given her as a present, Clare decided she'd read the first chapter before heading back downstairs to get breakfast started. But she barely made it to the bottom of the first page before her eyes drooped and the book dropped to the floor.

When Clare woke again, it was to the sound of Ben and Lucy running down the hallway. Mmmm, that was a great sleep, she thought, stretching her arms up above her head. Rolling onto her side, she picked up her watch from the bedside table. Eleven thirty. Wow. She hadn't slept that late for a long time.

Arriving downstairs fifteen minutes later, Clare was shocked to see the dining room table beautifully arranged with leftover Christmas food. Lillian stood at one end, counting out the plates, while Emma was setting out the cutlery. Seeing Clare, she smiled. 'Good morning, sleepyhead.'

Exchanging a quick glance with Lillian, Clare smiled back. 'Morning. I can't believe I slept half the day away.'

'Well, you have been working very hard, trying to sort the rest of us out,' said Lillian. 'I think you deserved a sleep in.' Looking up, she exchanged another look with Clare, this one much more meaningful.

'Thanks, Lillian. How are you feeling today?'

Stepping back to let Lucy run past her, Lillian smiled. 'Better than I have for a long time.'

Being Boxing Day the beach was packed, but the housemates spent most of the afternoon down there, anyway. Lillian even came down to watch when everyone went for a final swim just before six o'clock. Peter carried a beach chair from the veranda down to the sand and she sat there, surprised at how restful being so close to the waves was.

It was close to the end of patrol hours and the lifeguards and surf lifesavers were beginning to wind down their operations for the day.

Lillian was taken aback when the head lifeguard came over to speak to her. 'How's your granddaughter?' he asked.

'My *what?*'

'The little blonde girl. Lucy, isn't it? She had a bit of an adventure the other day. Lucky Grandad came to the rescue.' Jim nodded in Peter's direction.

Lillian was about to correct Jim's misconceptions, but he spoke again before she had the chance.

'Sorry, I should have introduced myself. Jim Stewart.'

'Lillian Kilsyth. You've met my husband, then?'

'Well, not exactly, but I met Emma when we were looking for Lucy and I've seen your other daughter around and your grandson. I suppose the other chap is the son in law?'

Lillian was too stunned to try and set the record straight so she just agreed. 'Yes, we're quite a bunch all right.' She wasn't sure how Emma would feel about being paired off with Ron, but the real story was far too complicated to try and explain.

'How has your stay up at the house been?'

'It's been lovely, thank you,' Lillian answered, while thinking wryly about all the drama that had ensued over the past eleven days.

Jim looked out into the water where the others were splashing around. 'It's great to see a family group up there over Christmas enjoying the house and all that it stands for.'

Lillian nodded. 'Yes, well…,' she began, but Jim wasn't finished what he wanted to say.

'You see so many broken relationships these days, so it's just good to see a decent family group spending time together. Enjoy the rest of your stay now,' he finished with a nod.

Lillian just smiled politely in return, only mildly insulted that Jim thought she looked old enough to be a grandmother.

Emma was subdued when she and Clare played SPIT that night. She missed several opportunities to throw cards down and didn't seem very bothered when Clare won five rounds in a row.

'What's up, Em?' Clare asked as she put the cards in two piles.

Emma's bottom lip trembled and a tear ran down her cheek. 'It's Boxing Day,' she said.

'Okay,' Clare replied. 'And that makes you sad because…?'

Emma wiped the tear away, but another took its place. 'We always have a big family reunion on Boxing Day,' she sniffed. 'My grandparents have a place in Tauranga, it's right on the beach. It was always so much fun seeing our aunts and uncles and cousins. They're probably all there now, playing cards and singing around the piano.'

'I bet they miss you.'

Emma sniffed again. 'I don't know about that, but I miss *them* so much,' she whispered.

Clare came around to the other side of the table and put her arm around her. 'Emma, it sounds like you have a really nice family. Sure, they might be angry and hurt that you ran away, but I bet they would get over it really fast if you got in touch.'

Emma started to cry harder. 'It was such a stupid thing to do.'

Clare handed her a tissue from the box on the table. 'Yeah, it was, but you were sixteen. Who doesn't do stupid things at that age? You were in love and that can cloud your judgement.'

'My parents had such high hopes for me. They thought I would be a teacher or an accountant and instead I'm an uneducated single mother. They'll be so disappointed.'

'Emma, you're twenty-four, you've got all the time in the world to finish your education *and* you're a wonderful mother with two delightful kids. How could they possibly be disappointed about that?'

'I've caused them so much pain.'

'And you're causing them more by staying away. If you can't bring yourself to ring them, then write a letter. I'll help you if you like. Can you do that?'

Emma blew her nose. 'I think so,' she gulped.

'All right, we'll do it tomorrow.'

Clare walked slowly back from town the next morning, amazed at how much she was sweating. While Victoria sometimes had heatwaves that lasted for days with temperatures in the forties, it was rarely humid like this.

'Oh, Clare there you are, we were wondering where you got to.' Lillian was sitting on the veranda, drinking a cup of tea.

Clare jogged up the back steps. 'I've just been in town,' she said. 'I had a few things to do and thought I'd get off to an early start.'

'Good idea.'

Clare sat down on one of the loungers and put her feet up. 'Whew, it's nice to be in the cool again. It's a hot walk to town on a day like today.'

'Yes, it's warm all right,' agreed Lillian. 'I was just talking to Michael on the phone and they've had a blizzard where he is.'

'Oh, of course, it would still be Christmas day there, with the time difference. Is Peter talking to him now?' Clare asked. She could hear him talking animatedly and laughing heartily.

'Yes, those two could talk all day. They've always been very close.'

'Did Michael have a good Christmas?' Clare asked.

'Yes, he seemed to, although he said he missed us.'

'I'm sure he did.' Clare opened her bag and pulled out a piece of paper. 'Uh, Lillian, I thought you might like to have this,' she said, extending the page.

Lillian looked at her before taking it. When she read what was on the paper, the colour drained from her face. 'Clare, where on earth did you get this information?' she asked.

'A combination of the internet, electoral rolls and directory assistance. It helped that she had an unusual surname and still lives in Melbourne. It's been a busy morning,' Clare said.

'And you're sure it's her?'

'Positive. I spoke to her daughter, Mrs Astor lives with her now. She's getting on a bit and is frail, but is still very mentally alert, apparently.'

Lillian stared out at the ocean for a moment. 'You know, I thought she was old back when I worked for her, but she was probably only a few years older than I am now. It's funny how your perspective on age changes as you get older.'

Clare nodded. 'You're right, it does.'

'I always meant to stay in touch. I even wrote a couple of letters but didn't send them. In the end, I just thought it would be less painful to cut all ties.'

'Her daughter said that she loves having visitors and that she has kept all her photos. Boxes and boxes of them.'

Lillian put her hand to her mouth and closed her eyes for a second. 'I'd be able to see my baby again,' she whispered. 'Mrs Astor had a camera and took lots of pictures of us.'

'I think it would help you a lot, not only to see the photos, but also to talk to her about it,' Clare said. 'She undoubtedly suffered as well, you know.'

'Yes, I'm sure she did, she loved Teresa too.' Lillian put the piece of paper in her pocket. 'I'm sorry I can't talk about this anymore with Peter just in there, but thank you so much,' she said softly.

'You're very welcome.' Clare stood, then walked over to the door and went inside.

The housemates gathered around the kitchen table that night and talked openly. Looking to Clare for guidance they all wanted to get something off their chests. 'What if everybody makes one resolution that they know they can keep?' Clare said. 'I have to make one too.'

Everybody nodded.

Emma went first. 'I'm going to contact my family by letter. Maybe even move back to New Zealand if I can save up the fare.'

'I'm going to look for more constructive ways of dealing with stress than the bottom of a bottle,' said Peter.

Ron was next. 'I'm going to try to find my daughter. It shouldn't be that hard; I've just never looked. If she is half as nice as you girls I'll be as happy as a lark.'

Clare and Emma beamed at him.

Lillian's voice was much quieter than normal. 'I'm going to catch up with an old friend, it's been far too many years since we last saw each other.'

Finally, it was Clare's turn. 'I'm going to complete my training ASAP,' she said with a smile. Then she raised her glass in a toast and everybody joined in with her. 'To the Beach House,' she said with a grin.

'The Beach House,' the others echoed.

As each of them left, they all found at least one anonymous gift from one of their other housemates.

Ron found a pile of pamphlets and printed pages with information about searching for a missing relative.

Lillian found the book *In Memory Of My Daughter*.

Peter found a framed photograph of himself riding a wave on Christmas day.

Emma found three airline tickets to New Zealand. She didn't have to guess where they came from.

The good byes were poignant, but happy, in the sense that they were all leaving in better emotional shape than when they arrived.

Clare found it strange to be in the house by herself, even if it was for just one day, until Joanne's family arrived. She enjoyed the solitude, even though she did miss the others.

It wasn't until the late afternoon that she got her surprise. She was sitting on the veranda and noticed a commotion on the beach. Everybody was peering up to the sky and pointing.

She looked up and saw a plane doing skywriting. How sweet, she thought, intrigued by the message. So far, she could read 'Thank You'. Then came a C, an L, an A, and then Clare realised who it was for.

With tears running down her face she hugged her knees up under her chin. 'No, thank you,' she said

Jack

2003

𝒯he traffic was very light as Jack Nolan headed into work at six forty-five on a Monday morning. Although now considered a regional city, Millvale hadn't quite shaken off its country town image, and there was never much activity before eight. Stopping at a red light, he watched a group of commuters sprint towards the Sydney Direct bus that was about to depart, thankful he didn't have to make that ninety-minute trek to the city each day.

Like most mornings, Jack was the first to arrive at Kendall and Masters Solicitors. The security guard buzzed him in and he walked briskly through the silent building, switching on the main lights and opening some of the blinds. At thirty-six, he was a senior associate and occupied a corner office overlooking the entrance to the botanical gardens. Dropping his briefcase and laptop on the desk, he took a moment to appreciate the view, before consulting his daily planner. Jack enjoyed the hour of silence before the office got into full swing. With a staff of thirty, it was a busy workplace and once the phones started ringing, there was never much uninterrupted time.

None of Jack's workmates were surprised to see him at his desk when they started trickling in after eight o'clock. Mr Kendall Senior gave him a good morning nod as he walked past. He had worked in law for fifty years and knew how rare it was to come across an employee of such high calibre. Jack's remarkable technical knowledge, his skill in planning strategy and his ability to think on his feet in court had earned him a stellar reputation and there was a waiting list for his services. Mr Kendall planned to offer him a partnership before the year was out.

Kelly Burke sipped her take-away coffee as she walked through the front door of the office. She was enjoying her new role as Jack's secretary, after being stuck in the junior typing pool for almost a year. But, as much as she liked her new job and Jack himself, she was finding it difficult to really get to know him.

Dumping her empty cup in the bin, Kelly sat down at her desk, removed her keys and water bottle from her bag and shoved it in her bottom drawer. She watched as Jack walked over and selected a reference book from the bookcase. Slightly above average height with a lean build, dark hair and intense dark brown eyes, Jack was a good-looking guy who also had impeccable dress sense. Kelly had calculated he must have at least ten designer suits, a benchmark that none of the other male staff came close to matching.

Picking up the document on top of her in tray, Kelly glanced at the corrections Jack had made in pencil. He never signed off on anything that wasn't perfect and she was used to doing numerous drafts. He must be a Virgo, she thought, they're supposed to be perfectionists.

Kelly switched on her computer and rested her chin on her hand while it booted up. 'Why is it that the only guy in this office who is classy enough to wear Armani and Hugo Boss is also a social recluse?' she said to her workmate, Abby, who had just arrived at her desk.

Abby frowned. She had long harboured a secret crush on Jack, despite his reserved manner. She didn't like to hear him bad-mouthed or gossiped about. 'I wouldn't say he's a recluse,' she replied.

'Are you kidding? He eats lunch at his desk most days, he rarely comes to social functions unless he has to and he never gossips or even listens to gossip.'

Abby turned her computer on. 'He's just quiet,' she said.

'Yeah, he is, but he's not shy, as such. I mean, he talks to people easily enough, he's so approachable and I've heard he's amazing in court.'

'Oh, yeah, he is,' Abby agreed, more enthusiastically than she meant to.

Kelly looked at her.

'I had to take some documents over one day and I sat in for a while,' Abby answered casually, not wanting to reveal it was her own careless driving charge that Jack had been defending.

'Oh, right.'

Abby glanced up at the clock. 'We'd better get to it,' she said.

'Yeah, yeah.'

It was almost five o'clock when Kelly went to clear Jack's out tray. Most of the staff were winding down and preparing to leave but Jack was still hard at work. His desk was covered with files and he was typing something on his laptop. He had his jacket off and Kelly noted that he was wearing a new pair of black cufflinks. They're nice, she thought to herself and they look great with that shirt. Blue really is his colour. Kelly smiled to herself, knowing that Jack would be mortified if he knew how the women in the office scrutinised and commented on his wardrobe on a daily basis. He was such a private person.

Jack looked up, his dark eyes focusing on Kelly as she walked over to his desk. He always maintained eye contact when he spoke to people. It was probably the only way he let his guard down. Whether Jack realised it or not, his eyes were very expressive. Looking at them now, Kelly could tell that Jack was tired and stressed.

She picked up the stack of documents and flicked through them to make sure there wasn't anything that needed to be urgently mailed.

'Thanks Kel. Good work on the Karlson documents, sorting that paperwork out has been like wading through glue and I appreciate how frustrating it can be to type it all up.'

'No problem, that's the secretary's lot in life. You're not going yet?'

Jack shook his head. 'Nah, a solicitor's lot is to get everything done yesterday and I've got court tomorrow.'

'You work too hard, you know.'

'So I've heard. It's just how I am Kel, a bit of a drudge. Have a good night,' Jack said, with a smile.

He had a nice smile and on the few occasions that Kelly had seen him laugh she saw how it changed his whole demeanour. Sometimes she had the urge to tickle him, just so he would lighten up a bit.

Kelly smiled back. 'Yeah, you too,' she said, although she knew he would be at the office for a couple more hours at least. Kelly loved her job and understood that people put their heart and soul into their work, but she did have a life beyond it. Apparently, Jack's work *was* his life.

It was almost eight thirty when Jack walked through his back door, still in his gym clothes. He'd worked out for an hour on the way home and was exhausted, as well as hungry.

Dropping his briefcase and laptop in the study and his work clothes in the laundry, Jack headed for the fridge. He smiled when he saw the dish of lasagne his cleaning/ironing lady had left him. He neither asked nor expected Edna to do it, but she didn't believe a single man living alone could possibly feed himself properly and regularly prepared him food.

After flipping through *The Sydney Morning Herald* while he ate, Jack collapsed onto his recliner and picked up the remote control. He stopped flicking channels when he came across *Surf City*. Originally billed as *the* new primetime show of the year it had been slammed by the critics for its far-fetched storylines and mediocre acting. Jack had only come across it after it was shunted to a later timeslot.

He wasn't sure exactly what it was about the group of elite lifeguards that captured his interest, but he found himself watching it almost every night. So far removed from the work he did, Jack couldn't fathom having the beach as an office.

When the late news finished, Jack spent an hour reviewing his paperwork for the next day. Eventually shutting down his computer at eleven thirty, he leaned back in his desk chair and rubbed his eyes. He was wrecked. It was hard to remember the years when he had genuinely loved his job, despite the long hours and the stress. These days it required much more effort to maintain the high standards that he prided himself on. Jack fought against this career discontent by working harder. He just didn't have time for a mid-life crisis right now.

The alarm had reached its highest pitch when Jack finally silenced it with a well-practiced thump the next morning. As he contemplated another half hour of sleep, the radio sprang to life. 'Good morning all you early risers, it's five thirty-five and a chilly ten degrees outside.' Jack tuned out the chirpy banter between the breakfast show hosts and dragged himself out of bed.

He tried to ignore the discomfort in his right knee as he ran steadily along the dark, deserted streets and thought about the day ahead. Running was his pressure valve when he was under the pump out and he had been doing a lot of it lately.

Standing under the shower half an hour later, he could see that the knee had started to swell as well as ache. Great, he thought, knowing his old high school rugby injury had flared up again.

By two thirty, the pain level had increased markedly. Discreetly swallowing another two Panadol, Jack shifted uncomfortably in his chair. He was glad he'd given his closing arguments before lunch, when he could still stand without grimacing in pain. His opponent, Marcus Firth, was pacing dramatically as he gave a long-winded explanation as to why he couldn't give his closing arguments without a final set of documents that had been held up in the mail.

The magistrate peered down at him sternly. 'All right Mr Firth, we will reconvene at nine in the morning with or without the documents. I've already given you more than enough leeway with this.'

Jack glanced at the woman beside him and rolled his eyes sympathetically. This was a fairly cut and dried case that had already dragged on too long and he felt sorry for his client, having to take another day off work.

After being formally dismissed for the day, Jack packed his briefcase and hobbled outside. The one upside of the adjournment was that he could go to the doctor and get some pain relief.

Dr Brian Wilson examined the knee and shook his head. 'No magic wand here, Jack. As I've told you before, until you take my advice and lay off the running and heavy gym work for at least three months, it will never heal properly.'

Jack flinched as the doctor applied pressure to the swollen knee. 'Yeah, I know, I know. I do wear the knee guard and most of the time it holds up well.'

'This is the second time in less than a year.' Doctor Wilson glanced at his notes. 'You can't keep re-inflaming it without some long-term damage.'

Jack sat up, exhaling sharply as another stab of pain hit.

'This is your stress point Jack. It's a physical weakness and when you put yourself under a lot of pressure, it's going to be the thing that buckles, literally.'

'How else am I supposed to get an aerobic workout? Didn't you tell me exercise is the best way to de-stress?'

Dr Wilson laughed. 'Don't get all lawyerly and convict me with my own words. Swimming would be perfect for your injury and you can get your heart pumping just as much in the water without further damaging your knee. The pool is open long hours these days, to cater for workaholics like you,' he said, as he wrote in Jack's file.

Nodding, Jack gratefully took the script that Dr Wilson had written for Panadeine Forte.

· · · · ·

Kelly and her netball team-mate Amanda went for a drink after their game one Thursday night.

'I've got a bone to pick with you,' Amanda said, as she settled onto her stool and took a sip of merlot.

'What?' Kelly sat on her seat and raised her eyebrows.

'I'm always asking if there are any decent men in your office and you tell me there aren't. So, I was pretty surprised when a new guy joined my swimming squad and he told me he worked at Kendall and Masters. *Then*, I say how my friend works there and it turns out that you're his secretary. And you never told me about him.'

Kelly's eyes widened. '*Jack* joined your swimming squad?'

'Yeah, he did, and stop avoiding the question.'

Taking a swig of her rum and coke, Kelly shrugged. 'Well, I would have said something, but I just didn't think he was your type.'

'Since when has a good-looking guy with a killer wardrobe, a decent job, lots of money and a great body not been my type?'

'Great body?'

'Yeah, definitely. He's lean but he's very toned.'

Kelly pondered this for a moment. 'He's just really quiet, reserved, you know,' she said eventually. 'You're so outgoing; I just don't know how that would go.'

Amanda took another sip of wine. 'Quiet and reserved I can work with. What are his other good points?'

'Well, he's our personal injury specialist and he pretty much never loses a case. You wouldn't want to mess with him in court.'

'I'll keep that in mind. How about him, personally?'

'Uh, he's really polite, perfect manners, very intelligent, respectful,' Kelly said. 'He drives a Lexus and he's got an amazing house up on the range.'

'You've been to his *house*?'

'Don't get too excited, I just had to drop some papers up once after hours.'

'All right, now you've built me up, you'd better knock me down. What's the catch?'

'Well, firstly, the reason he's so successful is because he's a workaholic, so you'd be lucky to ever see him. Secondly, he doesn't let you get far below the surface. It's kind of like everything is in place on the exterior, but there's not a lot of substance underneath.'

'Maybe he just needs the right surroundings to loosen up a bit.'

Kelly took another sip of her drink. 'I know you guys in the squad are really social, but I bet he'll just politely decline any invitations you extend.'

Steepling her fingers, Amanda smiled. 'Forewarned is forearmed. I'll ambush him tomorrow night, tell him we always take the new team member out for drinks.'

'Good luck with that.'

Amanda enlisted the help of Davo, a fellow squad member, to help convince Jack to come to drinks. Tall and heavily built with a shaved head, full beard and ruddy, weather-beaten complexion he looked downright scary, although he really had a heart of gold. He cornered Jack as they rested between sets of freestyle drills in the shallow end.

'You'll be at the pub later, right?' he asked. 'I haven't bought you a drink yet and my dad always told me you can never trust a bloke who won't have a drink with you.'

Jack eyed Davo carefully, taking in his thick chest, sizable beer gut and bulging biceps that were covered in tattoos. He must be in his fifties and Jack wasn't sure exactly what line of work he was in, although being a member of a bikie gang seemed more than likely. 'Okay,' he said. 'Maybe just the one.'

Kel's right, Amanda thought, as the squad sat talking an hour later. He doesn't let you delve too deep. Jack had been friendly and polite, but had given little about himself away. I'll just have to keep working at it she decided. I can be very determined when I need to be.

• • • • •

After heading off at three a.m. and travelling for the better part of a day, Jack smiled wearily when he saw the turn off for Sunset Point. 'Finally!' he exclaimed, as he exited smoothly onto a two-lane road with a gravel shoulder. He had recently traded his Lexus for an Audi and while he'd enjoyed putting the new car through its paces, twelve hours behind the wheel today, coupled with four the previous evening, was long enough.

Motoring along the coast road, Jack was captivated by the beautiful scenery. Even though it was a cloudy day, the sight of the ocean rolling gently into shore helped him forget his exhaustion for a while. He felt carefree as he cruised around the base of the cliff and wished for a moment he was in a convertible.

The high spirits vanished when Jack walked into the big, empty house. In fact, the size of it seemed to amplify the sense of isolation he always carried. Although he was used to being alone and doing things by himself, it was different when you were in a strange place. A wave of uncertainty hit him. What on earth am I doing here? Jack wondered, as he hauled his suitcase inside.

Sinking wearily onto the couch, he answered his own question. Desperation had brought him there. A series of eighty-hour weeks dedicated to a high profile, workplace accident case had led to five days in bed with severe bronchitis. Even after two courses of antibiotics, the cough had lingered on for weeks, leaving Jack physically weak and approaching burnout. He knew he had to take a break for his own sanity.

It had been Davo who came up with the idea of doing his lifeguard training. *Surf City* had come on in the pub one night and Jack had admitted his fascination with lifeguards and the work they did. He hadn't expected Davo to tell him that he had a cousin in Queensland who worked as a lifeguard and ran a training program.

'It's a great job, Jack,' Davo enthused. 'I did surf patrol for years when I lived in Sydney. Course, I was younger and fitter then,' he said, with a smile that made him look much less intimidating.

Jack had dismissed the idea out of hand at first, but Davo kept insisting it was just the kind of change he needed to shake his life up. When he was sick, he contemplated the idea seriously for the first time. Two weeks later, Jack submitted his leave form and now he was here.

Even though it looked old, the shower had great water pressure. Jack stood under the hot spray and let the water run over him. Gradually he relaxed a little and felt some of the weariness leave him. He could do this.

Down in the kitchen, he popped open the can of Coke he had bought at the servo in Rosethorn, and took a long draught. The sugar and caffeine hit his system with a welcome jolt. He gulped another mouthful and looked at his watch. It was nearly four o'clock, but he decided to take a walk down to the beach, anyway and get the ball rolling before he chickened out.

Like his cousin Davo, Jim Stewart was tall and his complexion weather-beaten, but that was where the similarities ended. Although he must be in his mid-fifties, Jack's thick brown hair was only tinged with grey and he had the trim, muscular build of an athlete.

After introducing themselves, Jim eyeballed Jack, apparently trying to sum up if he was serious about what he was getting himself into. 'This job isn't some fun hobby, you know, we deal with life and death. I'm prepared to teach and teach well but only if you put in one hundred percent effort,' Jim said, his green eyes still watching Jack's face closely.

Jack nodded. 'I fully intend to. I wouldn't be here if I wasn't serious about it.'

'You know you're at a real disadvantage? Most people in this job have grown up near the beach and are already naturals in the ocean. I've never trained a complete novice before.'

Jack met Jim's gaze, hoping he looked more confident than he felt. 'Fair enough. But is there a rule that says you can't do the job without the benefit of a childhood and youth spent at the beach?'

Crossing his arms, Jack shook his head. 'No, these are non-discriminatory times we live in, as I'm sure you know. Anybody who meets the basic health and fitness requirements is eligible to do the training program.'

'Well, consider me advised that it will be an uphill climb.'

'You could do the surf lifesaver bronze medallion instead, you know. It's not as tough as the professional lifeguard program and the work they do is just as important.'

'I know. I like to do things the hard way.'

'Be warned, Jack. I like to push people further than they think they can go. If you train under me, you won't get an easy ride. I make no apology for it either, no matter what your background is.'

'Message understood.'

'All right then, orientation is tomorrow. Nine o'clock.'

'I'll be here.' Although he'd come across as confidently as he could,

Jack walked away feeling uneasy. Although he could do the eight hundred metre pool swim within the time limit, Jack knew his biggest challenge would be learning to deal with the ocean itself. Now that he was actually here, it seemed a more daunting prospect than it had been when the whole thing was just a crazy idea.

Jack sat on the couch to eat his Chinese takeaway that night. It just seemed less lonely than sitting alone at the large dining room table. He had the radio on but only as filler noise. After switching between a Charlie Pride marathon and a talkback debate about feral cats in the area, he realised there wasn't anything too exciting in the local AM range. The ancient stereo didn't even have an FM dial.

He wasn't sure what to make of Jim. He'd been polite enough and straightforward, but Jack had detected a bit of a hostile vibe. He was obviously a man's man as well as being physically imposing, so maybe he expected the same qualities in his trainees and was disappointed that Jack didn't fit the bill.

Realising he hadn't heard his mobile phone ring or beep since he arrived, Jack picked it up off the coffee table and studied the screen. No reception. That was obviously why the committee didn't have a ban on people bringing them to the house. He'd ask around and find out where the reception hotspots in town were and check his messages tomorrow.

As he sat there eating his chicken and cashews straight from the container and listening to Charlie sing *Kiss an Angel Good Morning*, Jack thought about the movie *About a Boy*. He'd watched it on DVD while he was sick and remembered how the quote "No man is an island" had touched a nerve. The realisation that he was an exception to that rule was an uncomfortable truth.

In fact, right at this moment - with the exception of Jim and the local real estate agent - nobody else in the world knew exactly where he was, and, without his mobile phone, nobody could reach him. It was a liberating, yet depressing thought.

• • • • •

It was policy for new trainees to complete a basic fitness test before they commenced the lifeguard training program. Jim sat in on Jack's test the next morning and didn't hide his surprise at his trainee's good fitness test scores.

'Didn't think you office types had time for exercise,' he said, as Jack completed the required twenty push-ups with ease.

'Have you ever been in a gym at night? They're full of office workers.' Jack started doing the chin-ups that the doctor asked him to.

'Any exercise I need is done outside,' Jim said.

The doctor smiled to himself. Mr Stewart was always telling him gym fitness was inferior to anything the great outdoors had to offer.

'Well, I swim too,' added Jack.

Jim gave him a withering look. 'Don't tell me, you go to an indoor heated pool?'

'Most of the time.' Jack couldn't lie.

'When I was a kid, I could swim the width of the river against the current, summer or winter. There was no such thing as heated pools back then.'

Jack raised his eyebrows. 'I'm suitably impressed.'

Suspicious that his new trainee was mocking him, but unable to prove it, Jim wrote some notes in a file and motioned for Jack to follow him down to the sand.

The first morning was taken up with the usual admin kind of tasks. Jim showed Jack around and explained how the program was run, the hours he was expected to work and the tests he would need to pass along the way. He also emphasised once again the serious nature of the work and how he expected Jack's full attention on the job at all times.

Jack nodded seriously throughout his induction, and asked the occasional question, trying to appear more confident than he felt. His eyes widened when Jim handed him a couple of sets of the official lifeguard uniform. Accepting the navy board shorts and navy and white polo shirts wordlessly, Jack wondered just what he was trying to prove to himself. He'd assumed he would be in the background to begin with, not out there in uniform like an official lifeguard, as far as the public was concerned.

Jim stared at him. 'What? Not fancy enough for you?'

'No, it's fine.'

'Then what's that look for?'

'I didn't think I'd be in uniform yet.'

'Why not? You want to be a lifeguard, don't you?'

'Yeah.'

'Then you've got to dress like one. I thought a smart bloke like you would have figured that out.'

Jack didn't respond to that comment, realising that he hadn't imagined the hostile vibe. Apparently, Jim was going to make this as hard as possible and would gain some kind of satisfaction out of watching him struggle to make the grade.

Jack was relieved when the afternoon was also taken up with other tasks, like familiarising himself with the first aid equipment and learning the ins and outs of driving the four-wheel drive and ATV on the sand. Although it was only delaying the inevitable reality of hard, physical training, it made Jack feel that at least there would be something he would be able to do proficiently.

Surprised when Jim dismissed him at three o'clock, Jack said, 'So, I just have to show up here tomorrow morning then? There's no other initiation tests or anything?'

Jim shook his head.

'All right, I'll see you tomorrow then.'

Jim nodded curtly in reply and Jack could feel the older man's eyes boring into his back, as he headed back to the house. He had no idea what he'd done to rub Jim the wrong way, but he wasn't going to let it put him off. Now he'd started his training, he was determined to see it through.

Strolling into town half an hour later, Jack had a good look around the place that was to be his home for the next two months. Walking past the jewellers, he noticed a diver's watch similar to the one that Jim wore in the front window and on impulse he went in and bought it. He might as well try and look the part, even if he didn't feel it.

The small IGA supermarket was bustling when he walked in and selected a trolley. Given the limited takeaway options, he was going to have to stock up on some proper food. He was putting some apples into a bag when he noticed a man with a mobile phone on his belt.

'Excuse me, is there anywhere around here you get reception for your phone?' Jack asked.

'It depends how fit you are,' the man said.

'How so?'

'The top of the cliff will give you three bars, but you've got to walk up and it's a bit of a climb. Or else there are random backyards and some areas along the beach that will get you a bar or maybe two.'

'Right. So, Telstra hasn't bestowed you with a tower yet?'

'Nah, most people here aren't too worried about it. I work over in Rosethorn, so I get all the reception I need over there. It's kind of nice to switch it off when I get home.'

Jack nodded his thanks and continued shopping.

Although the sun was shining at seven o'clock the next morning, the air was still cool when Jack walked across the sand towards the lifeguard tower. It was only August, after all, and the start of spring was still a couple of weeks away. Jack felt self-conscious in the uniform and was glad there weren't too many people on the beach yet.

A middle-aged woman walking her dog gave him a long, hard gaze when they crossed paths. Jack smiled politely, but she only nodded curtly in response. Maybe Jim had already put the word out that there was an impostor in his ranks, who knew little about the ocean and even less about how to rescue people.

Jack almost laughed out loud when a Japanese tourist ran over to him, just before he got to the tower. 'Please may I take a picture with you?' she begged. 'I think lifeguards are so brave.'

'Um, sure,' Jack said. The young woman handed her camera to another passer-by, who took several snaps. Despite his embarrassment, Jack was intrigued when the woman turned her camera over to reveal an LCD screen. He'd heard about digital cameras, but had never used one. The tourist scrolled through the photos delightedly. 'My friends will be so envious when I email them,' she said with a nervous giggle. 'You're so cute.'

Smiling self-consciously, Jack waved her off, before walking over to where Jim was setting up the flags. 'Good morning,' he said.

'Mornin'.' Jim continued grinding the flag into the sand, without looking up.

'Great day for it.'

'Yeah, it's the best bloody office in the world.'

'Can't argue with that.'

Jim picked up the other flag and motioned for Jack to follow him, as he walked about thirty metres down the shoreline. 'Are you sure you want to do this?' Jim asked, as he ground the second pole deep into the sand. 'Like I told you, it's not an easy ride.'

'Yes, I am.'

Finished with the flag, Jim folded his arms. 'Did you enjoy your photo shoot?'

'She asked me if I'd be in the photo, I didn't volunteer. There's no rule against having our photos taken is there?'

'No,' Jim said. 'But just looking good in the uniform and wearing a four-hundred-dollar watch and fancy shades won't help you out in the ocean, you know.'

'I got the watch on sale for three twenty and I already owned the Ray-Bans.'

'You know what I mean.'

'Yeah, I know what you mean and, no, I haven't changed my mind. I really do want to do this.'

'All right then, let's get started.'

• • • • •

The first week of the training program was hell. Jim pushed Jack to his physical limit and threw him in the deep end, literally, in the water skills component. Confident at least in his swimming ability, Jack soon realised that doing laps in a pool had nothing on surf swimming. He even had to be rescued twice on the third day, when larger than normal waves pummelled the Sunset Point shoreline and a strong rip formed south of the flags.

Jim shook his head when his trainee was escorted back to shore the second time. 'I thought we just covered how to swim out of a rip.'

'Theory and reality don't always coincide, exactly,' said Jack, reaching for his towel.

Ignoring Jack's attempt at humour, Jim continued to glare at him. 'You're too timid with the big waves as well. Just dive under them. I told you, all the power is at the top.'

Jack's reply was curt this time. 'Okay, got it.'

'Good. Maybe I won't have to keep repeating myself then.'

Jack soon learnt to tune out Jim's unyielding criticism, but it still stung. After so many years in a career he excelled at, being incompetent at something was difficult to deal with. He wondered if it was just him personally that Jim objected to or if he treated all his students the same way. From what he could tell the other lifeguards got along well with Jim and respected him highly.

The lawyer jokes and comments about the inadequacies of the legal system started to get old after a few days, but Jack didn't flinch. He knew Jim was trying to rattle him and was determined not to give him the satisfaction.

'How long does it take to become a lawyer?' Jim asked one morning.

'It's a four-year degree,' Jack said, not bothering to explain the other requirements the job entailed.

'So, added to twelve years of school, you've had sixteen years of education.'

Jack nodded, deciding not to mention the Master's degree and three other post-graduate diplomas he had earned. Or kindergarten, for that matter, which added another year to his formal education.

'I only had ten years of schooling and I reckon it's done me right. Kind of funny that I'm the one teaching you, isn't it, when you're the one who's done all the learning.'

'Life is full of ironies.' Jack smiled through clenched teeth. Although Jim's people skills were sadly lacking, the man was a genius when it came to the ocean and Jack knew he was learning from the very best. If Jim was hoping to break him, he could think again.

Unlike most new trainees, Jack enjoyed the day-to-day chores involved in being a lifeguard. It was a welcome respite from the physical punishment. As the lowest man on the totem pole, it was his job to set up and pack up, clean the equipment, stocktake the first aid supplies and update the log book each day.

Steve, a fellow lifeguard in his early thirties, gave Jack a hand stacking the equipment one afternoon when rain was threatening.

'It doesn't seem right putting you through the same initiation we give the young kids. For them it's to teach some respect and work ethic, but you're in a different category.'

'I don't mind, really. At least I can do all this stuff competently. After making a fool of myself in the water, it lets me scrape together some dignity.'

'Mate, you're a brave man to give it a go and I don't doubt you'll get through the program.'

Jack closed and locked the equipment room door. 'Yeah, I hope so. I'm pretty persistent when I set my mind to something.'

'Are you really a lawyer?'

'Guilty as charged.'

Steve stared at him for a moment. 'Can I ask why you're doing this? It's not one of those undercover TV shows, is it?'

Jack shook his head. 'No, nothing that exciting. Mid-life crisis I guess. I just needed to do something that actually matters for a while.'

'Well, saving people's lives definitely matters,' said Steve.

• • • • •

Jack took a swig of orange juice straight from the bottle and shoved two pieces of bread in the toaster. Mother Nature had thrown a last burst of winter at Sunset Point and he had overslept without the sun streaming in the window to wake him up. It was the start of his second week and Jack didn't want to get off on the wrong foot by being late.

He glanced out the window at the low grey clouds. The house had rattled all night as gale force winds howled outside. It had calmed down this morning, but it was still cold and bleak. It felt like a Melbourne winter's day and Jack wasn't looking forward to going in the water.

The acrid smell of burning toast assaulted his nostrils and he leapt back over to the toaster and hit the cancel button. Two pieces of charcoal popped up. Dropping them in the bin, Jack grabbed a banana and ate it as he hustled out of the house, banging the door behind him.

Jim stared at Jack's fleece jacket, making him feel like he had broken a sacred law of lifeguarding. Jim was wearing his usual shorts and t-shirt, apparently not bothered by the cold.

Jack ignored the pointed look. 'Morning,' he said.

'You're five minutes late,' Jim growled.

'Yeah, sorry. I didn't sleep well and…'

Jim cut him off. 'Not interested in excuses, just get here on time.'

'Right.'

Jim motioned towards the equipment room. 'Week two,' he said, 'Time to conquer the rescue board.'

After setting up all the equipment, Jack picked up a rescue board and studied it. He had watched the other lifeguards use them with little apparent effort and thought that paddling one must be easier than swimming in the surf. Steve had told him they were heavy and bulky to carry on the sand, but in the water, they were buoyant and stable, which made them ideal for ferrying swimmers back to shore.

Walking over to where Jack was standing, Jim extended his arms. 'Well, what are you waiting for?'

'I thought you might give me a few pointers first.'

'You're not at uni now sonny, not everything in life comes with instructions. A bright boy like you should be able to work it out.'

Jack was grateful the beach was deserted that morning, as he battled to even stay on the rescue board, let alone manoeuvre it through the waves. As yet another wave pushed the board backwards, which in turn flipped him off the side, Jack felt like he was in a *Three Stooges* routine. Surely it couldn't be this hard? He was lying on his stomach, paddling hard with his arms, just like he'd seen the other lifeguards do, with apparent ease. So why couldn't he get even a few metres into the surf? The other option was paddling from a kneeling position and Jack didn't even attempt that.

Every time Jack caught a glimpse of Jim on the shore, he seemed to be shaking his head in disgust, but Steve finally took pity on him and waded out to give him a few pointers.

'I take it you've never surfed before, either?' he asked.

Shaking his head, Jack attempted to hold the board steady, as it banged against his legs. 'That obvious, huh?'

'It's okay, you'll get there.'

'You reckon? How long did it take you?'

'It was different for me, I learnt as a kid, when I did nippers. You're a lot more fearless then.'

'I'll say. This is way harder than it looks.'

'Yeah, it is for the uninitiated. Keep at it Jack, you're already driving the old boy nuts by not throwing in the towel.' Steve grinned.

'Really?'

'Yeah, really.'

Jack smiled back. 'That's good to know.'

'All right, let's get down to basics,' Steve said. 'Your main problem is that you're too far back on the board, so you've got no power and not enough forward movement. The other issue is that you stop paddling as soon as you get to a wave. What you need to do is paddle faster, to get over the top of it.'

'Okay, that makes sense. But what happens if the wave is too big to get over?'

'That's when you have to roll your board *under* the wave.'

'Under?' Jack said warily, catching a glimpse of Jim watching him.

'Forget about him,' said Steve. 'Come down here a bit further and give it another go. I'll show you how to roll.'

'Sounds like a plan.'

The weather improved marginally that afternoon. A few weak shafts of sunlight filtered through the cloud cover and the ocean breeze felt a few degrees warmer. Jack still wore his fleece. He wasn't about to get pneumonia just to prove a point to Jim.

He was working on the logbook in the tower, when Jim called him down to the sand again. Dropping his pen, Jack climbed down the ladder, steeling himself to get wet again. It wasn't that the ocean was colder than normal, on the contrary, it was warmer than the air today. It was the wind that caused Jack to shiver.

Down on the sand, Jim was talking to a boy who looked about nine or ten. Wearing a Sunset Point Primary School t-shirt, the kid had a beach towel slung over one shoulder. Thin and wiry, he had light brown hair and his eyes were a similar shade.

'Jack, this is Danny,' Jim said. 'He's the training partner I mentioned the other day. He's one of Sunset Point's best nippers and I reckon you can learn a lot from him.'

Studying Jim's face, Jack realised he was serious. Not wanting to offend Danny, or openly question Jim's plan, he extended his hand.

'Hi Danny, I'm Jack. Nice to meet you.'

Taking Jack's proffered hand, Danny eyed him curiously. 'You're a lot older than I thought.'

'I'm sure I am,' Jack said. 'I'd appreciate your help though; I'm not much good at this, yet.'

Danny thought for a moment. 'Okay, I'll help you. It can be hard work, you know,' he said.

Amazed to see a smile on Jim's face, Jack nodded. 'That's all right, I can live with that.'

'All right lad, off you go and get changed, and then you and Jack can start training,' said Jim.

Danny scampered off in the direction of the surf club and Jim motioned Jack to walk with him over to the tower.

'He's a good kid and the responsibility of helping you will be a positive thing for him. You have any problems with him, just let me know.'

'All right.' Jack sensed that Jim was probably testing him in some way and was wary of rising to the bait. He didn't dislike children; he just hadn't had much exposure to them and was a bit concerned how he would go relating to the boy.

In reality, Jack was surprised by how quickly he struck up a rapport with Danny. Amazed by his fitness and skills in the water, Jack soon realised he would learn a lot from him. Initially fearing it would be hard work to reduce his conversation to a child's level, Jack found that wasn't the case at all. If anything, Danny was wise beyond his years, and, like Jim said, he was a genuinely good kid.

Reading between the lines, Jack soon worked out that Danny's home life was not ideal. Between an absent father and a mother who enjoyed a busy social life, Danny was left to his own devices a lot of the time. For all Jim's gruffness and old-school views, he had obviously stepped in to keep the kid out of trouble, by having him down at the beach, under his watchful eye, as much as possible.

Jack couldn't help but compare his own childhood with Danny's. As a doted on only child, his parents would have given him the moon if they could. The idea of being left unsupervised after school at

Danny's age was something he couldn't comprehend.

After a few days, Jack and Danny had slipped into a comfortable routine that suited them both. Danny came to the Beach House after school for a snack and then he and Jack played chess for fifteen minutes. Wanting an opportunity to turn the tables and teach Danny something, Jack had assumed it might take a while for him to get a handle on the game. But, yet again, the boy had surprised him. Picking up on the rules quickly, Danny needed no specialised coaching. They now had an ongoing game set up on one end of the table, which was proving to be quite competitive. After a few well considered moves from each of them, they headed down to the beach. Jack had come to terms with the fact that a nine-year-old was his training partner and tried to learn all he could from him.

Jack had come to enjoy the conversations he and Danny shared as they ate afternoon tea on the veranda each afternoon, although he still wasn't used to the candour of children, or the way they asked personal questions as a matter of course.

'Did you get fired from your other job?' Danny asked one day, as he nibbled on a Jatz cracker, topped with Jarlsberg cheese.

Taken aback, Jack shook his head. 'No, I'm just having a break. Kind of like school holidays.'

'Aren't holidays for having fun, though? You don't normally do another job, do you?'

'No, not usually,' Jack said.

Danny continued to look at him expectantly.

'I'm thinking about changing my job and I wanted to see what being a lifeguard is like, before I make up my mind.'

'How come you don't like your other job anymore?'

Jack exhaled slowly. Fair question, he thought. 'Well, I've been doing it for a long time now and I work from early in the morning until after dark. I guess I'm just a bit tired of it.'

'Is it kind of like getting tired of school? I'm always tired of school.'

'Yeah, something like that. Now, come on, let's play chess,' Jack said, happy to have a change of topic.

Jack liked the way Jim met with both of them at the end of the afternoon training sessions, to discuss his progress. He could see Danny was gaining confidence and a sense of importance as the sessions progressed. Jim listened to Danny's observations and asked his opinion on what Jack needed to improve on, and then suggested the best way to go about it.

'He's still not dolphin diving quite right,' said Danny, as the three of them stood near the lifeguard tower late that day. Jack had to fight not to shiver visibly, as a stiff breeze whipped around them. There was nothing quite as cold as an afternoon sea breeze when you were in the shade and dripping wet.

'I reckon he's not grabbing the sand,' Jim said.

'Yeah,' agreed Danny. 'He's not pushing up hard enough with his feet, either.'

Jack nodded, making a mental note to work on his sand grabbing. At that point he would have agreed to anything, if it meant he could go back to the house and have a hot shower.

'His swimming is getting better,' Danny said.

Jack smiled to himself and thought about how many hours of training it had taken for his swimming skills to get the tick of approval from a child.

'Yes, he's improving now that he's given his goggles away,' Jim said.

Danny giggled. 'You wanted to wear goggles at the beach?'

Sending a pointed glance Jim's way, Jack shook his head. 'Jim soon put me right on that.'

$$\bullet \ \bullet \ \bullet \ \bullet \ \bullet$$

In true Queensland style, spring arrived right on time. The last days of August were warm with a balmy breeze, which made ocean swimming much more pleasant. Jack knew he was making progress but Jim never acknowledged it. He just pushed harder and reminded his trainee how much more he had to learn.

He's wasted in this job, Jack thought, as he ran out of the choppy knee depth surf one morning. He should be in the army running a boot camp. While they sounded benign, ins and outs were their own special kind of torture.

'Move it, Jack!' yelled Jim. 'You've got five to go and stop slacking off when you get behind the tower, I can still see you.'

Yeah, I can just see him with a crew cut and a clipboard, Jack mused as he ran back into the water, trying to ignore the way his lungs were burning. I'd like to see him out here sometime.

Finally, the session ended. Leaning against the lifeguard tower, Jim folded his arms folded and raised an eyebrow. 'That was almost acceptable,' he said. 'You didn't fall over every time you ran in.'

Jack, who was leaning over with his hands on his knees, gasping for breath, could only nod weakly. Much as he would like to, he knew he wasn't in a position to challenge Jim's authority.

'You've still got a lot of ground to make up, Mr Lawyer. If you'd started when you were Danny's age, it wouldn't be such a shock to the system. You can see much easier it all comes to him. In fact...,'

Jim's voice cut off abruptly and Jack looked up to see why.

Ripping off his shirt and hat, Jim sprinted towards the water. Sensing the urgency of his movements, Jack ran to the water's edge, converging with Steve who had run back from further down the shoreline. He could see Jim in the water, towing in an apparently lifeless figure. Jim's movements were sure and confident. He had no need of a rescue board. Steve pulled his shirt off and raced into the surf to help Jim carry the victim back to the shore.

Jack watched in awe as the two men quickly lay the slightly built young man on the sand and immediately began CPR, working so efficiently together it was as if they were one. Jack's own heart was galloping much faster than it had been a few minutes before. He felt useless standing there, but was frozen with inertia, the CPR training he'd done over the past two weeks just a blur in his mind.

Attracted by the commotion, a growing number people clustered around. Jim looked up from where he was performing chest compressions. 'Get onto Surf Com, Jack!' he yelled impatiently, 'and disperse this bloody crowd.'

'Right,' Jack replied, feeling the sting of his reprimand. Grabbing Steve's discarded shirt, he un-holstered the two-way radio and depressed the call button. Once he'd given the details to the operator, he herded the onlookers back away from the scene.

The ambulance arrived within minutes. A young man and an older woman stumbled across the sand, weighed down with portable equipment. Once the ambulance officers had set up their portable defibrillator Jim and Steve stood back and let them do their job. After two shocks the male paramedic exclaimed, 'We've got a pulse!'

There was an immediate energy shift from high tension to relief. The ambos continued to work on their patient, but at a less frantic pace. Steve patted Jim on the shoulder. 'Good work, Boss,' he said quietly.

Jack carefully recorded the details in the logbook while he waited for Jim to return to the tower. Although he had done the first aid training, Jack had been unprepared for how confronting an emergency situation was and felt bad that he'd had to be told what to do. Jim was right, he still had a long way to go.

Jack was waiting for Danny to arrive from school when Jim called him up to the tower. 'We'll have to call training off this afternoon, that king tide is moving in fast,' he said.

'Sure. No worries.' Jack held back his sigh of relief.

Jim bit into a Granny Smith apple. 'Just talked to the hospital,' he said, as he chewed. 'The kid has regained consciousness and is doing well. Not quite out of the woods yet, but it's all looking positive.'

'That's a huge relief. I've never seen real CPR like that before, it literally is life and death.'

'Well, it's the first time I've had to do in a long time. I can't say I like doing CPR, but the power to bring someone back to life is about as good as it gets and defibrillators have upped the survival rate by a good margin.'

'You guys were all over it. Didn't hesitate for a second.'

'That's why we're always practising. I know you think it's overkill, but it's the only way to stay sharp with it.'

'Lesson learned. I'll practice twice a day from now on,' Jack said. 'Do they know why it happened?'

'Apparently he's got some kind of medical condition that causes him to pass out and he shouldn't have been in the water alone. It was lucky we got to him so quickly.' Jim took his last bite of apple and threw the core in the bin.

Jack studied his feet. 'Sorry I wasn't much use out there, I should have set things in motion faster.'

'The only way you can really learn to cope with an emergency situation is to experience one. You didn't do too bad,' Jim said gruffly. Pausing for a beat, he looked over at Jack. 'You didn't think I still had it in me to do a rescue like that, did you?'

'Of course I did, you're the team leader, the boss.'

'You're a smart bloke, Jack, you think before you open your mouth. But I've sensed your resentment at how I train you. You've been thinking to yourself that I had a cheek to push you so hard when I was past it myself.'

Jack shook his head, trying to look sincere. He couldn't believe the old boy had totally nailed him. He *had* wondered many times if Jim was just a figurehead, who supervised the other staff but never got in the water himself. Obviously, that wasn't the case and never would be as long as he worked there.

'One thing you should know about me Jack; I never expect any of my team members to do things that I wouldn't do myself. Remember that.'

'Yeah, I will.'

Danny was excited about their afternoon off. 'You could do with a break from training,' he said, when he heard the news. 'And we can play chess for longer.'

Jack smiled. Children had a great way of stating the obvious.

When they had taken the chess game to a stalemate, Jack tossed Danny his car keys. 'I need to get some petrol, do you want to come for a ride?' he asked, knowing how much the kid admired his Audi.

Danny used the remote to unlock the car and was inside within seconds, settling back into the leather seat and grinning with excitement. Following his careful directions, they were soon at Sunset Point's only servo, on the outskirts of town. Pulling up at a bowser, Jack was taken aback when the proprietor walked over and greeted him, before he had a chance to get out of the car.

'I wondered if I'd get the chance to check out this fine machine sometime,' the man said. 'I haven't seen an Audi in a long time. It's the latest model, isn't it?'

'Sure is. Only four thousand k's on the clock,' Jack replied.

The man peered in the passenger window. 'Hello young Danny, you've come up in the world, riding in this beauty.'

Beaming with pride, Danny made the introductions. 'Jack, this is Gus. He's got the best ice blocks in his freezer.'

Gus smiled. 'That's a hint if I ever heard one. You take premium unleaded?'

'Yeah, thanks.' Jack pressed the fuel cap release, amazed that driveway service still existed.

Gus filled up the tank, washed the windscreen and checked the tyre pressures. When he came back with Jack's change, he handed Danny a pine-lime Splice and a few napkins. 'Careful with drips, young man, on these fine leather seats.'

'What do you say, Danny?' Jack prompted.

'Thank you, Gus,' said Danny.

'You're welcome, buddy.' Gus slapped the roof twice. 'Drop in before you leave and I'll make sure she's ready for the return trip.'

'Sure thing.' Jack gave a friendly wave as he pulled out of the driveway.

Back in town, they parked in front of the Sunset Café, where a middle-aged woman with her hair in a bun was sweeping the footpath. The doorway had the vinyl fly strips that Jack could remember from his own childhood. He literally hadn't seen any in years, though. Pausing in her sweeping, the woman smiled at Danny.

'Hello Danny, I heard you have a new friend,' she said, giving Jack and his car a wary gaze.

Jack was surprised that so many people in town seemed to know of him. Not sure what kind of rap Jim was giving him, Jack decided to turn on the charm.

'I'm Jack Nolan, pleased to meet you,' he said with a warm smile and a slight nod, guessing that the woman would not appreciate a handshake.

'Marge Granger,' she replied, thawing a little.

'I heard you have the best coffee in town,' Jack said, having actually stopped to buy a paper at the newsagent next door.

Marge smoothed her hair back. 'Yes, well, I do take pride in my coffee. I was getting ready to close, but if you'd like a cup?'

Jack nodded and he and Danny followed Marge inside.

The next morning, Jack sat alone in the tower at ten past seven. It wasn't like Jim to be late, but Jack was enjoying the chance to monitor the patrolled area without feeling like he was being closely scrutinised. Not that there was much to look at yet anyway, the beach was almost empty. Steve was down on the sand and Jack knew he could handle anything that came up.

Jim arrived soon after, carrying a travel mug and wearing a grim expression.

'Morning,' Jack said, keeping his eyes on the water.

'Hmm,' was the response as Jim paced around, making sure everything was set up just right. Unable to find fault, he sat down on the other chair and pushed the mug over to Jack.

Jack raised an eyebrow. 'For me?' he asked.

'Yes, for you,' Jim replied. 'Marge waylaid me on my way through town and insisted I deliver this cup of coffee to you. I felt like a fool carrying a cup up the main street.'

'So, you're not a take-away coffee fan, then?'

Jim's face remained steely. 'No, I'm not. Unlike you city people, I drink my coffee at the kitchen table, with my breakfast. I don't feel the need to cart it all over the place.'

Taking the lid off, Jack had a sip; doing his best not to grimace at the strong, bitter taste. Once he'd got inside the café yesterday, Jack soon realised Marge didn't have a coffee machine, just a pot of brewed coffee on the counter. Putting the latte he'd been hoping for out of his mind, he'd laced his drink liberally with milk and sugar, to make it palatable. Seeing that Jim was apparently not going to offer any such accompaniments, he was going to have to drink this cup black.

Jim examined the logbook and seemed annoyed to find it perfectly up to date. 'What did you say to Marge anyway? I've never seen her hand out free anything to anyone, let alone a visitor.'

'Maybe I just smiled at her the right way.'

'Well, that might work with women, but not with me.'

'You don't say,' Jack muttered, feeling the caffeine jolt his system as he choked down another mouthful.

Jim shook his head dismissively in reply. 'Once you've finished your coffee break, you can do six circuits around the buoys on the rescue board. Maybe you might even manage to stay on *and* catch some waves in today. There's not much point getting someone onto a board if you can't get them back to shore.'

'Yeah, righto,' Jack mumbled, giving Jim a salute when his back was turned. He was managing to get out beyond the wave zone on his board now, but coming in was still another story.

Even though Jim obviously didn't like him, Jack was confident that he and Danny had developed a genuine friendship. He looked forward to seeing him each day and was fairly certain that Danny felt the same way. So, he had a rude awakening that afternoon when he answered the door with a smile and was greeted by a sullen, non-communicative child.

After dropping his schoolbag on the floor, Danny sat silently at the table and nibbled a Tim Tam. Jack had bought them specially and hoped for a more enthusiastic response.

'You like the bikkies, Dan?'

'Yeah.'

Jack took a biscuit for himself. 'How was school?'

'Fine.'

Remembering how his father used to jolly him out of bad moods by telling a joke, Jack gave that a try. Danny responded by putting his head down on his folded arms.

Jack told another joke.

'That's stupid!' Danny growled, without looking up. 'You're stupid! You're a grown up and you can't even paddle on a board properly.'

Jack had no knowledge of child psychology, but his legal training had taught him to use a cooling off period when accusations were being hurled around. He sat silently and waited.

Danny raised his head briefly. 'Didn't you hear me? I said you're stupid!'

'I heard you, but I know you didn't really mean it.'

Danny's head bobbed up again. 'I did so mean it. You're bigger than me and I'm teaching you things!'

'Did you get in trouble at school today?'

'No!'

'Did somebody tell you that you were stupid?'

Danny didn't respond so Jack waited a minute and repeated the question.

'It was just a dumb girl who doesn't know anything,' Danny mumbled eventually.

It didn't take too much questioning for Jack to work out that homework was the problem. Danny's mother wasn't around enough to supervise and he didn't like to bother anyone else with it. So, it was mainly left undone and that was getting him into trouble.

'Hey Danny, we're all good at different things,' Jack reassured him. 'You're great at beach stuff and I'm pretty good at homework. Seeing that you're helping me in the surf, how about I help you with your homework?'

'I try and do it but I just can't work it out,' Danny mumbled, his eyes downcast. 'I am stupid.'

'No, you're not, Danny. Don't ever say that. How about you bring your books over and we'll have a look.'

As they walked across the sand fifteen minutes later, Jack reassured Danny that he would sort everything out.

After bolting down a sandwich as he walked to town, Jack spent his lunch hour the next day on the internet. Despite its small size, Sunset Point had a well-equipped library and outside school hours the internet terminals weren't heavily booked. He trawled through information relating to the Queensland primary maths syllabus and printed everything that looked promising. Glancing at his watch, he closed the browser and hurried over to the counter.

Moira Bell did a double take when she saw the thick stack of paper and checked her computer screen. 'You do realise it's forty cents a page to print?' she said. 'That will be $27.60.'

'Yeah, that's fine,' Jack said, reaching into his back pocket for his wallet.

Moira didn't know what to make of this handsome young man in the lifeguard uniform who was staying up at the house. She'd heard the stories about him training with Jim and that he wasn't making great progress. So why was he bothering to stick it out?

She hesitated when Jack handed her his platinum MasterCard. *Here we go;* she thought, resisting the temptation to roll her eyes.

'If you can't take the card, I can go down to the bank and get some cash,' Jack said. 'I should have thought about it before I came in. I just didn't realise I would be printing so much.'

Moira softened at Jack's perfect manners and polite smile. Marge is right, he is very charming, she thought and he's got the most beautiful eyes. 'No, this is quite acceptable,' she said, rummaging in the cupboard under the counter. Eventually she unearthed an old-fashioned click-clack machine and processed the payment. She also made a mental note to order more paper, given that Jack had burned through a week's supply in one sitting.

After his third late night studying the printed information and making notes and lesson plans, Jack was sure his obvious lack of energy was going to earn him a lecture from Jim. The Berocca and Panadol he had supplemented his breakfast with helped to blow the early cobwebs away, but his arms and legs were aching and his head had begun to pound again by the end of his morning training session. His run-swim-run time was mediocre and he'd wiped out on just about every wave he'd caught on the rescue board. And, to top it all off, Jack could see yet another bruise forming on his shin. He'd never had so many bruises in his life.

Pulling on a dry shirt and wrapping his towel around his waist, Jack sat down wearily in the tower and steeled himself for the inevitable criticism.

It didn't come.

Instead, Jim said, 'Danny tells me you've been helping him with his schoolwork.'

'Uh, yes, I have been. Is that all right?'

'Yes, of course. It's decent of you Jack. I don't really have time to help him and, to be honest, I hadn't noticed he was struggling.'

Jack kept his expression neutral, even though it felt like the stern school principal had just engaged in friendly chitchat. 'He hid it pretty well. I've got some time on my hands, so it seems like a fair trade with him helping me with all this.'

'True enough.' Picking up a corned beef sandwich, Jim took a bite.

'It seems the boy has learned some manners too,' he said, still chewing.

Jack feigned surprise. 'Really?'

'Yes indeed. The other day he jumped up and opened the door for my wife when she left the room and, yesterday, he met her walking up the street with some shopping and insisted on carrying it home for her.'

'Kids hey? You try and teach them well.'

'Gloria was tickled by it, wanted to know who'd been instructing him.'

'If you want me to keep it strictly maths and English, just say so.'

'I didn't say that. Fact is, there aren't enough good manners around these days. The little scamp challenged me to a game of chess, too and almost beat me. Seems like he's had some expert tuition. He couldn't even play before.'

Before Jack could respond, Jim snatched up the binoculars and trained them on a point outside the flagged area. He then picked up the two-way radio and spoke into it urgently. 'Phil, that bloke on the north side is flagging fast.'

'On my way,' replied Phil.

Jack watched the lanky, ex pro-surfer pick up the rescue board and paddle out at speed. Like all the other lifeguards, he made the job look easy. Jim stood up and watched until the swimmer was safely back ashore.

Jack waited patiently for Jim to sit back down and continue their unprecedented friendly conversation. Making himself comfortable, he was brought back down to earth when Jim's gruff voice penetrated the small room again.

'So, what the hell was going on with you out there today?'

Danny was fascinated when he discovered that Jack was left handed, like him. 'Nobody else in my class at school is,' Danny said, as they sat at the dining room table that afternoon working through subtraction with regrouping. 'When I was a *little* kid I used to wish it would change by magic and I'd be like everyone else,' he said.

'Don't ever wish that Dan, we're part of an elite group,' Jack reassured him.

'What's elite?'

Jack thought for a moment. 'Special,' he said, eventually.

'Really?' Danny beamed.

Jack nodded.

'Nobody ever told me that before.'

'Well, just because nobody has said it doesn't mean it's not true. Maybe nobody has told you you're smart, but I know you are.'

Danny shook his head. 'No, I'm not smart. If I was, I'd be able to do my own homework.'

'There's nothing wrong with getting help, Danny and when you catch up, you'll be fine on your own. You *are* smart.'

'You mean it?'

'Yeah, of course I do. Now let's get back to these sums.'

• • • • •

He was going to die.

Jack had been in a couple of dangerous situations before. He'd been robbed at knifepoint in Rome and had narrowly escaped a mini-avalanche while skiing in New Zealand. But he'd never felt his lungs constrict like they were right now. The surface of the water was too far. There was no way he could make it back up. He'd always heard that drowning was a peaceful death, but that was wrong. It was terrifying.

Just when he thought he couldn't go on, a shaft of sunlight penetrated the water and he saw the outline of the inflatable rescue boat just above him. With a last bout of frenzied kicking, he exploded through the surface and gulped in huge mouthfuls of air.

As usual, Jim's expression was bland. 'That wasn't too bad,' he said, 'although I thought an *elite* guy like you might make it a little bit further.'

Jack was still desperately sucking in oxygen. 'What?' he gasped.

Extending his hand, Jim hauled Jack back into the boat. 'Danny was over at my place for tea last night,' he said. 'I heard all about how elite the pair of you are.'

Despite his physical discomfort, Jack couldn't hold back a smile. 'He used elite in conversation? In the right context?'

'Yes, he did. Several times.'

'That's great!'

'Yeah, I suppose it is,' Jim said. 'He also made me recite the six times tables with him.'

'Really?'

'Yes, really. Lucky that was something I actually remembered from school.'

Jack let out a chuckle, which he immediately regretted when he saw Jim fold his arms and eye him critically.

'Right, now you've caught your breath, let's do it again.'

Once he had the maths lessons under control, Jack turned his attention to getting Danny some books to inspire him. When he arrived at the library at lunchtime, Moira escorted him to the best internet terminal. Ignoring his growling stomach, Jack googled on-line bookstores and scrolled through their catalogues. He knew Danny loved dolphins, dinosaurs and boats and eventually ordered a dozen books on all three topics after making sure they could be express couriered to a regional area.

When the first lot of books arrived the next day, Jack was unprepared for just how touched Danny was by his gift. He looked at the pile of books in awe, stroking the covers and spreading them out on the table to get a better look.

'They're all brand new, straight from the shops,' he said.

Jack nodded, trying to ignore the lump in his throat.

'The ones from the library at school aren't interesting like these ones and I don't have any of my own at home.'

Jack thought of his own childhood bookshelves, that had overflowed with every title imaginable, and fully realised for the first time just how blessed his life had been.

Clearing his throat, he had a drink and ruffled Danny's hair. 'Well, mate, you have to read them all, okay? And you have to do your book reports for homework.'

Danny nodded excitedly. 'Oh, I will. This big one tells you how they make ships; I always wanted to know that.'

Unused to the ways of children, especially their impulsive actions, Danny took Jack completely by surprise when he enveloped him in a hug. He couldn't remember the last time he'd had small arms thrust around his waist and a little head resting against his chest. He returned the embrace a little clumsily and once again fought against the lump in his throat.

• • • • •

Almost a week later, Jack sat with Jim in the lifeguard tower, watching the lashing rain outside. Despite the inclement weather, the beach was not officially closed and there were a few people in the water. Jim had Jack's first written test in front of him. Jack was confident he had done well and was sure that even Jim would find it difficult to criticise a good test result.

'You're a dark horse sometimes, Jack, I'll say that for you.'

Jack was puzzled by that comment. Jim was always ribbing him about his level of education, so he must have expected that Jack would do well on a written test, even if his physical skills were still lacking. He chose not to respond, waiting instead for Jim to continue on with whatever was on his mind.

'Danny was up here the other afternoon, dancing around like he had ants in his pants and he told me about the books you got him. Seems like it's been Christmas every day this week and you've been playing Santa.'

Jack smiled, not sure of what to say.

'Nice books like that cost a fair whack and delivery doesn't come cheap either. You've made a big hit with that boy, Jack, there's no two ways about it.'

'I'm not trying to buy him or impress anyone by flashing money around.'

'Well, the very fact that you haven't mentioned a word of it to me proves that point rightly enough. I'm just saying that it was generous of you to do what you've done.'

'To be honest, I'd forgotten how good it feels to give. It can get boring only spending money on yourself.'

Jim cast his eyes out to the water. 'That fool out there will need rescuing before the day's out,' he muttered and then turned to face Jack again. 'Moira tells me you're down there in the library playing on the computers for hours. Never understood them myself, but I'm guessing it's got something to do with young Danny.'

'I'm being very well monitored. Just as well I didn't ask who the local drug supplier was; I would have been run out of town by now.'

Jim actually laughed at that comment. 'You would have been too. Welcome to a small community, where everybody knows your business whether you tell them or not.'

They sat in silence for a few moments before Jack spoke again. 'You took a bit of a chance on me, though, didn't you? How did you know I wasn't some kind of undesirable character?'

'Well, for starters, Davo is a private investigator. I had you thoroughly checked out before you ever came here. Secondly, I'm a fairly good judge of character so after that first week I had a pretty good idea of if you were safe to have around Danny. Besides which I question him pretty intensely.'

'I don't think I've ever been checked out by a PI before.'

'Just as well I did, you're like a bloody bank vault when it comes to giving away personal information.'

Jack shrugged. 'Too many years being entrusted with other people's secrets.'

'I never said it was a bad character trait.'

'So, what kind of dirt did Davo dig up on me?'

'You're an only child, posh English parents, school at St Ignatius', a law degree from Sydney University and now you're a well-respected lawyer in a ritzy firm. Anything you want to add?' Jim asked.

'Well,' Jack said, 'My favourite colour is blue, I don't like pumpkin but I like pumpkin soup, I won a chess competition when I was nine...'

Jim folded him arms and gave one of his best withering looks. 'Anything relevant, I meant.'

'No, it sounds like you've got me all worked out.'

Jim threw Jack's test paper down on the table. 'You've still got a long way to go in the water but I've never had a perfect written test score before. You must have listened to some of the things I've taught you.'

Opening the log book, Jim flicked through it. Apparently, that was the end of the compliments for the day. Jack took his cue to leave and treated himself to lunch at Leo's to celebrate his success.

As Jack dawdled down the main street on his way home, he noticed a sign for a small solicitor's office. He did a double take when he read the words "G. Jackson Solicitor and Notary". Jack stopped in his tracks and walked closer to read the lettering on the door, 'Gerard Jackson, B.Comm, LLB.' The name G. Jackson had given him a jolt.

Jack adjusted his scarf, buttoned his overcoat and pulled on a pair of gloves before leaving the relative warmth of the underground car park. Bracing himself against the freezing Hobart winter wind, he put his head down and walked as quickly as he could along the city streets that were almost deserted at quarter to seven a.m. He had accepted that he would probably never fully acclimatise to Tasmania's harsh winters.

Jack loved the historic building that housed Jackson and Nolan Solicitors and, as always, he felt a frisson of pride on reading the plaque bearing his name on the office door. At twenty-eight, and a partner in the small firm for six months, he genuinely loved the challenges it constantly presented. His gloved hands caused him to fumble with the keys and it was a welcome relief to finally enter the warmth of the reception area. Walking down the hall further he wasn't surprised to see George Jackson already ensconced at his desk, making notes in longhand.

'Using a computer doesn't make you any less a legend in the legal world, George,' Jack said to his partner and mentor, as he leaned against the doorframe. George was strictly old school, but was also a legal genius, and Jack was honoured to be his protégé.

George shook his head and smiled. 'Ah Jack, I was young once too and not afraid to embrace change. I'm glad you get such great use out of your contraption and I agree it certainly has not hindered your development, but for me, it's too stressful.'

'Fair enough. I got a call from Redwin and Parke just after you left last night, they're willing to settle for forty-five grand after all.'

George leaned back in his chair. 'I've taught you well, but I can't take all the credit. You've got real natural talent for this job, Jack, as well as a great work ethic and it makes me proud to know that when I retire, this firm's reputation will be maintained.'

'Retire - you? I'll be on my second round of long service leave before that happens.'

George chuckled. 'I guess we'll have to wait and see.'

Jack continued his walk back to the house, lost in the memory. At the time, he'd believed his long-term future was in Hobart. He took a deep breath, determined not to dwell on depressing thoughts. Feeling the warmth of the sun on his back, Jack also acknowledged that there was no way he would be wearing shorts and a t-shirt and swimming in the ocean in September, down in Tasmania.

Walking along further Jack stopped to read the message of the day posted outside the Methodist church. It said, "Know that in this moment you are exactly where you are supposed to be."

Jack pondered this for a moment. The fact he was in a place that six months ago he had never heard of, doing a job he had never dreamed he was capable of, was enough evidence for him to acknowledge the message might just be right.

• • • • •

During his first couple of weeks at the house, Jack had trekked up the southern cliff almost every day to check his phone messages. But now he only ventured up every third or fourth day. He was on sabbatical, after all, and needed to distance himself from the office.

When he went up the cliff on Saturday morning, he took Danny with him. Jack was proud of the way he could do the climb without raising much of a sweat, but Danny still made him feel like he was dragging the chain. He scampered on ahead as frisky as a young puppy.

Having walked along the beach to reach the cliff, Jack had bypassed the car park. So, he didn't realise how many people were doing the cliff climb, until he was halfway up. Usually he met a handful of people along the way, but today there were dozens. What's the big attraction? he wondered, as he clambered up the last section.

Danny answered that question when Jack emerged onto the flat cliff top. 'There's whales in the water!' Danny informed him excitedly, grabbing Jack's hand and dragging him over to a better vantage point.

As awesome as the sight of the three whales frolicking in the water was, Jack was even more touched by the way Danny had taken his hand so easily. From his own observations, Jack believed a child willingly taking an adult's hand was a sign of great trust. This kid really likes me, he realised, surprised at how touched he was by that thought.

Jack checked his messages, happy to see that the work related ones had slowed to a trickle. He didn't return any of the calls, deciding instead to send a few emails the next time he went to the library.

Walking back down the path, Jack felt buoyant, as Danny chattered excitedly about the whales. He was right to come here, despite how hard Jim was making things for him. All the hard work was worth it to experience a morning like this one.

They made their way to the lower lookout near the base of the cliff, hoping to see the dolphins that often played there. It was teeming with people and Jack soon realised it would be too difficult to try and push their way to the front.

'Never mind Dan, we'll come back another day,' he said, stepping back to let a woman with a baby on her hip move past him. He started making his way back to the path. 'Are you right, matey?' he called back to Danny.

There was no reply. Jack turned around, a pang of alarm jolting him when he couldn't see Danny anywhere. The cold hand of fear clenched Jack's gut like a vice and his heart started to pound at what seemed like twice its normal speed. It felt like it was bouncing off his rib cage. He had only taken his eyes off Danny for a few seconds.

Horrific stories about abducted children assaulted Jack's mind. It could happen anywhere, even in a small town like Sunset Point. Danny was such a trusting child too, the kind an abductor probably targeted.

Jack shoved his way through the throng of people crowded around the lookout, desperately seeking out the bright green shirt Danny had been wearing. He must have walked back down the path, Jack decided, he's not up here anywhere.

He broke into a run. 'Danny!' he shouted, as he weaved his way back to the base of the cliff. Jack studied every child he met along the path, willing them to be the boy he had grown to care for so much. The boy who *he* was supposed to be responsible for. None of them were. The car park was jammed and Jack looked into each car frantically, but Danny was nowhere to be found.

Pulling out his phone, he cursed when he saw the "no signal" notification. There was another number you could call instead of triple zero if you were in a low reception area but Jack couldn't remember what it was. His hand was shaking as he shoved the phone back into his pocket.

Jack paced back and forth for a few seconds, trying to work out what to do. The police station wasn't that far away, but they didn't always take these things seriously right away. There would be questions as to why Jack was reporting him missing instead of his mother. Precious time would be lost.

'Jim,' he said aloud. Jim would know what to do. He could get people looking immediately. Everyone knew Jim and would do what he said, no questions asked.

After scrambling down the boulders at the base of the cliff, Jack sprinted to the water's edge. Even though he hadn't done any serious running for months, muscle memory kicked in and he pounded the damp sand steadily, covering the two kilometres without having to stop or even slow down.

Jack was soaked in sweat and red faced when he finally came upon the patrolled section of the beach. Frantically, he raked his eyes around the tower and surrounds, looking for the familiar tall, imposing figure of Jim. He wasn't there. A young kid called Lucas was up in the tower and Steve was standing on the sand. Noticing Jack, he waved, but soon realised something was amiss. Taking in the dishevelled appearance and desperate, wild-eyed look, he came over.

'You all right, mate?' he asked.

It wasn't until Jack tried to speak that he realised how out of breath he was. 'Jim,' he gasped. 'Where is he?'

'He's not working today.'

'Are you kidding me? I really need to talk to him!'

Steve put his hand on Jack's shoulder. 'Hey, take it easy, Jack. Can I help you with something?'

Jack shook his head. 'I've really messed up and I need his help.'

Steve was still staring at him with a worried frown. 'Right, uh, do you where his house is?'

'No!'

'It's not far, it's the blue one on the corner of Shore Road. But try the playground at the caravan park first. He usually takes his grandkids there on the weekend.'

Nodding his thanks, Jack took off again.

The playground was crowded, but Jack spotted Jim straight away, standing over near the swings. Dodging his way around play equipment and small children, Jack came up alongside him, dreading what he knew he had to say.

Jim looked him up and down, apparently amused by his dishevelled state. 'You want me to push you on the swings too?'

'I uh, I...,' Looking down, Jack stopped short. There, alongside Jim's granddaughter and two grandsons, was Danny, patting a golden retriever. Looking up, he grinned. 'Hi Jack,' he said.

Relief washed over Jack like a wave. He felt his heartbeat slow back to its regular rhythm. He could breathe again. Hoping his voice wouldn't give him away, Jack cleared his throat. 'Hey Dan. I wasn't sure where you got to.'

Danny kept playing with the dog. 'I saw Banjo down on the rocks and knew he must have run away again. I had to chase him all the way back up the beach before I caught him.'

'He's my dog,' Jim explained. 'The kids next door keep leaving the gate open and he's off like a shot. He loves the beach, so we know we'll usually find him here. Danny's become quite an expert at spotting him.'

'Right,' Jack said. 'Good on you mate. Do you still want to come fishing with me?'

'Yeah, course I do,' Danny replied.

'Great, then we'd better head off.'

Jack stayed to have a drink at the surf club, after he delivered Danny back to Jim's custody. Taking his beer out to the veranda, he sat and looked out at the water, still shaken by the events of the morning. Well aware he'd dodged a bullet, Jack couldn't stop thinking about what might have been.

He was shocked when Jim came out to join him. Even though they spent hours together each day, they never socialised.

'You recovered yet?' Jim asked, by way of greeting.

'From fishing? Well, yeah, it wasn't too taxing; we just went out on the rocks near the lighthouse.'

'No, I mean from this morning. The kid really gave you a scare, didn't he?'

'Not really, I kind of figured he must have come back here,' Jack said.

387

'I wasn't born yesterday, Jack. I saw the look on your face. It's the kind of pure panic only a lost child can bring about.'

'Well, I was hot, I'd just run up from the beach and…'

Jim cut him off. 'Give it up, Jack. Steve told me what state you were in when you spoke to him.'

'All right, fine. Apparently, I'm even worse at babysitting than I am at lifeguarding. I've never been so scared in all my life.' Jack took a long drink of beer.

'I know how it feels, Jack. Once, I found my son at Gus's servo, when I was left in charge of him. I doubt there's a parent alive who hasn't felt what you felt this morning.'

'Well, I gained a new respect for parenthood today.'

'I'm not saying I'm glad it happened, but that half hour of panic taught you more than I ever can. If you want to be a lifeguard, you have to know that kind of terror is what we're trying to avoid. It makes you much more watchful.'

'One of those tough but valuable lessons, huh?'

'Yeah, to put it plainly. It also showed me, finally, that there is some emotion locked inside you somewhere and you're not just a piece of granite.'

'Thanks, I think.' Jack set his glass down on the table.

Jim set his glass down alongside. 'I'll see you Monday,' he said and walked back inside.

• • • • •

Jack was in good spirits when he walked across the sand to work on Monday morning. After his conversation with Jim on Saturday, he decided they had come to a new understanding. Maybe things were going to be different now.

'Good morning,' he said, after climbing up the ladder into the tower.

Jim had a pile of papers in front of him and a look on his face that would sour milk. 'Nothin' good about it yet.'

Feeling like he had just slid down a snake on a life-sized snakes and ladders board, Jack took a deep breath. Apparently they had regressed back to the stern headmaster/bad student scenario. 'I'll just go and set up,' he said, more than ready to escape the negativity in the tower.

Things didn't improve during the morning session and Jack reported back to the beach after lunch to find that Jim had gone home, without explanation. Steve had been left in charge and was apparently enjoying his stint of authority. 'You're welcome to hang around, Jack, but if I was you I'd enjoy a rare afternoon off. It's pretty quiet here today.'

Meandering back to the house, Jack thought about how to spend his free afternoon. He threw a load of washing on, including the shirt was wearing, and surveyed the downstairs area. The house really needs a good clean, he thought, but decided that he just couldn't be bothered with chores.

Jack was lounging on the couch, eating a packet of chips and reading the paper, when there was a knock on the door. As he didn't know anybody who might visit, except Jim and Danny, Jack got up to answer it as he was. Seeing the attractive, middle-aged woman standing there, he was immediately conscious of the fact that he was shirtless and covered in crumbs. The woman was dressed very nicely but looked uneasy, as if she was somewhere she shouldn't be.

'Jack?' she asked hesitantly, as she took in his lean, yet nicely muscled, physique, while trying not to be obvious about it.

'Yes, I'm Jack Nolan.'

'Oh, okay, I've got the right person. You just don't look like I imagined you would,' she said, with a smile. 'I'm Gloria Stewart,' she said. 'Jim's wife,' she added, reading Jack's puzzled look.

'Oh, of course. Nice to meet you, Mrs Stewart. Please come in.' Jack led her into the lounge room, gathering the paper and the chips in one swoop and unearthing himself a clean shirt from the pile of washing he'd been meaning to fold for days. Slipping it on, he turned back to his guest.

'Can I get you something, Mrs Stewart? Tea or coffee?'

'No, thank you, Jack. It's kind of you to offer but I don't have a lot of time. I just need to get your advice about something.'

'Please have a seat,' said Jack, showing her to the couch.

'Thank you.' Gloria sat down.

Jack sat on one of the recliners. 'What can I do for you, Mrs

Stewart?'

'Oh, call me Gloria, please.'

'All right.'

'Jim's got himself into a bit of trouble. Well, it's quite serious actually and, of course, he's too stubborn to tell anybody. He thinks it will tarnish his reputation or something equally as foolish.'

'Okay.' Jack nodded.

Gloria smoothed her skirt and clasped her hands together. 'It's all so silly, really. Jim got a parking ticket months and months ago over in Rosethorn. He always said the ticket wasn't right because it was issued outside the parking restriction times. But, being Jim, he didn't query it, he just ignored it and said they could sort it out themselves. A follow up letter came a bit later but he ignored that too. Then we didn't hear anything for months, until this morning, that is.'

Jack nodded again. No wonder Jim had been like a bear with a sore head that morning and had cancelled afternoon training.

'He got a court summons,' said Gloria. 'He was mortified. Thought somebody might have seen it at the post office and be gossiping about it. If this goes through and Jim is convicted, the news would be all over town. Besides that, the council take a harsh line with their employees and unpaid fines because there was some kind of racket a few years ago. Jim would be publicly disgraced and, you know him, his reputation is so important.'

Shoving his feet into his shoes and sticking his wallet into his pocket, Jack shepherded Gloria towards the door. 'I'll follow you over to your house right now.'

'Oh, thank you, Jack!'

For the first time since arriving at Sunset Point, Jack was in control, and it felt good.

Surprised and embarrassed in equal measure to see Jack walking in his front door, Jim immediately went on the offensive. 'Gloria, I told you not to ask him!' he growled, his face reddening.

Following Gloria into the lounge room, Jack raised his eyebrows at Jim. 'Got yourself in a bit of trouble, hey?'

Jim's face reddened further. 'You don't need to be here, Jack. Gloria is always meddling in my affairs when I tell her not to. She had no right to tell you,' he blustered.

'The summons,' Jack said, holding out his hand.

Folding his arms, Jim adopted a combative stance. 'I'll sort it out myself.'

Jack kept his hand extended. 'Give me any other paperwork too - the follow up letter and the original ticket if you have it.'

Standing firm for another few moments, Jim finally stomped off, Gloria trailing behind him. Jack could hear the two of them arguing heatedly in another room. Eventually, Jim re-emerged, holding a sheaf of papers in his hand. Reluctantly, he handed them over.

Jack scanned each official letter addressed to James Ernest Stewart. He resisted the urge to lecture Jim about the stupidity of his actions and the fact that unpaid fines didn't simply vanish. Nor did he give him the well-practised line about seeking legal advice before things got to such an advanced stage. Looking at the dates, Jack let out his breath slowly, but kept his cool.

'There's nothing like a last-minute battle plan, I suppose. It's fortunate that I'm a lot better at this than I am at lifeguarding. And you're lucky that I've got some contacts in Queensland. I don't suppose you have a computer with internet access?' he asked.

Jim's stony glare indicated that the answer was no.

'A fax machine?'

Jim shook his head.

'There's one at the post office,' said Gloria.

'All right, if I can use your phone a while, I'll go down there when I need to.' Jack smiled at Gloria. 'A cup of coffee would be much appreciated, please.'

'Of course, coming right up. Decaf?'

'No, full strength, thanks. Milk and one sugar, please.'

Gloria bustled into the kitchen and Jim showed Jack to the spare room he used as an office in silence.

• • • • •

Jack didn't expect his relationship with Jim to magically evolve to a whole new level after he sorted out the parking ticket. But he didn't expect it to deteriorate, either. After all, he'd had to pull out all the stops and use his best diplomacy skills to prevent the court action from taking place. Apart from a gruff 'thanks', the incident was never mentioned again and Jim reverted to an even meaner version of his original self over the following week.

Jack felt that any ground gained between the two of them had now been lost. He began to dread the morning training sessions, where Jim often worked him to the point of collapse and then dismissed him abruptly afterwards. The almost-friendly chats that had begun to happen occasionally had also disappeared. At least the afternoons were more bearable with Danny there as a buffer. Like all children, he was very perceptive, though, and picked up that something was not right between them.

'Why are you two mad at each other?' Danny asked one afternoon, as Jack paddled him to shore on the rescue board, under Jim's critical eye.

'It's a grown-up thing,' Jack replied, repositioning himself a bit further back on the board. 'I'm not mad at Jim but I think he's frustrated with me because I'm not much good at this.'

'But you are good, Jack. You were a bit slow to start with but now you're heaps better. You can paddle much faster and you haven't nosedived the board for ages. I think you could do a real rescue now,' Danny said, as they caught a little wave right to shore.

Jack smiled gratefully at Danny as they both dismounted the board. 'Thanks Dan, I'd like to think that I'm getting better. Jim's the boss, though.'

'I can talk to him if you want. He's not mad at me,' Danny said.

Feeling Jim's stern gaze on them, Jack shook his head and dragged the board up on the sand. 'No mate, don't worry. I'll sort it out.'

Danny's words played on Jack's mind as he dressed the next morning. He was proud to wear the lifeguard uniform, but he still didn't feel official in the role, even after five weeks on the job. Jim allowed him to monitor from the tower, man the first aid station, give directions to beachgoers and answer questions down on the sand. But, as yet, he hadn't let him do a water rescue, even a minor one under supervision.

Even though he thought about it all day, Jack didn't have the nerve to confront Jim. I'll do it next week, he decided, as he loaded the rescue boards onto the equipment trailer. It was Friday afternoon and he didn't have the energy to start something that might get ugly.

Watching Jack closely as he took down the flags, Jim seemed disappointed when he completed the task correctly. 'You getting the boy to fight your battles for you now?' he asked.

'Huh?'

Folding his arms, Jim glared at Jack. 'Danny's just been telling me you reckon that you should be out in the water rescuing people.'

Jack carefully stacked the flags on the top of the trailer. 'No, I didn't say that, exactly. We were just talking generally. I told him not to say anything to you.'

'Well, he did. There's a lesson for you, kids can't keep a secret.'

'Fine, I'll remember that.'

'What makes you think you're capable of rescuing someone?'

'Danny thinks I'm up for it.'

'Last I heard, I'm in charge around here and that means I get to decide who goes out in the water.'

'I'm not questioning that, I'm just asking for a chance to prove myself.'

'You've got a way to go yet, sonny. Not everything in this world is cut and dried and black and white.'

'Yeah, so you keep telling me. But, you know that I've done the hard yards, here. I've worked like a Trojan and nothing I do is good enough for you. The goal posts just keep on moving.'

'Maybe you're just used to having everything handed to you on a plate. You're a privileged only child who's never had to work for anything. This is the first time you've had to do something on your own, isn't it?'

Looking at the sand, Jack shook his head. 'You've got it all worked out, haven't you? Was there any point in me even trying to do this if you had already made your mind up that I couldn't?'

Jim's jaw clenched and his ruddy face reddened further. 'That sounds like an accusation.'

'Take it any way you like.'

'I told you that first day how it is and you agreed to those terms. I'll decide if and when you go in the water,' Jim said, before storming off towards the tower.

Jumping into the ATV, Jack slammed the door and turned the ignition key. Driving towards the equipment shed, he soon caught up to Jim. Jamming his foot on the brake, Jack pulled up alongside him. 'You know what, Jim? I don't have months and months to do this, so consider your services terminated,' he said.

Stopping in his tracks, Jim threw Jack a look of disdain. 'I might have known you'd quit. Take you out of your prissy office and you crumble in a heap.'

'I'm not quitting, as it happens. I'm going to find another more reasonable trainer and continue with them. Thanks for your efforts.' With that, Jack planted his foot on the accelerator and looked straight ahead all the way up the beach.

Jack sat on the veranda that night and listened to the crashing waves. It was a balmy night and he felt relaxed, despite the drama of the afternoon. The crickets were chirping noisily and the croak of a lone frog penetrated the still evening air. It was a comforting sound, reminiscent of his childhood.

He pondered what he'd gotten himself into. Despite his bravado on the beach, Jack was at a bit of a loss as to what to do next. The comment about finding another trainer had been a spur of the moment answer, but it was a possibility. If he did that, though, he'd have to leave the Beach House much earlier than planned. Jack had another four weeks left on his lease and it seemed a waste to give it away.

Maybe he could commute. If he went an hour or so up the coast, surely there would be someone he could train with.

Jack thoroughly enjoyed his lazy Saturday. Rolling out of bed at nine thirty, he wandered down to the Sunset Café and ordered breakfast. Uninspired by the *Sunset Point Sentinel,* he went into the newsagent next door and paid a steeply inflated price for a two-day old *Sydney Morning Herald* and picked up a *Courier Mail* and *The Australian* for good measure. He had finished his deluxe breakfast special and was on his second free cup of coffee (compliments of Marge), when Moira from the library came in with a young woman that Jack guessed must be her daughter. He could see them talking and feel their gaze upon him. He took that as his cue to leave.

That afternoon, Jack took the Audi for a burn further up the coast, enjoying the sight of the gently unfurling coastline and noting down the towns within driving distance. As Jack headed back south in the late afternoon, he couldn't help but enjoy the moment, despite what had happened. The new car was handling beautifully and it was great to give it a proper workout. It was a treat to be able to listen to his CDs again, especially on such an awesome stereo system. Jack felt that there was something symbolic about singing *Echo Beach* at high volume, as he drove with his window down and the vast expanse of the Coral Sea to his left.

I'm going to enjoy these last four weeks, he decided, as he overtook a slow-moving silver Tarago. Jim Stewart is somebody I don't even have to think about anymore.

Being a Saturday night, Leo's was busy. Jack realised he'd been lucky to get a table at short notice. Taking in the elegant interior of the restaurant, Danny's eyes widened. 'I've never been to a *real* restaurant before,' he said, as they stood in the reception area, waiting to be seated.

Jack smiled. 'Well, there's always a first time. And this is a pretty nice one to start out with.'

If the waiter was surprised to see a nine-year-old boy wearing shorts and a t-shirt in the upmarket eatery, he didn't show it. 'This way, gentlemen,' he said, leading them to a table near the window.

Danny beamed. 'He called us *gentlemen*,' he whispered loudly.

Grinning in reply, Jack shepherded him past the bar area.

Once they were seated, Danny studied the menu. 'This food costs a lot of money,' he said. 'Are you sure you can pay for it?'

'Yes, I've been saving up,' Jack said. 'Have whatever you want.'

They managed to avoid the topic of Jim until Danny was halfway through his seafood basket. 'I thought we were going to do more training today,' he said, as he munched on a king prawn. 'I waited a long time for you to come.'

A pang of guilt hit Jack. I should have told him I wasn't coming, he realised. 'Uh, I decided to take a day off,' he replied. Jack hadn't even considered how his disagreement with Jim might affect Danny.

'It's probably good that you did,' Danny said. 'Jim was cranky.'

'Really?'

'Yeah. He got mad with Steve when he asked why you weren't there.'

That's interesting, thought Jack, as he relished his last bite of lobster thermidor. I thought he'd be celebrating to see the back of me.

'You'll be back on Monday, right?' Danny asked.

Jack studied the boy's earnest face, wondering how he could avoid disappointing him. Danny had already been let down too often for somebody so young. 'Hmmm,' he murmured.

The waiter appeared again. 'Everything all right, sir?' he asked Danny.

Danny grinned. 'Yeah, it's awesome! You have ice-cream here, don't you?'

'Oh yes, I think we can rustle you up some ice-cream,' the waiter replied, smiling in return.

Jack steered the conversation away from Jim, as Danny worked his way through a large bowl of Double Chocolate Delight. They then joined the crowd at the cinema to watch *Finding Nemo*. Jack, who had never seen an animated movie, was surprised how much he enjoyed it.

It was eleven thirty when the first bang sounded. Jack's eyes popped open and he lay there in the darkness, trying to work out if he had dreamt it or not. He strained his ears, but only silence greeted him. Jack was just drifting back to sleep when two more bangs shattered the peace. He realised someone was knocking on the front door. Bleary eyed, he stumbled downstairs.

'Who is it?' he called.

'It's your team leader.'

Jack opened the door. Taking in Jim's glassy eyes and beer breath, he held his right hand out in a *stop there* gesture. 'Go home Jim. I don't need to hear any further comments about my inability to meet your standards.'

'No, no, no I can't go home yet!' Jim said. 'I have to talk to you, right now. It's important. I'm not going to criticise, I promise.' He placed his hand on his chest, as if swearing a solemn oath.

Despite Jim's intoxicated state, he was coherent and Jack was curious what he might say with his inhibitions lowered. Flicking on a couple of lights, he steered Jim to the lounge room and parked him on the couch.

'Can I get you something? Coffee? *Beer*?'

'No more beer. I think I had a few too many.'

'Yeah, I reckon you did,' Jack said, sitting himself on the nearest recliner. 'In the interests of us both getting some sleep tonight, may I ask what brings you over at this hour?'

Jim folded his arms and shook his head sadly, as if to say he'd been hard done by. 'I told Gloria what happened yesterday. Thought I might get some sympathy. Might have known she'd take your side. She thinks you're the bee's knees.'

Jack stifled a smile and waited.

'She wouldn't make my breakfast or my tea and said I had to come and talk to you. I knew if I didn't do it sometime today she'd make me sleep on the couch tonight.'

'Well, you left it to the last minute, but you're here now. What do you want to talk about?'

'Why I've been so hard on you,' Jim said, as if it should be obvious.

Eying Jim warily, Jack realised he wasn't as drunk as he first thought. Sure, he'd had a few, but he'd obviously sobered up a bit before coming over. 'All right, keep talking.'

'Some days I think I'll give in and tell you I'm pleased with your progress, but I can't bring myself to do it. Can't do it,' he said again, shaking his head for emphasis.

'Why not?'

'Because I'm jealous,' Jim said, hanging his head for a moment, before casting a sidelong glance in Jack's direction.

'*You're* jealous of *me*?' Why would that be, exactly?'

Closing his eyes, Jim leaned back on the couch before speaking. 'I was a tearaway kid,' he said. 'Never had any time for books or school and got out of there as fast as I could. I was lucky, I s'pose. I've always worked around the water and didn't need the books after all.'

He sat still for a few moments, before speaking again.

'I know I'm good at my job, I'm one of the best in the business.'

'Yeah, you are,' Jack said, still unsure how this related to him.

'Because I'm good at what I do I've gotten by. People listen to me; think I'm smarter than I am. I've gotten good at bluffing my way through things outside my area of exsep.., esperese… what's the word?'

'Expertise?'

'Yeah, that's it. Truth is, there have been lots of times when I wished I had listened more at school and been more book smart. So, when I see someone like *you*.' Jim paused to point at Jack.

'Someone like me?'

'Yeah, someone who is *smart*. When I meet a smart person, I set out to bring them down a peg or two, you know, try and ruffle their feathers a bit?'

Jack nodded. 'I did notice that.'

'You know, usually it works. I make them realise that in my world *I'm* the expert and *I'm* in charge.' Jim stabbed his chest with his forefinger. 'Most of them give up, can't hack the pace. But you were different. I just couldn't rattle your cage.'

'Oh, you rattled it all right; I just didn't let you see that you did.'

'But you stay so calm all the time! It's really hard to intimidate someone when they don't react.'

'I know. It's maddening, isn't it?'

Jim nodded. 'Yeah, it is maddening. When I couldn't get a rise out of you I really slammed you with the physical stuff and that didn't work either. You just put your head down and kept trying. And trying. You weren't much chop those first couple of weeks, but you wouldn't give up. I realised I wasn't going to scare you away.'

Jack had to laugh at that. 'Are you kidding? I was terrified of you. Still am,' he said.

'You don't act like it.'

'I probably shouldn't have told you, then.'

'I guess the long and short of it is that I was sure you would fail. And then I could tell myself that I'm one up on you. I might not be smart, but I'm a bloody good lifeguard.'

'But you are one up on me. I'm a terrible lifeguard.'

'No, no, you're not terrible. Just inexperienced. You're getting there. Considering you came in with no surf background whatsoever, you're doing really well. Once you get past the breaking waves you're a pretty decent board paddler and your run swim run time is more than acceptable.'

'Thanks. I appreciate you telling me that.'

'That's why I'm jealous. Because you're already good at what you do in your normal job and now you're getting good at *my* job.'

'How do you know I'm good at my job?'

'I told you, Davo checked you out. Sounds like you're a bit of a star of the legal world. Anyway, I could tell by the way you fixed the parking ticket. You knew exactly what to do and who to talk to.'

'That's only because I've spent years training and honing my skills. Just like you have with lifeguarding. Sure, I'm finally starting to master the physical tasks associated with the job, but that has taken lots of determination and hard work. Anyone who put their mind to it could do it. But I'm one hundred percent certain I don't have the natural instincts that you do. I've seen the way you watch the water and can spot rips, current direction and tidal changes in seconds. You can mobilise your staff instantly, perform CPR, handle any emergency, without breaking a sweat. There will always be trained people like me who can perform rescues and follow instructions, but you need a natural leader to guide them through it.'

Jim's weathered face softened. 'You reckon?'

'Absolutely. I could study every book written about being a lifeguard and still never have your natural talent for the job. Besides, I'll never be as tough as you.'

'No, you won't be son, I hate to tell you. You don't scare people.'

'I'm too soft, right?'

'No, I was just stirring you when I said that. You're a gentleman and people like that.'

'That's good to know.' Jack looked expectantly at Jim, hoping he would head off now that he'd cleared the air.

Catching Jack's eye, Jim nodded. 'All right, I'm going. But can I tell you one more thing first?'

Jack yawned. 'Sure, spit it out.'

'You've got it all going for you Jack, but you're buttoned up. You don't let people near you. I was kind of surprised when you took so well to Danny, but it's been good for you. I can't work out why you keep people at arm's length, but there's a barrier there alright.'

'Come on, what about basic psychology? I'm an only child, older over protective parents, a serious and steady career path? Am I not just a product of my life experiences?'

Jim eyed him carefully for a moment and then shook his head slowly. 'Nuh, it's not that. I reckon something has spooked you and you've shut down emotionally. You don't say much, but your eyes give you away.'

'My eyes?'

'Yeah. Some peoples are kind of flat and a bit empty. Yours are really intense. People can see there's a lot going on inside your head.'

'It's an intriguing theory Jim and I'm sorry to disappoint you, but I'm really not that interesting. I guess I'm just a natural born conservative and a bit of a loner.'

Holding his hands up, palms out, Jim nodded wearily. 'All right, you don't want to tell me. I probably wouldn't tell me either. But you should sort it out, whatever it is. You should enjoy life more.'

'Fine, I'll take it on board.'

Jim hauled himself to his feet. 'I'm going home now.'

'Good idea. You okay to walk back?'

'Yeah, can do it with my eyes closed.'

Jack believed him. He knew anybody who tried to take on Jim, drunk or not, would come off second best. He escorted him to the door. 'Thanks for dropping by. Does this mean I can do some rescues now?'

'Come and see me tomorrow.'

Jack went back to bed but didn't sleep. His mind was too busy. He'd worked so hard to keep the lid on the past, but now Jim had stirred it all up again. Had it really been six years? In some ways it felt like another lifetime entirely, but in others it seemed like only yesterday.

Jack blew out the candles on his thirtieth birthday cake and kept a smile fixed on his face as dozens of camera flashes lit up the darkened room. Looking out at the sixty guests that had come to wish him well, he felt proud of the life he had created for himself in Tasmania. Jackson and Nolan had expanded and taken on two new associates in the past eighteen months, he'd bought a house, he had a great social life and then, of course, there was Christine – the girl of his dreams. Waiting until the cameras stopped flashing he beckoned her over to stand beside him and his parents in the next round of photos.

Jack didn't like the term "the perfect couple", but that was the title he and

Christine had earned themselves in their large circle of friends, who all agreed they were made for each other.

Later they stood arm in arm, looking at the photo board that Jack's cousin Julia had put together. Pointing a perfectly manicured fingernail at Jack's university graduation photo, Christine chuckled softly.

'Gosh, look at you there, so young and baby faced.'

'Oh, as opposed to the old man I am now?'

'No, not at all. If anything, you're much more dashing now.'

Julia had come over to join them. 'That's because I taught him how to dress properly. When he started work he had one grey suit, one black suit and he only wore white shirts.'

Christine gave him a mock horrified look. 'Mr Armani himself? And here I was thinking what a great fashion sense he had for a guy.'

'Uh, no,' Julia laughed. 'It took me six months of dragging him into Sydney's finest menswear shops before he started to learn the ropes and I still oversee his major purchases.'

Jack gave his cousin a fake punch on the arm. 'What can I say Jules, you helped make me the man I am today.' Looking at some of the other photos he laughed at one of him with Julia and her twin brothers Jason and Paul. Their families had always been close, and his three cousins were like the siblings he never had.

Christine pointed to another shot of Jack with Jason and Paul on the rim of the Grand Canyon. 'I've never seen you with your hair that long or with three days' stubble.'

'That's my travel persona,' Jack said. 'After six months living out of a backpack, our personal grooming standards had understandably slipped a bit. It's all part of the fun.'

Christine shuddered a little. 'I'm glad you did all that before you met me, I'm strictly a five-star girl.'

Gazing adoringly at his girlfriend, Jack smiled. 'Oh, come on Chrissie, you're capable of much more than you think. We had some amazing experiences on that trip. I'd love to show you Europe.'

'Maybe someday when you can afford to take me first class.'

Jack switched on the light and picked his wallet up off the bedside table. Reaching behind several business cards, he retrieved the photo that had been taken that night. He rarely allowed himself to look at it because the pain was still there, not far under the surface. He shook his head, remembering the happiness of that time and how he had thought it would always be that way. A year later he was even more certain that he and Christine would be together forever.

Christine was inconsolable as she and her family lined up ready to board their plane. Jack held her tight and did his best to comfort her.

'Come on Chrissie, it's only for six weeks. You'll have a great time over there, I promise.'

'But I'll miss you so much and I hate flying. I need you Jack, you know that.'

Christine's cousin was getting married in Edinburgh and her whole family was going over for a holiday as well as the wedding. Jack had initially planned to join them for three weeks but George had been injured in a car accident and was still convalescing. It was disappointing, but he knew he had to stay and man the fort.

Eventually Christine calmed down. Just before she walked away, she whispered to Jack, 'Remember it's my birthday a month after we're back. I hope you're getting me a good present.'

Smiling, Jack nodded. 'Just wait and see.'

Christine had long been hinting that she wanted an engagement ring for her twenty-third birthday. They had been together almost three years and Jack's only reason for holding back in proposing was because of their age difference. He was more than ready to settle down and have a family, but he was concerned that Christine was still too young. After reassuring him for the past six months that it had always been her goal to marry and have her children young, Jack thought that the time might just be right.

Jack got out of bed and sat on the window seat. Pulling the curtain across, he looked out onto the moonlit water and concentrated on the noise of the crashing surf. He hadn't let himself think about this for so long. Becoming a workaholic might be exhausting, but it was certainly an effective way to keep painful thoughts locked away.

Don't go there, he thought. Focus on the here now, especially since I've taken this huge gamble and done something different. I'm learning new skills that might lead to a career change. Jim has just proven that he is actually human. That was enough to cope with, Jack decided. He didn't need ghosts from the past cluttering this new reality. Stepping back over to his bedside table, he picked up the novel he was reading and brought it back over to the window seat. Finding his page, Jack started reading and managed to lose himself in the story by sheer force of will.

After dozing fitfully on the window seat until dawn, Jack crawled back into bed just as the sun came up and managed a few hours of sleep. Still feeling flat, he didn't bother showering or shaving before wandering down to the surf club just after eleven. He found Jim sitting on the lower deck, downing a cup of strong, black coffee. He looked as rough as Jack felt. They eyed each other warily before Jim invited Jack to sit down.

'Gloria wasn't very happy when I told her I visited you last night after I'd been out drinking. She said the only way she is going to cook the Sunday roast lunch is if you come over and join us. None of our kids can make it today and she won't do it just for me.'

'Well, far be it from me to deprive you of your food. Tell Gloria I would be happy to accept.'

'Good answer. She's right, I shouldn't have landed on you like that, so, my apologies,' Jim said gruffly.

'Apology accepted, as long as I get to have a go in the water.'

Jim narrowed his eyes. 'I'm not saying I was wrong by not putting you out there before.'

'Let's say it's not an admission of guilt but rather an act of goodwill.'

'I'd say I can live with that. Go and get yourself looking decent and be at my place by one.'

'What, you don't think I can carry off the stubble look?'

'No,' Jim replied bluntly.

After tasting Gloria's roast beef with all the trimmings, Jack understood why Jim had invited him to lunch. Forfeiting a meal like this, especially after Gloria hadn't fed him last night, would have been crazy.

Laying down his cutlery neatly in the centre of his plate, Jack smiled at Gloria. '*That* was a veritable feast. Thank you so much.'

'Oh, go on, it was just a roast. Are you sure you've had enough? There's plenty more. How about another potato or some more meat?'

Shaking his head, Jack rubbed his stomach. 'Really, I couldn't eat another bite as delicious as it all is.'

Jim pushed his own plate aside. 'Yes, Love, you've excelled yourself again.' Turning to Jack, he said, 'I hope you've saved some room for dessert.'

'Dessert? Wow. If you give me fifteen minutes, I'll be up for it.'

'That's perfect, the apple crumble is still in the oven,' Gloria said. 'More wine, Jack?' Gloria held up the bottle of Shiraz.

'Sure. I don't have to drive anywhere.'

Jim held out his glass as well. 'Don't look so surprised,' he said, giving Jack a sidelong glance. 'I may not have had your rearing, but I'm not a total redneck.'

'You've got me pegged all wrong, you know.'

'What, you're not a rich lawyer after all?'

'Okay, sure I make good money, but I worked hard and earned my way to where I am, you know. That's why I got so mad the other afternoon. You've just made so many assumptions about me.'

'Assumptions? I was just going on what Davo told me. Being an only child with posh English parents and going to one of Sydney's leading boys' schools adds up to well-to-do in my book.'

'My parents were ten pound migrants. Neither of them finished high school and they only ever worked unskilled jobs. They only had one child because it took them twenty years to conceive and I guess having English accents in a country town in the 1970s made them sound posh, but they weren't.'

Jim furrowed his brow. 'Well how'd they afford to put you through St Ignatius' and a law degree?'

'I went to St Ignatius' in Millvale – not Sydney - and I was at the tail end of the free university era. That's not to say my parents didn't work hard to support me, or that I didn't work part-time myself to cover my expenses, but it wasn't like it is now with HECS.'

'Hold my apple crumble,' Jim said. 'It looks like I'm getting a big serve of humble pie right here.'

Gloria smiled. 'It's not often that I get the chance to hear this man admit he's wrong.'

'Well, what about your fancy manners?' Jim asked.

'I guess that's a credit to my working-class parents,' Jack said. 'To be fair, though, Jim, when you said I was a privileged only child, I guess I was. I had two parents who adored me and gave me everything they could. That's more than a lot of other kids get.'

'Gloria's right, I don't say I'm wrong very often, but when I am, I'll admit it. You're a decent bloke Jack and I like you a lot. Even if you are a Blues supporter.'

• • • • •

The conditions were perfect for Jack's first day in the water. The sun shone warmly, but not too hot, and the waves were just big enough to cater for the school holiday crowds, without being dangerous. Lots of tourists meant lots of inexperienced swimmers, so the lifeguards were still kept busy.

Adrenalin surged when Jim gave Jack the nod to assist a forty-something woman, just outside the flags. Right, act cool, he thought, as he pulled off his shirt and picked up the rescue board. As far as this lady is concerned you've got years of experience. Wading to knee depth, Jack threw the board down, mounted it smoothly and paddled out.

Reaching the woman quickly, Jack sat astride the end of the board and assisted the woman to climb up in front of him. 'You're safe now,' he said. 'Just lie face forward,' he instructed, glad that she wasn't panicking. I'm rescuing somebody! he thought proudly, as he lay back down to paddle in. What an amazing feeling.

'Thank you,' the woman said, once they were back in the shallows. 'I shouldn't have gone outside the flags.'

Dismounting the board, Jack helped her to her feet. 'You're welcome,' he replied.

Taking a closer look at her rescuer, the woman smoothed her hair and gave Jack an admiring gaze, but he was too caught up in the glory of the moment to notice. Unable to stop smiling, he dragged the rescue board back to its rack.

Jim gave a single nod. 'Not bad,' he said.

Danny was much more effusive. 'Awesome Jack!' he exclaimed, raising his hand for a high five. 'See, Jim, he *can* do it.'

'Yeah, so he can,' Jim agreed, a little less enthusiastically than Jack would have liked.

Jim's response remained lukewarm when Jack carried out another two textbook rescues over the course of the day. He decided not to let it affect him. He knew Jim hated admitting he was wrong, there was no point rubbing it in.

Conditions the next day were much less favourable. Several flash rips lurked along the shoreline and the waves were bigger. It was also very humid, enticing even more swimmers into the water. From the moment he arrived on the beach, Jack could feel the change in atmosphere. Whereas the lifeguard team had taken an almost casual approach yesterday, today it was much more intense.

Jim marshalled his troops near the tower. 'All right, this could be a very busy day, so everybody needs to stay sharp. We need to really watch that north side. People think it looks calm, but we know how sharply that sandbank drops off. It always makes me nervous when kids play there.'

Maybe I should just volunteer to stay in the tower, Jack thought. When he suggested this, Jim shook his head. 'You wanted to be in the water, you're in the water. Lucas can take care of the tower.'

A wave of uncertainty hit as Jack realised there was some kind of teaching opportunity behind Jim's decision.

It didn't take long to see the lesson. While Jack carried out his first rescue without incident, his second was a disaster. The first wave pummelled him before he was even halfway there. I should have rolled it, he realised, as he was pushed backwards in the white-water. Jim was always telling him to attack the big waves head on and, while Jack agreed in theory, facing an oncoming wall of water still freaked him out. Rolling the board under the wave was a better option for him, but required split second timing he hadn't quite mastered yet.

Clambering back on the board, Jack paddled a little further and, once again, mistimed his roll when the next wave crashed. Knowing how incompetent he must look, he clung desperately to his board as it turned sideways. Caught on the other side of the waves, the teenaged boy he was trying to rescue started to panic. 'Help me!' he yelled.

Jack weighed his options. Caught in the strong side sweep, he doubted he'd be able to turn the board around fast enough. Attempting a rescue in breaking waves with it facing sideways was too dangerous. Meanwhile, the boy started thrashing around.

'Hurry! I can't stay up!'

Abandoning his board, Jack dived under the next wave and swam towards the boy, realising as he did so that he now had no flotation device. Great! Now *I* need help, Jack realised. But before he even had time to turn back towards shore and raise his arm for backup, Jim was by his side.

'I'll get the kid,' he said. 'Grab that board before it hits someone.'

Jack collected his wayward board and watched as Jim easily towed the victim back to shore with a rescue tube. The guy really is a legend, he thought. *And* he was right all along. I wasn't quite ready to go it alone and he could see that.

'You don't need to say it,' Jack said, as Jim came to stand alongside him a few minutes later. 'Never leave your board.'

'Yep, that's right. Even Danny knows that. Any person working under me needs to follow that rule to the letter.'

'So, I guess you want me back in the tower, then?'

'Nope.'

Jack's jaw dropped. 'You're kicking me off the beach all together?'

'Of course not. Like I said before, you wanted to be in the water, that's where you're gonna stay. Sometimes a baptism of fire is the best way to learn.'

· · · · ·

That Saturday night Jack was invited to the surf club to celebrate his first week in the water. As Jim predicted, it had been a baptism of fire, but his skills had improved markedly over the past few days. Arriving just after seven, Jack was very surprised to find himself the guest of honour of the whole bar. He'd assumed it would just be his fellow lifeguards there to congratulate him.

Jack had no idea the surf club was such a happening place on Saturday nights. There was a DJ playing some decent music and once the dining hours were over, the tables were cleared away to make a dance floor. Cara, Sunset Point's only female lifeguard, wasted no time dragging Jack to his feet. He resisted at first. 'Nah, Cara, I'm not much of a dancer.'

Cara clamped her hands around his elbow. 'You have to dance! You're the only really cool guy on the lifeguard team.'

'I'm not cool.'

'Yeah, you are. You're wearing label clothes and decent shoes *and* you've got product in your hair, right?'

'Well, yeah, but only a small amount. You see I've got this weird cow's lick and…'

Cara cut him off. 'Anything besides Brylcreem makes you cool around these parts.'

Jack kept his feet planted firmly on the spot. 'What about Lucas? He's young like you.'

'*Puhlease*! I went to school with him, he's so *not* cool.' Cara made a gagging gesture.

'What about Jim? He looks like he might have a few moves.'

'Yeah, he's a real groover. *Come on,* Jack,' she wheedled, hauling him closer to the dance floor.

'Okay, fine. But you have to go and tell the DJ to put on some eighties stuff.'

'Sure!' Cara made her way over to the music booth.

Jack eventually made his escape when Cara met up with some friends. He found himself a bar stool in a quiet corner and was enjoying some time out, when Jim came over, beer in hand. Jack had noticed him among the throng of patrons when he first arrived but thought he had long gone home.

Taking a seat on an adjacent stool, Jim motioned to the dance floor. 'Good to see you having fun.'

'Yeah, the good old YMCA is always a crowd pleaser.'

'I think Cara is a bit sweet on you.'

Jack shook his head. 'She's just a kid.'

'Yeah, true. I'm not saying you should encourage her.'

'Don't worry, I'm not.'

They sat in silence for a few moments before Jim spoke again. 'So, what's her name?'

Jack's gaze flickered around the room before it came back to Jim.

'What?' he said.

'Come on, Jack, you're not talking to Danny now. The reason you've built a little compound around yourself is because some woman burned you, right?'

Jack stared at Jim for a moment, then shook his head. 'If you'd asked me what was wrong I would have been able to deflect you. But coming in with the direct question, it always catches you off guard. That's a real court room strategy.'

'I'm right, though.'

'Yeah, you're right. But how did you know? I definitely haven't told Danny that story.'

Leaning back against the wall, Jim smiled. 'Let's face it, most male problems are either about money or women. You seem to have no financial issues so a woman seemed like a sure bet.'

'Well, I guess that makes me just another statistic, hey?'

'Look, Jack, I know I was a mean old bastard to you, but I'm not that bad. Honestly. I can lend you an ear, if you like?'

Picking up a coaster, Jack spun it several times. 'I'm sure you've got better ways to spend your Saturday night than listening to my tale of woe.'

'I'm right here and I've got a fresh beer. Seems like an ideal opportunity to get it off your chest. Let's face it, we've all been there.'

Spinning the coaster again, Jack studied the table top for several moments. Then he started talking.

Throughout the meal, Jack was aware of the little box in the breast pocket of his jacket. Christine had not been subtle in dropping hints about the kind of ring she wanted, so he was fairly confident she would like it. He smiled, recalling the previous day they had spent together at the races. Christine had been in her element and he was relieved that she seemed to be back to her old self. It had been a surprise when she stayed an extra three weeks overseas and although she had walked into his waiting arms at the airport, he could sense something was amiss. She had been moody and out of sorts ever since, which Jack put down to post holiday blues. He was glad she had enjoyed the trip so much and figured she would get over it soon enough.

After they finished their dessert, Jack reached across the table and took Christine's hand in his. 'I've got your present here.'

'But my birthday isn't until tomorrow.'

'What's a few hours?'

Christine glanced around their table. 'But you don't have anything with you.'

'Small presents can sometimes be the most exciting.' Jack's smile died on his lips when he saw the expression on Christine's face. It wasn't the look of somebody who was anticipating a proposal; rather it was a stricken expression that made him very uneasy.

Removing her hand from Jack's grasp, Christine shook her head. 'Jack, please don't ask me. I don't want to hurt you and I'm so, so sorry, but please don't say it. I can't be with you anymore.'

Jack had heard the analogy of feeling like you had iced water running through your veins, but had never understood it until that moment. The conversation that followed was surreal. It didn't seem possible that Christine was telling him that travel had opened her eyes and broadened her horizons. The girl who had once told him that Hobart was plenty big enough for her was now saying that she was moving to the Gold Coast while she saved some money and then planned to travel for at least a year after that. She had come to realise that getting married and having children now would be a huge mistake for her, for both of them. She refuted all Jack's suggestions of him moving to Queensland with her or of them travelling together.

'Please, Jack, don't make this any more difficult. I've just got to do this for me.'

Fighting hard to hold it together, Jack resisted the temptation to throw the ring, with great force, down the length of the elegant restaurant.

'Well, at least there wasn't anybody else,' he said quietly.

It was only a fleeting expression that crossed Christine's face, but Jack caught it. He shook his head. 'Ah, but there was, of course there was. What's a holiday without a bit of infidelity?'

Christine started to cry. 'Please Jack, it wasn't like that. I didn't... I never...'

'No, Christine, I didn't and I never, but you did, apparently.'

'It was stupid, we were both drunk and it didn't mean anything. I'm sorry, okay?' she sniffled.

'No, it's not okay, actually, but there doesn't seem to be much point in being here with you when you obviously don't want to be with me.'

With that, Jack stood and put on his overcoat. He handed Christine a linen napkin to wipe her eyes and a twenty-dollar note. 'I'll ask the doorman to call you a cab,' he said, willing himself to stay in control.

After paying the bill on the way out, Jack hailed a taxi for himself and went home with a broken heart.

'That's a tough break, mate,' Jim said. 'Sounds like that young lady poleaxed you good and proper and you didn't see it coming.'

Jack nodded. 'I just couldn't understand why she let me get as far as buying the ring and almost saying the words. That restaurant in Hobart is well known as a place you go when you're going to propose, she *knew* what was coming.'

'Maybe she didn't decide until that moment that she couldn't go through with it,' Jim said. 'Women are a different species, there's no two ways about it.'

'Yeah, you're right about that. But, you know, I probably would have dealt with it better if a couple of other things hadn't happened. Four days later I lost a big case on appeal. It was one of those crazy legal loopholes and I couldn't do a thing to stop it. I felt that I had let my clients down badly because I'd assured them it would be okay and it wasn't.'

'I can understand that.'

'It was my first major career setback and because it was such a high-profile case, the press coverage of it was relentless. I had reporters outside the office and my house demanding to know why I had allowed a guilty man to walk free.'

'It wasn't a murderer or something, was it?'

'No, it was a crooked accountant who fleeced dozens of retirees of their nest eggs.'

'Well, that can generate a lot of fury too.'

'Oh, yeah. But worse was to come. A month later, my dad died suddenly. We were really close and it absolutely devastated me.'

'Sounds like a pretty rough trot.'

'Yeah, it was. I went from having a really great life, to everything collapsing around me in a matter of weeks. I literally felt numb, but seeing my mother so distraught, I had to put my own grief aside and help her through it. By that stage I was already desperate to escape Hobart and all its memories and Mum's health wasn't good, so I sold up and moved back.'

'I'm sure she appreciated having you close by.'

Jack nodded. 'Yeah, she did. I don't regret it. I haven't been unhappy back home and career wise it's been great. That's the thing about my work, if you put in sixty or seventy hours a week, you don't have time to feel.'

'That's no way to live though, is it? As hard as it is sometimes, you have to experience emotion. It's part of being human.'

'I don't know Jim, if you don't let yourself get too happy, then when something bad happens it's not so far down. When Mum died three years ago, I was better equipped to handle it.'

Jim nodded. 'Sure, it sounds reasonable. But how's that whole philosophy working for you now?'

Taken aback, Jack had several defensive replies on the tip of his tongue. But, thinking for a moment, he shook his head. 'It's not working. Not at all.'

Two days later, Gloria arrived at lunchtime, with a basket of baking. 'I just thought you might enjoy some home cooked things,' she said, pulling back a tea towel to reveal a selection of scones, muffins and biscuits.

Holding open the door to let her inside, Jack smiled. 'You are an angel, Gloria. The best thing I had to offer Danny today was the boring leftovers in the family assorted pack. He'll be thrilled with this magnificent spread.'

Gloria made no protest when Jack invited her to stay for lunch and then banished him to the lounge room while she prepared the meal. When they sat down to eat on the veranda, they talked of inconsequential things at first, but Jack knew that Gloria had something on her mind.

'It's all right. I'm guessing Jim told you about Christine,' Jack said, as he set about making himself another sandwich.

'He's not a gossip, Jack, really he's not.'

'I know. I figured he'd tell you. I didn't tell him he had to keep it a secret.'

Gloria buttered a slice of banana bread. 'He's actually a pretty good listener when he needs to be.'

'Yeah, he is. He's also surprisingly astute. He had it all worked out.'

Gloria fiddled with the tablecloth for a minute. 'I just wanted to say a couple of things, you know, from a woman's perspective,' she said.

'Fire away.'

'I'm a firm believer that things happen for a reason. I'm not saying that Christine didn't genuinely love you or that she wasn't completely sincere in saying that she wanted to spend her life with you. You've probably said to yourself that if she didn't go on that trip then you would still be together now.'

'Only a million times or so.'

'Something that I have learned over the years is that if something is going to happen, it will happen eventually, one way or another. Sure, that holiday awakened Christine's restless side and, you're right, if she hadn't gone then you probably would have gotten married. But you know what, Jack? If it hadn't been that trip, then it would have been something else. Somewhere, at some point, those feelings inside her would have come to the fore.'

'But she never said anything. In fact, she didn't even want to go on the trip when I couldn't go.'

'Jack, she obviously didn't realise herself until she was over there. Don't you think that it was better that this all happened before you got married and had children? You may very well still consider Christine the love of your life, but she might not even be the same person now, in fact she probably isn't. Have you ever considered the possibility that there might be someone else for you?'

'No. I really believe that was my one chance and it's gone. I can't imagine feeling that for anyone else.'

'Oh Jack, there are always second, third and fourth chances in life if you are open to them. Promise me you'll think about looking out there a bit?'

Jack nodded, unconvincingly. 'Maybe.'

• • • • •

When school resumed the following week, Jim allowed Jack to finish his shift at three thirty each afternoon so he could continue working with Danny. On Tuesday, Jack was doing a walking patrol along the sand, his eyes keenly watching the swimmers in the water, when he was almost bowled over by a force from behind. Startled, he turned to see Danny, still fully dressed in his school uniform, including shoes, waving a piece of paper in front of him.

'Hey, hang on Dan, I'll just get Cara down to take over.'

By the time Jack officially handed over, Danny was almost jumping out of his skin. Taking the well-handled sheet of paper, Jack looked at it. It was a maths test. At the top was the result 17/20 and next to it was a gold star and the words "well done Danny!"

It took Jack a second to realise that Danny's excitement was more about the star than the result.

'I've never had a star before! You only get them if you're one of the best.' Danny beamed at Jack, pride in his achievement patently clear.

Jack ruffled Danny's hair. 'I'm so proud of you, mate! Didn't I tell you that you were smarter than you thought?'

'I thought you were just being nice, though,' said Danny. 'I didn't know you *really* meant it.'

'Course I meant it.' Jack blinked back the unexpected tears of pride that welled up.

As he gathered his gear together, Jack could hear Danny excitedly telling Jim his news. When he walked back over to collect Danny, he saw that Jim had presented him with an official Lifeguard cap.

'Well, what about our boy here, quite the scholar hey?' said Jim.

Still fighting the unexpected swell of emotion, Jack could only nod and motioned for Danny to come up to the house with him.

When Jack saw an advertisement in the surf club for a beginner's surfing workshop, he thought immediately of Danny. The boy had mentioned several times that he would love to learn to surf, but his mum couldn't afford a board or lessons.

When Jack ran the idea past Jim, he readily agreed. 'It will be good for the lad and you to do something together, just for fun.'

'Oh, you think I should go too?'

'Sure, come on, even I will admit you're more than competent in the water now. You could definitely handle a surfing lesson.'

'No, I was just wondering if Danny would want me to tag along?'

'Of course he would. That boy thinks you get up every morning to let the sun up. In his eyes, you wear a cape and have a big red S on your chest.'

'And you're still trying to convince him I'm really Clark Kent.'

Jim shook his head. 'Sometimes I think I liked the silent version of you better,' he said.

'You can't have it both ways.'

'Yeah, yeah, I know. Look, to be honest, I was a little bit miffed when I got replaced as Danny's hero, but I'm over it now.'

'I think hero is overstating it a bit.'

'No, it's not. Kids look up to adults and seeing that his dad isn't worth mentioning, I'm glad he found someone worthwhile to idolise.'

'What is the story with his father, anyway?'

'Local kid from a troubled family. Could never manage to keep himself out of strife. He cleared off a few years ago, now.'

'Right. That's pretty much what I gathered.'

Not wanting to miss out on the workshop, Jack headed straight over and made the booking. As Jim predicted, Danny was thrilled about them learning to surf, together.

'It's like a dream come true!' he exclaimed, engulfing Jack in another unexpected hug. 'And I've got five dollars in my piggy bank I can give you. I know it costs a lot.'

Jack hugged him back, pleased that this time he didn't feel so awkward. 'Keep your money Dan, it's a thank you present for all the help you have given me.'

Jack was well used to being outshone in all surf related activities, so he wasn't surprised when Danny picked up the technical skills almost immediately and was standing up on his board when Jack was still mastering the crouch.

At least I've got the paddling under control, Jack thought, as he watched the man next to him struggle to move through the water, while he surged ahead. All those hours on the rescue board have done me some good and these surfboards feel so light in comparison.

By mid-afternoon Jack, too, was standing, albeit not for very long. This is fun, he realised, as he wobbled unsteadily on a calm little wave almost all the way to shore. I might have to come back another time to Sunset Point for a surfing holiday.

Eventually falling off his board, Jack waded into shore and watched proudly as Danny confidently rode yet another wave. He had already perfected the stance and maintained his balance seemingly effortlessly. It wasn't just that he had a wiry build and was light on his feet, Danny had true athletic ability that could take him a long way in life. That kid deserves the best, Jack decided, and one way or another I'm going to make sure he gets it.

As they packed up that afternoon, the young instructor came over to talk to Danny and Jack. Giving Danny a playful punch on the arm, he smiled. 'Well, we all know who the star of this course was. You keep practising, mate, and you'll be a top-class surfer.'

Danny beamed at the praise. 'Thank you,' he said.

'Don't forget your dad, though, he did pretty well too,' the instructor added, nodding at Jack before moving away.

Neither of them mentioned the mistake then, but Danny obviously contemplated it. He brought the topic up later that evening as they sat eating fish and chips on the balcony of the surf club.

'How old are you, Jack?' he asked.

'Thirty-six.'

Danny mulled it over for a moment. 'That's old enough to be a dad, isn't it?'

Jack nodded. 'Yes, it is.'

'Our surfing teacher thought you were my dad.'

Not sure where Danny was going with the conversation, Jack nodded. 'Well, we do kind of look alike,' he said. 'And usually parents take their kids to these kinds of things.'

Danny poured some tomato sauce onto his plate and dunked a chip. 'My dad doesn't come and see me very much. He sends me money sometimes, but I think he's pretty busy.'

'I'm sure he loves you, though,' Jack said, wondering if his voice conveyed the contempt he felt for a man who thought that twenty dollars in a birthday card, when he could be bothered, constituted fatherly duties. He also felt genuine pity that Danny's father had made no effort to get to know such an amazing child.

Danny chewed through the rest of his calamari before he spoke again. 'I know you can't be my dad, but I think you'd be really good at it. See, you didn't think you would be a good lifeguard but you are and maybe you think you wouldn't be a good dad but I reckon you would.'

Jack smiled wistfully. 'You really think so, Dan?'

'Yeah, of course. You're good at homework and you like doing fun things like playing games and going surfing. And you're nice too; you don't yell and get mad all the time.'

'Well, in fairness to parents everywhere, that's much easier to do when you don't have the day to day responsibility of childcare.'

Danny stared at him. 'What does that mean?'

Laughing, Jack shook his head. 'Don't worry about it, mate.'

'So, do you reckon you'll have some kids one day?'

'Who knows, Danny?' Jack sighed and gazed out to the horizon.

Worn out after their busy day, Danny was almost asleep when Jim arrived to take him home. Waving them off, Jack headed out the front entrance of the surf club, onto the sand. Although the sun had set, it was a full moon and the beauty of the light on the water was transfixing. Smiling at another couple as they walked past, Jack looked over towards the Beach House, but decided to keep walking. As much time as he'd spent on this beach over the past weeks, he'd never walked north towards the lighthouse and this was the perfect night to do it.

Strolling along, Jack thought about the conversation he'd just had with Danny. Although it hadn't occurred to him, he supposed that most of the people at the workshop thought he and Danny were father and son. It didn't bother him that they did, in fact, he was pleased that he could pull off passing for someone's father. I still want that, Jack acknowledged. As much as I've created a lifestyle that excludes children, it's not how I want to live, anymore.

It suddenly struck Jack, then, just how much power he'd given Christine over the past five years. While she was out there living her life, here he was, working himself into the ground and existing like a sad, social recluse, just because she didn't want him anymore. Get a grip, Jack, he thought. Jim is right, you're not the first guy to be cheated on and dumped and you're not going to be the last.

Jack's bare foot struck rock then, as he arrived at the northern most end of Sunset Point Beach. Looking up, he took in the majestic, century old lighthouse, with its beaming light shimmering across the water and, in that moment, he felt the proverbial weight lift off his shoulders, just a bit.

Walking up the narrow path, Jack made his way to the platform at the base of the structure. Standing there, he raised his arms above his head. 'I'm back!' he yelled out into the still night, and then stood looking out at the water for a long, long time.

The next morning Jack made his first appearance at Stella Maris church. Like many other things in his life, church attendance had been pushed aside as he let work dominate more and more. Speaking about his parents to Jim last night had reminded Jack of the peace and ritual of Sundays, back when he was growing up. Determined that this day would be the first in a new chapter of his life, Jack decided that taking some time to pray was a fitting way to move forward.

Arriving early and choosing a seat in the back row, Jack felt a gentle calmness descend upon him, as he re-immersed himself in the familiarity of Mass. He liked historic churches like this small, timber one and was highly impressed with the stained-glass window above the altar. Jack noted the familiar faces that filled the pews – Moira from the library, Gus from the servo and Jim and Gloria, who made sure they caught him before he left. Jack had to stifle a smile at the unfamiliar sight of Jim in his Sunday best. His own outfit was much more casual.

'I wondered if you'd make an appearance here eventually,' Jim said, with a grin.

Furrowing her brow, Gloria nudged him.

'It's all right, Gloria, Jim has obviously appointed himself my spiritual adviser as well as my lifeguard instructor. How did you know I haven't been attending the local Methodist or Anglican services?'

'With you having an Irish surname like Nolan, wearing a St Christopher medal and being educated at St Ignatius', it would have been pretty long odds that you weren't a Mick. Besides, I would have heard if you went somewhere else.'

'Well, I'm glad I came, the choir was very nice,' Jack said with a smile to Gloria, who was a member.

'You know, we don't get too many hundred dollar notes on the collection plate around here,' said Jim.

Gloria nudged him again, sharply this time.

'What?' Jim shot her an exasperated look. 'I was just saying.'

'Sunset Point has been pretty good to me, I just wanted to give a little something back,' said Jack.

Gloria smiled. 'Well, I'm sure the parish will put your contribution to good use,' she assured him.

After partaking of morning tea with the rest of the congregation, Jack walked home slowly, enjoying the freedom of an unstructured day. It was so much easier to implement change here, away from the pressures of his normal life. He just hoped he could transition back, without relapsing back to full throttle.

• • • • •

As an ongoing reward for his improving schoolwork Jack and Danny often played pool at the surf club in the late afternoon, just before Danny went home. While Jack was impressed at how well the child could play, he was secretly relieved that his own, admittedly average, skill level was better.

On Friday afternoon, Steve and his son, Alex, came to play as well. After a couple of games of doubles, one of the other tables came free and Alex suggested the kids and adults part company for a while.

'Good idea,' said Steve.

Frowning, Danny's gaze flicked between Alex and the adults. 'But I like being on your team, Jack.'

'Yeah, but Steve doesn't believe I can beat him without you to help me. You don't mind if I just give him one game by myself, do you?' asked Jack.

'All right,' Danny agreed, reluctantly, heading over to the other table.

'Nothing like a bit of hero worship, hey?' said Steve, as he arranged the balls in the rack.

'Yeah, it's good for the soul.'

Steve lifted the rack and hung it on the hook on the edge of the table. 'He's gonna miss you.'

Leaning on his cue, Jack watched the boys for a moment. 'I'm going to miss him too. He's a great kid.'

'Yeah, he is.' Steve broke, sinking number five. 'I reckon Jim's going to miss you as well,' he said, as he lined up his next shot.

Raising his eyebrows, Jack smiled. 'I don't know about that.'

'Well, he'd never admit it, of course, but I think he will. You haven't thought about staying on? Summer is pretty busy here, we could use you.'

Jack took his first shot, slamming both thirteen and ten into the top corner pockets. 'You know, it is kind of tempting. But I've got to get my old life sorted out, before I can start a new one. There's a lot of me invested in law.'

'Fair enough.'

· · · · ·

When he'd first arrived at Sunset Point, Jack had numbered the weeks on the calendar in the kitchen. In the beginning nine weeks had seemed an eternity, but now it was mid-October and it was the Monday of his last week. He couldn't believe it was almost over.

Taking his bowl of cereal out to the veranda, Jack sat down and looked out on the beach that had become so familiar to him. As always, the flags were up and a fair crowd was in the water. Even though he had the morning off, Jack felt a genuine desire to be down there and part of it all. He was going to miss this house, this beach and this town, for that matter.

In fact, it was going to be a big upheaval to put his solicitor's hat back on and Jack wasn't even sure if he wanted to. Yesterday, Kelly had emailed him the fully booked calendar, for his first week back. It was a jolt that he wasn't quite ready for and Jack decided to put it out of his mind for now.

Wandering down to the beach later, Jack stood on the sand for a moment and took in the cobalt sky and water that was clear as crystal. Amidst all the technological advances and endless entertainment options of the modern world, he finally understood why people still flocked to the beach. It had a simplicity and beauty that you just couldn't find anywhere else.

Wading into the water, Jack dolphin dived under the smaller waves and swam out to the breakers. The water temperature was perfect and the gently spilling waves were just the way he liked them. Even though Jack had worked hard at overcoming his fear of big surf, the huge waves still rattled him, especially on the rescue board. If he did decide to make a permanent career of lifeguarding, Jack knew it was something he'd have to overcome.

When he walked over to get his towel, Cara gave Jack a wave and an appreciative glance. Remembering Jim's words, he'd deliberately ignored the signals she'd been sending, seeing all too clearly the pitfalls of getting involved with a nineteen-year-old who was just out for fun. Yet, the attention *was* flattering, and, given the way Cara was eyeing him now, getting back into the dating game was obviously possible. But Jack knew it might take a while to work up the courage.

• • • • •

Jack made the most of his last days on the job. He savoured each moment in the tower, and the hours spent down on the sand, knowing that an amazing experience was almost over. On his second last day, Jim came over and stood beside him, near the water's edge. 'I reckon things are going to be a bit different around here next week.'

'Yeah?'

'Uh huh. The equipment room has never been in such good shape, since you've been here and the log book is actually legible,' Jim said. 'And that new inventory system you set up for the first aid supplies is great.'

'Is that your way of saying you'll feel my absence?'

'I suppose it is,' Jim said, before heading back to the tower.

Jack watched him go, smiling at the fact that Jim hadn't mentioned he'd miss his water rescue skills. Ah well, he was under no illusions that he was still very much a beginner in that department.

Two teenaged girls walked past, giggling as they sang the theme song to *Surf City*. Jack smiled to himself, realising that he'd hardly given the program a thought since he'd been at Sunset Point. He'd soon realised it was not a particularly accurate depiction of the job he'd devoted the last two months of his life to.

Yet, despite its many shortcomings, *Surf City* had got one thing right. Being a lifeguard *was* a noble profession and he felt a great pride at being part of it. There was something very humbling about a job that's only premise was helping people, and saving lives, and Jack was truly grateful for all that it had given him.

· · · · ·

Jack insisted on hosting dinner on his last night at the beach house. After the first Sunday lunch, he had eaten at Jim and Gloria's numerous times and wanted to repay the favour. Despite what his cleaning lady, Edna, thought, and what he suspected Gloria thought too, Jack could actually cook. He couldn't help but smile at Gloria's reaction to her first mouthful of his chicken curry.

'Gosh, there's more than a pinch of Keen's Curry Powder in that,' she gasped, reaching for her glass of water. 'But I like it.'

Jim didn't seem bothered by the heat of it. 'Nothing like a good curry,' he agreed, shovelling more into his mouth.

'He's always had a cast iron gut,' Gloria said, shaking her head.

When Jack set dessert down on the table, Jim eyed it suspiciously. 'Don't tell me you whipped up a pav as well.'

'No, it's compliments of Marge.' Jack pushed the frosted glass pie dish over to Gloria. 'I'll let you do the honours,' he said.

Gloria cut into the pavlova expertly. 'Jim hasn't stopped raving about his drive in the Audi,' she said, handing the first huge slice to Jack. 'The way he tells it, you went for a burn around Mount Panorama.'

Jack laughed. 'Yeah, well, I won't be surprised if a speeding fine turns up in the mail.'

'Don't let the mild-mannered persona fool you,' said Jim, reaching out to take his slice of pavlova. 'Mr Nolan here has got quite a lead foot, himself.'

'I'll be sending you the bill for the clutch replacement.' Jack grinned as he poured cream over his dessert.

'It handles a bit differently to the Falcon,' Jim replied, defensively. 'And, I was so confused about the blinkers and windscreen wipers being back to front, I didn't have my full attention on the gear changes.'

Sorry she had raised the subject, Gloria rolled her eyes, as she served herself a slice of pavlova. 'Men and cars,' she murmured.

After the meal was over, they sat on the veranda and enjoyed a post dinner drink.

'You'll miss this view, Jack,' said Gloria.

'You're telling me. I've got a mountain view at home, which is pretty spectacular, but there's nothing quite like the ocean on a beautiful night.'

Jim took a long draught of beer. 'So, what's ahead for Jack Nolan, Boy Wonder?'

'I wish I knew. I don't believe in burning bridges so I'm not going to resign from my job and become a beach bum just yet. But, doing this job has reminded me what it's like to have a passion and finish a day's work with true satisfaction. Law used to give me that. My job was always the constant force that drove me, no matter what personal stuff was going on. Then it got tainted too, and I guess that's how I ended up here.'

'For what it's worth, I'll give you my advice,' said Jim, taking another sip of beer. 'First and foremost, you really saved my bacon with that parking ticket and it hasn't been forgotten. On my recommendation, you could get a job on pretty much any beach in the country and I'll do that for you, if it's what you honestly want. You're still a junior in terms of skill level, but you're willing to work hard to gain more experience.'

Jack nodded. 'Thanks.'

Holding a finger up, as if to illustrate a point, Jim thought for a moment before speaking again. 'The fact that the surf lifesavers are part time volunteers doesn't mean they're of any less value. They were out there saving lives long before professionals every got appointed and they do exactly what we do. I never appoint anyone on my team who hasn't been a clubbie. So, you don't need to split hairs about who is the more superior.'

'Oh, yeah, I get that,' said Jack.

'Good to hear, because I think that's the way for you to go. Join a surf club in Sydney. You'll still get to use the skills you've gained but you won't have to leave the rest of your life behind.'

'It's a good option.'

'You're a smart bloke, Jack. One of the smartest I've ever met. While you might have lost the fire in your belly for your job, you're good at it, really good. You shouldn't let all that education go to waste.'

'I know my parents would turn in their graves if I gave it all away. My problem is that I've specialised in an area of law I'm really not passionate about. I thought personal injury would be all about fighting for the underdog, but a lot of it is fighting with insurance companies, or explaining to people that signing an iron-clad waiver pretty much takes away your right to sue.'

'Can't you just specialise in something else?' Taking his last sip of beer, Jim set the glass on the table.

Jack sighed. 'The short answer is yes, I can. The reality is that it will upset the applecart at my firm. They've invested a lot in me becoming a specialist. My name is on all their advertising. My expertise generates a lot of business for them.'

Folding his arms, Jim eyeballed Jack. 'Come on, now, that sounds like an excuse to me. If your bosses value you as much as I reckon they do, I'm sure they'll accept you want to change direction.'

Giving a mock exasperated look, Jack held out his hands in surrender. 'Put like that, I'm all out of excuses, aren't I? I need to work out the direction I want to go in and do something about it.'

'That's about the size of it,' said Jim.

Gloria interjected at this point. 'Whatever you decide Jack, you have to slow down. Twelve-hour work days are just plain crazy.'

Jack nodded. 'Yeah, I know. I've got another week off before I go back to work and I'm going to really think things through. The only thing I know for sure is that I can't go back to how I was.'

They chatted long into the night and Jack wasn't surprised when the topic of conversation turned to his personal life. To his credit, Jim hadn't mentioned the Christine situation again, but Jack knew he was itching to give him some advice.

'Young Cara's going to be disappointed to see you leave,' said Jim, a mischievous grin playing at his lips. 'And Moira's daughter down in the newsagent has had her eye on you as well.'

Shaking his head, Jack couldn't stop an exasperated smile.

'Come on Jack, you've got to get back out there. A good looking young bloke like you, a real gentleman, a nice car, plenty of money… you tell him love, what woman could refuse him?'

Gloria smiled from ear to ear. 'You know I adore you, Jack. If I was twenty years younger...,'

'Hey, come on now.' Jim put on an affronted look. 'I was just as good a catch in my day. Gloria had some stiff competition back then.'

Jack laughed. 'Haven't you heard? It's a real jungle out there these days. There's some statistic about your chances of finding love decreasing every year over the age of thirty-five.'

Shaking her head, Gloria gave Jack a playful poke on the arm. 'That's for women. Men, as ever, are in the box seat. Like Jim said, you're quite the catch.'

Putting an arm around Gloria, Jim pulled her close. Snuggling in, Gloria kissed him on the cheek.

'Find yourself a woman Jack, have some kids,' Jim said. 'That's what life is all about, you know. My life wouldn't be anything without this lady right here.'

'Mine either,' said Gloria. 'Even though he can be an old grump.'

'You kids make it all look so simple.'

'Come on Jack, you've shown me how determined you are,' said Jim. 'You don't want to end up one of those rich, lonely, old blokes, do you?'

Smiling at the two of them, Jack shook his head. 'No, I don't.'

Saying goodbye to Danny was bittersweet. Jack felt such a deep gratitude towards the child for helping him out of his self-imposed exile. He knew he would miss him. Although he couldn't control Danny's circumstances, he had made some provisions to help him wherever possible. Among these was a bank account in Jim and Gloria's custody to discretely provide the things that his mother couldn't or wouldn't give.

Danny helped Jack load up his car and took his role of checking every room to make sure nothing was left behind very seriously. Jack laughed when he came out holding a roll of paper towel and an unused bar of soap. 'That's all right, mate, we'll leave them as a present for the next people.'

Eventually the house was empty and Jack's car was packed ready for the journey home. Danny sat on the front steps with a sad look on his face. 'It's going to be so weird not to have you here anymore. It's just not the same.'

Jack sat down beside him. 'Yeah, I know, Dan. I'm going to miss you a lot. But we can still stay friends even though we won't see each other every day. I'll come and visit sometimes and remember how we talked about writing letters and emails? Moira said to go and see her if you want to use the internet.'

Looking a little bit happier, Danny nodded.

As they stood next to the car, Jack extended his hand. 'Thanks Danny, for everything. I know I couldn't have done it without you.'

Taking Jack's hand, Danny shook it firmly, the way Jack had shown him. 'That's okay, Jack. I really liked helping you. Thanks for all the things you gave me.'

'You're welcome.'

They stood there for a moment. Jack was just about to get into his car, when he noticed the tears in Danny's eyes. Blinking back his own tears, Jack leant down and hugged Danny tight; proud that this time he had initiated the embrace.

Jack didn't like to drive off and leave Danny upset, but he knew that he would bounce back, as kids did. Besides, once Danny went back to Jim's place and saw the surfboard Jack had bought him, he'd be too preoccupied with that to fret too much. Glad for the shield his sunglasses provided, Jack waved until Danny was just a speck in the distance.

Having fuelled up the night before, Jack navigated his way back out to the highway, then headed south, with a smile on his face. Sunset Point, and the Beach House, in particular, had given him back his life. Now he just had to live it.

Epilogue

$\mathcal{J}$ ack rubbed his eyes and yawned, before glancing at his watch. Ten o'clock already and he was nowhere near finished. He hadn't even changed out of his work clothes, yet. He'd only got as far as taking off his tie. It was still draped over the coffee table, where he'd dropped it two hours earlier. Jack's left hand was cramped from writing at an awkward angle and his shoulders tense from sitting in the same position on the couch for too long.

The late-night news came onto the TV and he used the remote to turn the volume up. It was weeks since he'd seen a news bulletin, the world could have stopped turning and he wouldn't know it. At forty-two he was still caught up in round-the-clock dedication to duty, surviving on minimal sleep and considering the five minutes he spent in the shower his 'me' time. Jack was thankful he'd recaptured the passion for his legal career and had no regrets about staying with Kendall and Masters, but the idea of another sabbatical was very appealing right now.

He could have said no to the case, everybody knew how busy Jack was, but the thought had never crossed his mind. It was for the Beach House and he had committed himself to doing whatever it took to win. Eager to help, Jim and Gloria had come to see him with a suitcase full of documents and plenty of anecdotal information. Preparing for the case long distance wasn't ideal, but it was the best he could do for now.

$\bullet \bullet \bullet \bullet \bullet$

Jim was holding court at an informal meeting of the Beach House committee. 'Well, the legal side of things is shipshape. I got all the documents to Jack and he's been working solidly on it ever since,' he said, taking a sip of beer.

Arthur Evans sniffed. 'That's all very well, Jim, but are we sure this bloke is even up to it? He's not even from Queensland. I told you Tania would have been happy to look the documents over. Legal secretaries have a wealth of knowledge, you know.'

Resisting the urge to roll his eyes, Jim mentally counted to five. He couldn't believe Arthur was still miffed about bypassing his daughter. 'I know, Arthur, but we needed an actual lawyer to get working on it. I can assure you Jack won't let us down.' He handed over a piece of paper. 'If you care to take a look at this feature article from *The Australian*, you will see that his credentials are impeccable. He's one of the best in the business.'

Arthur took the paper and glanced at it. 'Well, if he's so good, why is he willing to do this for free?' he asked, unwilling to concede completely.

'Because he's a genuinely decent bloke. Besides, we go right back and he owes me a favour.'

Gloria smiled to herself. She wasn't sure that six years constituted 'way back' or that Jim was the one owed a favour. Still, his ability to mobilise people was one of his special talents and, in this case, it was very helpful.

Moira Bell was much more direct. 'Give it up, Arthur. If there was ever a case of not looking a gift horse in the mouth, this is it. We'd never be able to afford this calibre of legal representation.'

Folding his arms, as if to say that he had done his best to instil some sense into the group and it hadn't worked, Arthur sighed. 'Fine, fine, let's get on with it,' he said.

The committee talked strategy for the next hour. When the meeting broke up at ten thirty, they were pleased with their progress. They made plans to re-convene the next week, and bid the Stewart's goodbye.

• • • • •

Tom and Kate McKay were both hard at work in their study. Now that their youngest child was at kindy, Kate had gone back to work full time and they both had things to be done by the next day.

'You know how unimpressed I was to get allocated that junior legal studies class?' Tom asked, as he typed into his laptop.

'Yes, you did mention it the odd hundred times,' Kate replied, busy at her own computer, which seemed to be in a go-slow phase as she tried to move a picture to a better position on the science worksheet she was creating.

Tom loaded some paper into the printer and turned it on. 'Okay, I know I was a pain about it, but I'm suddenly enthused about the whole idea. The Beach House case has become our term project. We're going to have a mock trial, the works.'

'Well, you know I'd never say I told you so, but I did mention that it could turn out all right.'

'Just like you having to teach grade seven instead of grade three, like you hoped?'

'Yes, well, that was completely different, of course, but all right, I've found a silver lining as well.'

Tom grinned as he hit print.

'Lose the smug smile or I won't tell you.'

'Yes, you will, you always do.'

Kate stuck her tongue out, but answered anyway. 'We're doing petitions. We found a random story in the paper and decided to create a petition about it.'

'Random hey?' Tom raised his eyebrows.

'Well, I did manage to lean the class towards a story concerning a certain beach house. I pointed out that our own school is on a piece of prime Gold Coast real estate and we wouldn't like it if someone tried to make us move.'

Tom leaned back in his chair and stretched. 'I still can't believe we both stayed there. What if we'd met back then, if we'd actually been there at the same time?'

'I don't know. I was having a major confidence crisis, didn't have a clue what to do with my life and was studying from dawn 'til dusk for subjects that I hated. I probably wouldn't have noticed you.'

'Thanks.' Tom feigned a hurt expression.

Kate threw a paper aeroplane at him. 'Come on, your brothers have told me what your taste in women used to be like. You wouldn't have noticed me either, I wasn't high-maintenance enough.'

'Yes, well, dating so many of the wrong women was character building. Besides I needed to experience what I didn't want so I could really know what I did want,' Tom said, with a grin.

Kate smiled back. 'Well, I'm glad you took your time. It's a bit like my career – I had to hate law, IT and business to be forced to turn in another direction.'

'I guess I just can't imagine you as anything other than a teacher. You're a natural.'

'A natural who took a while to find her vocation. Besides, if I hadn't wasted a year in various inappropriate degrees I never would have gone to the beach house and reconnected with Jane.'

Tom shook his head. 'You guys are besties. I can't imagine you not getting along.'

'Trust me, we didn't.'

'I *really* hope they win the case. How ironic would it be that we are finally taking the kids there this year and it might be gone?'

'They have to win. People power can still move mountains you know.'

'I know. We have to keep believing that.'

• • • • •

A flash of light woke Jack just before midnight. Blinking in the sudden glare, he was immediately aware of the crick in his neck. Ouch, he thought, massaging it with one hand. I can't believe I nodded off before I finished those last ten pages.

'Sorry to wake you sleepyhead, but it was just the sweetest photo. I couldn't resist.'

Jack managed a weary smile for his wife, Erin. She looked as exhausted as he felt, with her hair in a messy ponytail and dark circles beneath her eyes. But she smiled in return and, as always, it touched his heart.

Looking down, Jack gazed at their newborn daughter, Charlotte, who was sleeping on his chest. He knew he looked very rough, but this little angel was enough to transform any photo. 'I can't believe I used to voluntarily keep these kind of hours,' he said, gathering the papers into a pile with his spare hand.

Erin sat down next to him, yawned and rested her head on his shoulder. 'Neither can I. Maybe it was to prepare you for parenthood.'

Jack laughed. 'Yeah, maybe. You think if we just stay still and quiet we can all get a full night's sleep?' he said, gently stroking Charlotte's head with his thumb.

'Yeah, that's going to happen. I think we were spoilt just having one the first time round.'

'Oh, yeah, twins are a whole new reality.'

'We just need to remember that this phase of extreme sleep

deprivation doesn't last forever.'

'No, it just seems like it.'

They both smiled wearily.

'It doesn't matter how tired we are, I wouldn't swap this for anything you know,' Jack said, with a huge yawn.

Erin took his hand. 'I know. Besides, your leave starts next week and Edna said she'll come in every day until then.'

'I think she would have been delighted with anyone I married, but she absolutely adores you.'

'She's lovely,' Erin said sleepily. 'I'm so glad she's not one of those jealous types who feel threatened by the wife of the men they've looked after for so long.'

Jack smiled. 'Me too, good cleaning ladies are hard to find.'

The three of them dozed on the couch for the next hour, until the sound of their other daughter, Chloe, waking for her one a.m. feed saw them stumbling back to their room.

• • • • •

Gloria made herself and Jim a hot Milo. 'I don't doubt for a second Jack can do this, but I'm a bit concerned he's got too much on his plate,' she said, as she set the cups down on the kitchen table. 'You saw how tired they looked when we were there. I can't imagine how hectic things must be for them.'

'He'll do it. If he can go from a surf novice to a working lifeguard in nine weeks, he can juggle this and a couple of babies.'

Gloria didn't bother trying to explain that modern fathers were much more at the coalface of baby care than men of Jim's generation had been. Or that a "couple" of babies were more work than he could possibly imagine. Instead, she made a decision.

'I'm going to ring Erin tomorrow and offer to go and stay for a few days. I'll do all I can to help.'

'Help?' Jim said. 'But what about the committee?'

'You can keep that ticking over. We have to be practical. If we want Jack to do this as well as he can, then we need to lighten his load. I'll help with the babies, clean, run errands whatever they need.'

Jim rubbed his chin thoughtfully. 'You're a good woman, Love.

All right, you go and I'll see to things this end. We can't let that place go, we just can't.'

Gloria took a sip of Milo and nodded. 'I know.'

• • • • •

Dr Jill Ryan put a cup of tea in front of her colleague Jane Connelly and sat down at the table in the tearoom at the Royal Brisbane Hospital. It was Friday afternoon and they were both weary. 'How is little Mikael in room five going? He had me worried for a while there.'

Jane accepted the tea with a smile. 'He's doing really well now and so is mum. Don't worry, delivering babies does get easier with experience.'

'That's good to know. I felt like I was way out of my depth in there today and you had it all under control. You guys in maternity are amazing.'

'Come on, it's only the second week in your rotation. I've been doing this for ten years now.'

'Did being a midwife make you freak out when you had your daughter? I mean, knowing what could go wrong?'

'I guess it did a bit. But I also knew that stats were on my side, there's only a small number that don't go to plan.' Jane never liked to dwell on the heartache that had preceded conceiving and finally carrying to term a healthy baby and hadn't given up hope that she could have another.

'True enough. My sister Liz thought your pre-natal class was excellent, by the way. She really got a lot out of it.'

'She's lovely, your mother must be proud to have such great daughters.'

'She got lucky.' Jill grinned.

Jane took a mouthful of tea. 'Ah, that's really good. Only another two hours to go.'

'Lucky you, I'm on call tonight.'

'You should be fine. It's pretty quiet in here today. Only two have come in so far this afternoon.'

Jill opened the paper and looked at it briefly. 'I wonder how the Beach House is going? They've been a bit quiet about it lately.'

'Well, like any story, people lose interest after a while. The court case isn't for a few weeks yet, there's probably only so much they can say, at the moment.'

Resting her chin in her hand, Jill gazed out the window. 'I always thought I'd spend my honeymoon there, if I ever get married, that is.'

'Plenty of time for that, your age still starts with a two, remember?'

'Yeah, I know, and to be honest, I'm really in no rush. Did you and your cousin ever go back?'

Jane shook her head. 'Not together. Rick and I went there with his family when we got engaged and we took Amber there two years ago. I think Kate went with some other friends at some point too. How about your family?'

'Yeah, we went one more time together and we've all been back with other people at various times. I couldn't imagine it not being there.'

'No, I can't either.'

• • • • •

With Gloria, Edna and Erin's mother in residence at his house, Jack managed to get to Sydney for the day to do some research and meet with his cousin, Julia. She was also a solicitor and they often consulted each other about challenging legal situations.

'You could have worn jeans, you know,' Julia said, eying Jack's suit, as they sat in her office, working through some of the more tedious details of the case.

'In this place?' Jack said. 'As it is, I don't think your receptionist believes that I'm legit, she wouldn't have let me in the front door in jeans. Besides, you drummed into me all those years ago, how important it is to look the part. I didn't want you to think I'd lowered my standards.'

Julia laughed. 'Yeah, like that will ever happen. I'm just glad you married someone who shares my vision for your wardrobe.'

'Hey, I chose this tie myself you know.'

'Not bad,' Julia said. Glancing out the window, she noticed a man wearing shorts and a polo shirt walking towards the building. It was a stark contrast to the wall-to-wall suits that filled Martin Place. Besides

435

that, it was a cool day and everybody else was dressed warmly. 'I think your friend may have arrived,' she said.

By the time Jack emerged from the lift, Jim was pacing the foyer. Jack smiled to himself. It was the first time he'd seen Jim out of his depth and unsure of his surroundings. Jim was in Sydney overnight to see his nephew play in a rugby league game and Gloria had arranged for them to meet for lunch.

Jim was relieved to see Jack walking towards him. He wasn't nervous, exactly, but these big buildings and all these people hurrying everywhere, well, it just wasn't his scene. He had never seen Jack in full lawyer mode before, dressed in a dark suit, impeccably groomed and carrying a briefcase. Jim had always had complete confidence in his friend, but knowing Jack looked the part gave him even more reassurance that things would be all right.

They had a counter lunch in a nearby pub. 'Should we be worried that they have got three lawyers on their case?' Jim asked, as he tucked into his steak. 'Mr Walton made a point of telling us that.'

'No, it just means they've got plenty of money to throw at it.'

'As opposed to the grand sum that we're spending?'

Jack grinned. 'You can pay for lunch, if you like.'

'How is it going, really? Do you think we've got a show?'

'I wouldn't be here if I didn't think we had a show. I'm not sure I like the way it's being pitted as a David and Goliath battle, though.'

'But it is David and Goliath, isn't it? The big boys versus the small towners.'

'Yes, that's true enough. But I'm not one for an aggressive approach, so don't be concerned when I don't go in with all guns blazing.'

'You're our only hope Jack we have to trust you. If you want to tap dance on the roof of the court house, we'll cop it.'

'I'm no tap dog, but I'm glad to know you're behind me, in any event.'

Jim laughed, but then grew serious. 'I know it's a lot of pressure on you,' he said.

'It's par for the course. Gloria has been a Godsend, by the way. I feel like I'm living in a serviced apartment, with a maid thrown in.'

'Ah, you know Gloria, she's a very practical woman. Besides, she's crazy about Erin, we both are. She's a great girl.'

'You make me sound like a cradle snatcher when you say girl. She's only two years younger than I am.'

'Okay, a great woman then. She rescued you from your Robinson Crusoe existence and that's all that matters.'

Jack held up his glass. 'I'll drink to that.'

Gloria and Erin sat on the two recliners, each holding a sleeping baby.

'I can't thank you enough for this Gloria. Between you and Edna and Mum, I almost feel like I'm on holidays.'

'No thanks necessary, I'm loving it. My grandkids are all past the baby stage and I miss it. Besides, we know what a sacrifice this whole thing has been for you and Jack. The timing is awful for you but we really do need him.'

'There's no way he wouldn't have done it. Besides, we're managing and at least he's off work now. If these two hadn't decided to come three weeks early it wouldn't have been quite so hectic.'

'Ah, that's babies for you. I wonder if Jim managed to find his way into the city all right from the airport. He'd never admit it but he gets a bit nervous in crowds.'

'Well, we didn't get any phone calls or text messages, so I'm guessing they must have found each other and are probably having a gossipy lunch.'

'I'm sure you're right.'

'I listened in when Jessica did the interview and I can't believe that they didn't get on, to start with,' Erin said, adjusting the chair to a more comfortable position.

Gloria rolled her eyes. 'Well, we know whose fault that was. Honestly, the way Jim spoke about Jack, I imagined some pasty-faced, pretentious bloke who didn't know when he should just give up. Imagine my surprise when I actually met Jack and discovered what a charming, clever man he was. Funnily enough, Jim also never mentioned how good looking he was.'

'Well, I suppose it's the kind of thing a woman would notice more than a man. And, even if he did notice, he wouldn't admit it.'

Gloria nodded. 'We still talk about what a good time we had at your wedding. Jim was honoured to give that speech you know.'

'Jack was thrilled that he did it. He's really got the gift of the gab.'

'That he has.'

• • • • •

Emma Newman finally managed to get to the computer at ten p.m. Ben's current obsession was on-line chess and he would spend day and night playing it if she didn't have some rules in place. Logging onto her email account, she found another message from Clare entitled "Beach House Update."

It read: '….it all seems to be going okay at the moment. The lawyer that the committee has got has a lot of pressure on him, but I'm sure he'll do fine. I thought he looked familiar and then I remembered his legal firm came to one of our work/life balance seminars. He was a nice guy. I was just thinking we never got around to having our reunion, did we? Peter emailed me a couple of weeks ago and mentioned he got a Christmas card from Ron last year. I guess it's one of those things, life gets away and you never get around to it…. But we really should make the effort, don't you think??'

Emma read the rest of the message, smiling as Clare bounced from one topic to another. She had been over to visit Emma in Auckland three times in the years since their Beach House Christmas and loved to be kept informed about Emma's husband Nick, her five-year-old daughter Martha and, of course, Ben and Lucy. Emma was kept equally entertained about Clare's work as a motivational psychologist in the workplace and her dramatic love life, that always seemed to end in tears.

Emma checked through her other emails and laughed at one Peter had forwarded her about two blind pilots. She'd never forgotten his kindness in paying her way back to New Zealand. Her family had been overjoyed to have her home and she wondered why she had ever cut off contact the way she had. Her parents had tried to repay Peter the cost of the tickets, but he wouldn't let them.

A reunion at the Beach House would be great, or even in Sydney – just so they could all see each other again.

• • • • •

Liam walked into Budding Blooms at Toowong, glad he made it before closing time. He'd been out at UQ doing guest lectures most of the day and decided to pop in for a visit, while he was in the neighbourhood. *This really is a very inviting shop,* he thought, *and I know nothing about flowers, except that women love them.*

Simone looked up from the arrangement she was working on and smiled broadly, happy, as always, to see him. 'Mr Archer, you've come to visit me again?'

'Well, it was either come here or face the nightmare that is the M1 during peak hour.' Liam smiled broadly. 'Besides, I had to come and let you know that your bouquet worked a treat.'

Simone put the arrangement down and came around to hug him. 'I knew she'd say yes! That's fantastic news, I'm really thrilled.'

'Yeah, me too. I always thought I'd get married again one day. I didn't realise it would take me so long, though.'

Shrugging, Simone smiled. 'Some things just happen when they're supposed to happen Liam and you've certainly had some adventures in the meantime.'

Liam picked up a discarded carnation from the counter and twirled it in his hands. 'So, what about you Ms Budding Blooms? Do you think you'll ever take the plunge again?'

Simone went back to her arrangement. 'To be honest, Liam, I'm not that fussed. Don't get me wrong, if somebody very special came along and swept me off my feet I'd be delighted, but, if not, then I'm very happy with my life now. Owning and running the two shops and becoming a grandmother soon really is enough to keep me content.'

'Good for you, although, as I keep telling you, I think Larry in the newsagent is pretty smitten.'

'Smitten my foot, he's just looking for someone to keep house and cook for him.'

They looked at each other and laughed, the bond they'd formed so many years ago still very much in place.

Still grinning, Liam said, 'Don't ever tell Matt, but I had a crush on you for a while there.'

Simone grinned in return. 'Oh Liam, you flatter me sometimes. I can't imagine why; I was such a mess when we first met.'

'Well, to be honest it didn't start until the Hamilton Island trip for

Matt's twenty-first. Remember how we did that karaoke duet?'

'Yes, of course I remember. I was so nervous that I held your hand while we sang. It was a lovely holiday.'

'Yeah, we all had a blast. You really seemed to have found yourself again and when you insisted that I call you Simone instead of Mrs Ryan I just started seeing you in a whole new light. I don't know if you noticed, but after that I started dropping into your house a lot more.'

'You know, Liam, I was so caught up in preparing to open the shop that you could have moved in and I wouldn't have noticed.'

'I'm just glad you never knew, I thought I was being pretty transparent sometimes.'

'Well, if we're being completely honest here, there were a few times over the years when I had the passing thought that if only I was ten years younger or you were ten years older…'

Liam blushed. 'Now you're flattering me. Maybe if we lived in Hollywood it might have worked.'

'Yes, it might. But now you have the lovely Hayley and I have my friend Larry to keep me on my toes.'

They both laughed at that.

'I do love you dearly, Liam, you've been a very good friend to me.'

'As you have to me.'

'Don't worry, I won't ever tell Matthew. As open minded as he proclaims himself to be, the idea that you could have ended up as his stepfather would definitely freak him out.'

Liam's eyes widened. 'You know, I hadn't even thought of that angle.'

'Oh, make sure you get a copy of *The Reviewer* on Thursday,' Simone said, 'Our story is in this edition.'

'Do you reckon they did us justice?' Liam asked.

'Let's hope so.'

• • • • •

Jim rang a week before the trial, to check the state of play. Jack was in the midst of burping Chloe, and eighteen-month-old Josh had decided it would be fun to attach himself to Dad's ankle as he walked around the lounge room.

'Hope I didn't get you at a bad time,' said Jim.

Jack let it pass. After all, in a house full of small children there weren't too many moments that weren't chaotic. 'No, I can talk a minute,' he said, swapping Chloe to the other shoulder, so he could hold the phone better.

'Nothing last minute we should know about?' Jim asked. 'No dirty tricks from the other side?'

Jack smiled, thinking to himself that Jim had been watching too much TV. 'No, they seem to be playing a clean game so far,' he said, glancing into his study at the pile of papers that hadn't been touched for two days. Theoretically, being at home he should have more time to work on it, but somehow it wasn't happening that way. In truth, he wasn't quite sure how he was going to get everything finished in time, but that wasn't something to burden Jim with.

'You don't mind that it has been moved to Brisbane?'

'No, it makes it easier, cuts travel time back,' Jack said, wincing in pain, as he stepped on some Lego. Looking down, he hoped Josh wouldn't notice that he had just crushed the car he'd built him that morning.

'We've got a good contingent going down by bus. Don't worry, they're all behind you.'

Jack was momentarily distracted by a trickle of baby vomit running down his arm. 'Yes, I know,' he said, mopping up the best he could.

'All right then. Glad to hear we're all shipshape.'

'Yes indeed, don't worry about a thing,' Jack said, as he sat down on the couch and closed his eyes.

im had never known someone as outwardly calm as Jack Nolan. He felt like a cat on a hot tin roof as they sat in the cool, newly-refurbished courtroom and he was just a spectator. Jack was up at that desk by himself, having left home at the crack of dawn, after a broken night's sleep, *and* he had the huge pressure of a town's expectations riding on his shoulders. Yet, there he was, dressed to the nines, a folder of documents in front of him and a serene expression on his face. The team of lawyers at the other table were talking in low voices, writing notes and shuffling documents between themselves. Max Walton sat with them, looking composed and confident. If they were trying to intimidate their opponent, however, it wasn't working.

Having never been inside a courtroom before, Jim followed the rest of the spectators when the judge entered and they rose to their feet. He was too keyed up to listen properly as the case details were formally announced and everybody was seated again. But he was surprised when Jack stood and asked permission to approach the bench. Jim watched keenly as a seemingly involved conversation took place in muted tones. That didn't seem right so early in proceedings.

He nudged Gloria. 'I wonder what's going on?' he whispered. 'Doesn't the jury have to come in first?'

Gloria shrugged. 'I'm sure they know what they're doing,' she whispered back.

The judge's voice came over the microphone. 'Mr Evert, could you approach the bench please.'

Max's head lawyer did as requested and a further muted discussion took place at the front of the room.

Finally, the judge rapped his gavel and spoke again. 'I'm sorry to inconvenience you ladies and gentlemen, but it has become necessary to have a conference with the legal team in an outside office. We will reconvene at ten thirty.'

The following hour dragged on as the spectators in the gallery talked between themselves. Someone had a pack of cards and a quiet poker game got underway. A few of the women had brought their knitting and worked away industriously, seemingly unperturbed by the delay. Jim and Gloria went for a walk around the grounds to while away some time.

The judge and the lawyers returned to the courtroom at the appointed time. Once again everybody rose and sat, eager for things to get underway. Judge Mark Mason rapped his gavel. 'In this matter of Sunset Point versus Max Walton, the trial is hereby aborted.'

The low hum of conversation that filled the room was hushed by a further rap of the judge's gavel. 'Mr Nolan has brought evidence to our attention that nullifies the validity of this claim, and counsel for Mr Walton have hereby agreed it is in their best interest to withdraw their action.'

The Sunset Point contingent erupted into applause and Jim and Gloria were the first to reach Jack, as he stood at the desk, packing his briefcase. Jack was not surprised to get a warm hug from Gloria, but he was astounded to get one from Jim.

'You're a bloody marvel, Jack!' he said, his eyes suspiciously bright.

'I wouldn't say a marvel,' Jack said, with a smile. 'Just determined, like you said.'

Jessica finally managed to track Jack down for an interview about an hour later. Seating herself opposite him, in a café near the law courts, she stared at him, as he tucked into eggs on toast.

Glancing over, Jack paused, his fork halfway to his mouth. 'Sorry,' he said. 'I'm starving. I missed breakfast this morning.'

'Oh, no, please, go right ahead. I'm sorry for being rude, I just can't believe this whole thing could all be over so fast.'

Laying down his cutlery, Jack patted his mouth with a napkin. 'That's the thing about the law. It can be complex and it can be simple.'

'But what happened, exactly?'

'I always had my doubts about that extraordinary circumstances clause. The language of it was quite different to the rest of the document and it just didn't seem to fit with the vision of James McMaster.'

'So, there was fraud?'

'As it turned out, yes, there was. Luckily, I like to know the details, check all the facts, assume nothing and prove everything.'

'But you didn't tell anyone what you suspected?'

'No, I couldn't until I could prove it. I had the documents analysed carefully and there was definitely tampering, although professionally done. Plus, they kept their archived copies on microfiche in an off-site storage facility, so once I checked the original, I just had to track down the solicitor who drew it up. Unfortunately, he was dead, so I had to find the associate who witnessed it.'

'Was he hard to find?'

'I'll say, that's why it took me until now to present to the judge. This guy was living in San Francisco under a different name, but fortunately he was happy to help us out.'

'Why the name change? Is *he* running from the law or something?'

'Uh, no let's just say it was a … lifestyle change.'

Jessica nodded knowingly. 'Oh, I see. So, are you saying Mr Walton is crooked? Did he commit fraud just so his deal could go through?'

'No, not at all. I know everybody would love him to be the bad guy, but he knew nothing about it. One of the regional councillors has got a mate who works in real estate. After Max made some enquiries about the house, it seems they put their heads together and hatched a plan that would benefit both of them.'

'Which councillor?' Jessica asked excitedly.

'They mayor will be holding a press conference about it tomorrow.'

'Tomorrow?' Jessica wailed. 'I thought you'd give me the scoop!'

'The press conference is at eleven. Call me at ten and I'll give you some major clues.'

'All right, if that's the best you can do.'

Jack nodded. 'Yep, it is.' He took a mouthful of coffee. 'To be honest, I think they're all a bit miffed I robbed them of a big showdown.'

'Would you have won?'

'I think so.'

'But it's much simpler this way, right?'

'Definitely.' Jack eyed Jessica closely. 'I guess you must be a bit disappointed, though?'

'Huh?'

'Well, you were hoping that reporting on this trial would be your big break, right?'

'Why do you say that?'

'I could sense it the first time you spoke to me to arrange the interview. I got the feeling you were just going through the motions to keep your editor happy.'

Jessica's eyes widened. 'I guess that's why they pay you the big bucks, hey?' she said. 'All right, I'll admit my eyes were on the bigger prize in the beginning. I'll even admit I took some shortcuts when I chose who to interview.'

'The married couple?' Jack guessed.

'Yeah, it saved me heaps of time and I'd already interviewed Simone once before, so that was a no brainer too.' She shrugged. 'However, once I met all you guys and heard your stories I changed my mind. Although I hate it when Grant is right, he *was* right. The human-interest component was more important than the big headline.'

'Well, I'm glad you're not too disappointed.'

'No, not at all. How about you, though? You had to put in all that work and preparation for one short morning in court.'

'It doesn't bother me in the slightest. In fact, this would have been my first trial in almost two years. Most of my work these days is as a mediation consultant to keep things out of the court system.'

'Wow, really? What prompted the change?'

'Well, it kind of found me, really. I was mistakenly referred a case involving an unusual custody dispute and rather than pass it on, I decided to see if I could resolve it myself.'

'Why was it unusual?'

'A couple were killed in an accident and their will clearly stated that custody of their infant son should go to a close friend of theirs. The man's parents were contesting it.'

'That must have been tricky.'

'Yeah, it was. But we worked it out. Their motivation was completely understandable, they were the child's blood relatives, after all. But they eventually came to realise that the woman who was granted custody loved the little boy as much as they did and was better equipped to raise him, given their advanced ages.'

'And it's all still going well now?'

'Yeah, really well.'

'Do you always keep track of your clients after the case is over?'

'Well, this was a special case. I married her.'

Jessica's mouth dropped open. 'Oh, that was Erin! So, let me get this right – the baby from the custody case is your oldest? Sam, right?'

'Yep, that's right, he's four now.'

'Four kids under five, that must be a challenge.'

Jack smiled wearily. 'It can be. We didn't foresee having twins, of course, but we aren't complaining.'

Jessica took a sip of her cappuccino. 'Well, you wanted a different life and now you've got one. No regrets?'

'Not one.'

*J*essica was amazed that almost everybody made it to the victory party. The only one who couldn't get there was Chris, as he was deployed on an overseas naval mission. The others had all responded eagerly to her VIP invitations. Considering that six weeks was fairly short notice, it was no mean feat.

She had left most of the organisational details to Gloria, who had gone above and beyond what Jessica had originally envisaged as a simple get together, with a few of the guys manning the barbeque and the usual chips, dips and vegetable platters. The furniture had been rearranged to accommodate the crowd and several tables of beautifully presented canapés and other snacks were located strategically around the lounge room. Food for the evening meal was stacked in the fridge ready to be heated. Drink eskies were easily accessible. Blue and gold streamers and balloons decorated the house tastefully.

Jessica had arrived early, so she was on hand to welcome each party as they arrived. Now, an hour later, it was hard to believe that many of them had never met before as they all stood talking and laughing and various children ran around the grounds. The Beach House committee were there too and a few other invited guests.

Matt and Tom introduced themselves, each looking at the other closely. 'Your face is familiar,' said Matt. 'You didn't go to school at Terrace, did you?'

Tom shook his head. 'No, but I've seen you around somewhere. How about QUT between ninety-two and ninety-five?'

'No, I went to UQ,' Matt said, as he selected a sandwich off the table. 'You didn't do the Storey Bridge climb about three months ago? I remember a tall guy.'

'No, it wasn't me, but I would like to do it sometime. You're not a teacher too, are you?'

Matt shook his head. 'This is going to really bug us, isn't it?'

'I reckon.'

They were still puzzling it out when Jessica came over to get something to eat. 'Hey Tom, sorry, I had to move your surfboard. It's around the other side of the veranda.'

'No worries,' said Tom.

Jessica piled her plate with sandwiches. 'Enjoy the party guys, I'll chat to you later.'

'Ah,' said Matt, with a victorious grin. 'I've seen you down at Snapper Rocks.'

Tom nodded. 'Yeah, that's it. Small world, hey?'

'I still feel like a bit of a newcomer down that end, but you look like you know those waves pretty intimately.'

'I grew up there and there's nothing quite like your home break.'

'Well, I grew up in Brisbane so I can't claim a home break, but I'd like to think I've officially adopted Snapper's.'

'Yeah, plenty of waves down there for everyone, you're in.'

'Thanks.' Matt grinned.

Tom looked longingly out towards the ocean. 'I'm dying to get out here, look at those waves today.'

'I'm there, mate,' Matt replied. 'But we might have to mingle a while longer before we make the break.'

Clare and Emma were chatting to Kate and Jane. Jessica had changed names and some details in her stories, but they had placed each other easily enough.

'You're the cousins,' said Clare.

Kate and Jane exchanged a surprised look. 'How did you know?' Jane asked.

'I'm a psychologist, I know everything,' Clare replied, with a grin. 'Besides, when I was getting a drink earlier, I heard you talking about how peaceful it was to study here.'

Emma smiled at Kate. 'You became a teacher in the end, I understand? I was eavesdropping by the punchbowl as well,' she said.

Kate nodded. 'I did. I passed the dreaded exams I was studying for and then took some time off to work out what I wanted to do. It didn't take me too long to realise it wasn't criminal psychology.' She took a sip of punch and shrugged. 'I had four jobs in two years, none of which I was really happy with. Then I got involved in a volunteer charity program teaching disadvantaged kids to read. I loved it and couldn't work out why I hadn't chosen primary teaching in the first place.'

'As trite as it sounds, you can't put an old head on young shoulders,' Clare said. 'Sometimes things just don't occur to you until you're at the right maturity level. We're all guilty of beating ourselves up about choices we made when we didn't have enough life experience to know any better.' Realising how she sounded, she made a face. 'Sorry, end of lecture.'

'No that's okay,' Kate said. 'You're right, I spent ages wondering why I wasted so much time, but then realised that life is full of detours.'

'That's it, in a nutshell. So, you're married to the other teacher? "Jason"?' she said, using her fingers to indicate inverted commas.

'Yes. Jason from Maroochydore was really Tom from Coolangatta. We both got drafted onto a boring committee about educational reform that nobody wanted to be on, and the rest is history.'

Danny arrived as soon as he finished surf patrol. Although they kept in contact via regular emails, text messages and phone calls, the last time Jack and Danny had seen each other was six months ago. Danny was fifteen now and, after a major growth spurt, was almost a head taller than Jack. They embraced warmly, each delighted to see the other and spent the next five minutes catching up on general news.

'How's school?' asked Jack.

'It's good. I love rowing, I'm in the swimming team and we get to do a surfing elective for PE next term. It's a really great school.'

'Sounds like it. How about your non-sporting progress?'

Danny made a face. 'It's okay. I know I'm not smart enough to be a lawyer, but I'd like to be a fireman and a part-time lifeguard.'

'Dan, you're smarter than you think and if you need anything you just ask, okay? I'll help you do whatever you want to.'

'Okay, thanks Jack.' Danny nodded, not sure how to express his gratitude for all he knew Jack had done for him. St Joseph's in Rosethorn was renowned for its PE program. So excited to be accepted there, Danny had never questioned Jim's vague explanation about some previously unheard of scholarship. It was only when he accidentally saw the letter with Jack's name and address that Danny realised who really paid his school fees. He'd never disclosed that he knew, though.

'How about an iPhone?' Danny asked.

Jack shook his head. 'Dream on, kid. I'm not that much of a soft touch. Did you patrol today?'

'Yeah, I did. Are you still patrolling? You haven't let all my hard work go to waste?'

'Yes, I'm keeping my hand in.'

'I can't believe you patrol at Bondi.'

'The club is North Bondi, but it's the same beach. Tell you what, it's a bit different to here. Lots more action.'

'Sounds awesome.'

'It can be. It can be a bit scary, too.

'You still don't like the big waves, do you?'

'No, not really. But I'm a work in progress. It's like your schoolwork, you have to keep chipping away.'

Danny's eyes glazed over slightly. 'Yeah, I know. Where are Sam and Josh?'

'There's a bit of a kids club out on the veranda. Go and say hello, they'll be excited to see you.'

Simone and Lillian were discussing the lovely centrepiece on the table. They had placed each other and gossiped like everybody else, trying to fill the gaps. Simone revealed that she had designed and made the centrepiece especially for the occasion.

'Oh, so you're a florist?' asked Lillian.

Simone smiled. 'Yes, I am and I love it,' she said.

'And you really learnt to surf?' Lillian asked. 'I couldn't imagine doing that.'

'Oh yes, that's all true. I still go out on the board now and then when my son, Matthew, is around to supervise.'

'Well, you're braver than me. Did he become a writer?'

'You did read the stories thoroughly. Yes, he's the deputy editor of a travel magazine, actually, and he's writing a novel.' Simone took a moment to reposition the centrepiece so it looked its best. 'What about Bob, who was looking for his daughter?' she asked.

'Oh, that's Ron. Yes, he found her,' said Lillian, thrilled that she knew the details. 'She wasn't especially keen to reconnect at first, but after a while she came around. I think she was under the impression that he had abandoned her and her mother.' Lillian took another sip of her tea. 'Anyway, they're close enough now and that's all that matters. He's still a bachelor but he has four grandchildren.'

'Oh, lovely. How about you? Is your son married?'

'Yes, and we have two granddaughters. Now Peter is semi-retired, we spend a lot of time with them. How about you, are you a grandmother yet?'

'Well, my daughter Elizabeth is expecting her first in a couple of months. For someone who had her own children very young I've had to wait a while for the next generation, so I'm very excited. My other daughter Jill is concentrating on her medical career for the moment. Alas, Matthew shows no signs of settling down.' Simone sighed and gave a *what can you do?* gesture with her hands. Ironically, she hadn't noticed Matt and Clare's meeting over the punchbowl, nor did she see them talking animatedly in the corner now.

Erin was talking to Elizabeth and Jill. 'Isn't that guy Liam The Weatherman from *Kids News?*' she asked, motioning to where Liam was talking to Peter and Ron. Although he wore a variety of different costumes on the show, Erin was sure it was him.

Elizabeth and Jill laughed. 'Yes, that's him,' Jill said.

'I take it he doesn't really live in a tree house so he can be closer to the clouds?'

Elizabeth shook her head. 'No. He and our brother shared a place for a while that could have been classified as a cave, but he's getting a bit more respectable in his old age.'

'So, you're a fan of *Kids News?*' Jill asked. 'Liam isn't too convinced that it has a very big viewing audience. I think he wants to be mobbed at the supermarket or something.'

Erin laughed. 'It's a nice little show. Even though my kids are a bit young, my nieces and nephews love it. If Liam made an appearance at a day-care centre or a primary school, there would probably be mayhem.'

'I'll suggest it to him,' Elizabeth said. 'He's game enough to try just about anything.'

'And his name is really Liam? It's not a stage name?' Erin glanced over at him again.

'Yes, he really is Liam,' said Jill.

'It was a bit cloak and dagger with all the name changes in the stories, wasn't it? Jack can't really see himself as Hamish.'

'Well, our brother, Matt/Zac, often refers to us and Hannah and

Ellen and, to be honest, a lot of our friends had no clue the story was about our family,' Elizabeth replied.

'She did a good job then. I think it's great that she managed to use what were really personal stories in an inspiring kind of way, but still protected everybody's privacy.'

'Well, if there's a movie or a mini-series made, I want a say in who gets to play me,' said Jill.

Elizabeth raised an eyebrow. 'Yeah, I'm sure all the Hollywood heavyweights will be clamouring for the role.'

Smiling sarcastically at her sister, Jill turned to Erin. 'Come and I'll introduce you to Liam. He'll be so excited somebody recognised him.'

Jim and Gloria's fourteen-year-old granddaughter, Rachel, had been give the job of official photographer. Determined that everybody would be in at least a few snaps, she had no qualms about instructing various people to stand together and pose. Seeing Jack and Clare walking in the direction of the main food table at the same time, she grabbed each of them by the arm and had them stand next to the lavish mud cake that Gloria had made and decorated especially for the occasion.

'Gran is way proud of this cake,' she said, with a grin that showed the braces on her teeth. 'I'm trying to get it in as many pictures as I can.'

Jack and Clare posed obligingly and then officially introduced themselves, even though they had each worked out who the other was.

'I don't know if you remember me,' Clare said, as she selected a dainty cucumber sandwich from the table.

Picking up a mini quiche, Jack nodded. 'Oh, yes I do,' he replied in a mock stern tone. 'You made me do the chicken dance at that workplace team-building day my firm went to, even though I clearly didn't want to.'

'Yeah, well we make everyone do it and you have to admit it was fun once you got going.'

'I suppose it wasn't so bad. I'm surprised you do remember me, you must see thousands of people doing the work you do.'

'Well, I'm good with faces and I remember your firm in particular because you were the first group we did with our new program. We weren't really sure what we were doing the first few times,' she said. 'I realised that you were the lawyer for all this when I saw your picture in the paper, but I had no idea that you were Hamish until today.'

Jack laughed. 'I didn't realise I was Hamish until I got a fair way into the story – what with him living in Perth and driving a Commodore, it didn't sound much like me.'

'So, Jack, you have every right to tell me to mind my own business, but the psychologist in me can't help but wonder if you managed to resolve all that stuff with your ex.'

Taking his last bite of quiche, Jack took his time chewing, scrutinising Clare as he did so.

Embarrassed, Clare covered her face with her hands. 'Sorry, I shouldn't have asked that. I don't have an off switch, sometimes.'

'No, it's all right,' said Jack. 'Funnily enough, I ran into her on the beach when I was patrolling one weekend. She was there visiting her brother.'

Clare nodded, knowing that it was just as much the busybody in her as the psychologist that wanted to find out the details.

'Long story short we, had a coffee and caught up. Turned out she had met someone not long after she moved to Queensland. They had a whirlwind romance, got married on a whim in Fiji and had a couple of kids soon after.'

Clare sang a few lines from the Alanis Morrisette song *Isn't It Ironic?*

'Yeah, tell me about it,' said Jack, rolling his eyes. 'Anyway, the scales fell from my eyes, as they say. I was sitting there thinking, who is this woman? And why did I waste so many years pining after her?'

Clare's eyes widened. 'Oh, interesting.'

Exhaling, Jack gazed at the floor for a moment. 'That sounds a bit harsh, I guess. It was probably more that she'd changed and I'd changed and so much time had passed. But, it certainly killed any last lingering doubt that we were destined to be together.'

'Aren't you glad you did see her and finished that chapter properly?'

'Yeah, definitely. In fact, I met my wife about a month later and I've often wondered about the timing of it all.'

'Well, you know what they say about one door closing and another one opening?'

'Yep, I do. You know, I really did love Christine when we were together but, clearly, we just weren't meant to be. There was someone else out there for both of us.'

'Ah, now that's the kind of case history that keeps us mental health professionals inspired.'

Liam had struck up a conversation with Peter and Ron. 'Is this the first time you've been back here?' he asked the two older men, after establishing who they were.

Both nodded. 'My wife hasn't changed quite that much,' Peter said, with a smile. 'I might have to get my granddaughters to work on her - I'd love another holiday here.'

'I'm coming with my daughter and her family at Easter,' Ron said. 'I've got three grandsons who all love fishing, although their sister isn't very keen.'

'Yeah, it's the kind of place you can come back to all right,' Liam said. 'Matt and I came with a few of our friends just after uni, but it's been too long between drinks I reckon.'

Ron looked closely at Liam. 'Weren't you interviewed on that SBS documentary about Antarctica? What was it called?'

'The Icy Continent. Yeah, that was me. It was a pretty cool doco wasn't it?' Liam grinned, like an excited child.

Ron nodded. 'Yeah, it was very good, I really enjoyed it. Did you visit there?'

'I worked there for six months at the weather station. It was wild, literally and figuratively. You know, I actually had a photo of this house blown up and we mounted it on the wall. It was a little shot of irony while we froze our tails off.'

Peter smiled. 'I have a photo of it on my office wall. One of my clients actually got me to design a replica for a block of land on the New South Wales Central Coast.'

Liam raised an eyebrow. 'So, there's another beach house out there?'

'No, it's not a true clone.' Peter shook his head. 'Don't get me wrong the design was spot on, but it doesn't have quite the same feel. They use different materials these days and it hasn't got a century of history under its belt either.'

'Yeah, there'll never be anywhere quite like this.' Liam scooped up a handful of peanuts from a nearby table. 'Do you ever design observatories?' he asked Peter. 'I'm going to be building a new house soon and I want to have my own mini weather station in the back yard.'

'Well, to be honest, I haven't ever done one. But I'd love to.'

'Great, do you have a card?'

Lillian and Clare found themselves seated next to each other on the couch when Rachel assembled the 2000 group for a photo. 'How are you these days, Lillian?' Clare asked, once the others had dispersed.

'I'm good, very good. I've come a long way since we were last here.'

'That's what I like to hear. You're looking well.'

'Thank you, Clare, you're looking pretty fabulous yourself. I like your hair.'

Clare groaned. 'It only took two hours with the straightener, but thank you.' They smiled at each other. 'Great party, hey?' said Clare.

Lillian nodded. 'Yes, it is.' She looked around the room for a moment, apparently wanting to say something more, but hoping for some means of escape, at the same time. Catching Peter's eye, he nodded and gave her an encouraging smile. Taking a deep breath, Lillian turned to look at Clare again. 'Clare, I never really thanked you properly for everything you did for me. I meant to write to you or give you a ring, but you know, time just gets away somehow.'

'I didn't do that much, really, all the hard work would have come after. I was just the catalyst.' Clare smiled easily.

'Yes, but without you making me take that first step of acknowledging my problem, I hate to think where I'd be now.'

'You're very welcome, Lillian. Don't forget, you helped me too. I'm not sure I would have gone back to psychology if you hadn't responded to my attempt at counselling.'

'I suppose we were both in the right place at the right time.'

'Yes, we must have been.'

'I know Peter has invited you to visit us if you're ever in Sydney. Please do come sometime, we'd love to have you.'

'Thank you, I'd like that,' said Clare.

Lillian smiled mischievously. 'Now, off you go, back to Matthew. His mother is living in hope he'll find a lovely young lady like you.'

Blushing, Clare did her best to look affronted. 'Lillian! I really don't know what you mean,' she said.

'He's been trying to catch your eye for the past five minutes. Don't worry, I'll put in a good word with Simone.'

Clare gave an exasperated look, but couldn't hide a smile. 'What is it with mothers becoming such matchmakers?'

'We can't help ourselves,' said Lillian. 'Now off you go.'

Clare shook her head and headed off in Matt's direction.

Kate made sure that she introduced herself to Jeffrey and Aiden. 'It's nice to put faces to the names,' she said. 'The only photo I've ever seen of you guys was taken when you stayed here.'

'Please tell me we've changed since then,' said Jeffrey.

Kate smiled. 'Yeah, just a tad,' she said. Jeffrey's hair was still red, but he wore it very short to hide the curl and he also had a goatee, which hid some of the freckles.

Aiden shook his head. 'Man, I can't believe it was more than ten years ago.'

'Sure doesn't feel like that long, being back here.' Jeffrey glanced around the room.

Shepherding the two young men over to one of the sofa's, Kate sat down next to them. 'Do you mind telling me how it all worked out after you left here, last time?' she asked, her eyes darting from one to the other. 'I never really knew the full story until all the stuff with the court case happened and I'm intrigued.'

Smiling, Jeffrey took a sip of his drink. 'Well, once I freed myself from the whole rugby league shackle, I decided to hit the books and realised I had some academic ability. I ended up getting a pretty decent OP and did an engineering degree at CQU in Rocky. I work for a firm in Gladstone.'

'That's great. How about you, Aiden?'

'I work at a horse stud in Charter's Towers,' he replied. Aiden was even taller than Tom now. He had the look of a country boy, down to the Wrangler jeans and RM boots.

'And Chris really joined the Navy? I don't think Tom could have foreseen that,' said Kate.

'No, none of us did,' Jeffrey replied. 'To be honest, Chris still struggled when we went back to school. I guess it was hard for him to find his place knowing he had undergone a big shake up but the other kids hadn't. His mum ended up sending him to a private school and he seemed to do better there.'

'From what I've heard, he just didn't seem like the type that would embrace the military lifestyle,' said Kate.

'Well, you know, he admitted to me he only went in because he met this girl who was joining up. He'd been dabbling in music and had done some labouring work, so I guess he was looking for some direction. The only open training position they had was in the kitchen and he took it.' Jeffrey shrugged. 'Turns out he had a dormant cooking talent and he's loving it. I'm really glad for him, you know? He's always found it hard to settle, but I think this whole Navy thing has given him some contentment.'

'Horses for courses hey?' Kate smiled.

'Yeah, you'll find your way to where you're supposed to be eventually,' said Aiden.

Tom and Liam bumped into each other at one of the beer eskies. Tom, who had his hand in the depths of the ice, smiled affably. 'I think there's only Fourex left in this one. Will that do you?'

'Yep, that's fine.'

Tom fished out a bottle and handed it to Liam, before pulling out one for himself. He nodded his thanks when Liam handed him the opener that was sitting on a small table nearby. 'I've already spotted one familiar face in the crowd here today and now here's another.'

Liam gave an *aw shucks* look. 'Well, it's not like being a real celebrity. I mean kids TV isn't where the big bucks are or anything. But it's kind of cool when people recognise you.'

'Yes, it must be.' Tom took a sip of his beer.

'I know it's a fun show, but it's educational too. You're a teacher, right? You can see value in kids TV when there's an educational component?'

'Yeah, I am and yes, I do, but it's not TV that I recognise you from. And, I must add, that's not a reflection on you. My kids will no doubt kill me when I tell them I met a celebrity and didn't know who he was.'

'Oh, right. Did I do one of those weather talks at your school? It's a pretty fun gig too, for primary schools.'

'No, I'm in secondary.'

Rubbing the back of his neck, Liam looked at the floor. 'It's not that stupid bloopers video on YouTube, is it? I just have to say the whole thing was a set up and that snake looked real.'

Tom chuckled. 'Hey, anything involving snakes freaks me out too, but it's nothing so elaborate. I've seen you down at Snapper's. I already met your mate Matt over there. It took us a while to work out that connection, but I clicked right away when I saw you. You used to be a surfing instructor at Coolangatta, didn't you?'

'Yeah, I did.' Liam nodded slowly. 'Although it feels like another lifetime now.'

'Since I met Matt, I've been thinking about your story, in fact I just re-read it before.' Tom gestured to where the various editions of *The QLD Reviewer* with the interviews in them were spread across a long table. 'Would your wife, by any chance, have been Debbie Kirk?'

'Yeah,' Liam said softly. Although he smiled as he said it, Tom still caught the faraway look that briefly came across his face.

'I used to do surf patrol with her. She was quite a bit older than me, but all the young guys were pretty infatuated with her. We were devastated when we heard she got married.'

'I can understand that,' Liam said, with the same faraway smile.

'Anyway, she saved my life once when I was fifteen and full of bravado. I nonchalantly went out to get this docile looking guy out of the water and he suddenly went nuts. He grabbed me around the neck and dragged us both under the water. As you know, Debbie was about half my weight and not very tall, but she appeared out of nowhere and slugged the guy until he let go of me and then managed to get him into shore single handed.' Tom exhaled. 'It still gives me shivers to think about it and I learnt a big lesson that day about being aware of my own safety before rescuing anyone else.'

'That was Deb all over. I don't think a day has gone past in the last eighteen years that I haven't thought about her and missed her.'

'I can understand that. Anyway, I just wanted to tell you that story. I probably wouldn't be here today if she hadn't been there for me. I haven't upset you, have I?'

'Nah, just reminds me why I loved her. It's always nice to talk to somebody who knew her. Thanks for telling me,' Liam said and held out his hand.

Tom put his own hand out and they shook hands warmly. 'You're welcome. Now can I get a photo with you to show my children? I'm sure they'll recognise the celebrity in you even if I didn't.'

Jessica was talking to Jim and Gloria. 'You must be quite honoured about all this,' she said to Jim.

'Me, honoured?' asked Jim, putting a hand on his chest. 'Why? I didn't do anything that the other committee members didn't do.'

'No, I mean you must be honoured to have been involved in all of these people's experiences of this house.'

Jim furrowed his brow. 'Well, I was very involved with Jack, obviously, and Tom and I had a few talks. And, of course, I remember Matt and Liam. But I didn't feature in all your stories.'

'No, you didn't make it into all the stories, but you came up in every interview.'

'Well there you go. I hope it was all good.' Jim smiled proudly.

Jessica nodded. 'Oh yes, no bad press. I guess I could describe you as a constant presence. It really gave me a feel for the place, knowing that there were people here who were central to the town and all that happens.'

Jim grinned humbly at the praise and Gloria gave him a hug to show how proud she was.

Jack and Erin managed to steal a quiet moment on the veranda as the shadows on the beach started to grow longer. They stood there for a moment, holding hands and content to just be with each other.

'Isn't it amazing how one house in a small town has impacted the lives of all these people?' said Jack. 'Not to mention the thousands of others who have stayed here.'

'I know and it took something potentially bad to connect you all.'

'Just think, if I hadn't had a gammy knee, joined the swimming squad, been dragged to the pub one night or driven myself to the verge of burnout, you and I wouldn't be here today.'

'Well, if I hadn't selected your firm randomly from the phone book and ticked the wrong box on my client form, we might never have met.'

'Don't even imagine that, it's too scary a thought.'

'Yeah,' Erin agreed, 'but somehow I don't think we would have missed each other. Even when everybody was telling me I was being too picky and that I'd never meet anybody if I didn't join RSVP or go speed dating, I just kind of knew you were out there somewhere and I'd find you eventually.'

'Sorry I kept you waiting while I lived out my self-imposed exile.'

'There's a lot to be said for meeting at our age. We're not so hung up on career success, we've had time to do our own thing and "find" ourselves and we both knew what we wanted.'

Jack smiled, his dark brown eyes exuding the contentment he felt with his life.

The moment was broken when one of Rachel's friends came out and asked them if they wanted anything to drink.

Jack chuckled after she left. 'Gloria could have a career in events management, the way she's got this party running.'

'I know, this is definitely one of the best shindigs I've ever been to. Not to mention the fact it's great to have so many willing babysitters.' Erin looked into the yard, where Danny, Ben and Lucy were entertaining Sam and Josh.

'I haven't seen the twins for hours,' said Jack. 'Should I be worried?'

'Gloria has it all under control and I just fed them before. We're under strict instructions to enjoy ourselves.'

'You got to meet everyone?'

'Oh, yes, Hamish is quite a star around here it seems. Which is fair enough considering you really did save the day.'

'Well, you know how much I *love* the limelight. It's quite handy having an alter ego.'

Erin put her arms around Jack and hugged him. 'You're the nicest man I've ever met.'

'And you're not so bad yourself.'

'Wow, this is really kind of weird,' Tom said, as he, Jeff and Aiden shared a beer on the veranda. 'I still kind of feel like I'm in charge of you guys while we're here. I'm not sure we should all be drinking.'

'Sorry Mr McKay, we're all grown up now. You can't tell us what to do anymore.' Jeffrey leaned over and clinked his beer bottle against Tom's.

'No, I guess I can't. It was good while it lasted.' Taking another sip of his drink, Tom eyed both the young men. 'Now, you can tell me the truth on this one. Was Chris really not able to come, or did he just not want to see me again?'

'Seriously, he couldn't come,' said Aiden. 'He doesn't hate you anymore.'

'Really?'

'Yeah, really,' Jeffrey insisted. 'Chris has always been pretty complex, but he's gotten himself together these days and he speaks well of you.'

'That's good to hear,' said Tom.

Reaching over to the table behind them, Jeffrey picked up a corn chip and dunked it in salsa. Realising what he was doing, he looked over at Tom and grinned. 'Salsa, Mr McKay?' he offered.

All three of them laughed.

Tom rolled his eyes. 'Yeah, yeah, I'll never live that one down. But I challenge you guys to try a mouthful of that extra hot stuff. It was torture.'

'It was Jeffrey's idea.' Aiden reached over to take some chips for himself.

'Oh, I didn't doubt that,' Tom replied. 'No offence, but I knew you and Chris wouldn't have come up with something like that. You weren't creative enough.'

'All right, I'll take the blame,' said Jeffrey. 'But, you know, we couldn't work out why you let us get away with that but then totally lost it with the snake. We thought it was kind of corny in comparison.'

Tom shuddered. 'I hate snakes, I always have. If you'd even put a *real* spider or rat or toad I wouldn't have cared. But the snake was my Achilles heel.'

Laughing, Jeffrey grabbed some more corn chips. 'I actually wanted to get fake vomit, but our shopping choices were pretty limited. It was hard enough to find the snake.'

Tom shook his head. 'It's probably just as well you used the snake, otherwise I probably wouldn't have made any progress. I really didn't have a clue how to get through to any of you.'

'Yeah, we kind of figured that to start with,' said Aiden. 'But then you got it together and we thought you must have had it planned all along.'

'Are you kidding? I was totally flying by the seat of my pants. Here I was, with just two years teaching experience and no real grasp on teenage psychology. I don't know what Karl thought he was doing, but it somehow worked out in the end.'

'Good old Mr Sullo,' Jeffrey mused. 'He just retired last year, you know.'

'Yeah, we keep in touch. I went to his retirement party. He did a great job out there.'

Jeffrey and Aiden nodded. 'He wasn't such a bad guy,' said Aiden.

All three of them paused to look out at the water. 'You still surf?' asked Jeffrey.

'Oh yeah, every day,' said Tom.

Jeffrey looked out to the ocean again. 'You reckon you could take us out tomorrow, for old time's sake?'

'Absolutely.'

Emma finally managed to steal Clare away for a chat when some of the men started up a game of backyard cricket. 'Soooo?' she said, grinning, as she sat cross-legged on the sofa.

'So, what?' Pretending nonchalance, Clare took another sip of wine.

'Come on, stop playing coy. What's the deal with you and Matt?'

Clare blushed. 'You're as bad as Lillian! What makes you think there's a deal?'

'Clare, Clare, Clare. I may not be a psychologist, but I do know when a guy and girl hit it off. You've been talking to him for ages.'

'All right, he *is* kind of nice,' Clare agreed, blushing even deeper.

'Kind of? He looks very nice to me. Just your type.'

'Since when have journalists been my type?'

'Excuse me, Miss 'don't judge a person by their occupation'!'

'I do say that, don't I?'

'Yes. All the time. Now come on, I take it he's single?'

'Yes, he is.'

'No crazy ex or a tribe of children to different mothers?'

'No, or at least I don't think so.'

'Age?'

'Thirty-four.'

Emma clapped her hands in glee. 'This is so exciting!'

'I'm not so sure about that.'

'Why not?'

'Uh, geography? He lives on the Gold Coast.'

'So what? It's a two-hour flight and you do lots of work up here anyway.'

'Yeah, that's true.'

'Come on, Clare, are you telling me if you had a client who presented this case you wouldn't say, "Give it a shot"?'

'Yes, all right, I would.' Clare smiled dreamily. 'He *is* cute, isn't he?'

'Yeah, definitely.'

'He's smart too. He's writing a novel and he said he'd name a character after me.'

'Whoa, that's cool.'

'His sisters are lovely and Lillian said his Mum is too.'

Emma shrugged in delight. 'Oh my goodness, Clare! This is so amazing.'

'I always tell people that parties are a great potential meeting place.'

'Well, there you go.'

Clare patted her hair. 'How do I look? I haven't been able to get to the bathroom for ages.'

'You look great, you're positively glowing.'

'Now you're being silly.' Clare pulled her lip gloss out of her pocket and slicked some on. 'I barely know him yet.'

'*But you like him,*' Emma teased in a sing-song voice.

'All right, yes, I like him!'

Emma reached over to hug her friend. 'All right! Now you just have to go and get him.'

Rachel finally managed to get all the story subjects together for a photo after the dinner plates were cleared away. Everybody declared they were too full for dessert at that time, so Gloria announced they could have an hour of digestion time. As Rachel was finding out, people seemed far more interested in talking to each other and swapping information than posing for photos.

Seeing her frustration, Jessica came over and stood next to her. 'Let them chat for a few minutes,' she suggested. 'Then I'll bully them into getting into a proper formation.'

'I didn't think any of them knew each other.' Rachel perched on the edge of the coffee table. 'Well, I know some of them stayed here together and that, but the people from the other stories would have been strangers, right?'

Jessica sat down next to her. 'Yeah, pretty much. But you know, a shared experience gives people something to talk about, and I kind of like to think that the way I wrote the stories made them feel like they knew a bit about the other people.'

'That's true, I guess. I read the stories and I thought they were cool.'

'Thanks,' Jessica said, with a smile.

'I know Grandad acts like he doesn't like all the attention, but he kind of does.' Rachel looked over to where Jim was holding court near the front door.

'You think?'

They both laughed, then sat there for a moment, watching the seemingly disparate collection of people talk and laugh together with the ease of old friends.

True to her word, Jessica eventually called the group to attention and got them to arrange themselves for the group photo. She imagined how an outsider might dissect the photograph - Tom was the tall guy, Jack the good looking one, Elizabeth the epitome of a yummy mummy to be and Lillian and Simone breaking the stereotype of a grey-haired grandmother in a rocking chair. She herself had done that many times before. But looking now at these people she had come to know so well, she realised properly, for the first time, what a privilege it was to be a storyteller. It wasn't necessarily about having a breaking news story that every other news publication would also tell, or getting the best photographs. It was about getting the reader to understand the experiences that somebody else had been through and hopefully take something away from that. Something that might change the way they saw the world, even if just a little bit.

Whoa, I'm starting to think like Grant, she thought, smiling to herself.

Looking back over at the group, she conferred with Rachel and called out some instructions. 'Okay, back row squeeze in a little bit. Matt take the rabbit ears away from Liz's head.' The group laughed as Elizabeth turned around and punched her brother on the arm, while Simone gave him a mother's glare. 'Jack, we need you to be in the middle and Lucy and Ben can you kneel up a bit higher.'

Finally, everybody was in position and Rachel called out, 'Okay say cheese.'

'Cheese!' they all responded, with beaming smiles.

The party lasted well into the night. It had been a long time since the house had hosted such a gathering, but it rose to the occasion magnificently. Although things got a bit rowdier as the night wore on, it was a generally well-behaved crowd.

The only mishap of the night occurred when Matt missed his footing on the steps at the side of the house and rolled his ankle. Tom and Liam helped him back up the stairs and Jim, who had also witnessed the incident, called out, 'Is there a doctor in the house?'

Reluctantly excusing herself from the conversation she was enjoying, Jill came over. She shook her head at the sight of her brother sitting on a chair, with his leg outstretched. 'Trust you,' she said, kneeling down to look at his foot. 'What were you doing over there in the dark anyway? The back stairs are well lit.'

Matt shrugged exaggeratedly. 'There's only one bathroom in this house and lots of guys drinking beer.'

'You guys are so gross.' Holding his ankle Jill flexed it gently. 'Luckily for you, it's just jarred. Some ice will do the trick.' With that, she pulled over a nearby esky and stuck his foot in it.

'Hey!' yelped Matt. 'I'll tell Mum you're mistreating me.'

Jill couldn't stop herself from laughing. 'Yeah, you do that. I'm sure she'll care.'

Clare came over to see if he was all right.

'Her bedside manner stinks,' said Matt, throwing Jill a sour look.

Concerned there might be a domestic dispute amidst all the revelry, Clare patted Jill on the arm. 'He's really very proud of you,' she said. 'He told me before.'

Jill smiled. 'I know. Don't worry, we've just never really grown out of our teenage insult stage. We're really very close. And, may I say, you are the nicest girl he's met in a long time.'

Clare smiled in return. 'Thanks.'

Jim was supposed to be saying a few words at some point in the evening, but by ten thirty Gloria knew he wouldn't be up to it. Once he started joining in conga lines and embracing people that he usually only shook hands with, he was well past talking sense. She kept a wary eye on him, making sure he didn't do anything too silly.

Slinging his arm around Jack's shoulder, Jim smiled at Erin. 'I was the one who told him to get back out there, you know.'

Erin smiled back. 'Really?'

'Yeah, I really did. He was a bit of a misery guts, just quietly.'

'Well, thanks for getting him back on the market.'

'No worries.' Jim gave a hearty thumbs up.

Overwhelmed by Jim's beer breath, Jack attempted to step away, but the older man tightened his grip. 'Uh uh, Jack. You've been hiding all night. Now you have to face the crowd.'

'Seriously Jim, it's fine. I don't need—' Jack tried again to extricate himself from Jim's iron grip.

Tightening his hold on Jack's shoulder, Jim whistled shrilly. 'Hey a bit of shush!' he yelled. 'We have to give three cheers to Jack Nolan, here. He's our hero!'

The noise in the room died down and everyone turned to look at Jack, who was growing redder by the second. 'It's okay,' he said, holding up his hand. 'There's really no need.'

Gloria stepped in then. 'Yes, there is,' she said. 'Alright everyone you heard the man, let's give three cheers for Jack!'

Jim clasped Jack's right hand and raised it, like a boxing referee after a fight.

'Hip hip!' he boomed.

'Hooray,' came the rousing response.

'Hip hip!'

'Hooray!'

'Hip hip!'

'Hooray!'

The room erupted into applause and cheers, as Jack desperately tried to fade into the background.

'Hey Jim,' yelled Liam. 'Matt and I were thinking of going up to the Crow's Nest.'

Jim shook his head. 'I can't save you this time,' he said.

'Aw, why not?'

'I'm a bit drunk,' he stage whispered.

Simone poked Liam in the shoulder. 'Stop stirring,' she said.

Gloria handed Jim a cup of strong coffee. 'I think you've had quite enough beer for tonight,' she said sternly, steering him over to the couch.

Due to Jim's inebriated state, Moira gave the official short speech on behalf of the committee, as the night began to wear down. She thanked everybody who had helped in any way and advised the crowd to get their holiday bookings in early, as due to all the recent publicity, they were expecting a barrage of enquiries.

Because everybody was having such a great time, plans were made to have a recovery brunch the next morning. Simone and Lillian offered to help Gloria get it organised.

Thanks to Gloria's careful collection of fold up beds and air mattresses, everybody from out of town was able to stay the night in the house. The lounge room looked like it was hosting a huge teenage slumber party but nobody minded.

Matt, Liam and Tom made plans to go for an early morning surf, no matter what shape they were in. Clare said she might come along to watch.

Simone announced she was walking down to the southern cliff, if anybody wanted to join her.

Jack told Danny that he would escort him to shore on the rescue board, just to prove that he could.

Lucy and Ben had promised Sam and Josh that they would build them the world's largest sand castle.

And Jessica sent a text to Grant, thanking him for the best story assignment that he had ever given her.

DEVELOPER GO HOME!

By Jessica Stanton

jess_stant@qldreviewer.com.au

People power won the day in the Brisbane Magistrates Court on Monday when the case of Malton Construction vs The Sunset Point Beach House Committee was thrown out of court. It was a dramatic anti-climax to what was promising to be a protracted battle between millionaire property developer Max Walton and all 3000 residents of the small Queensland town, who, in a somewhat unique arrangement, are custodians of the century old holiday house, thanks to the generosity of former owner James McMaster.

Mr McMaster, who died in 1985, willed The Beach House to the town of Sunset Point, providing that certain conditions are met. Chief among these is the stipulation that the house must never be sold or removed from the site, nor the land it sits upon sold or subdivided. When Mr Walton first expressed interest in purchasing the site to construct a multi-million-dollar resort, he uncovered a clause in the ownership documentation that allowed the sale clause to be waived under "extraordinary" circumstances.

Counsel for the plaintiff, Mr Jack Nolan, was able to provide documentary evidence that the abovementioned clause had in fact been fraudulently added. Mr Walton was cleared of any involvement in the fraud, but was left with no choice than to immediately withdraw his claim to buy the land. It was later revealed that the tampering had been initiated by Councillor Ken McVeigh, of the Mid-Coast Regional Council. Mayor Roderick Wilson announced the sacking of Councillor McVeigh in a press conference on Tuesday morning. Mr McVeigh spoke briefly at the conference, tearfully insisting he was trying to help the small town.

"That ownership clause is bull****," he said. "It was written in a different time by an old man who had no concept of how real estate would grow and change in the coming decades. Building this resort would have allowed an influx of employment and attracted more tourists to the town. In this day and age, you can't just sit and shut the world out. That kind of small town living is over."

Max Walton also spoke briefly at the conference, insisting that he had no knowledge of the fraud, but echoing some of the sentiments of former Councillor McVeigh.

"Look, I absolutely do not condone what Mr McVeigh did. In all the years I have been in business I have never been involved in anything that is illegal in any way and I will continue to operate my company in that manner. However, I do agree that the ownership clause is counterproductive. It is preventing the town of Sunset Point from moving forward. We're well into the twenty-first century now and these folks are still in the seventies. People have changed. They can see that having a single dwelling on a large, under-utilised block with a hills hoist and bindies in a big patch of grass is not the best use of that space. Statistics don't lie – people want to spend their holidays at resorts where all the conveniences are available."

A spokesperson for the Committee, Mrs Moira Bell, refuted both men's comments.

"You only have to speak to the people who come and stay at The Beach House to understand just how much people DO want this kind of holiday," she said. "What we have here is a place where there is not even a TV. There is no internet access. You are asked not to bring your laptop or iPod. And you know what? Most people don't. They come here and enjoy a peaceful holiday, just like those magical times back in the sixties and seventies. The Australian coastline, and especially Queensland, used to be dotted with caravan parks and beach shacks that offered an affordable holiday for the average family. Now most of the caravan parks have been sold to developers and moved away from the beaches. In some areas, you have to walk five minutes to hit sand. So many of those old timber shacks have also been sold and replaced with mansions or holiday units. These places are expensive to stay at. A lot of people just don't have that kind of money. I'm not saying we shouldn't have them too, but we need some balance."

Both Mr Walton and Mr McVeigh dismissed Mrs Bell's comments.

"She's dreaming," Mr Walton insisted. You can't tell me nobody brings their laptop or iPod to Sunset Point."

"No," agreed Mrs Bell, "I can't say that nobody does, but I am saying that most people follow the rules. In fact, since the publicity we've received from the court case we have had a massive influx of enquiries. People are saying 'I love the fact you've got rules about iPods and other gadgets. It means my kids have to leave their stuff at home. I want them to have the kind of holiday I had when I was a kid.' I might suggest that Mr Walton would be better served to build some replica beach houses. He would be surprised by the demand."

"I very much doubt it," was Mr Walton's reply.

In an aside, Mrs Bell also refuted Mr Walton's claim that the backyard at The Beach House was infested with bindies.

"I can assure you that thousands of children have run barefoot in that yard over the years and very few, if any, of them have trodden on a bindi," she said. "The committee employs a gardener to ensure the grass remains in tip top condition."

Mrs Bell also praised the efforts of solicitor Jack Nolan, who volunteered his time and expertise to help the town maintain their iconic holiday house.

"We were so very fortunate to have Jack's assistance," she said. "Our committee was not in a position to fund an expensive legal battle and, unfortunately, we did not have anybody in our local community with the necessary level of trial experience to take on a legal juggernaut like Mr Walton's team. Jack himself stayed in the house back in 2003 and has maintained ties with the Sunset Point community. He was very gracious in offering his skills for no fee, despite having a very busy personal and professional calendar. He really is a hero to us and, although very modest, we just want to acknowledge his great contribution to our win. We really couldn't have done it without him."

Mr Nolan, 42, is an associate with Kendall Masters in the regional NSW city of Millvale. His pedigree as a trial lawyer over ten years is impressive, although he has since moved his focus to acting as a mediation consultant. When asked if he was nervous about returning to the court room, he replied, "Oh I didn't hesitate. Sure, I don't do much trial work anymore, but I was happy to put that hat on again for the people of Sunset Point. It's a great little town and the house holds a very special place in my heart. Besides that, I passionately believed in the cause. Beach Houses are embedded in the Australian psyche and there aren't very many of them left these days. We've got to hold onto the ones we've got."

He seemed embarrassed when the 'hero' tag was mentioned.

"Me a hero? Oh, I don't think so. I was just doing my job. Heroes are people who do something extraordinary in difficult circumstances. I just worked with my particular skill set. Generally, if you dig deeply enough into any paperwork, there is always a trail to follow. This particular fraudulent activity was very well carried out, but it wasn't perfect. I guess they're just unlucky that I'm a bit OCD with details."

He remained modest, yet confident when asked if he could have won, had the case gone to trial.

"Oh yes, I think we would have won. I know that's easy enough to say when the event isn't going to happen, but I really do believe it to be true. Mr McMaster was a very astute businessman and he was very clear in his instruction. One of the most sacred duties a lawyer has is to uphold the wishes of a client as expressed in his or her will, and I would have fought every inch of the way to do that for Mr McMaster."

When asked if the level of public interest and support would set a precedent for any similar cases, he insisted that he couldn't speculate.

"Oh, no, I really couldn't say that," he said. "Making those kind of comments can get you into a lot of trouble. But, my personal opinion is, that this case has hit a nerve. The general public are saying, 'hey we don't want to lose all our beach shacks. Let's hold onto at least a few of them.' Here in Australia, we've always been proud of the fact that there is no such thing as a private beach. Let's make sure that all our beaches remain very much in the public domain for anybody from any walk of life to access."

Mr Nolan also refused to comment on whether the long-term friendship of Ken McVeigh and Dennis Rowan of Rowan Real Estate may have come into play when Ken initiated the document tampering.

"I really can't say what motivated Mr McVeigh to do what he did and, I must insist, that there is no evidence to link Mr Rowan to this case. I guess some people will look at the facts and join some dots and that's their prerogative. Would both these men have stood to gain if the deal had gone through? Yes, definitely. But, once again, I am making absolutely no accusations towards Mr Rowan. That is a case for the police to sort out."

Ken McVeigh is now the subject of a fraud investigation. Mayor Roderick Wilson said the sacking of a councillor was a dark day for the Mid Coast Regional Council, but there was no other choice than to follow the course of justice.

"One thing I know for certain is that, as an elected member standing for the people of your community, you cannot afford to be anything other than transparent. Mr McVeigh says his actions were motivated by a need to help his electorate. Perhaps in a very misguided way they were. But this serves as a great reminder that honesty must always remain paramount in any form of government. I always remember my father telling me that there are no degrees of honesty in public office – you are either honest or you aren't. Unfortunately, Mr McVeigh chose the wrong path to go down and now he must pay for that transgression. I don't believe him to be a bad or evil man, rather he was somebody who made a bad choice and now he has to live with it."

Sergeant Anthony Reid of Sunset Point Police confirmed that a police investigation was underway involving Mr McVeigh but declined to comment any further.

Accommodation enquiries regarding The Beach House at Sunset Point can be made to Sunset Real Estate on (07) 84778593 or via their website www.sunset-real-estate.qld.net

About The Author

Helen McKenna lives on the Sunshine Coast in Queensland. She has a Bachelor of Arts degree from the University of Queensland and has worked in banking, local government and as a biographer. As well as writing, she currently works in learning support and as a swimming teacher.

Helen loves to hear from her readers, so please feel free to drop her a line:

Email: info@helenmckenna.com.au
Website: www.helenmckenna.com.au
Facebook: www.facebook.com/HelenMcKenna.Author
Twitter: www.twitter.com/helenmckenna_

All paperbacks are currently available directly from her website and all titles are also available as e-books at the major retailers.